THE CITY OF EMBER

THE GRAPHIC NOVEL

JEANNE DuPRAU

Adapted by DALLAS MIDDAUGH
Art by NIKLAS ASKER

Color by NIKLAS ASKER and BO ASHI
Lettering by CHRIS DICKEY

RANDOM HOUSE 🏠 NEW YORK

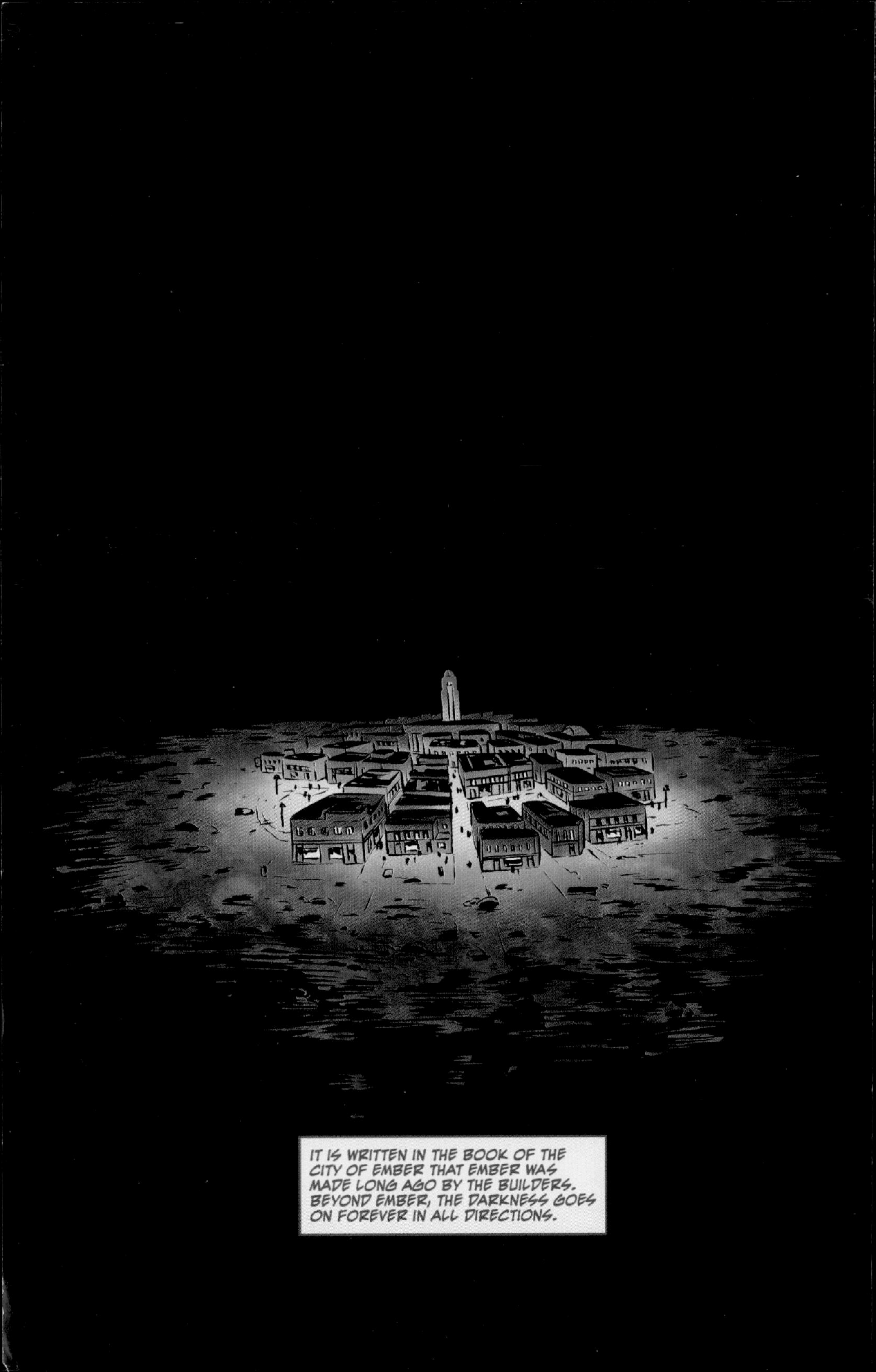
IT IS WRITTEN IN THE BOOK OF THE CITY OF EMBER THAT EMBER WAS MADE LONG AGO BY THE BUILDERS. BEYOND EMBER, THE DARKNESS GOES ON FOREVER IN ALL DIRECTIONS.

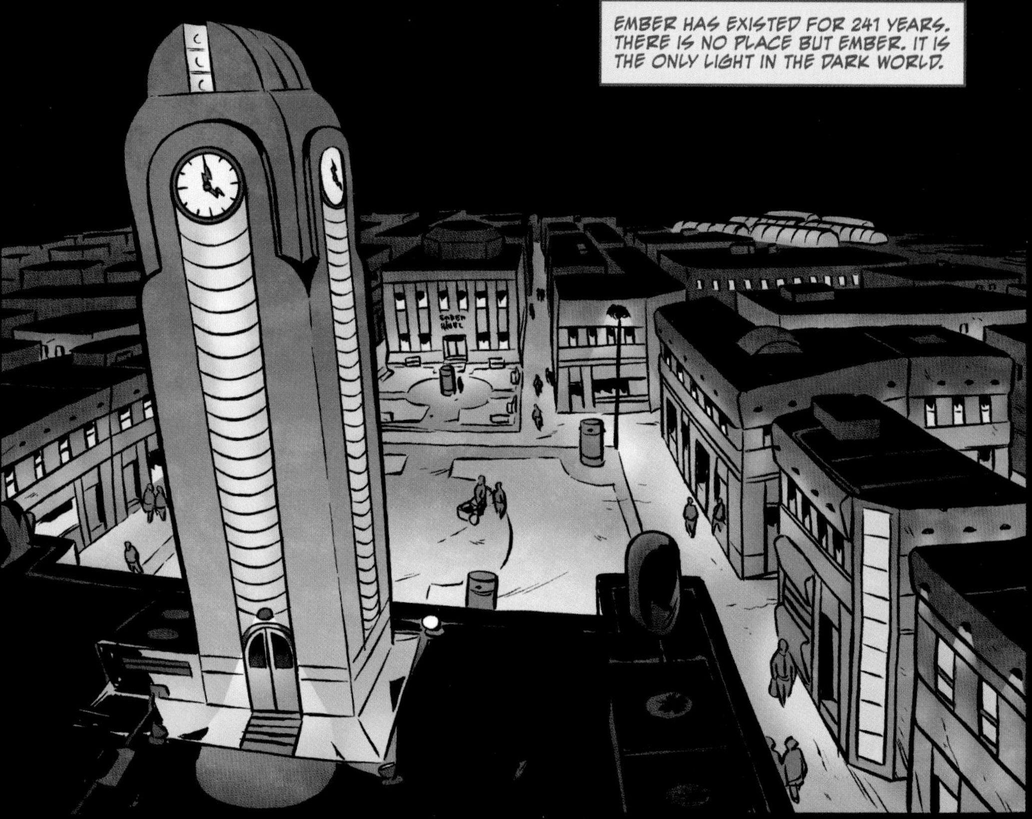
EMBER HAS EXISTED FOR 241 YEARS. THERE IS NO PLACE BUT EMBER. IT IS THE ONLY LIGHT IN THE DARK WORLD.

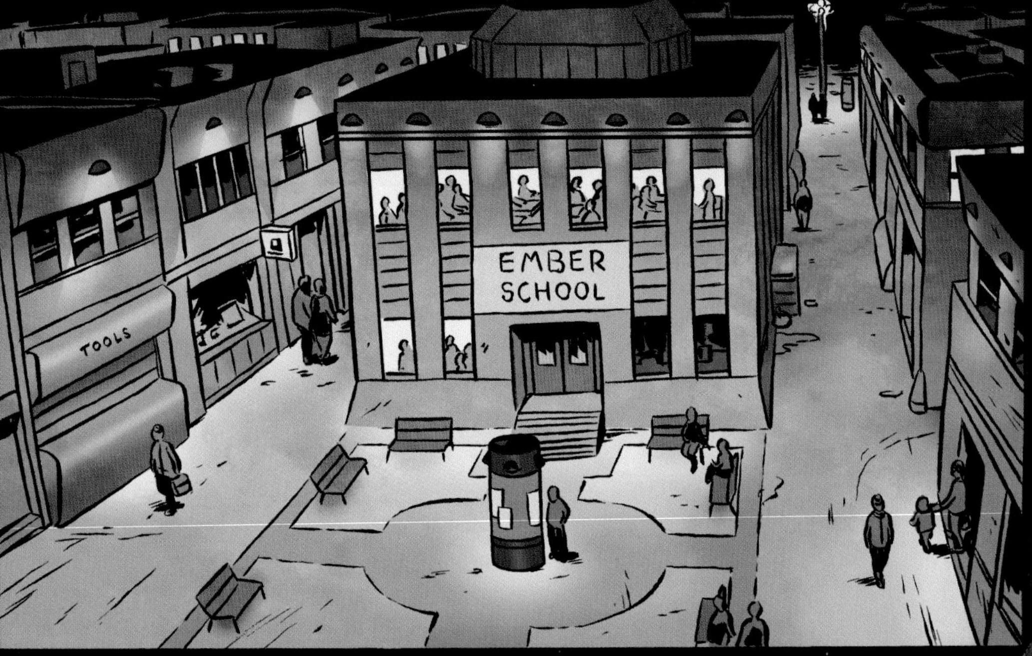
EMBER SCHOOL
TOOLS

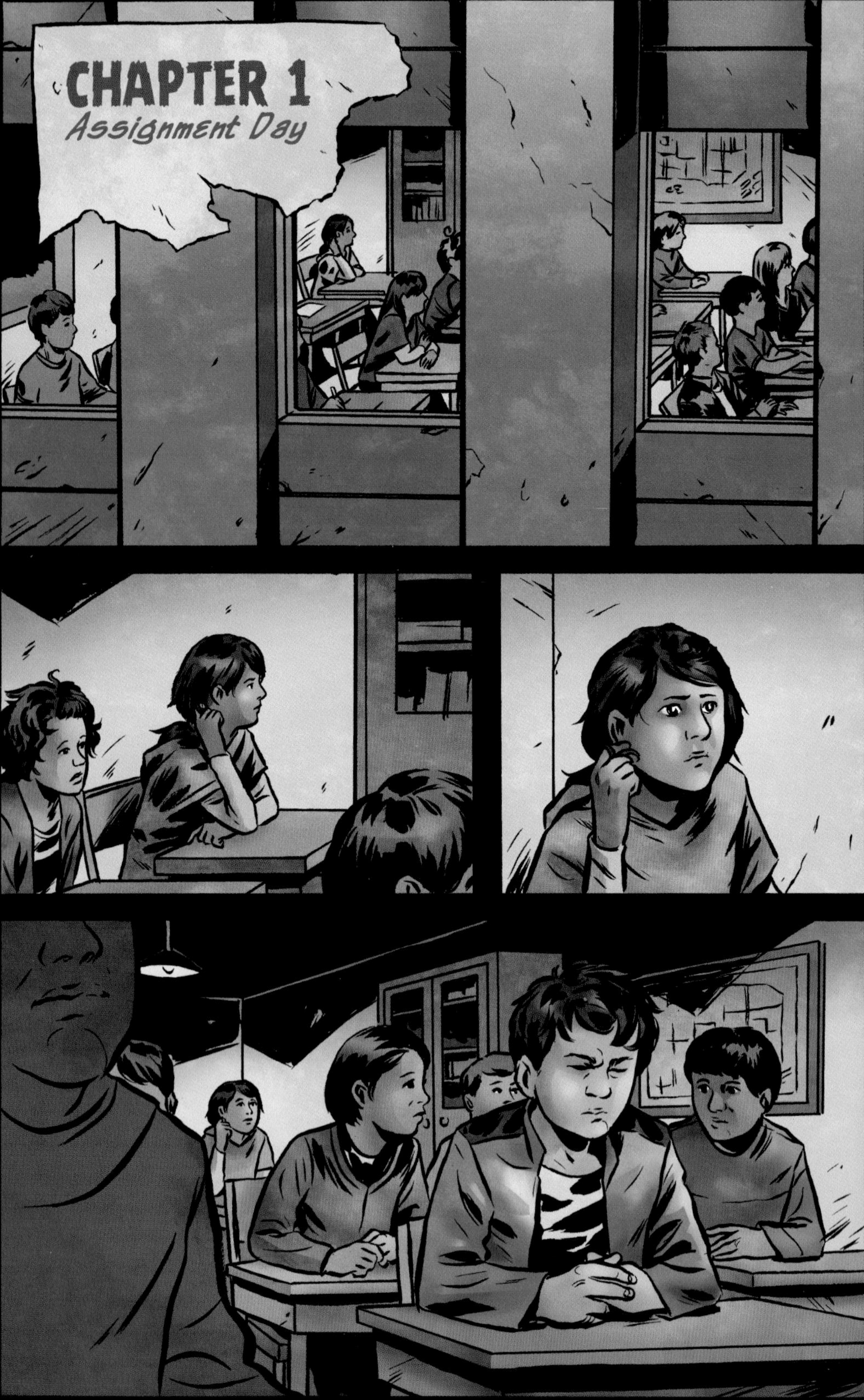
CHAPTER 1
Assignment Day

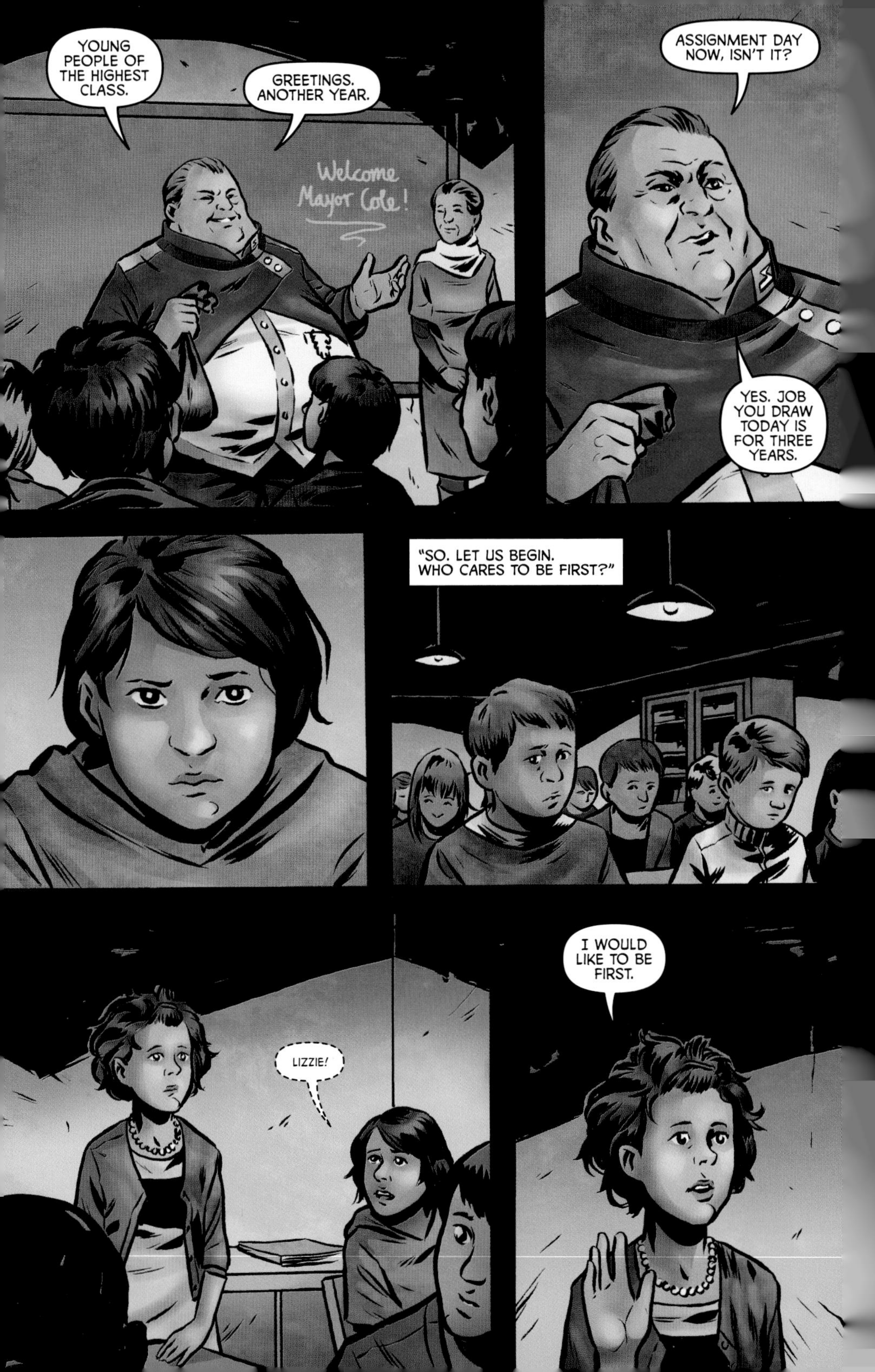
YOUNG PEOPLE OF THE HIGHEST CLASS.
GREETINGS. ANOTHER YEAR.
Welcome Mayor Cole!
ASSIGNMENT DAY NOW, ISN'T IT?
YES. JOB YOU DRAW TODAY IS FOR THREE YEARS.
"SO. LET US BEGIN. WHO CARES TO BE FIRST?"
LIZZIE!
I WOULD LIKE TO BE FIRST.

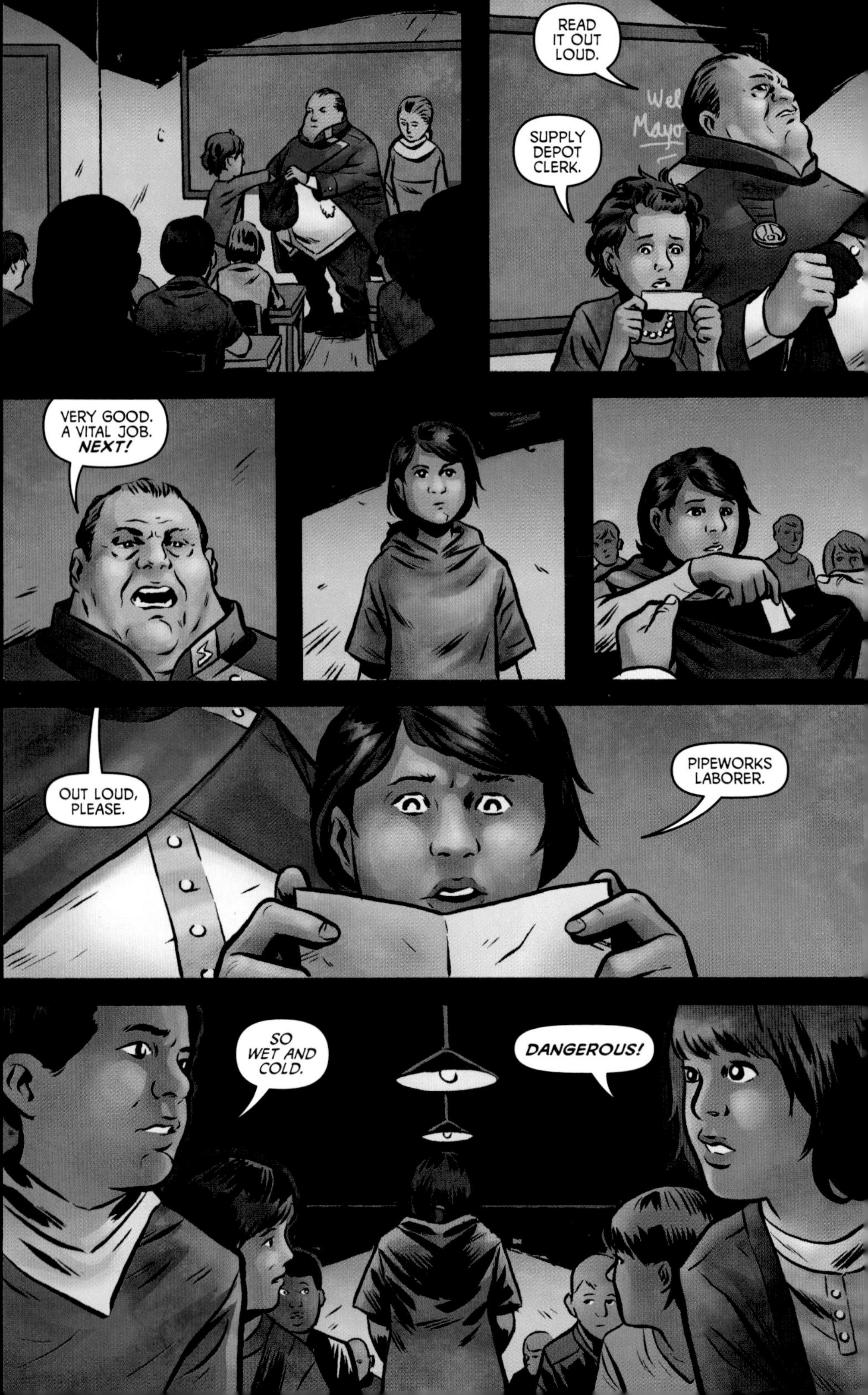
READ IT OUT LOUD.
SUPPLY DEPOT CLERK.
VERY GOOD. A VITAL JOB. *NEXT!*
OUT LOUD, PLEASE.
PIPEWORKS LABORER.
SO WET AND COLD.
DANGEROUS!

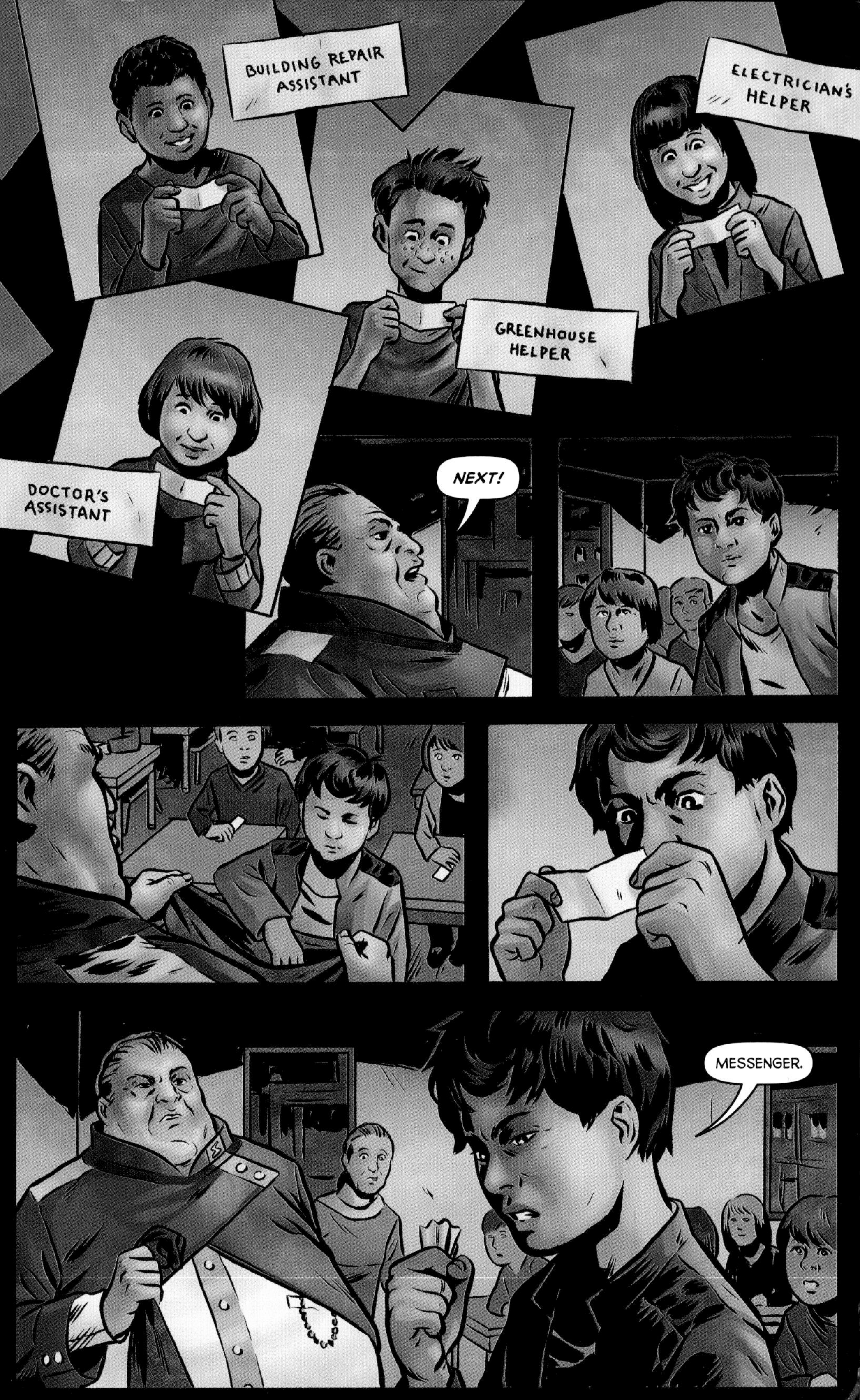
BUILDING REPAIR ASSISTANT
GREENHOUSE HELPER
ELECTRICIAN'S HELPER
DOCTOR'S ASSISTANT
NEXT!
MESSENGER.

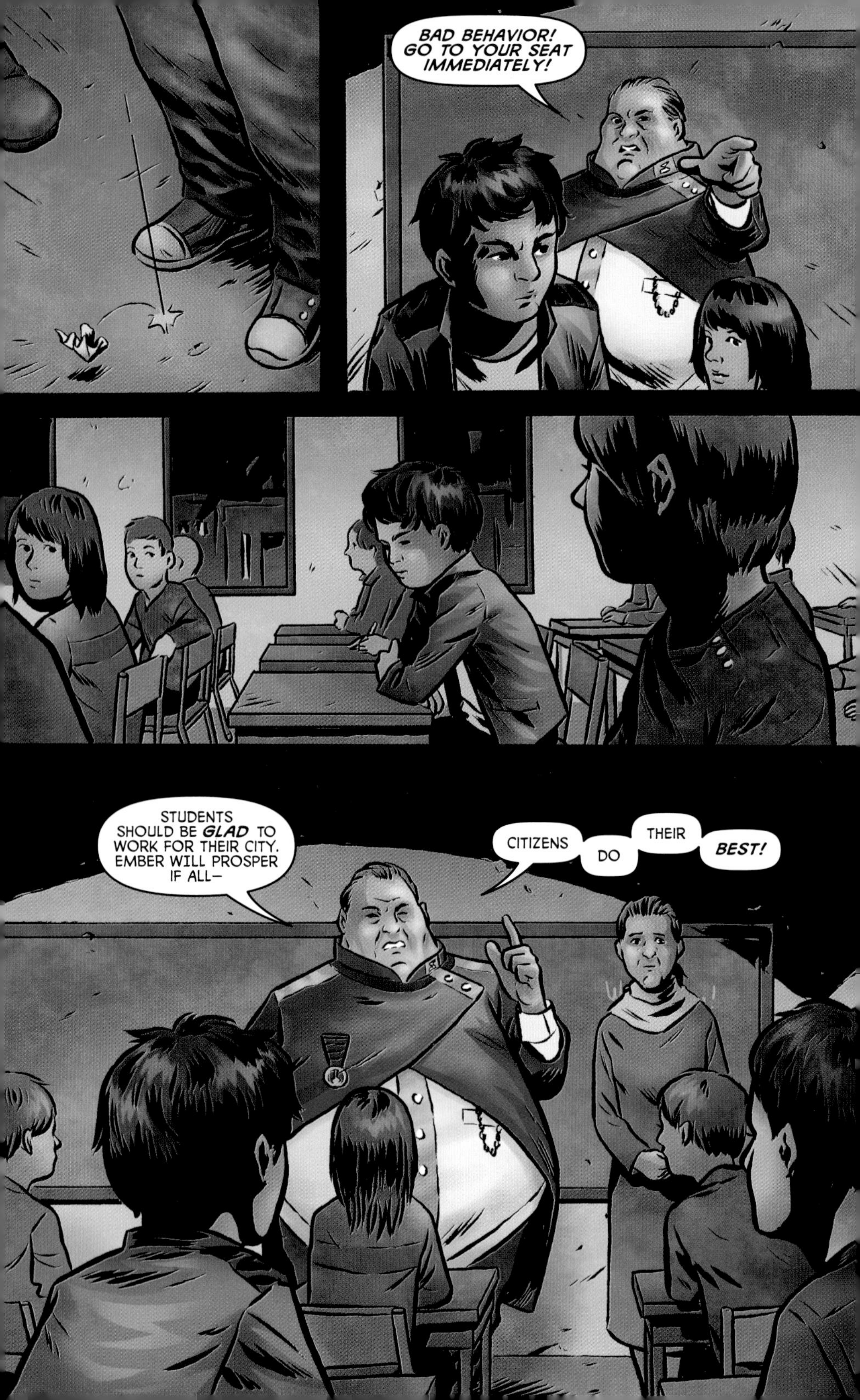
BAD BEHAVIOR! GO TO YOUR SEAT IMMEDIATELY!
STUDENTS SHOULD BE GLAD TO WORK FOR THEIR CITY. EMBER WILL PROSPER IF ALL—
CITIZENS
DO
THEIR
BEST!

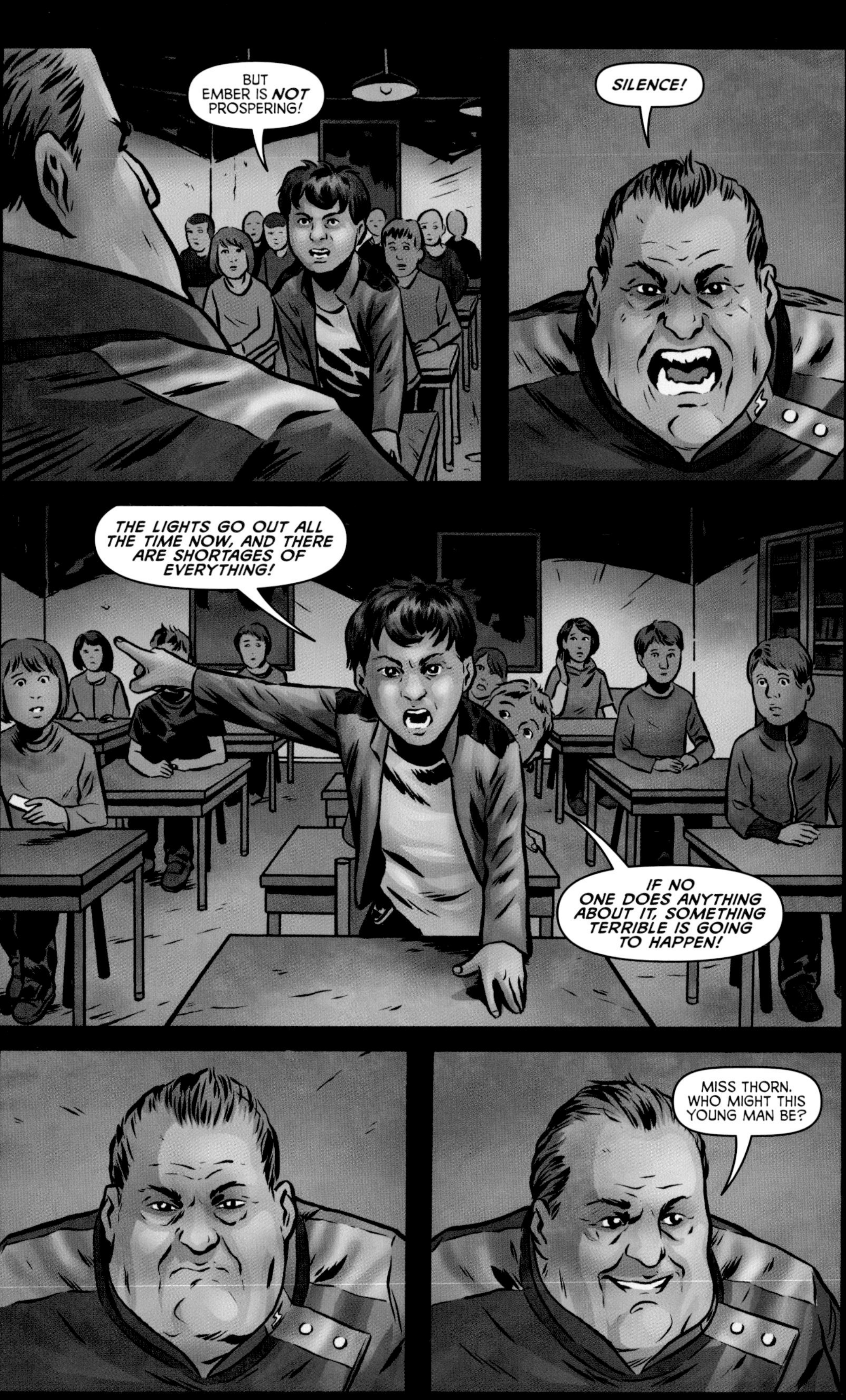

BUT EMBER IS **NOT** PROSPERING!
SILENCE!
THE LIGHTS GO OUT ALL THE TIME NOW, AND THERE ARE SHORTAGES OF EVERYTHING!
IF NO ONE DOES ANYTHING ABOUT IT, SOMETHING TERRIBLE IS GOING TO HAPPEN!
MISS THORN. WHO MIGHT THIS YOUNG MAN BE?

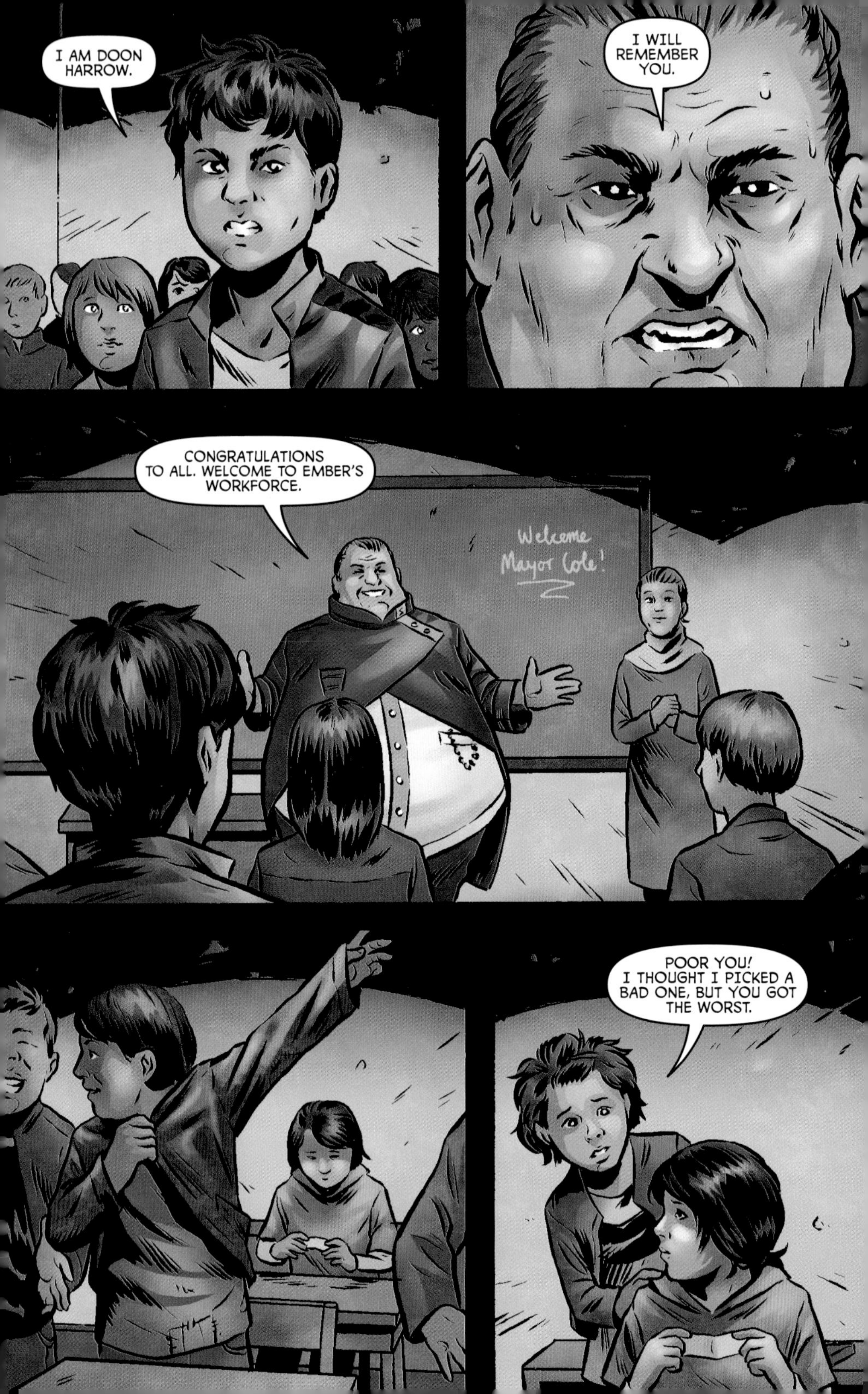
I AM DOON HARROW.
I WILL REMEMBER YOU.
CONGRATULATIONS TO ALL. WELCOME TO EMBER'S WORKFORCE.
Welcome Mayor Cole!
POOR YOU! I THOUGHT I PICKED A BAD ONE, BUT YOU GOT THE WORST.

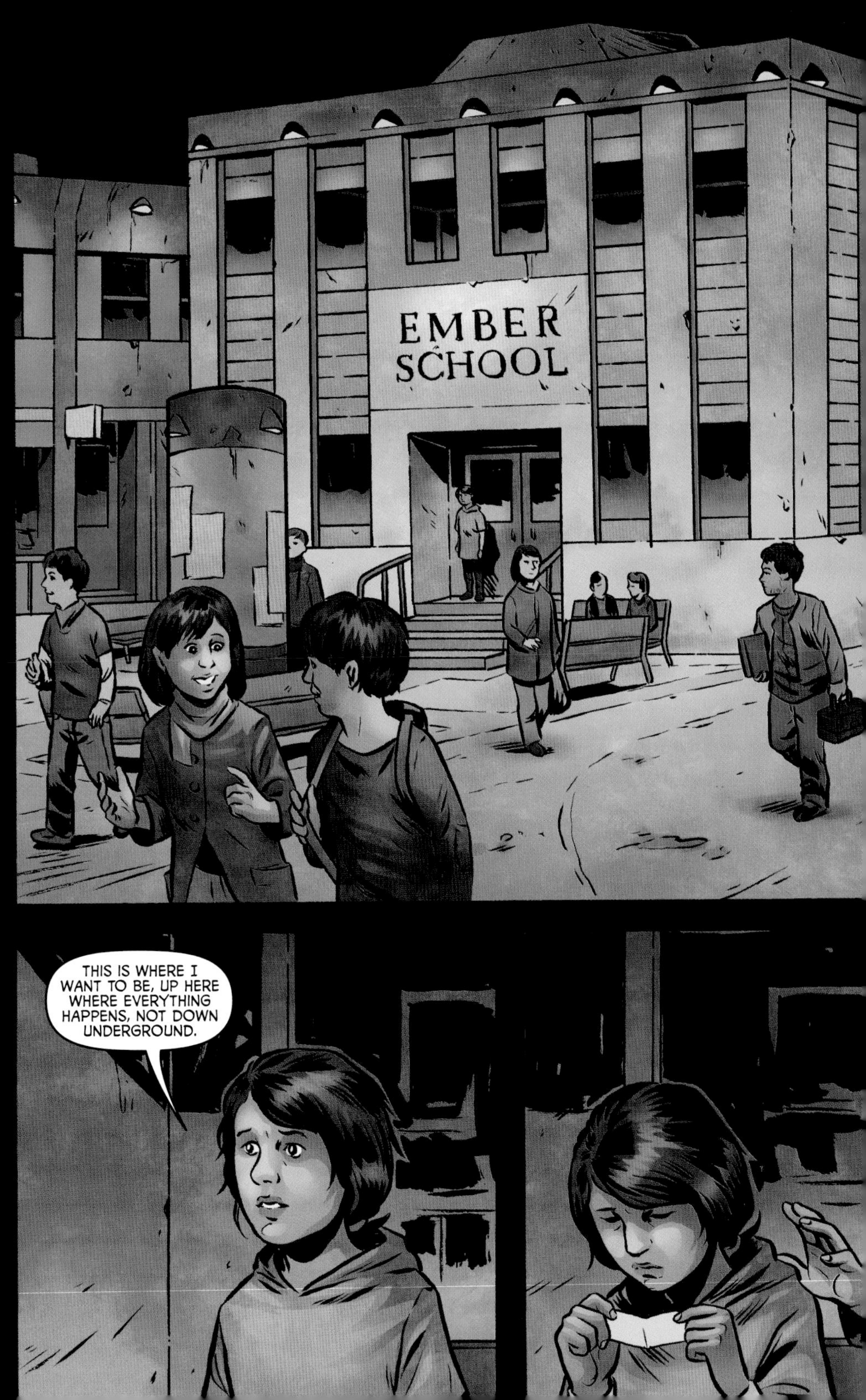
EMBER SCHOOL
THIS IS WHERE I WANT TO BE, UP HERE WHERE EVERYTHING HAPPENS, NOT DOWN UNDERGROUND.

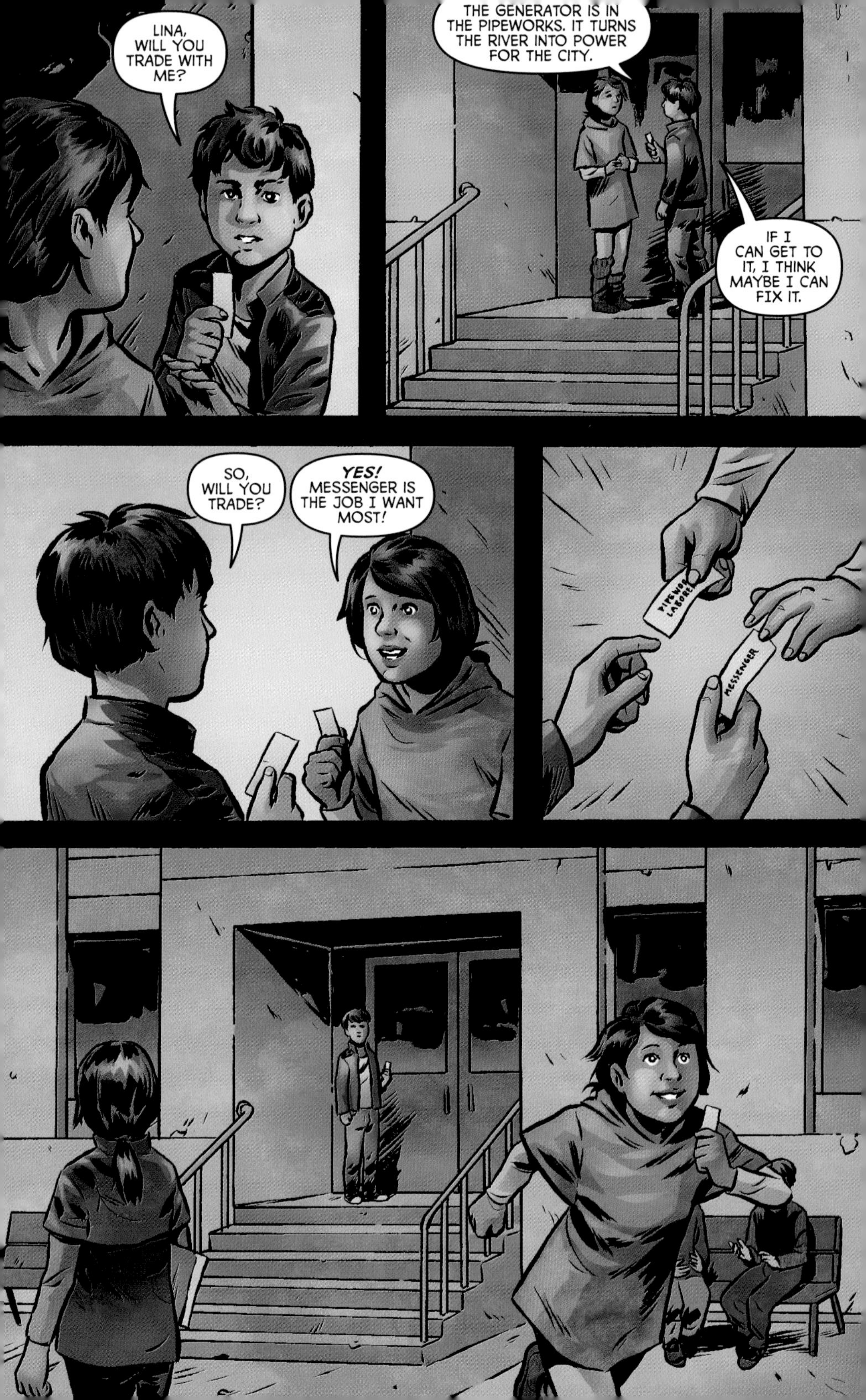
LINA, WILL YOU TRADE WITH ME?
THE GENERATOR IS IN THE PIPEWORKS. IT TURNS THE RIVER INTO POWER FOR THE CITY.
IF I CAN GET TO IT, I THINK MAYBE I CAN FIX IT.
SO, WILL YOU TRADE?
YES! MESSENGER IS THE JOB I WANT MOST!
MESSENGER

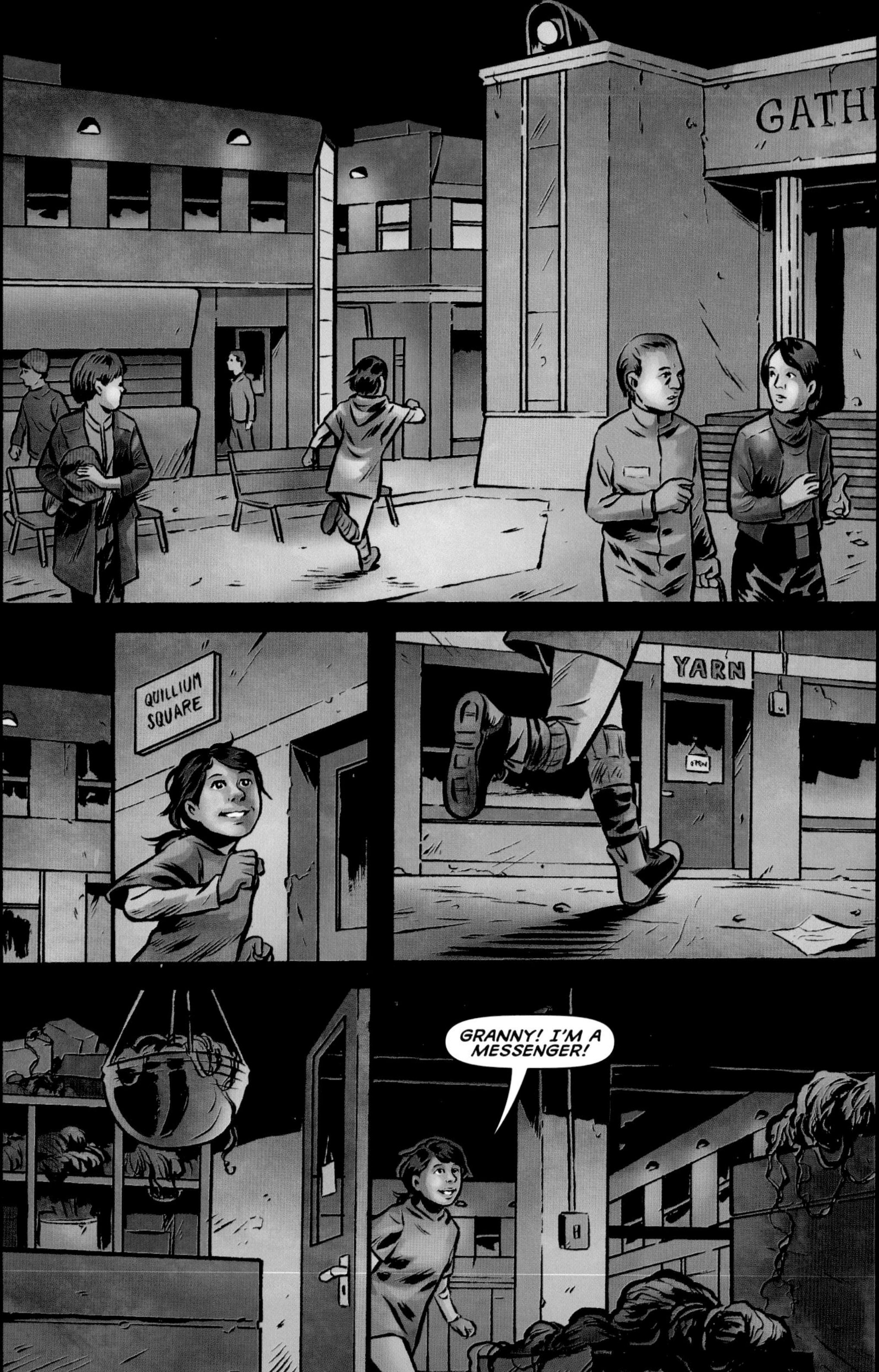
GATH
QUILLIUM SQUARE
YARN
GRANNY! I'M A MESSENGER!

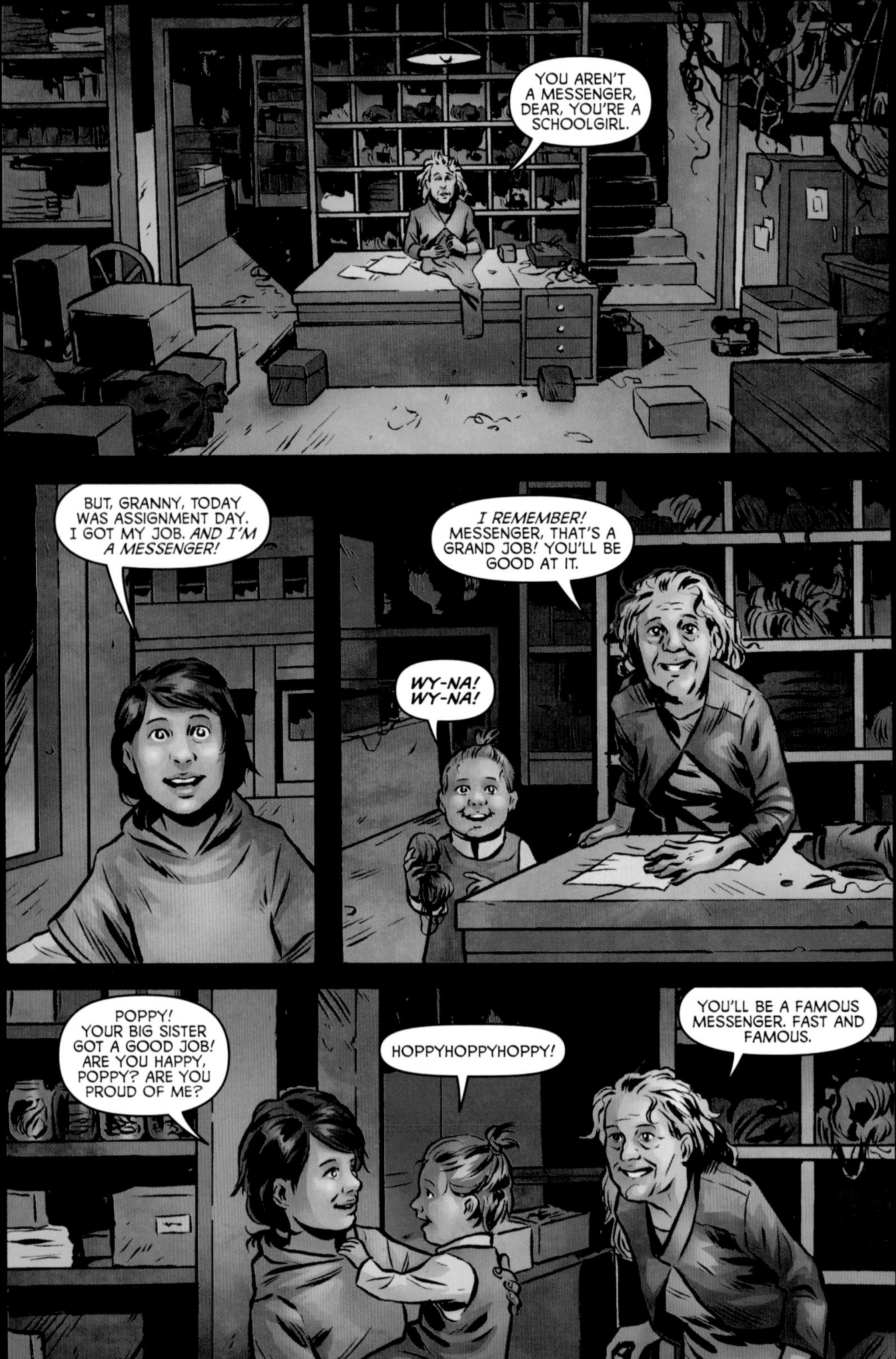
YOU AREN'T A MESSENGER, DEAR, YOU'RE A SCHOOLGIRL.
BUT, GRANNY, TODAY WAS ASSIGNMENT DAY. I GOT MY JOB. *AND I'M A MESSENGER!*
I REMEMBER! MESSENGER, THAT'S A GRAND JOB! YOU'LL BE GOOD AT IT.
WY-NA! WY-NA!
POPPY! YOUR BIG SISTER GOT A GOOD JOB! ARE YOU HAPPY, POPPY? ARE YOU PROUD OF ME?
HOPPYHOPPYHOPPY!
YOU'LL BE A FAMOUS MESSENGER. FAST AND FAMOUS.

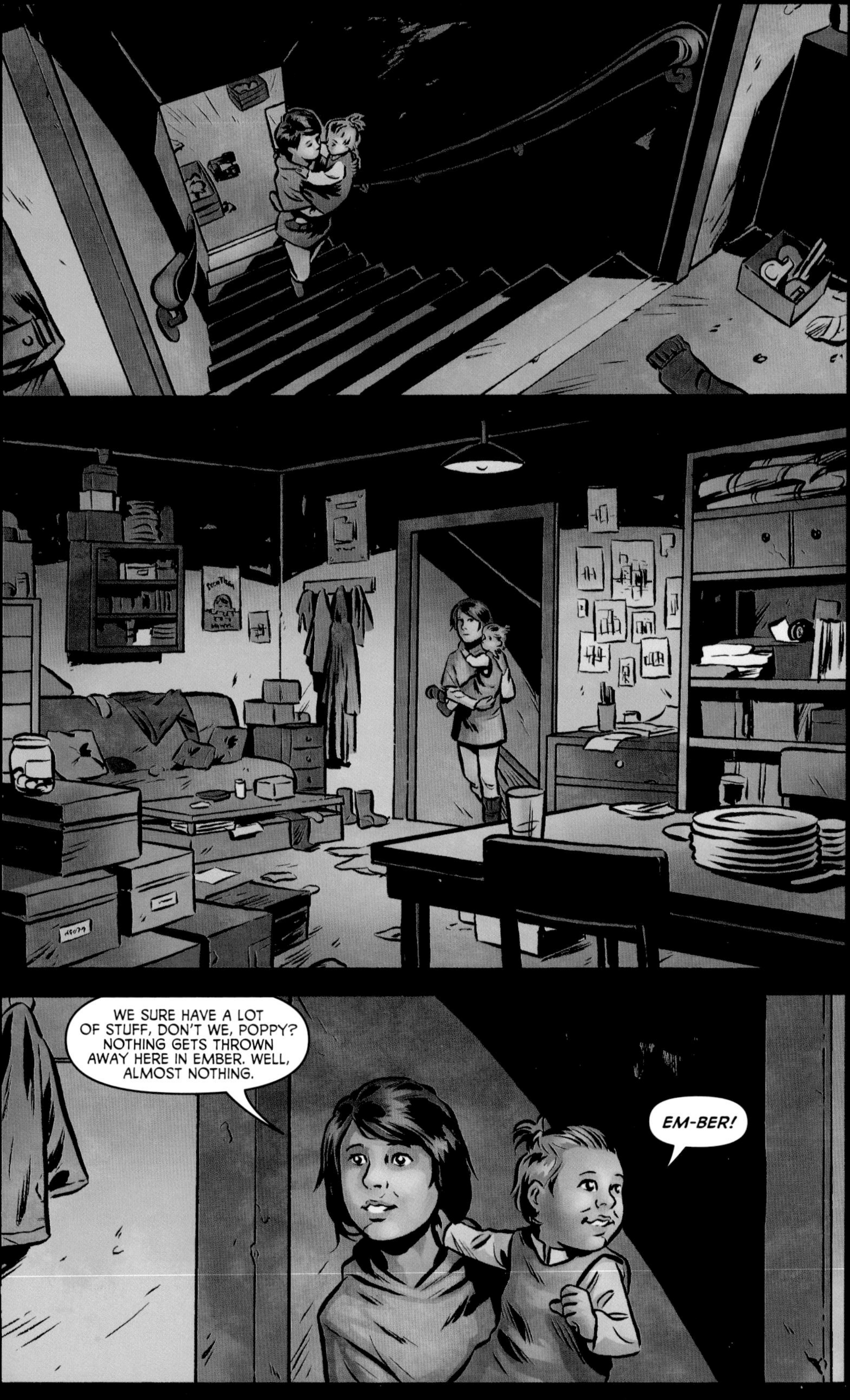
WE SURE HAVE A LOT OF STUFF, DON'T WE, POPPY? NOTHING GETS THROWN AWAY HERE IN EMBER. WELL, ALMOST NOTHING.
EM-BER!

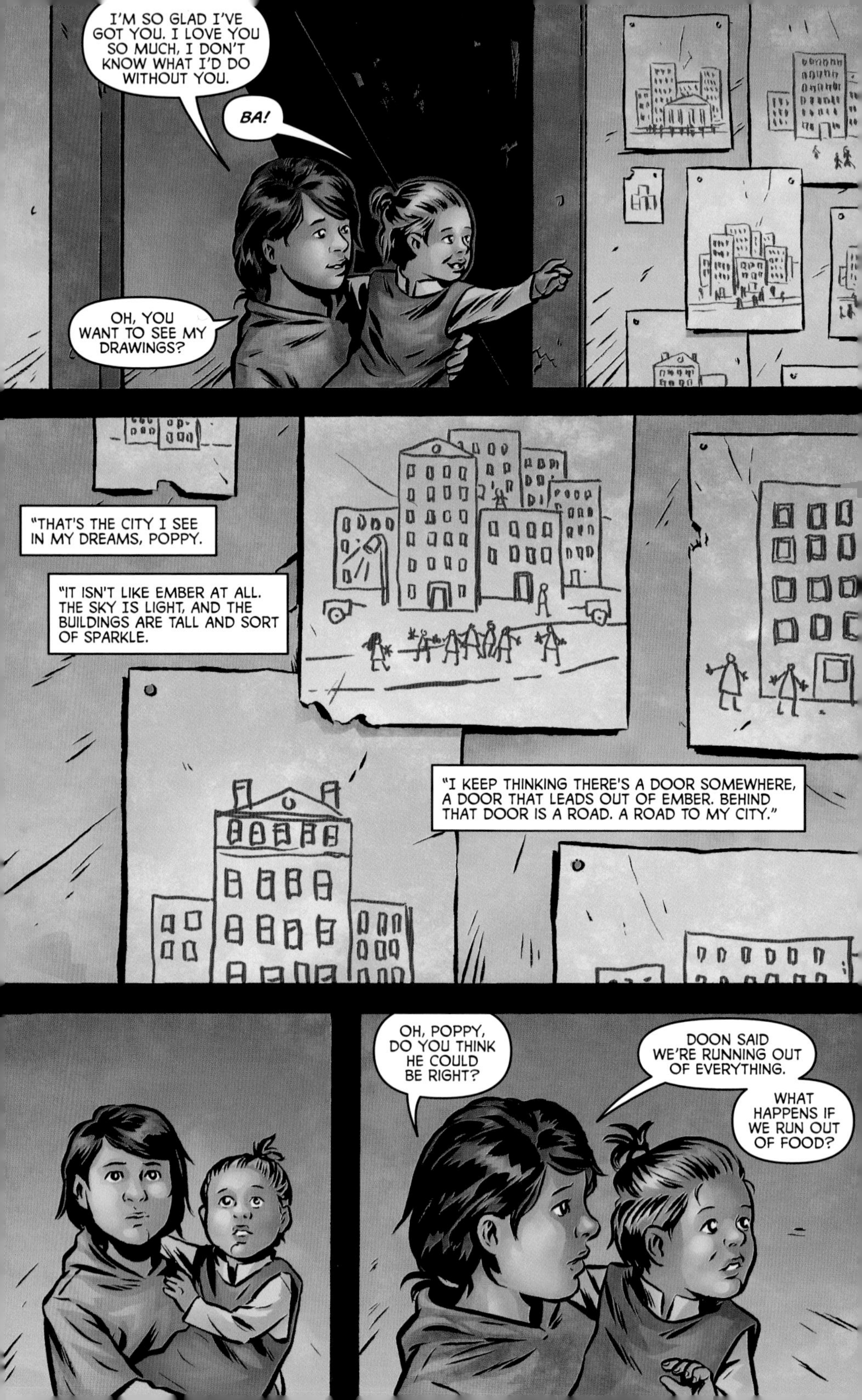
I'M SO GLAD I'VE GOT YOU. I LOVE YOU SO MUCH, I DON'T KNOW WHAT I'D DO WITHOUT YOU.
BA!
OH, YOU WANT TO SEE MY DRAWINGS?
"THAT'S THE CITY I SEE IN MY DREAMS, POPPY.
"IT ISN'T LIKE EMBER AT ALL. THE SKY IS LIGHT, AND THE BUILDINGS ARE TALL AND SORT OF SPARKLE.
"I KEEP THINKING THERE'S A DOOR SOMEWHERE, A DOOR THAT LEADS OUT OF EMBER. BEHIND THAT DOOR IS A ROAD. A ROAD TO MY CITY."
OH, POPPY, DO YOU THINK HE COULD BE RIGHT?
DOON SAID WE'RE RUNNING OUT OF EVERYTHING.
WHAT HAPPENS IF WE RUN OUT OF FOOD?

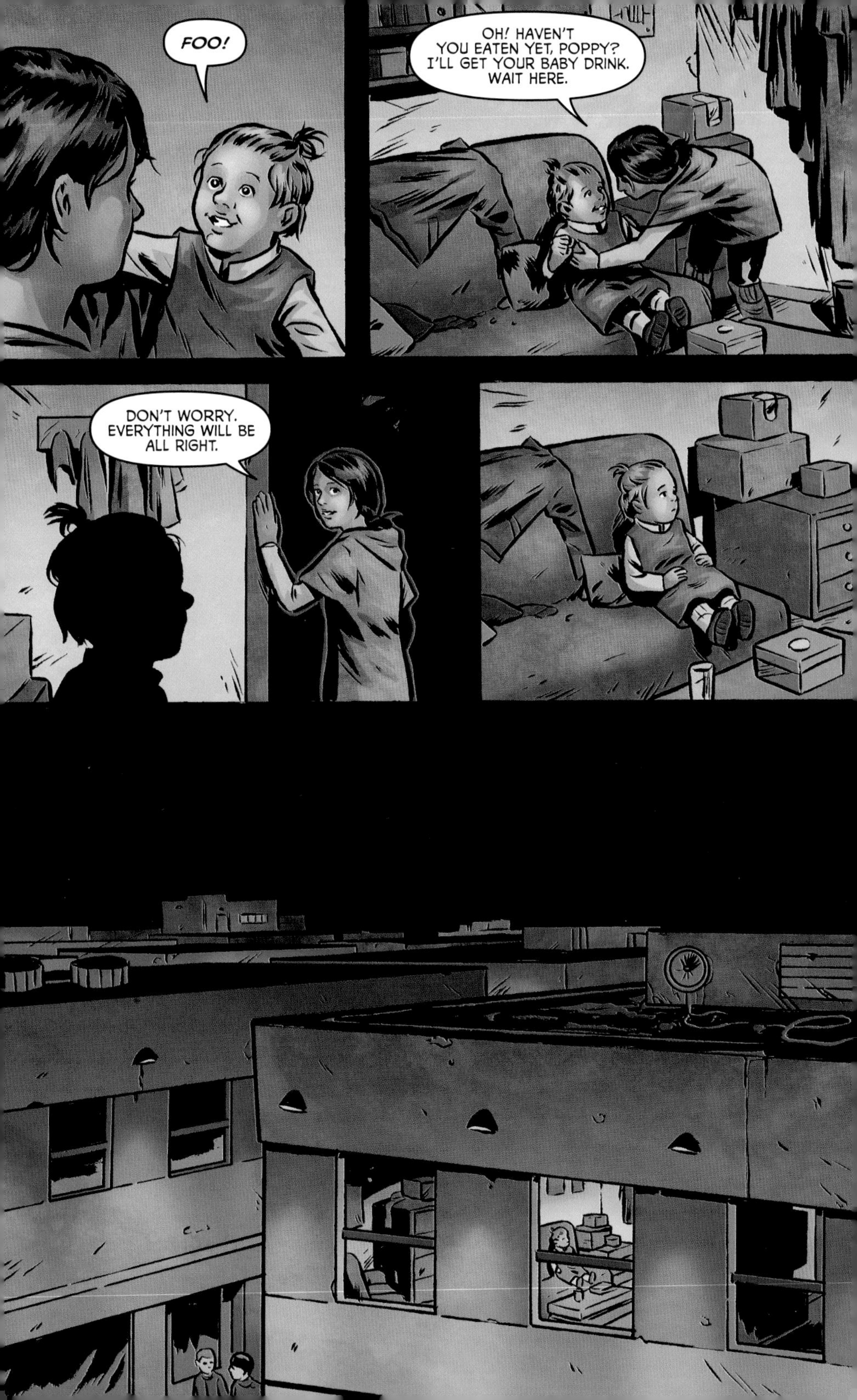
FOO!
OH! HAVEN'T YOU EATEN YET, POPPY? I'LL GET YOUR BABY DRINK. WAIT HERE.
DON'T WORRY. EVERYTHING WILL BE ALL RIGHT.

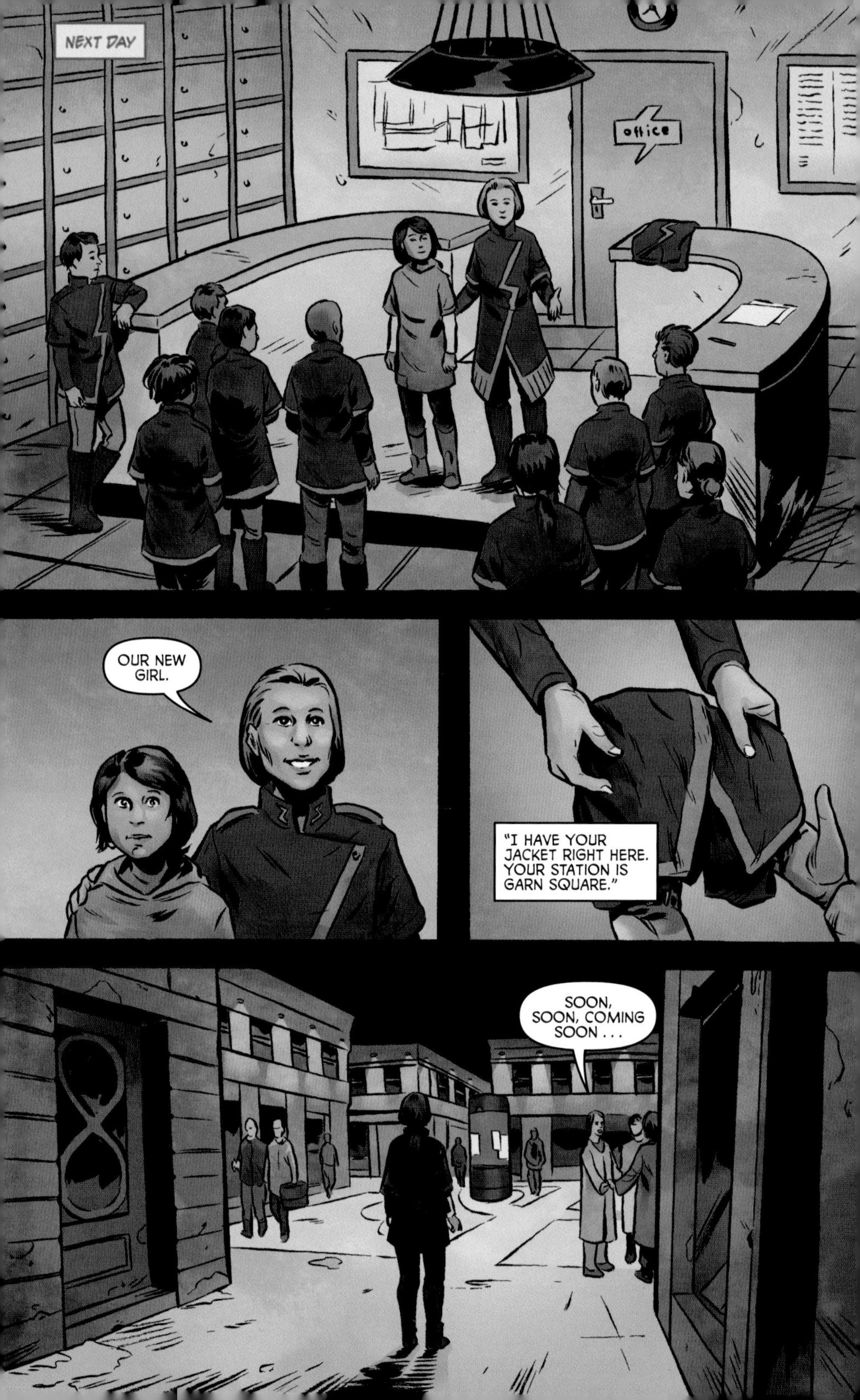
NEXT DAY
office
OUR NEW GIRL.
"I HAVE YOUR JACKET RIGHT HERE. YOUR STATION IS GARN SQUARE."
SOON, SOON, COMING SOON . . .

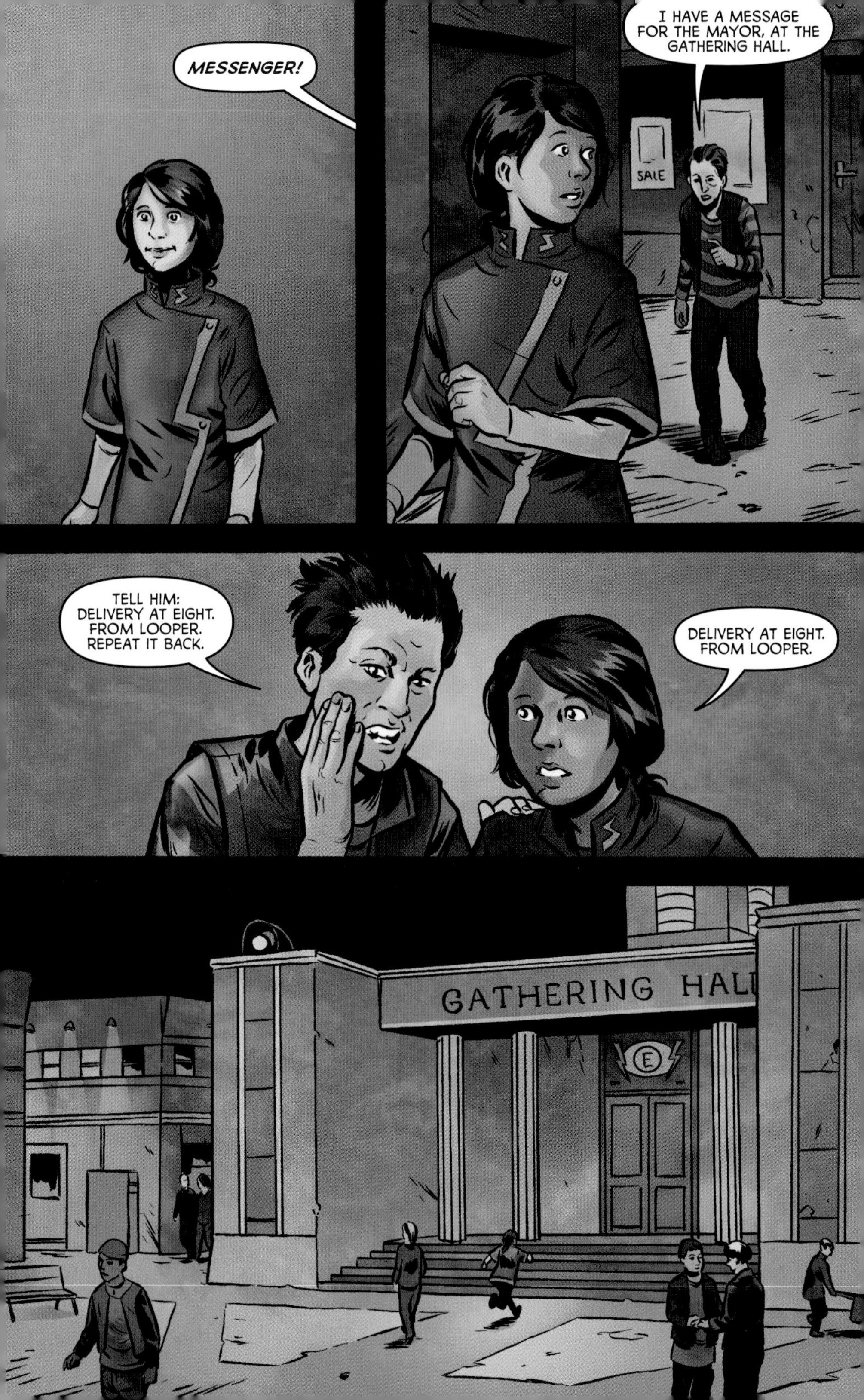
MESSENGER!
I HAVE A MESSAGE FOR THE MAYOR, AT THE GATHERING HALL.
SALE
TELL HIM: DELIVERY AT EIGHT. FROM LOOPER. REPEAT IT BACK.
DELIVERY AT EIGHT. FROM LOOPER.
GATHERING HAL
E

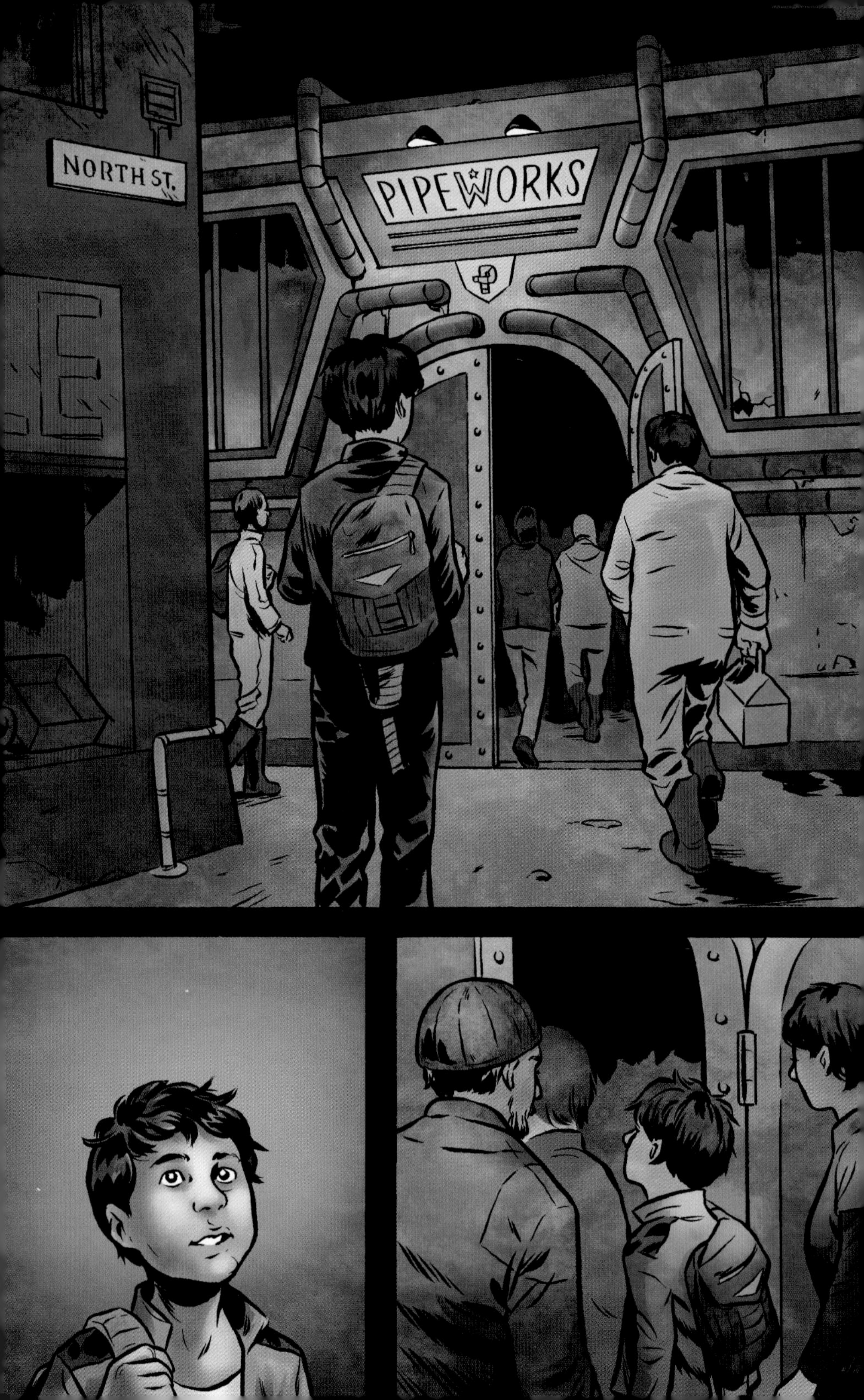
NORTH ST.
PIPEWORKS

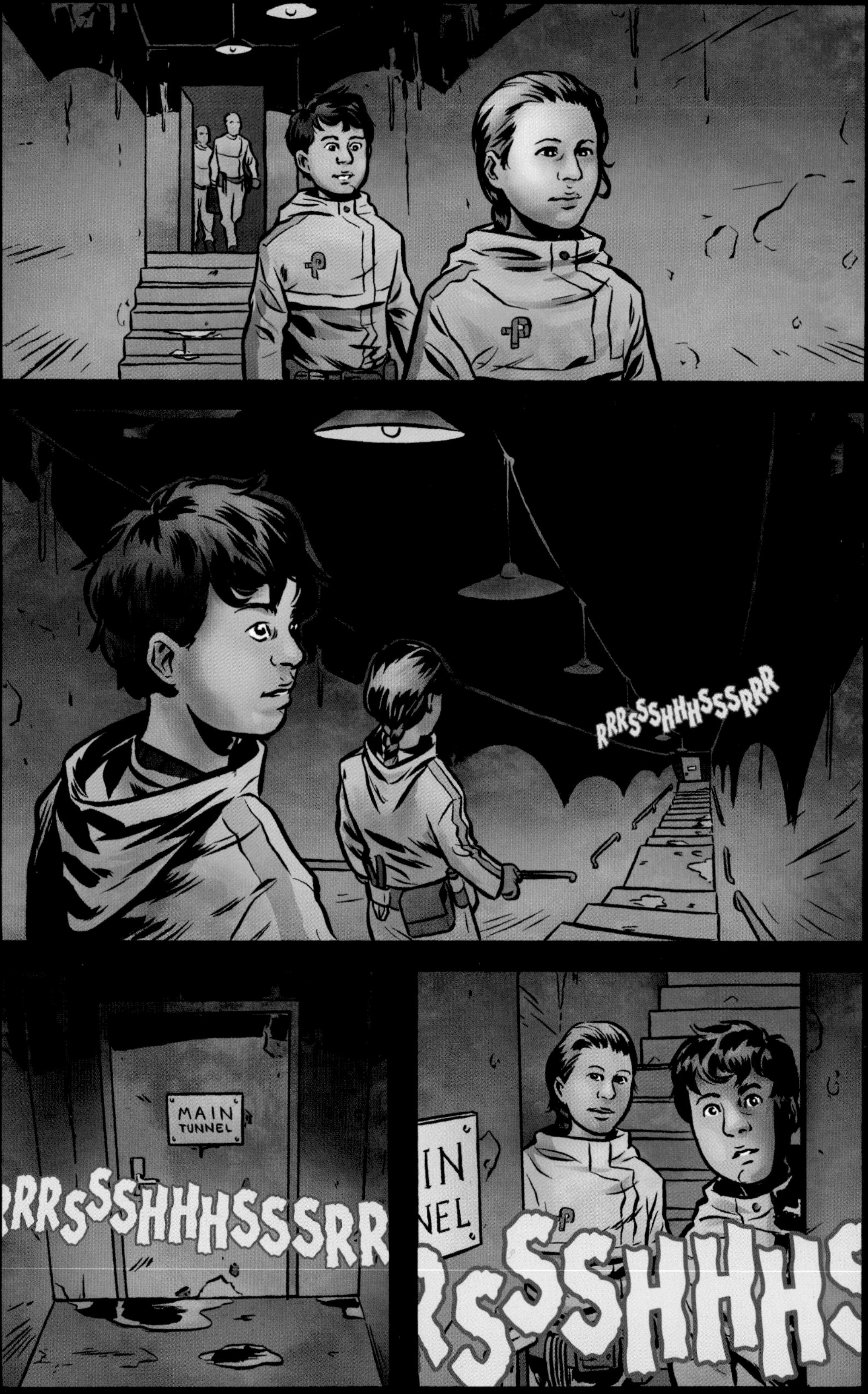

RRRSSSHHHSSSRRR
MAIN TUNNEL
RRRSSSHHHSSSRR
IN
NEL
RSSSHHHS

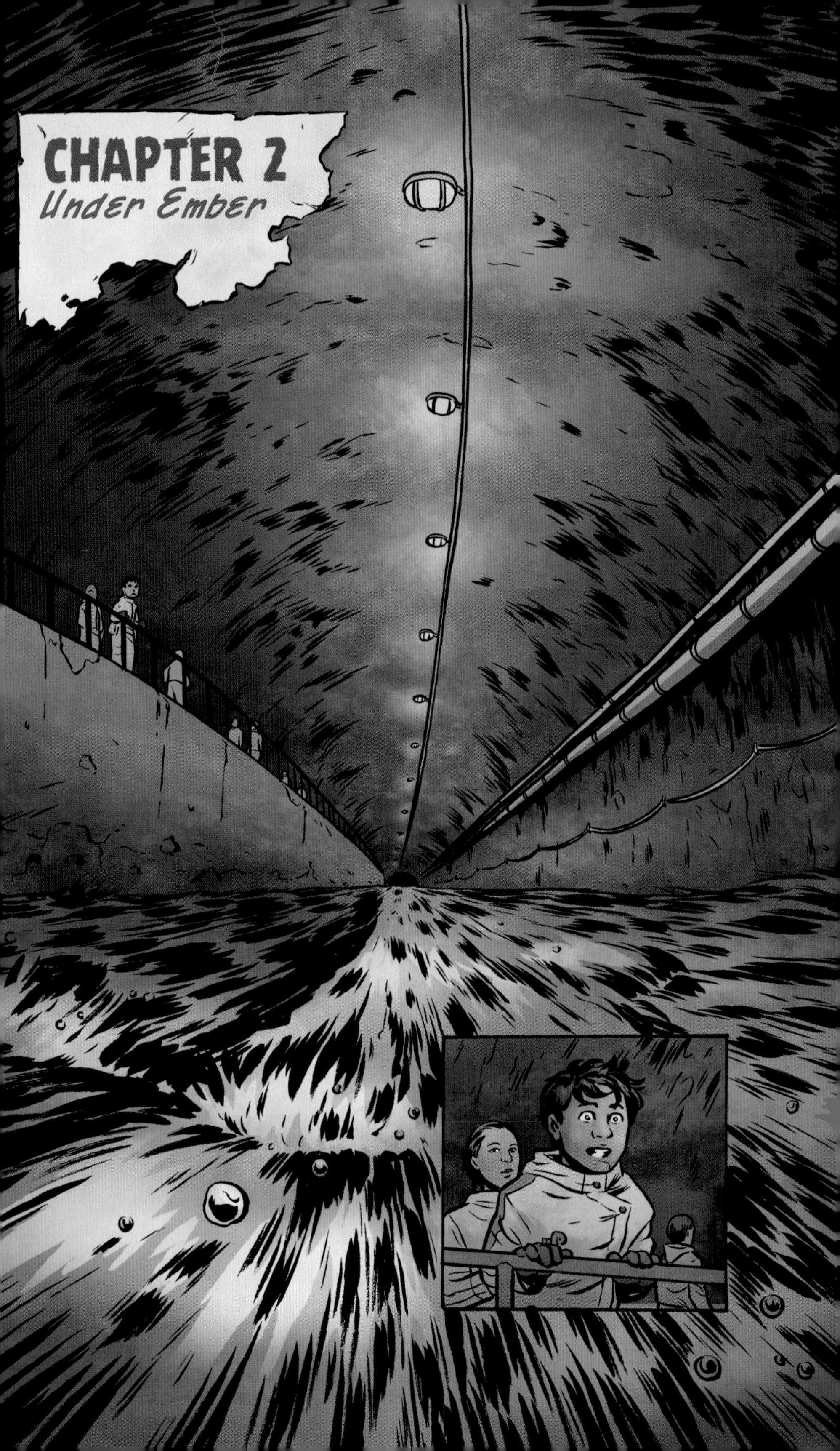
CHAPTER 2
Under Ember

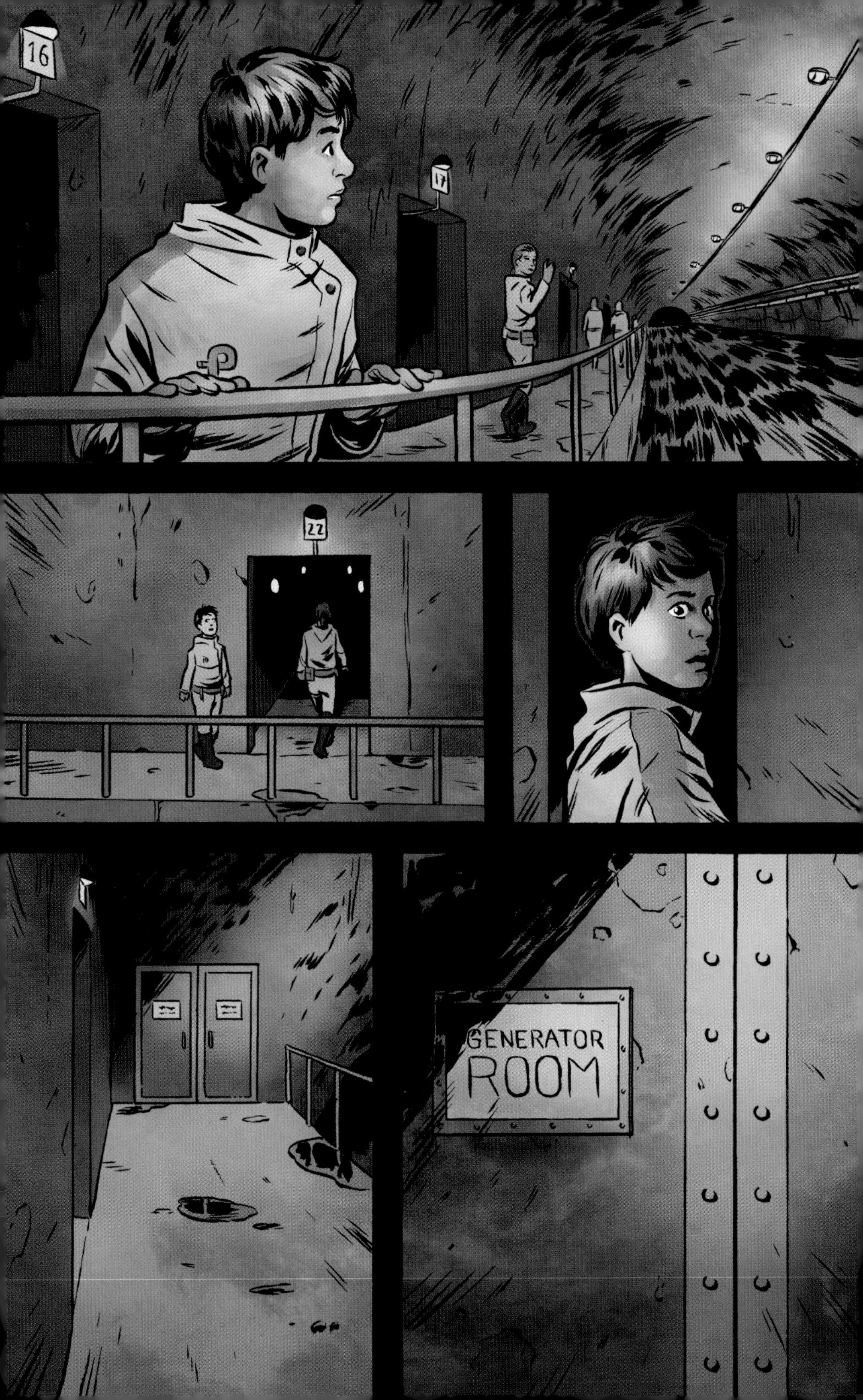
16
17
22
GENERATOR
ROOM

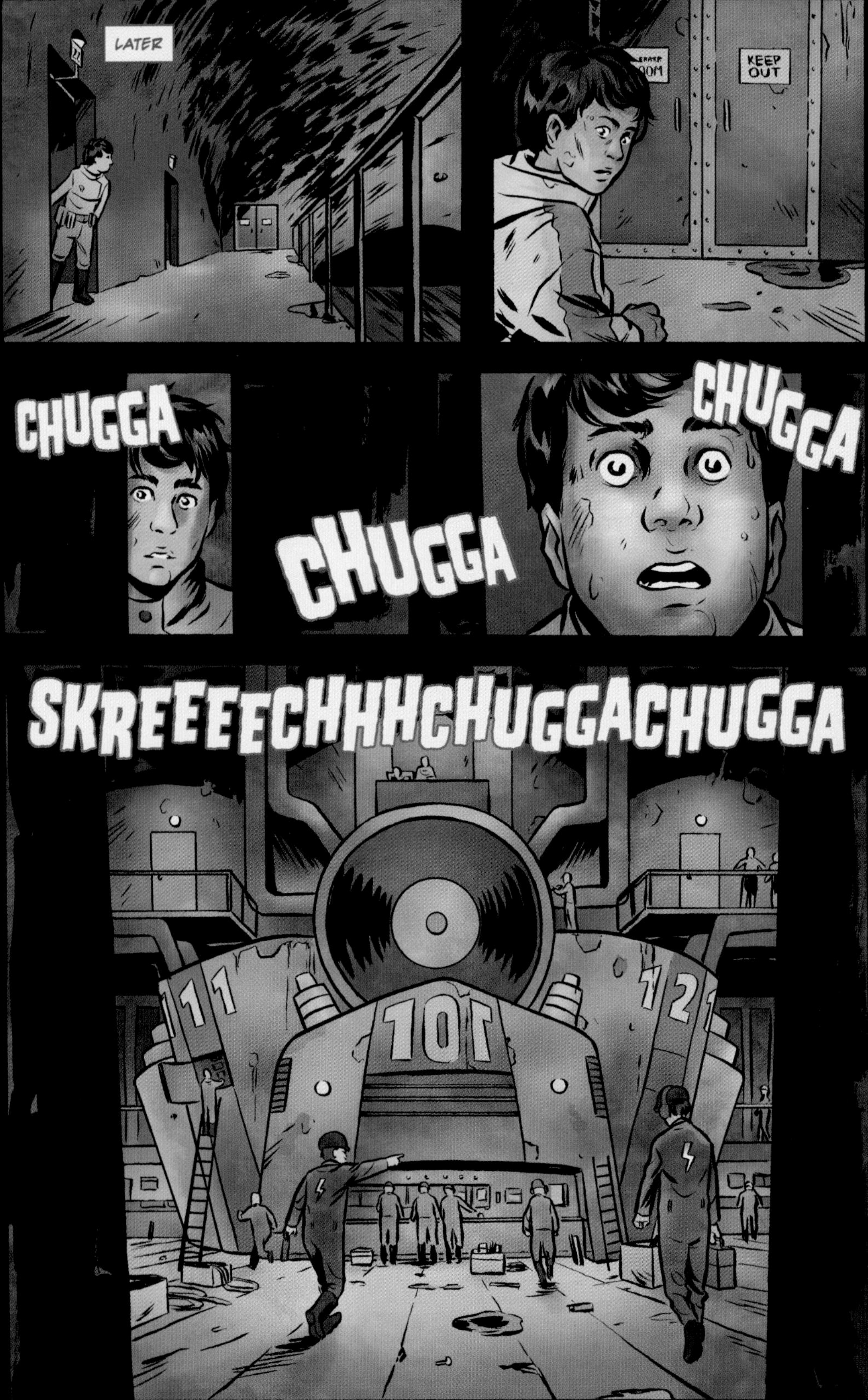
LATER
KEEP OUT
CHUGGA
CHUGGA
CHUGGA
SKREEEECHHHCHUGGACHUGGA
111
101
121

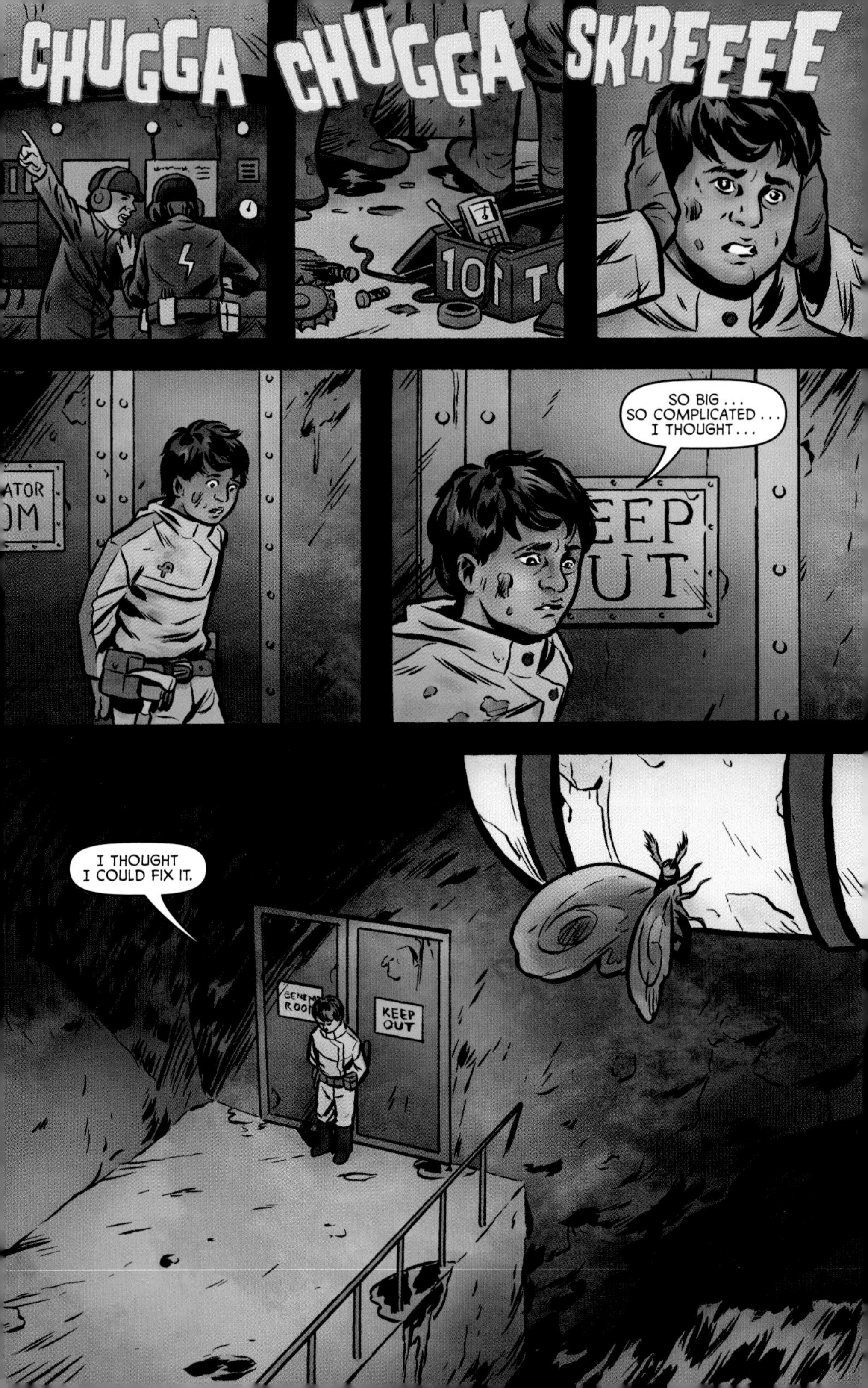
CHUGGA
CHUGGA
SKREEEE
SO BIG . . . SO COMPLICATED . . . I THOUGHT . . .
I THOUGHT I COULD FIX IT.
KEEP OUT

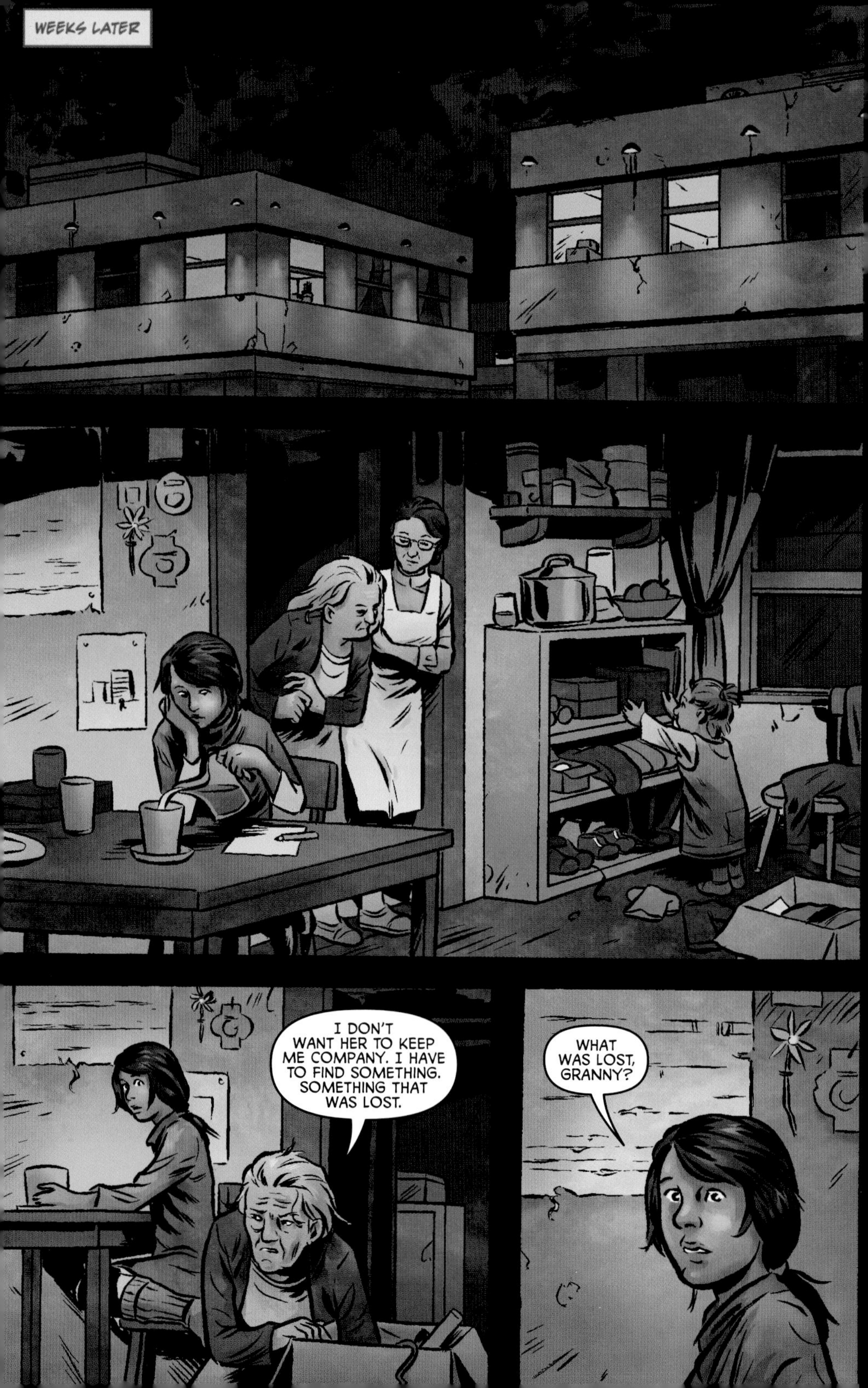
WEEKS LATER
I DON'T WANT HER TO KEEP ME COMPANY. I HAVE TO FIND SOMETHING. SOMETHING THAT WAS LOST.
WHAT WAS LOST, GRANNY?

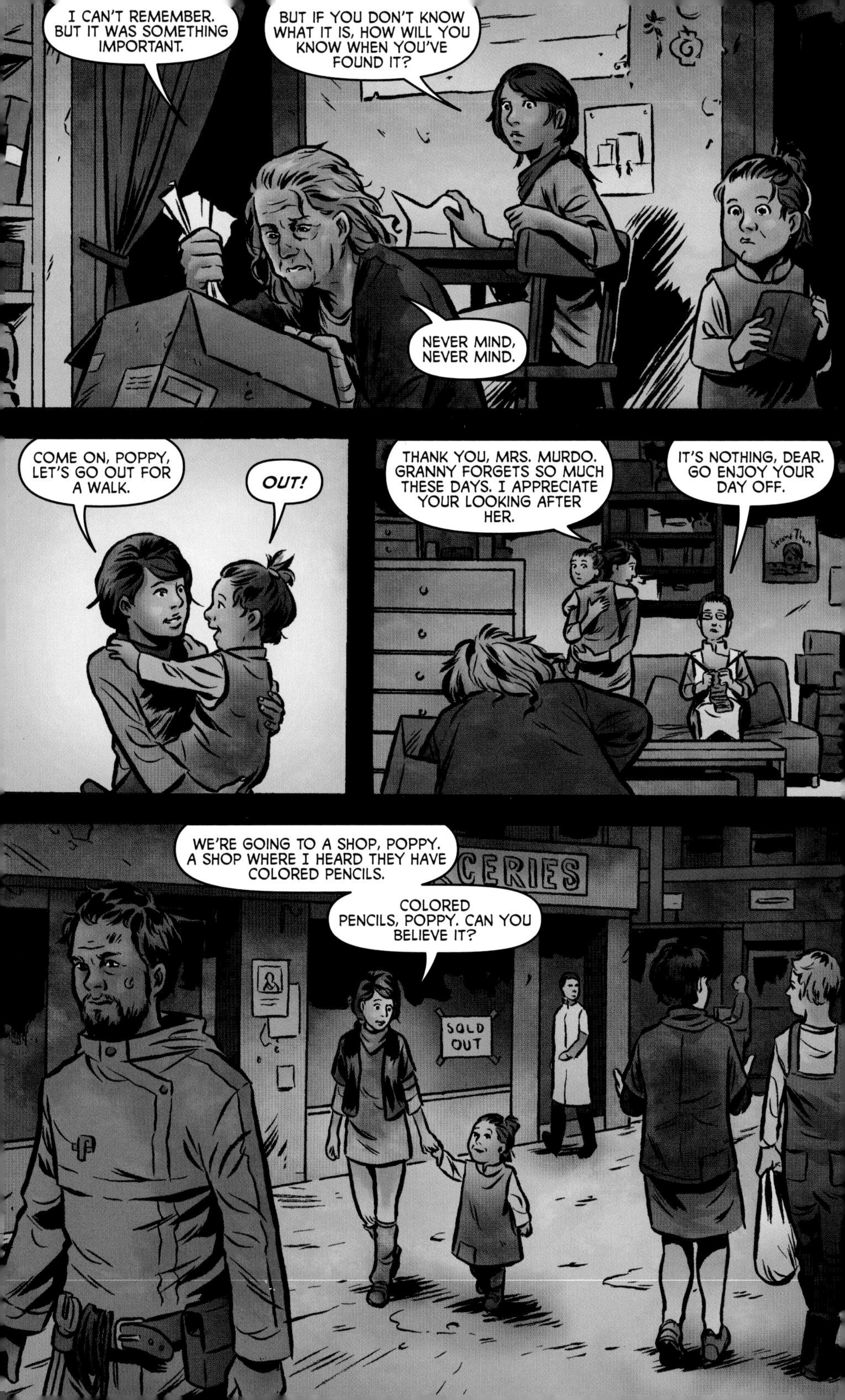
I CAN'T REMEMBER. BUT IT WAS SOMETHING IMPORTANT.
BUT IF YOU DON'T KNOW WHAT IT IS, HOW WILL YOU KNOW WHEN YOU'VE FOUND IT?
NEVER MIND, NEVER MIND.
COME ON, POPPY, LET'S GO OUT FOR A WALK.
OUT!
THANK YOU, MRS. MURDO. GRANNY FORGETS SO MUCH THESE DAYS. I APPRECIATE YOUR LOOKING AFTER HER.
IT'S NOTHING, DEAR. GO ENJOY YOUR DAY OFF.
WE'RE GOING TO A SHOP, POPPY. A SHOP WHERE I HEARD THEY HAVE COLORED PENCILS.
CERIES
COLORED PENCILS, POPPY. CAN YOU BELIEVE IT?
SOLD OUT

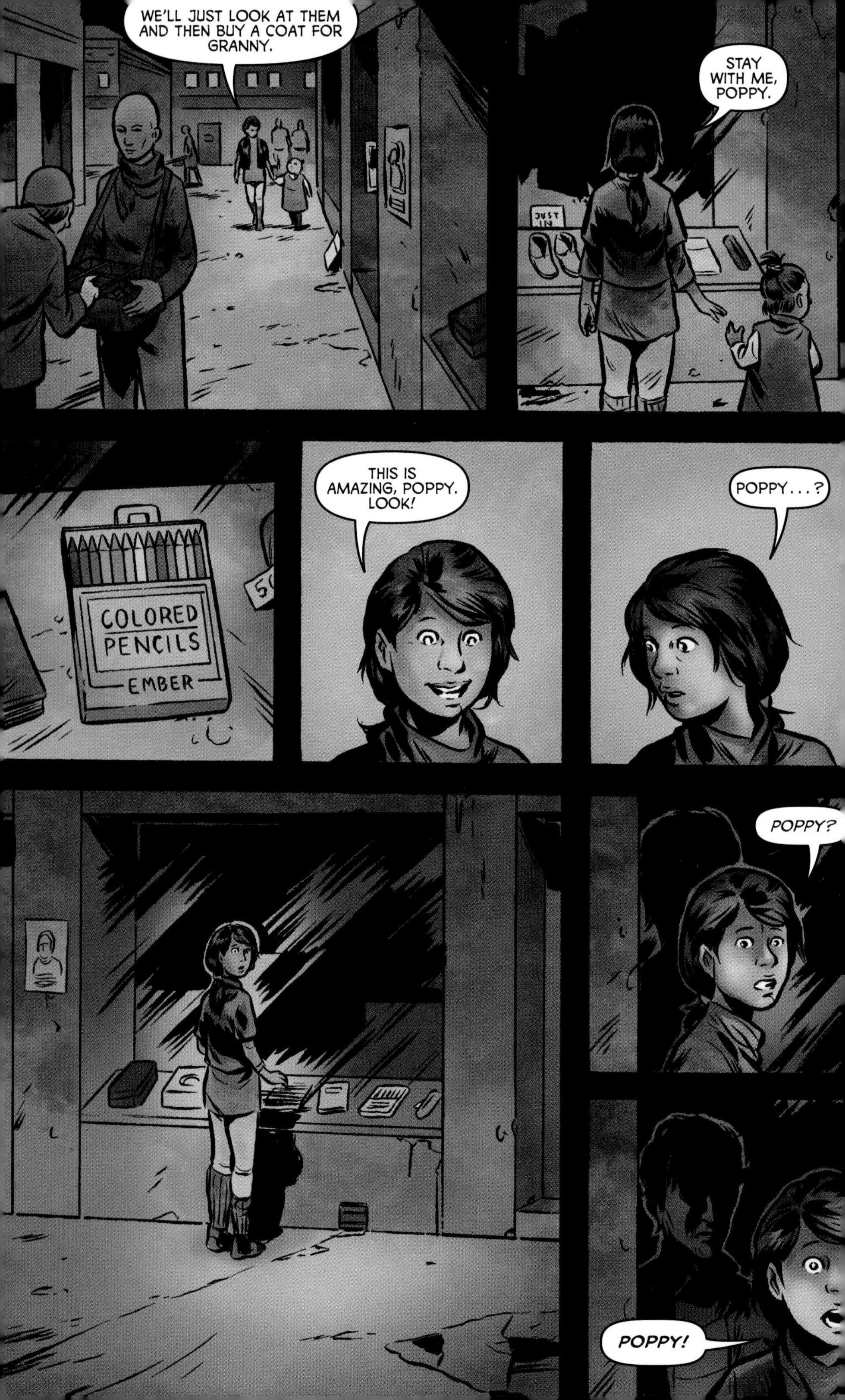
WE'LL JUST LOOK AT THEM AND THEN BUY A COAT FOR GRANNY.
STAY WITH ME, POPPY.
JUST IN
COLORED PENCILS
EMBER
THIS IS AMAZING, POPPY. LOOK!
POPPY...?
POPPY?
POPPY!

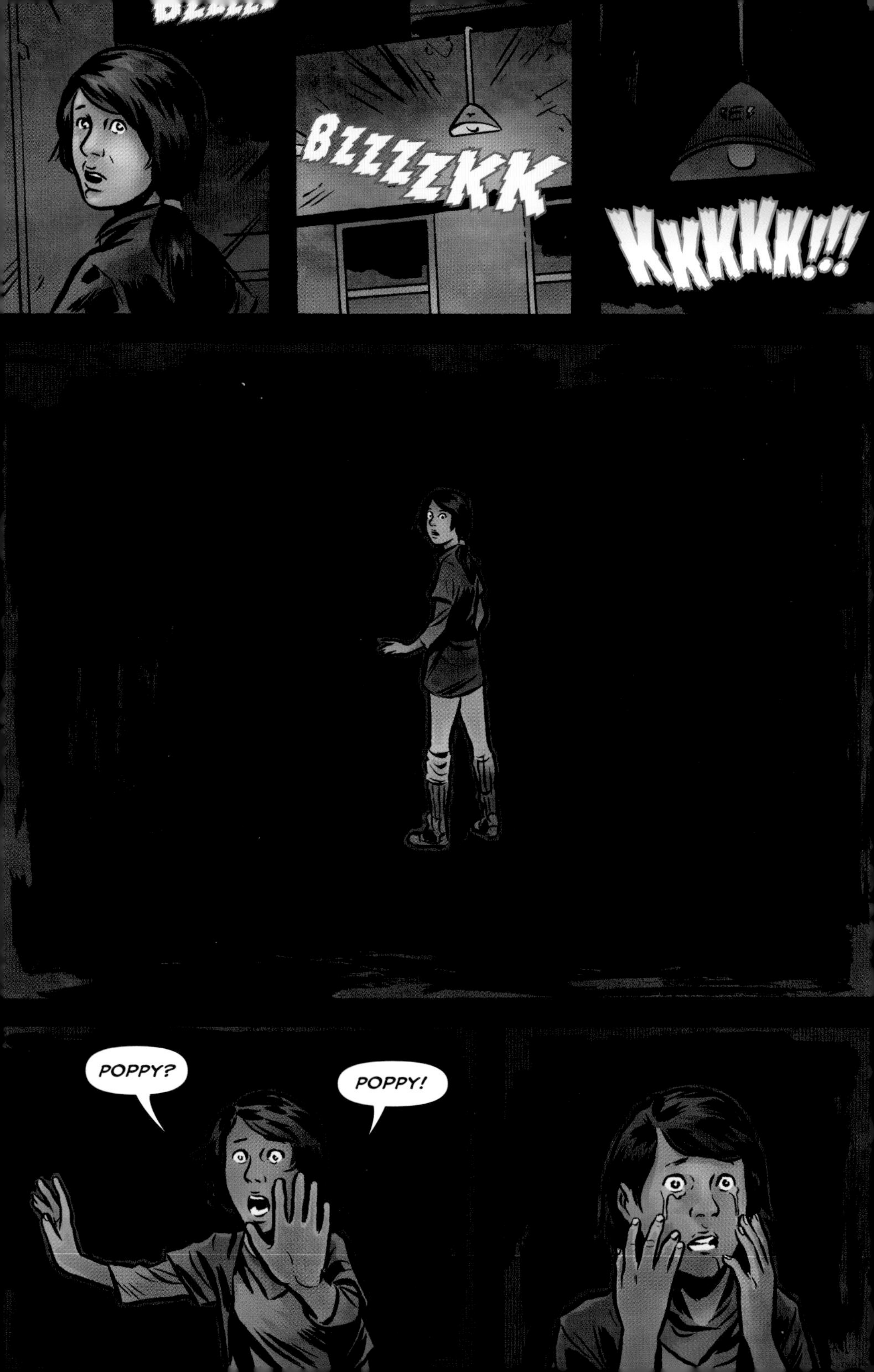

BZZZZZKK
KKKKK!!!
POPPY?
POPPY!

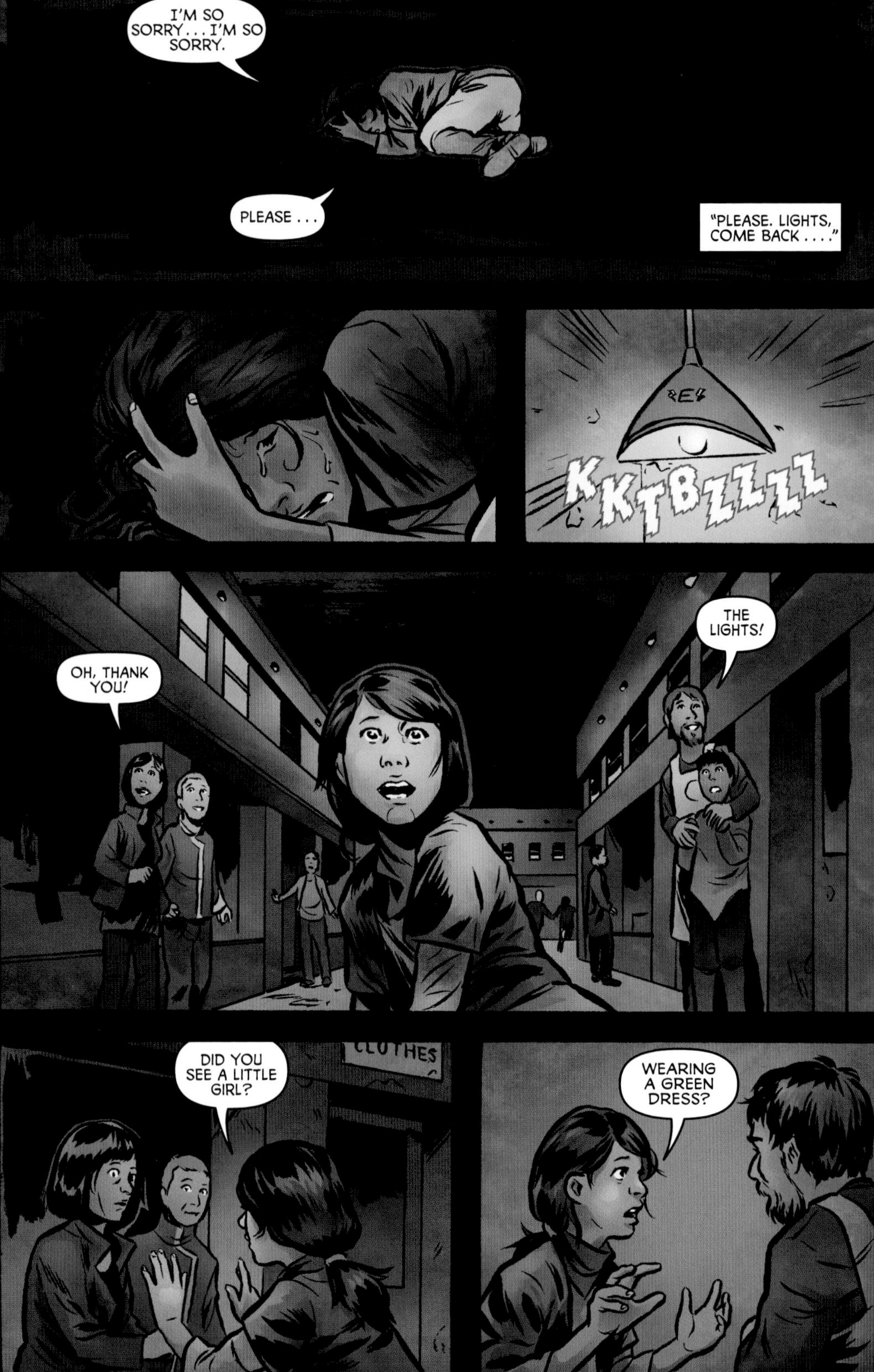
I'M SO SORRY . . . I'M SO SORRY.
PLEASE . . .
"PLEASE. LIGHTS, COME BACK . . . ."
KKTBZZZZ
OH, THANK YOU!
THE LIGHTS!
CLOTHES
DID YOU SEE A LITTLE GIRL?
WEARING A GREEN DRESS?

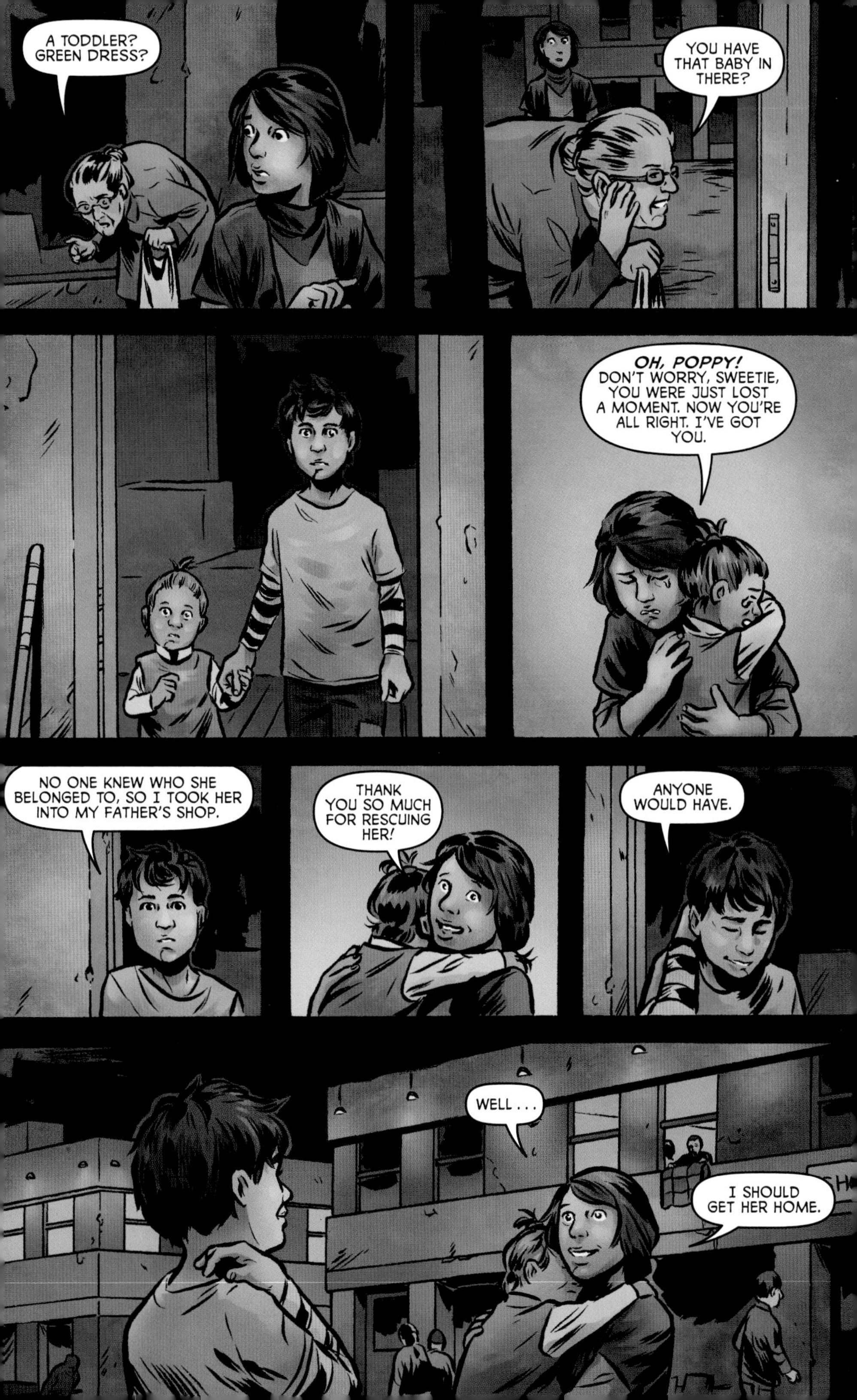
A TODDLER? GREEN DRESS?
YOU HAVE THAT BABY IN THERE?
OH, POPPY! DON'T WORRY, SWEETIE, YOU WERE JUST LOST A MOMENT. NOW YOU'RE ALL RIGHT. I'VE GOT YOU.
NO ONE KNEW WHO SHE BELONGED TO, SO I TOOK HER INTO MY FATHER'S SHOP.
THANK YOU SO MUCH FOR RESCUING HER!
ANYONE WOULD HAVE.
WELL . . .
I SHOULD GET HER HOME.

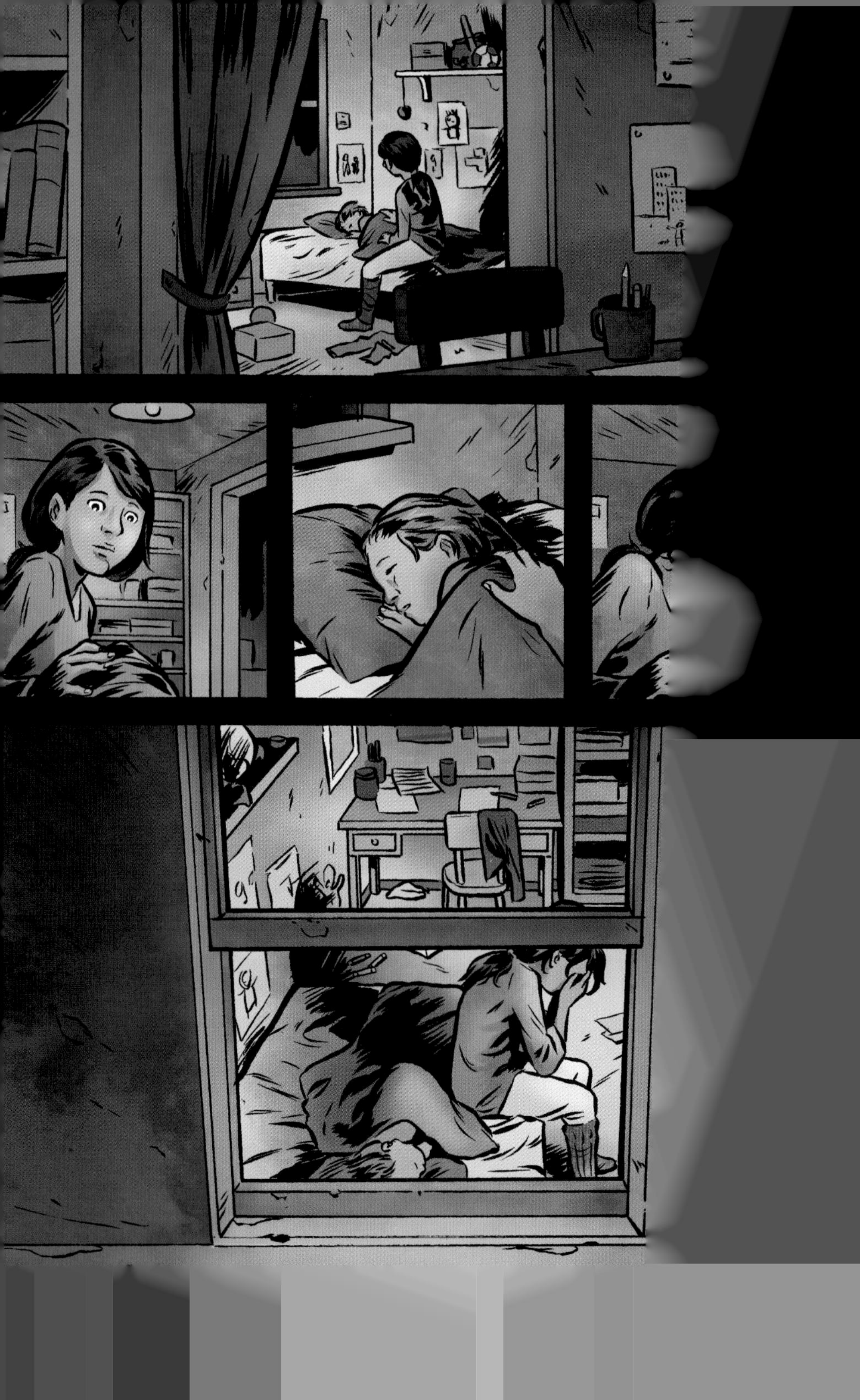

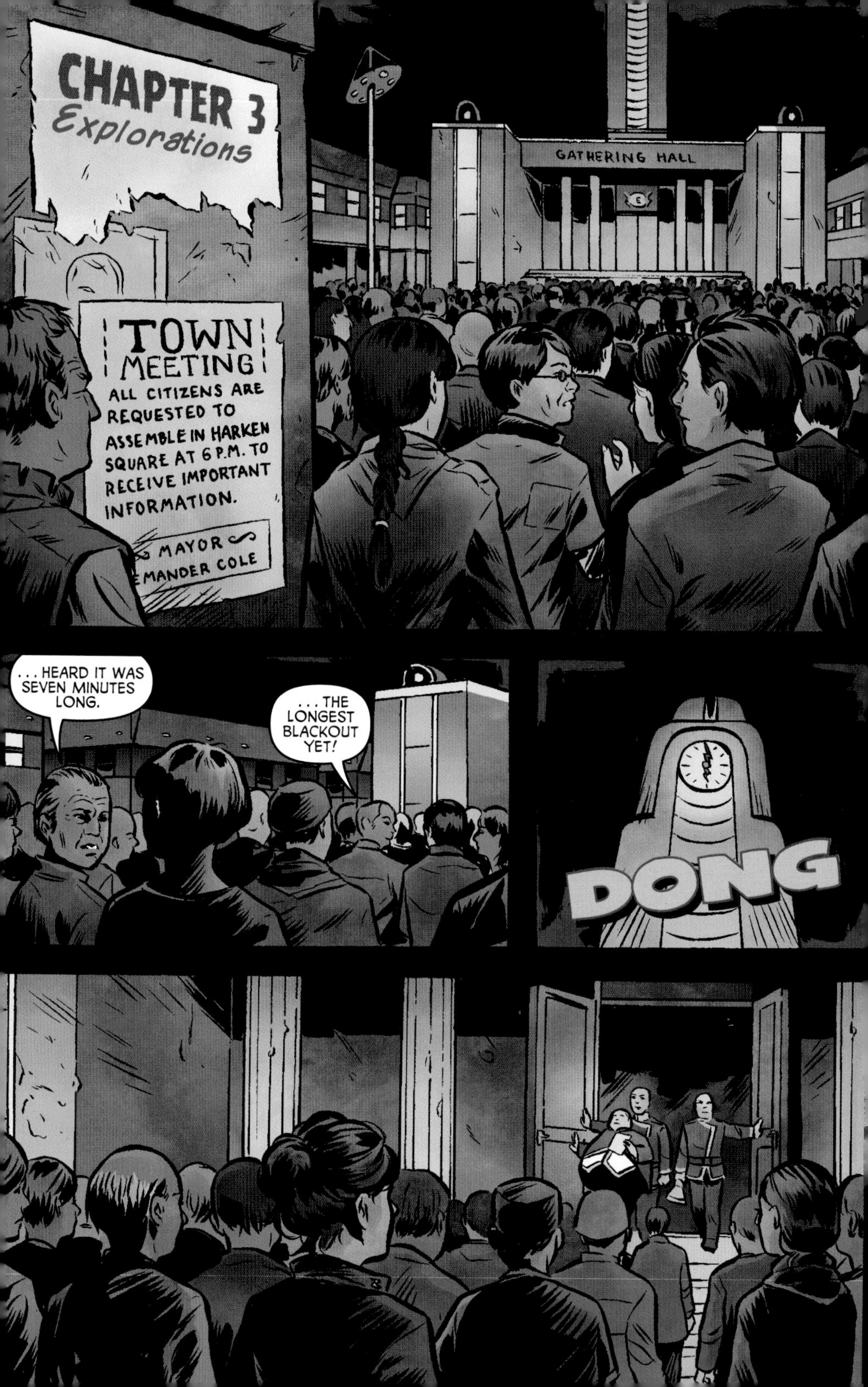
CHAPTER 3
Explorations
GATHERING HALL
TOWN MEETING
ALL CITIZENS ARE REQUESTED TO ASSEMBLE IN HARKEN SQUARE AT 6 P.M. TO RECEIVE IMPORTANT INFORMATION.
MAYOR
EMANDER COLE
. . . HEARD IT WAS SEVEN MINUTES LONG.
. . . THE LONGEST BLACKOUT YET!
DONG

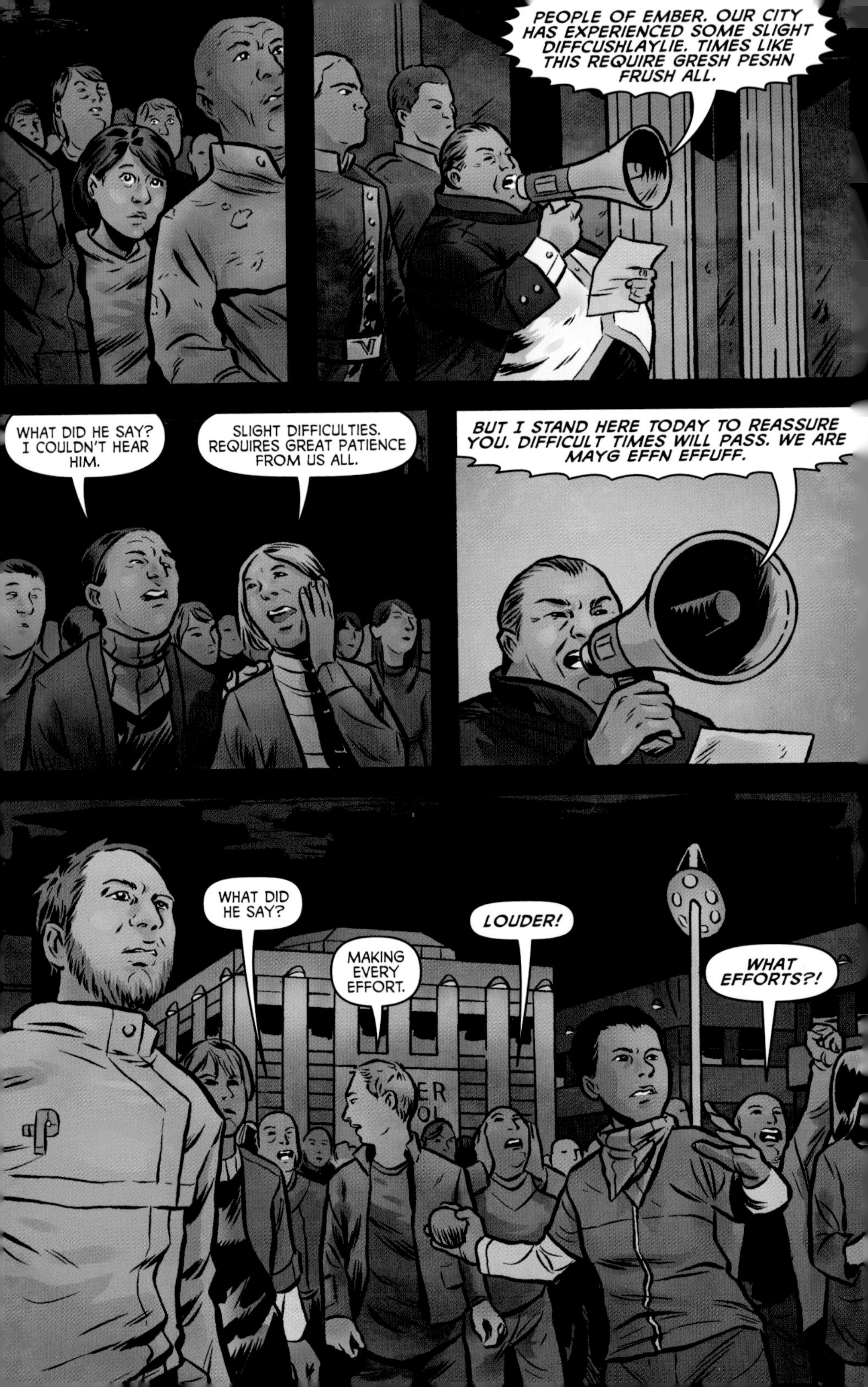
PEOPLE OF EMBER. OUR CITY HAS EXPERIENCED SOME SLIGHT DIFFCUSHLAYLIE. TIMES LIKE THIS REQUIRE GRESH PESHN FRUSH ALL.
WHAT DID HE SAY? I COULDN'T HEAR HIM.
SLIGHT DIFFICULTIES. REQUIRES GREAT PATIENCE FROM US ALL.
BUT I STAND HERE TODAY TO REASSURE YOU. DIFFICULT TIMES WILL PASS. WE ARE MAYG EFFN EFFUFF.
WHAT DID HE SAY?
MAKING EVERY EFFORT.
LOUDER!
WHAT EFFORTS?!

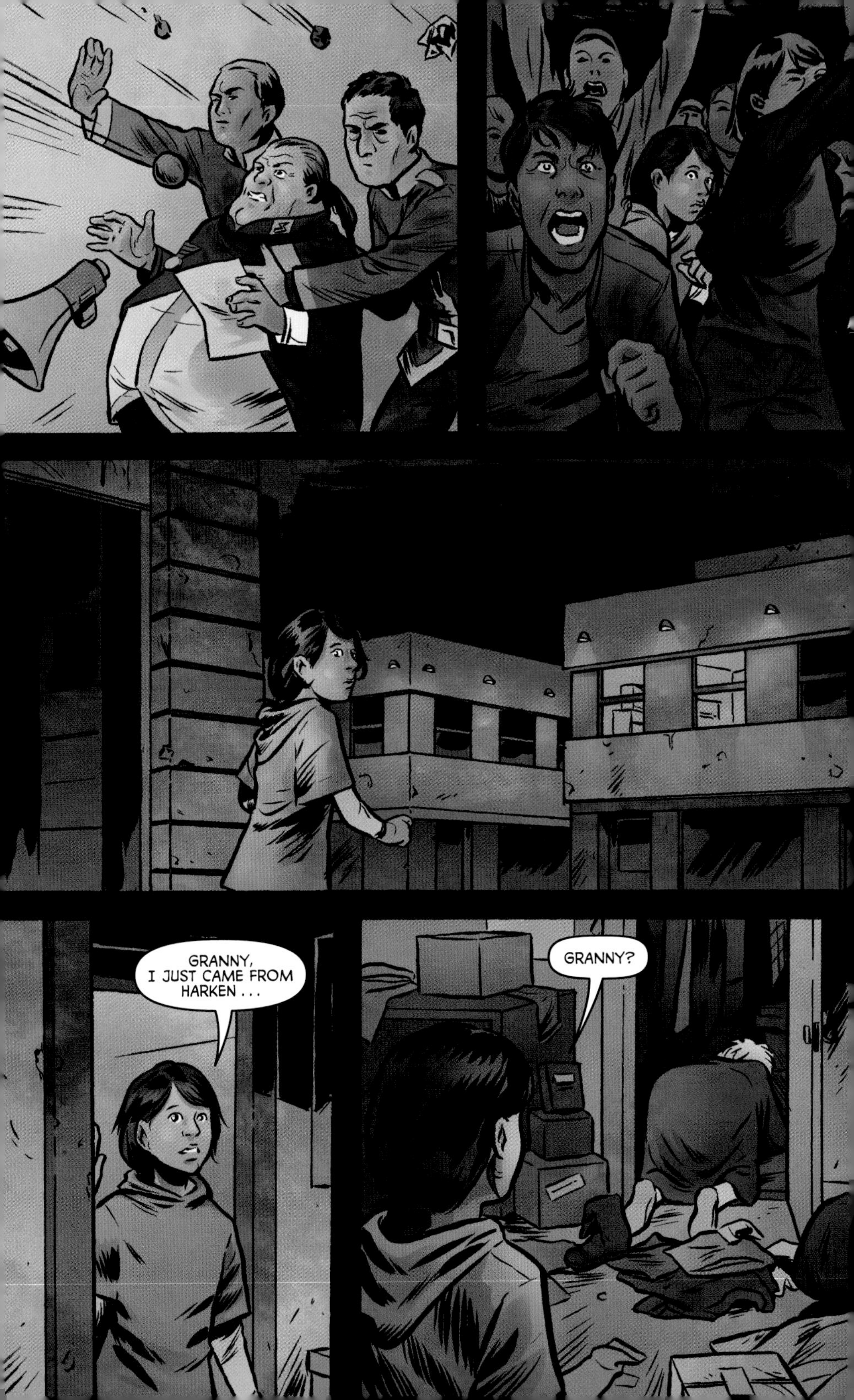
GRANNY, I JUST CAME FROM HARKEN . . .
GRANNY?

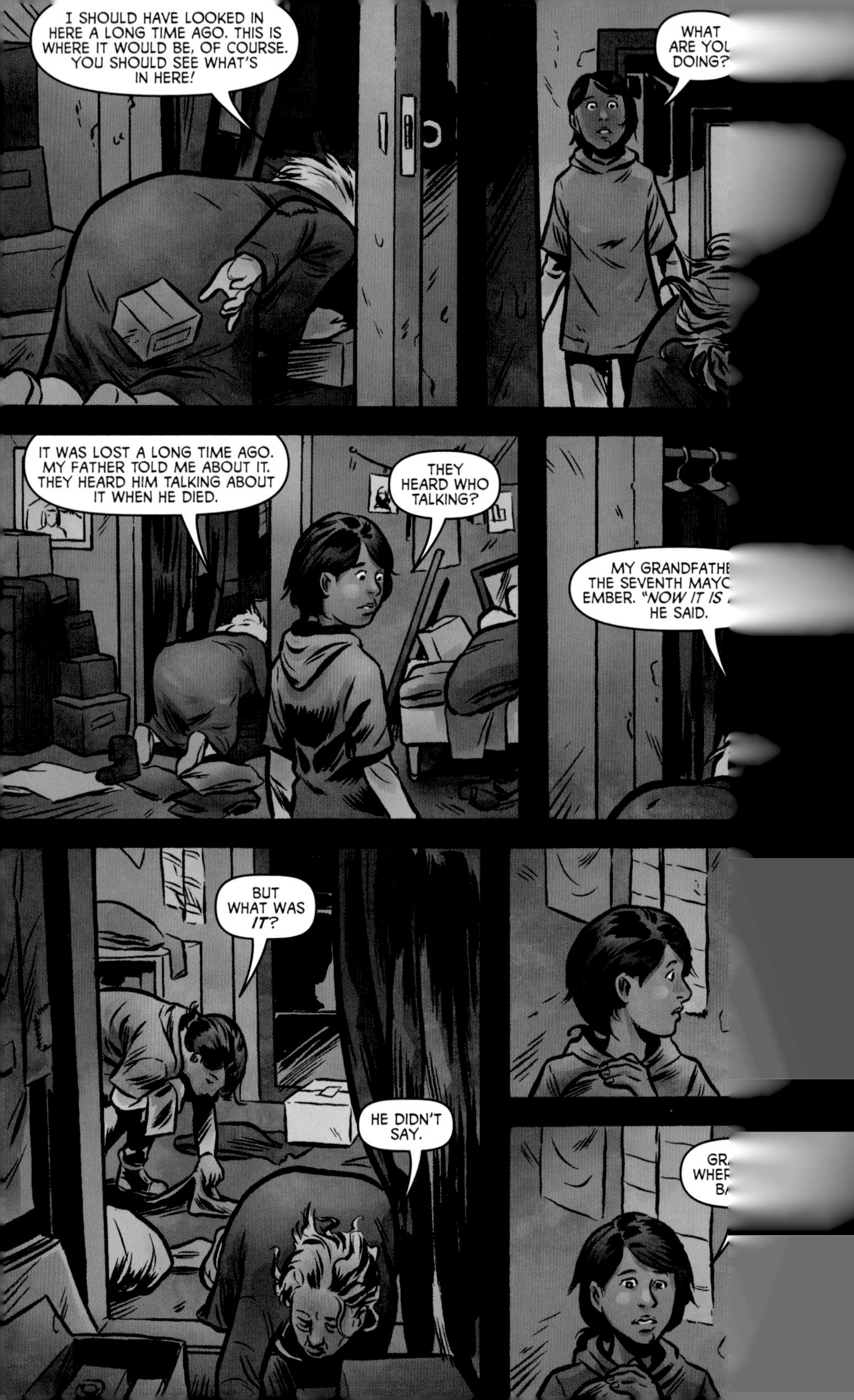
I SHOULD HAVE LOOKED IN HERE A LONG TIME AGO. THIS IS WHERE IT WOULD BE, OF COURSE. YOU SHOULD SEE WHAT'S IN HERE!
WHAT ARE YO
DOING?
IT WAS LOST A LONG TIME AGO. MY FATHER TOLD ME ABOUT IT. THEY HEARD HIM TALKING ABOUT IT WHEN HE DIED.
THEY HEARD WHO TALKING?
MY GRANDFATHE
THE SEVENTH MAYO
EMBER. "*NOW IT IS*
HE SAID.
BUT WHAT WAS *IT*?
HE DIDN'T SAY.

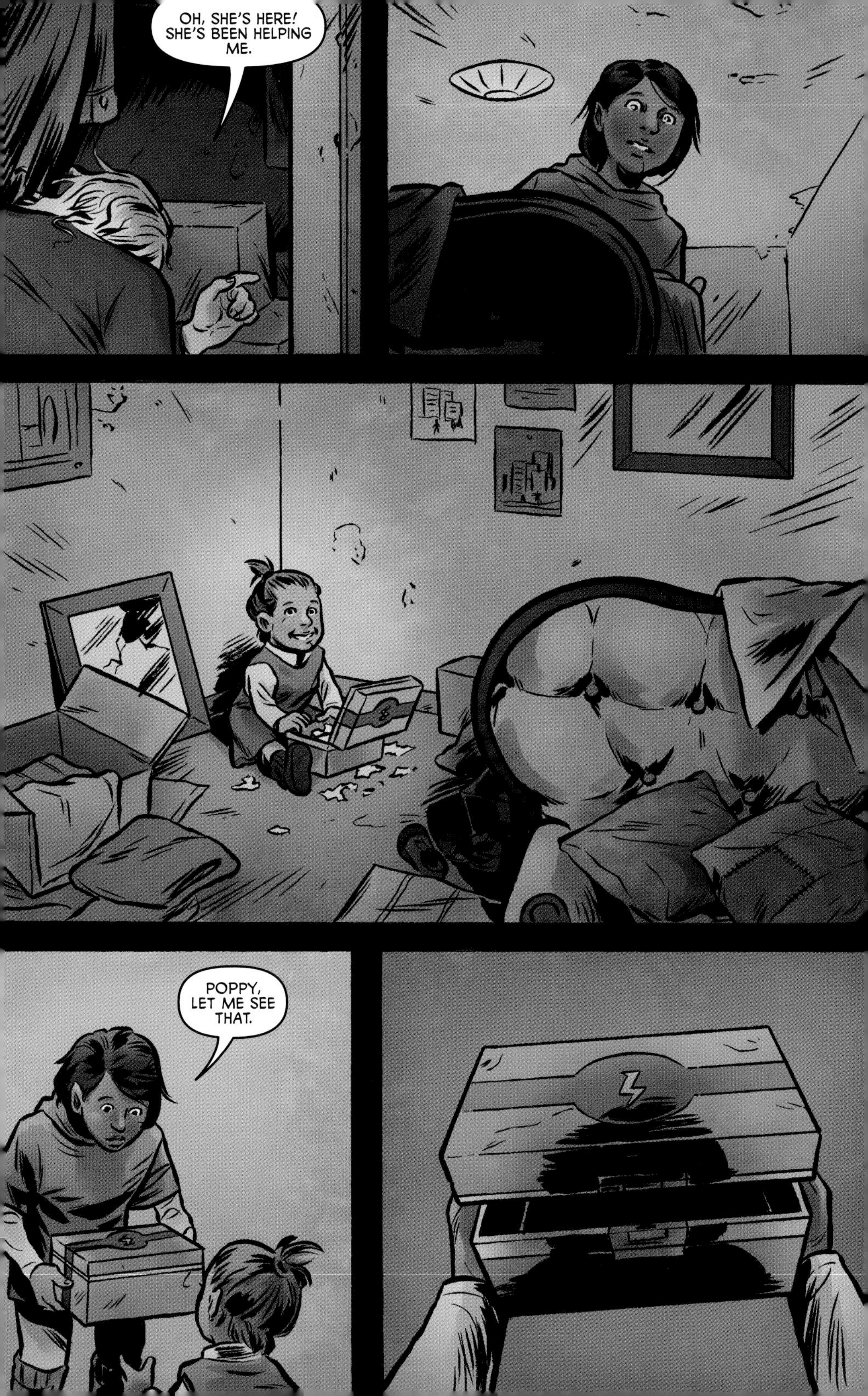
OH, SHE'S HERE! SHE'S BEEN HELPING ME.
POPPY, LET ME SEE THAT.

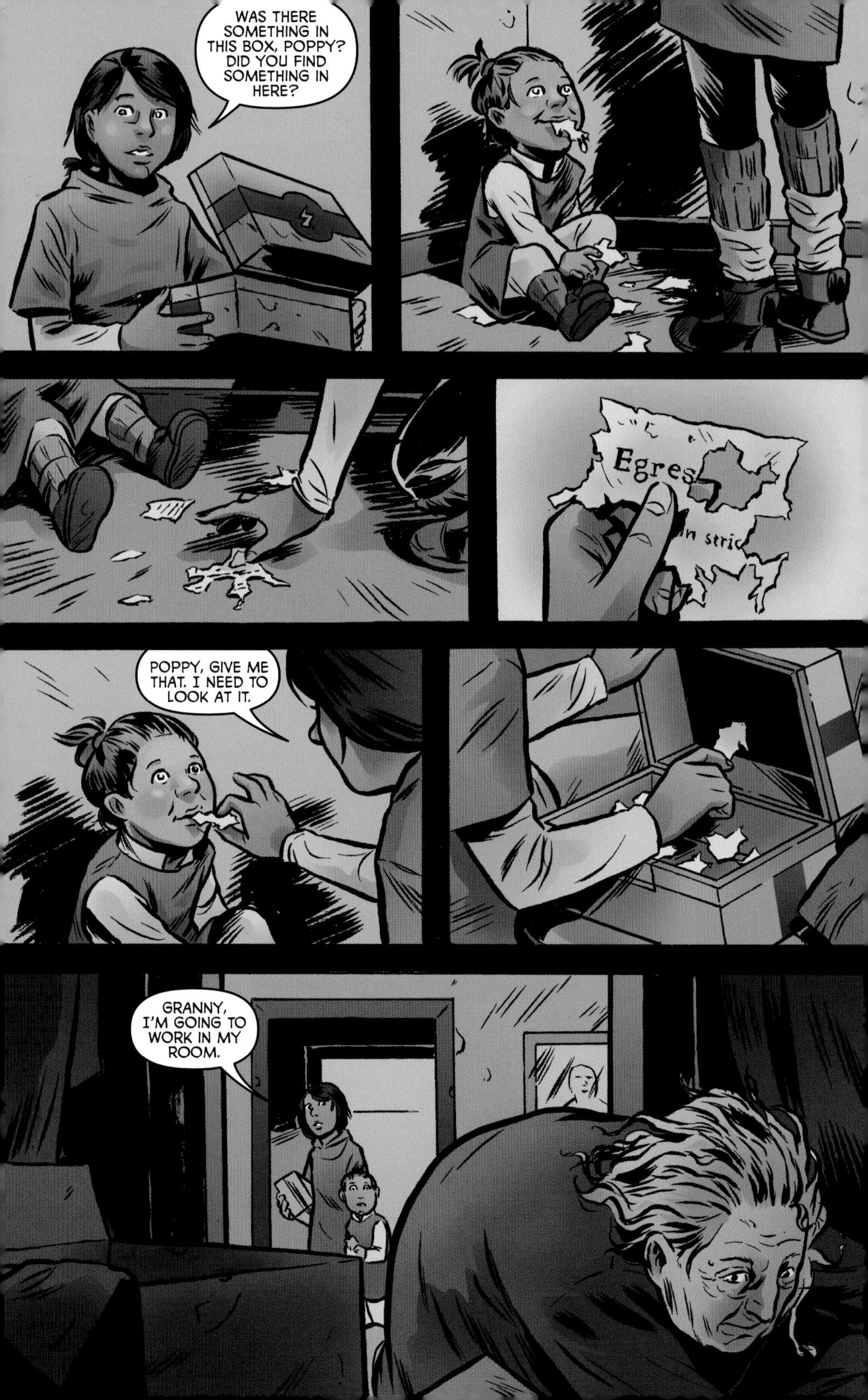
WAS THERE SOMETHING IN THIS BOX, POPPY? DID YOU FIND SOMETHING IN HERE?
Egres
in stric
POPPY, GIVE ME THAT. I NEED TO LOOK AT IT.
GRANNY, I'M GOING TO WORK IN MY ROOM.

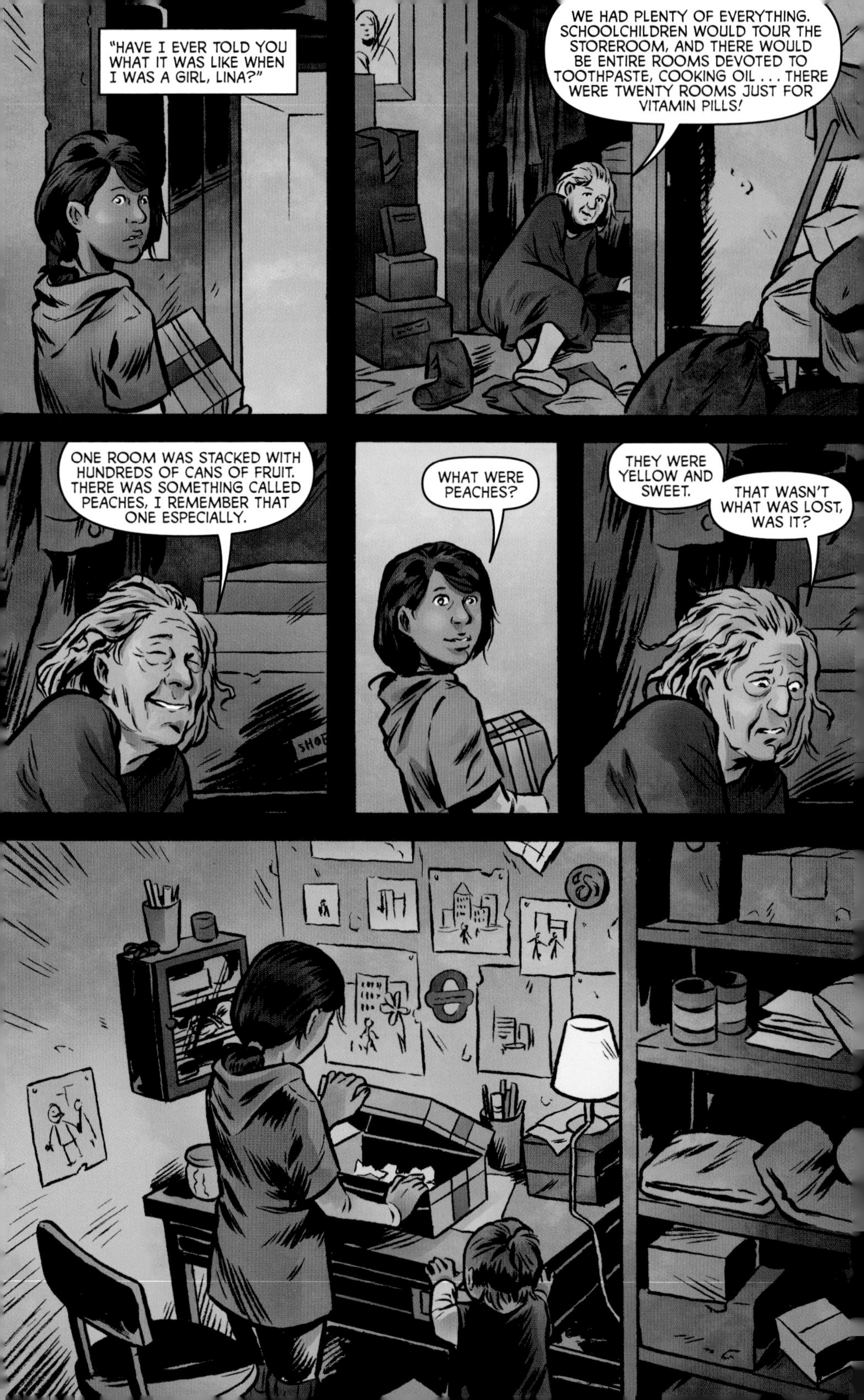
"HAVE I EVER TOLD YOU WHAT IT WAS LIKE WHEN I WAS A GIRL, LINA?"
WE HAD PLENTY OF EVERYTHING. SCHOOLCHILDREN WOULD TOUR THE STOREROOM, AND THERE WOULD BE ENTIRE ROOMS DEVOTED TO TOOTHPASTE, COOKING OIL . . . THERE WERE TWENTY ROOMS JUST FOR VITAMIN PILLS!
ONE ROOM WAS STACKED WITH HUNDREDS OF CANS OF FRUIT. THERE WAS SOMETHING CALLED PEACHES, I REMEMBER THAT ONE ESPECIALLY.
WHAT WERE PEACHES?
THEY WERE YELLOW AND SWEET.
THAT WASN'T WHAT WAS LOST, WAS IT?

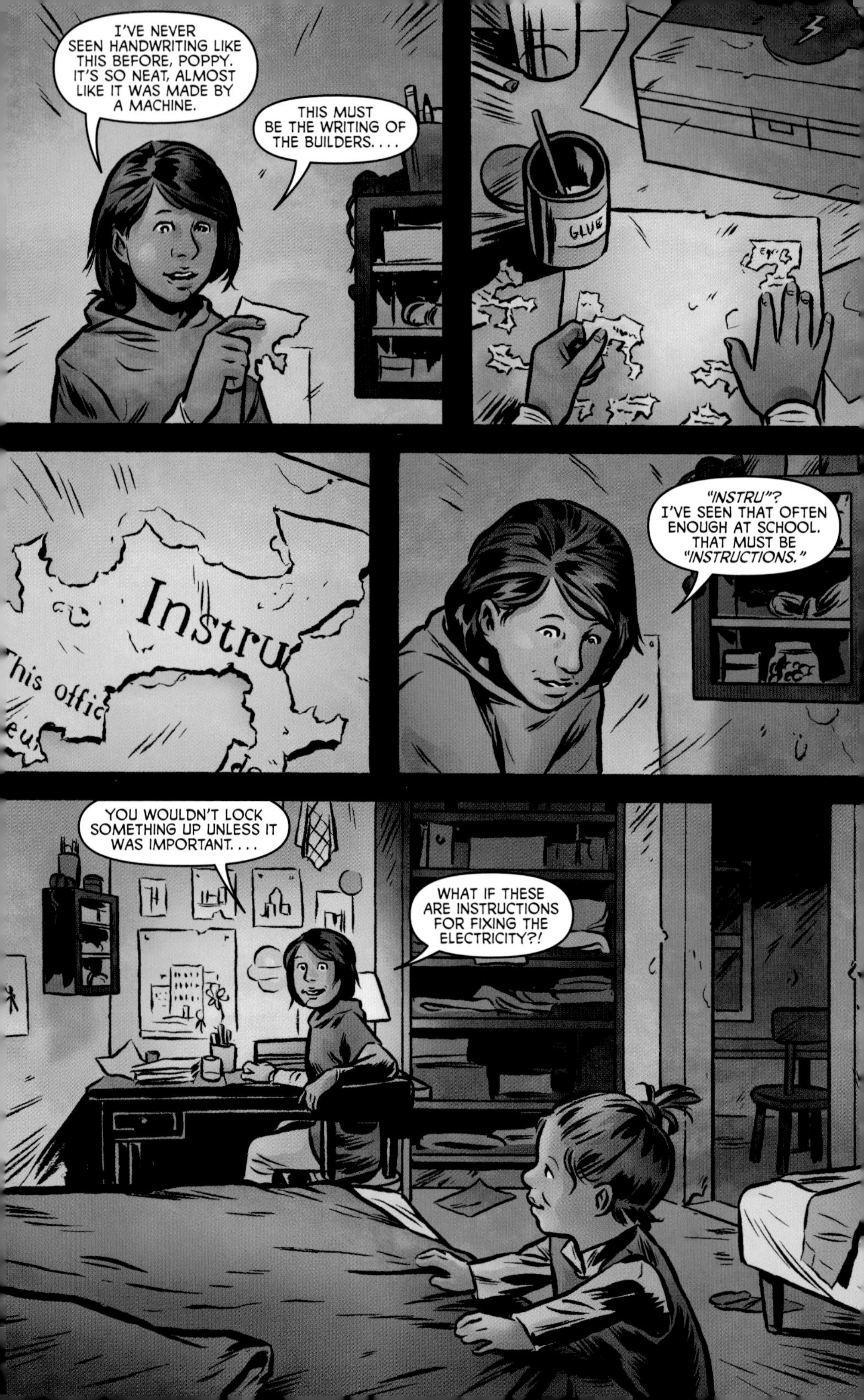
I'VE NEVER SEEN HANDWRITING LIKE THIS BEFORE, POPPY. IT'S SO NEAT, ALMOST LIKE IT WAS MADE BY A MACHINE.
THIS MUST BE THE WRITING OF THE BUILDERS. . . .
GLUE
Instru
This offic
"INSTRU"? I'VE SEEN THAT OFTEN ENOUGH AT SCHOOL. THAT MUST BE "INSTRUCTIONS."
YOU WOULDN'T LOCK SOMETHING UP UNLESS IT WAS IMPORTANT. . . .
WHAT IF THESE ARE INSTRUCTIONS FOR FIXING THE ELECTRICITY?!

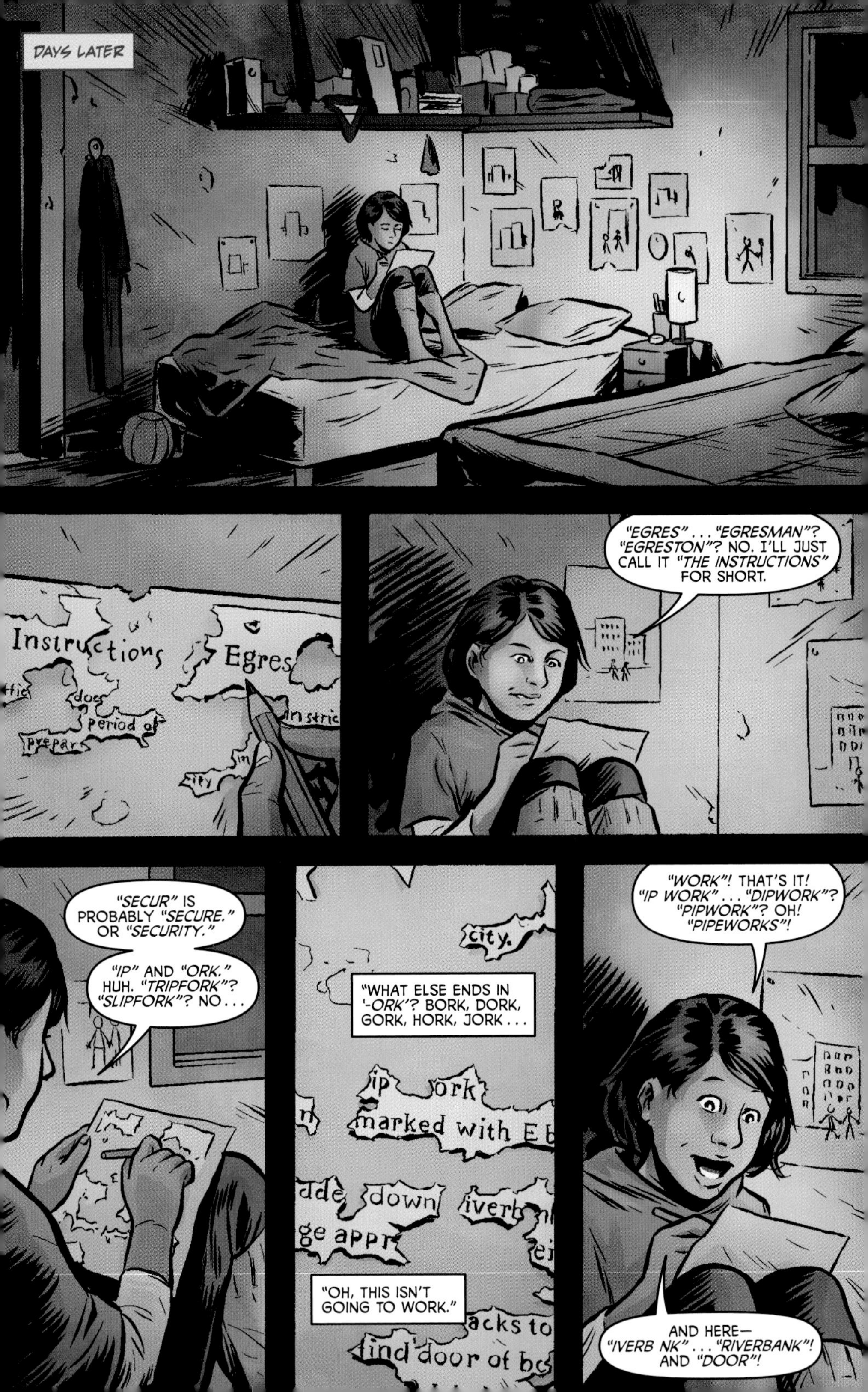
DAYS LATER
Instructions
Egres
does
period of
prepar
instric
in
city
"EGRES" . . . "EGRESMAN"? "EGRESTON"? NO. I'LL JUST CALL IT "THE INSTRUCTIONS" FOR SHORT.
"SECUR" IS PROBABLY "SECURE." OR "SECURITY."
"IP" AND "ORK." HUH. "TRIPFORK"? "SLIPFORK"? NO . . .
city.
"WHAT ELSE ENDS IN '-ORK'? BORK, DORK, GORK, HORK, JORK . . .
ip ork
marked with Eb
ade down iverb
ge appr
"OH, THIS ISN'T GOING TO WORK."
acks to
find door of bo
"WORK"! THAT'S IT! "IP WORK" . . . "DIPWORK"? "PIPWORK"? OH! "PIPEWORKS"!
AND HERE— "IVERB NK" . . . "RIVERBANK"! AND "DOOR"!

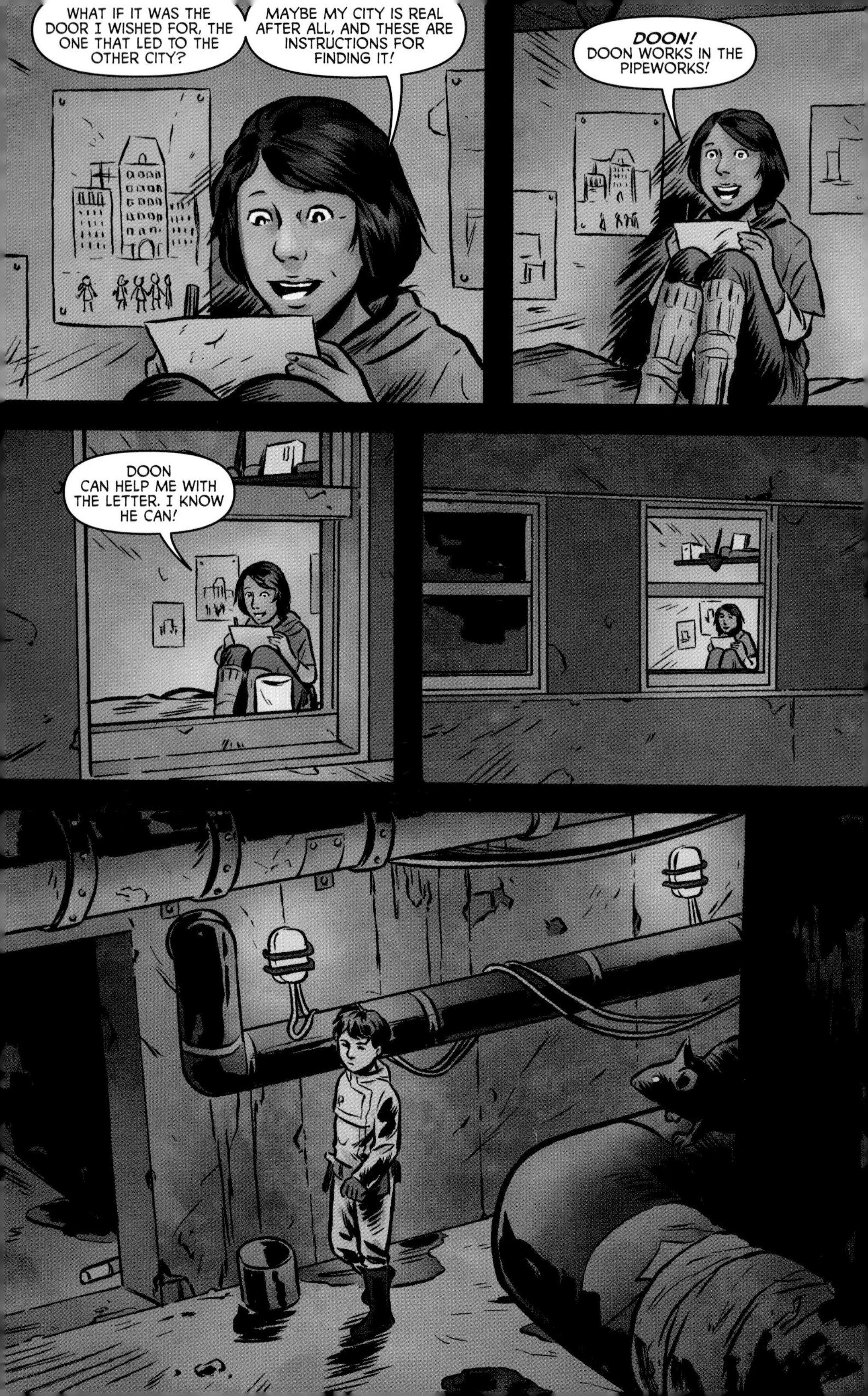
WHAT IF IT WAS THE DOOR I WISHED FOR, THE ONE THAT LED TO THE OTHER CITY?
MAYBE MY CITY IS REAL AFTER ALL, AND THESE ARE INSTRUCTIONS FOR FINDING IT!
DOON! DOON WORKS IN THE PIPEWORKS!
DOON CAN HELP ME WITH THE LETTER. I KNOW HE CAN!

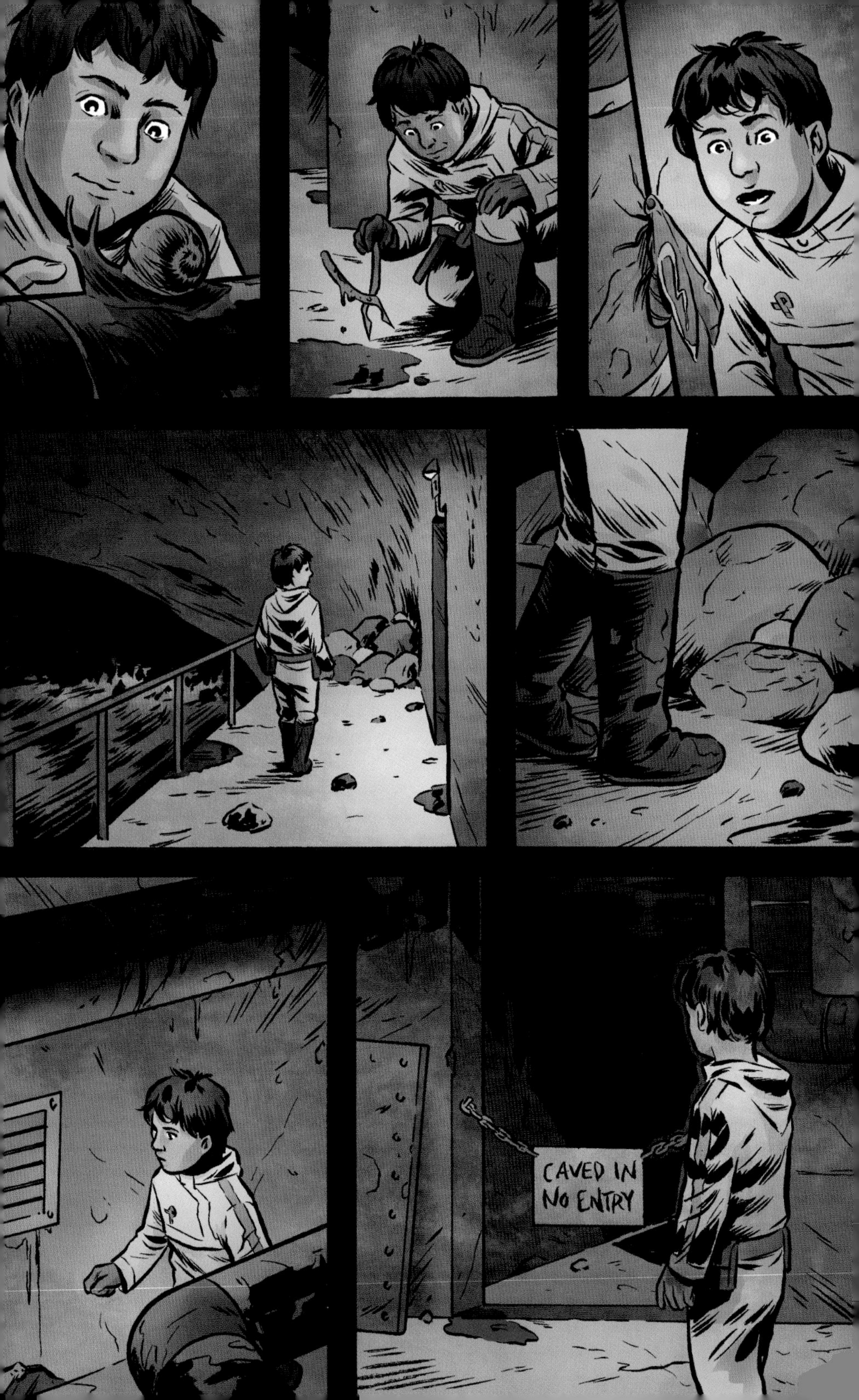
CAVED IN
NO ENTRY

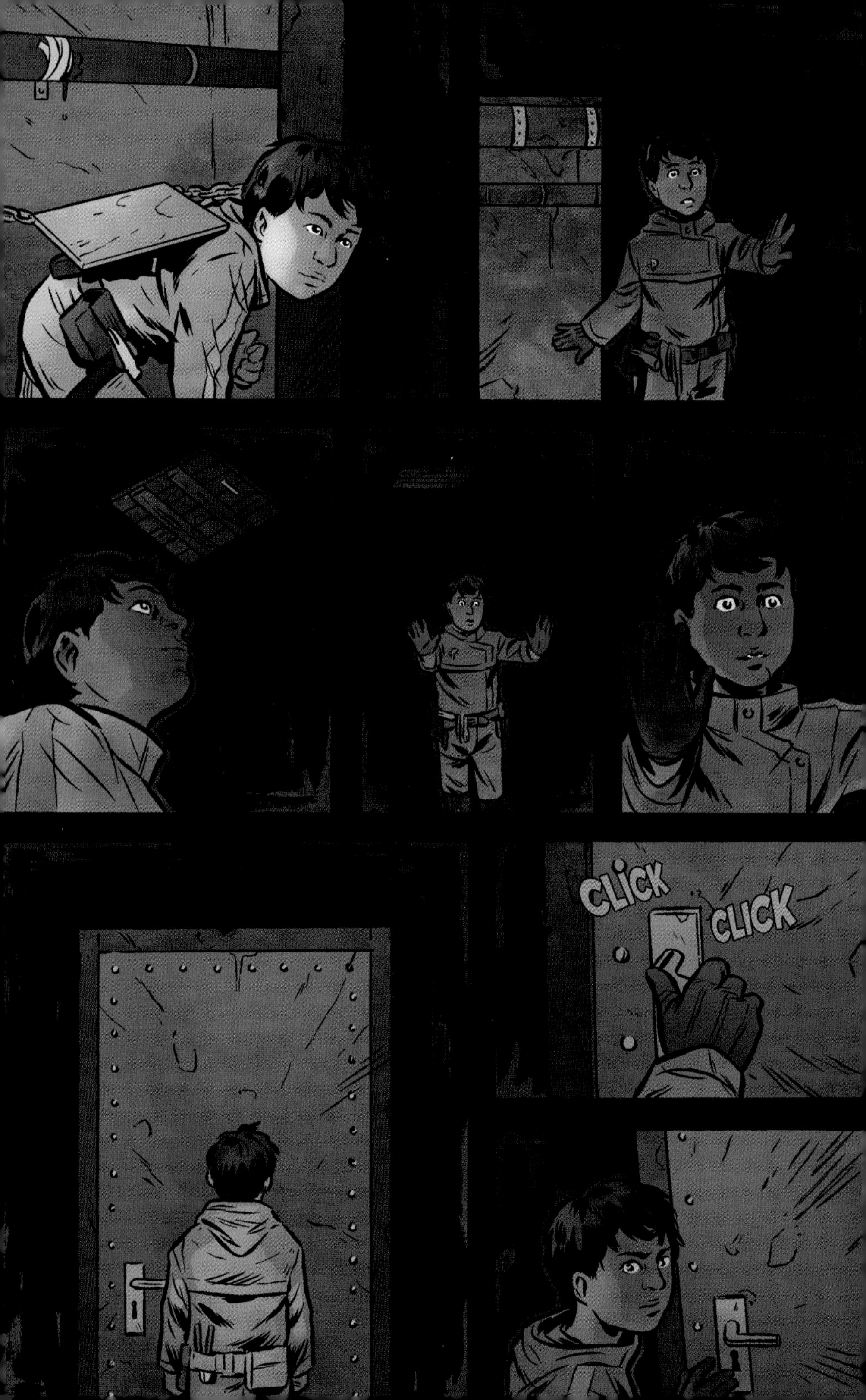
CLICK
CLICK

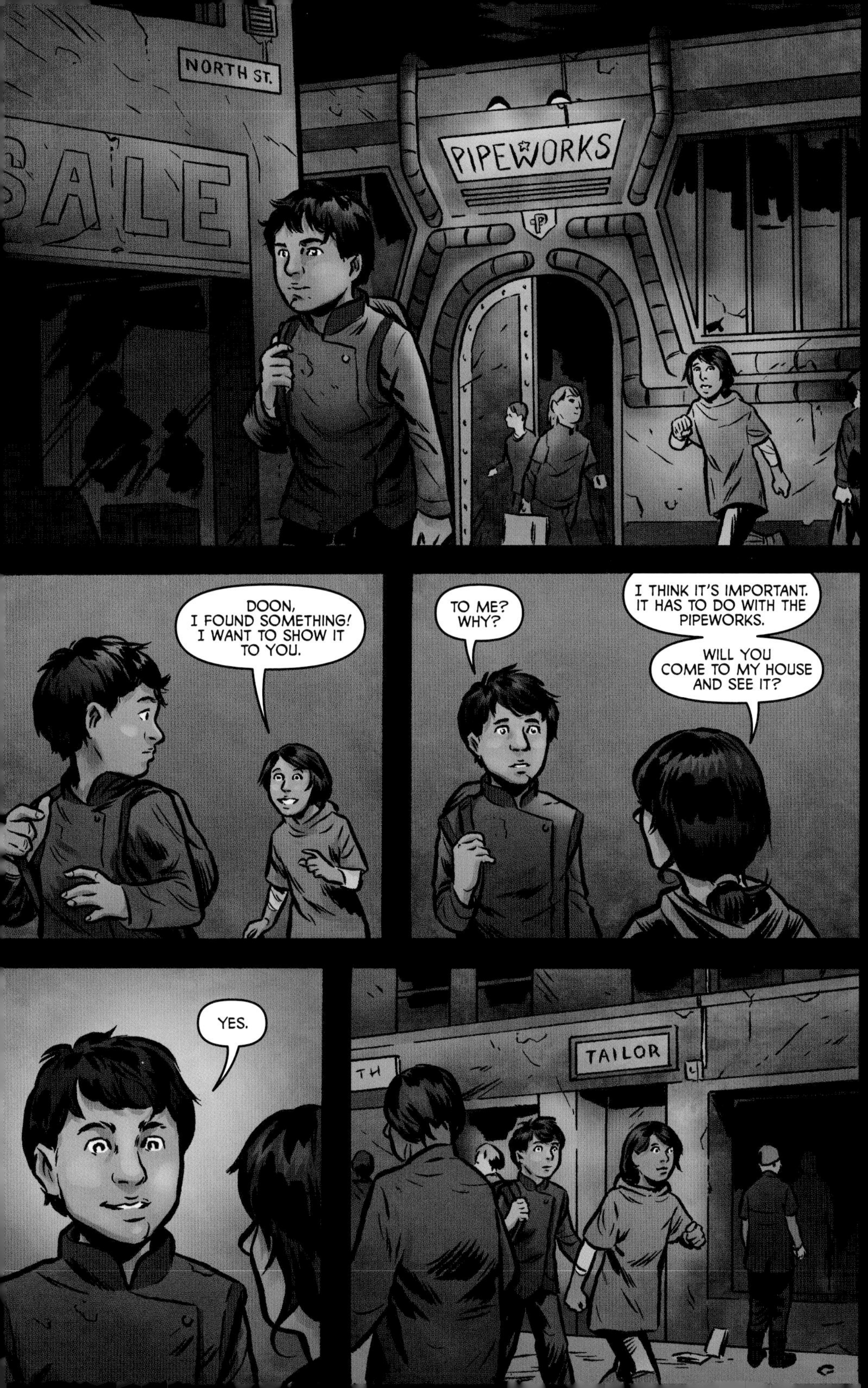
NORTH ST.
SALE
PIPEWORKS
DOON, I FOUND SOMETHING! I WANT TO SHOW IT TO YOU.
TO ME? WHY?
I THINK IT'S IMPORTANT. IT HAS TO DO WITH THE PIPEWORKS.
WILL YOU COME TO MY HOUSE AND SEE IT?
YES.
TAILOR

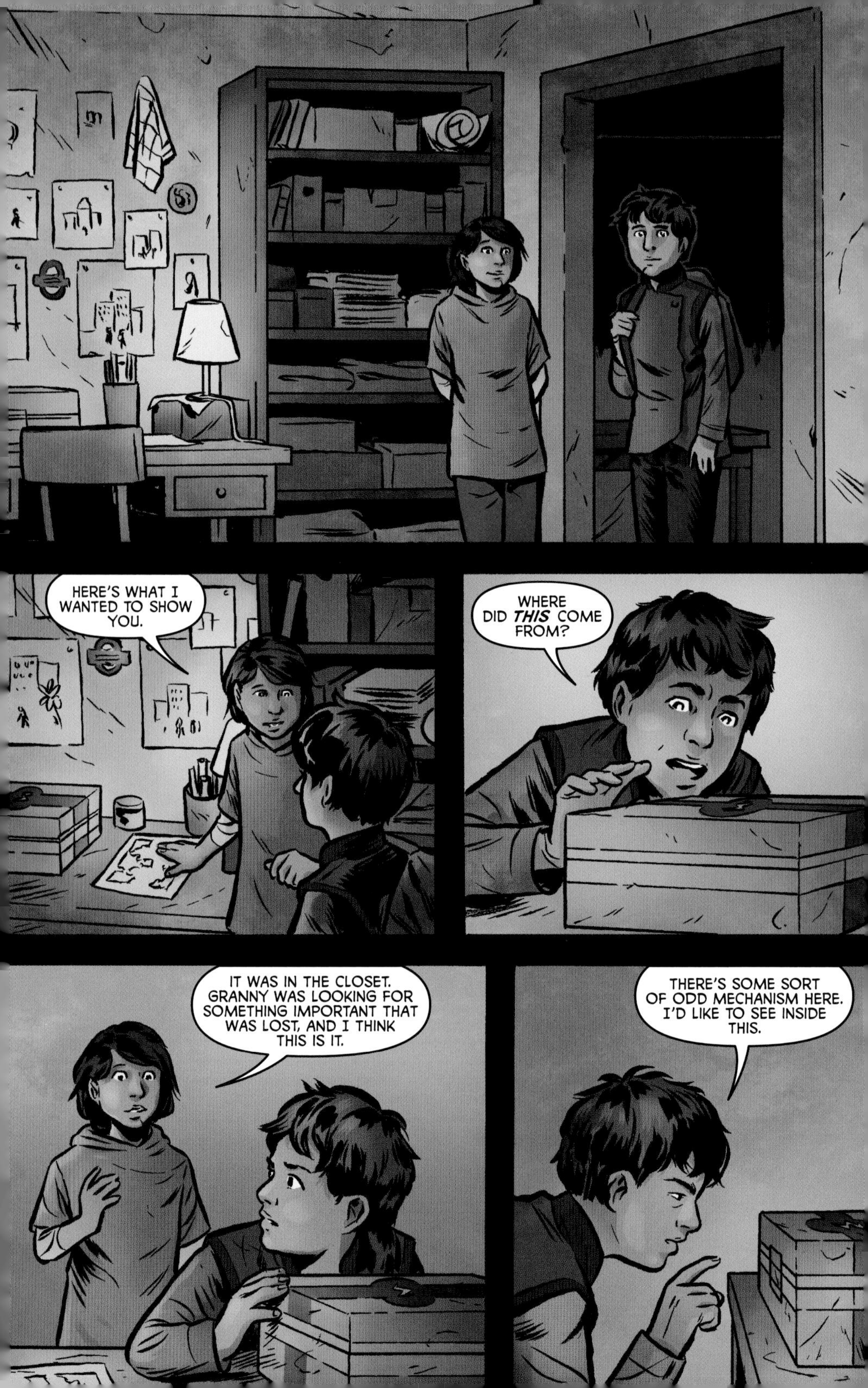
HERE'S WHAT I WANTED TO SHOW YOU.
WHERE DID *THIS* COME FROM?
IT WAS IN THE CLOSET. GRANNY WAS LOOKING FOR SOMETHING IMPORTANT THAT WAS LOST, AND I THINK THIS IS IT.
THERE'S SOME SORT OF ODD MECHANISM HERE. I'D LIKE TO SEE INSIDE THIS.

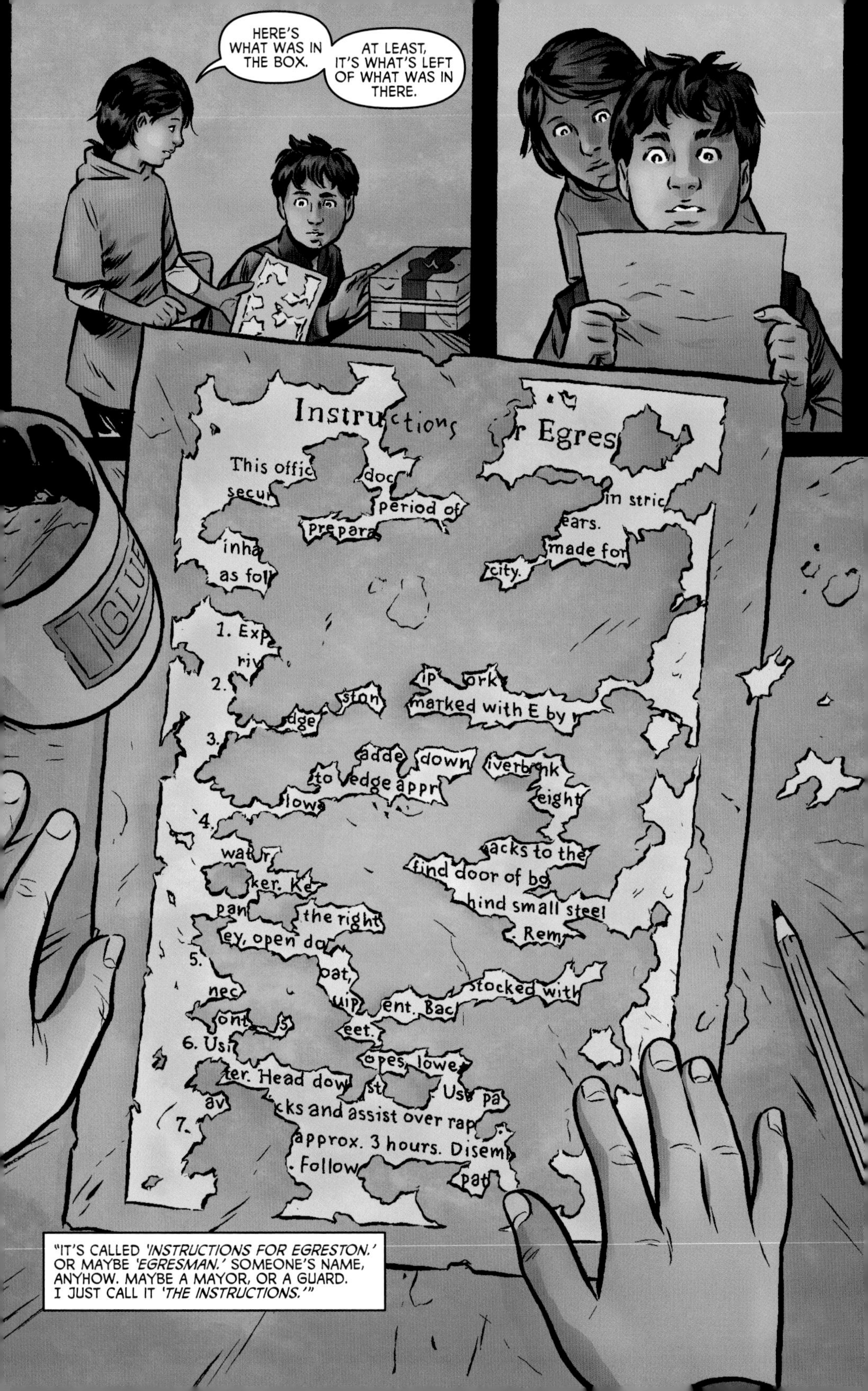
HERE'S WHAT WAS IN THE BOX.
AT LEAST, IT'S WHAT'S LEFT OF WHAT WAS IN THERE.
GLUE
Instructions r Egres
This offic doc
secur period of in stric
prepara ears.
inha made for
as fol city.
1. Exp
riv
2. ip ork
ston marked with E by
dge
3.
adde down iverbank
to edge appr
lows eight
4.
wat acks to the
find door of bo
ker. Ke
hind small steel
pan the right
ey, open do . Rem
5.
oat,
nec stocked with
uip ent. Bac
ont 5
eet.
6. Usi
opes, lowe
ter. Head dow st Use pa
av cks and assist over rap
7.
approx. 3 hours. Disem
. Follow
pat
"IT'S CALLED 'INSTRUCTIONS FOR EGRESTON.' OR MAYBE 'EGRESMAN.' SOMEONE'S NAME, ANYHOW. MAYBE A MAYOR, OR A GUARD. I JUST CALL IT 'THE INSTRUCTIONS.'"

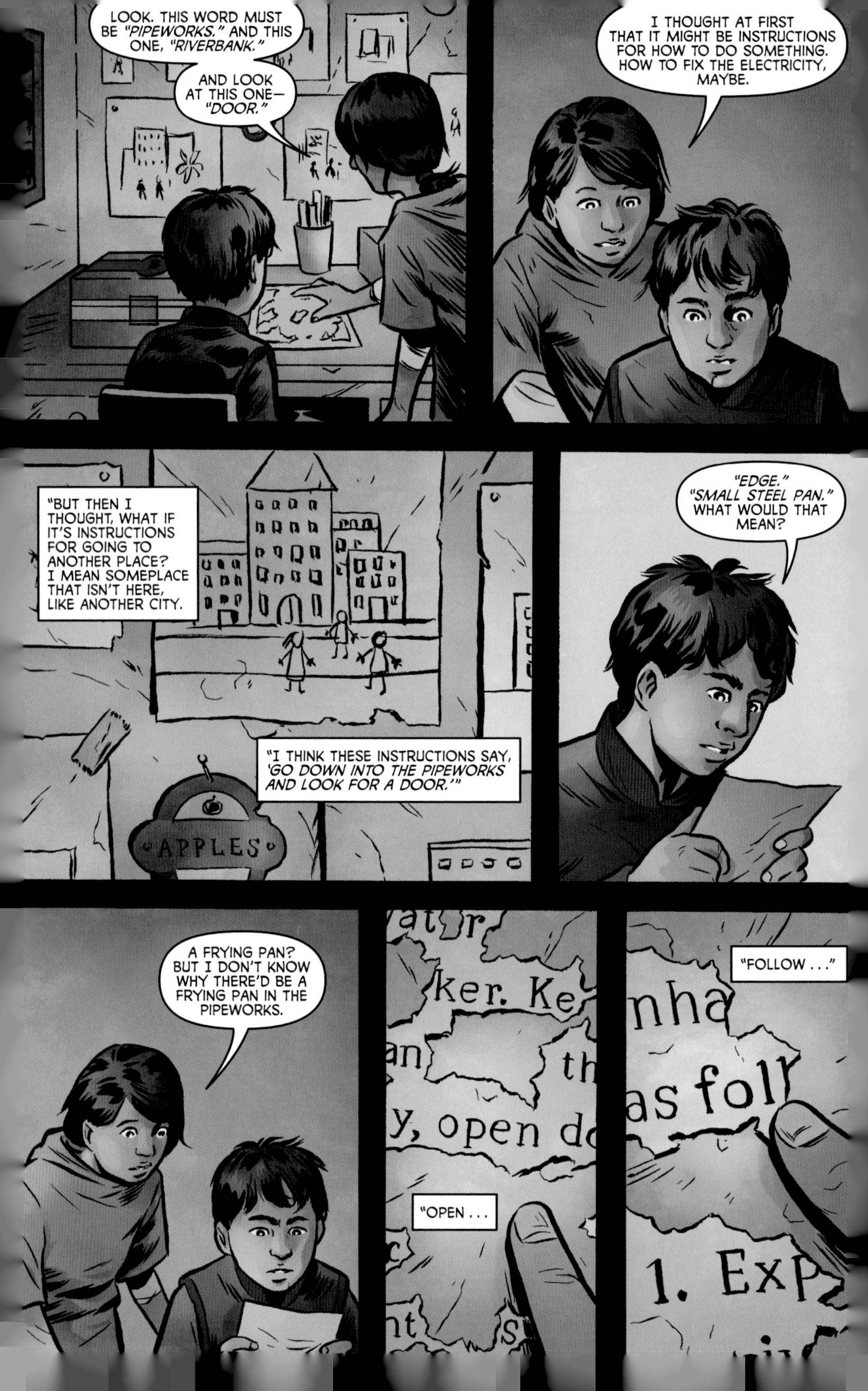

LOOK. THIS WORD MUST BE *"PIPEWORKS."* AND THIS ONE, *"RIVERBANK."*
AND LOOK AT THIS ONE— *"DOOR."*
I THOUGHT AT FIRST THAT IT MIGHT BE INSTRUCTIONS FOR HOW TO DO SOMETHING. HOW TO FIX THE ELECTRICITY, MAYBE.
"BUT THEN I THOUGHT, WHAT IF IT'S INSTRUCTIONS FOR GOING TO ANOTHER PLACE? I MEAN SOMEPLACE THAT ISN'T HERE, LIKE ANOTHER CITY.
"I THINK THESE INSTRUCTIONS SAY, *'GO DOWN INTO THE PIPEWORKS AND LOOK FOR A DOOR.'"*
APPLES
"EDGE." "SMALL STEEL PAN." WHAT WOULD THAT MEAN?
A FRYING PAN? BUT I DON'T KNOW WHY THERE'D BE A FRYING PAN IN THE PIPEWORKS.
at r
ker. Ke
an
th
y, open d
"OPEN . . .
"FOLLOW . . ."
nha
as fol
1. Exp

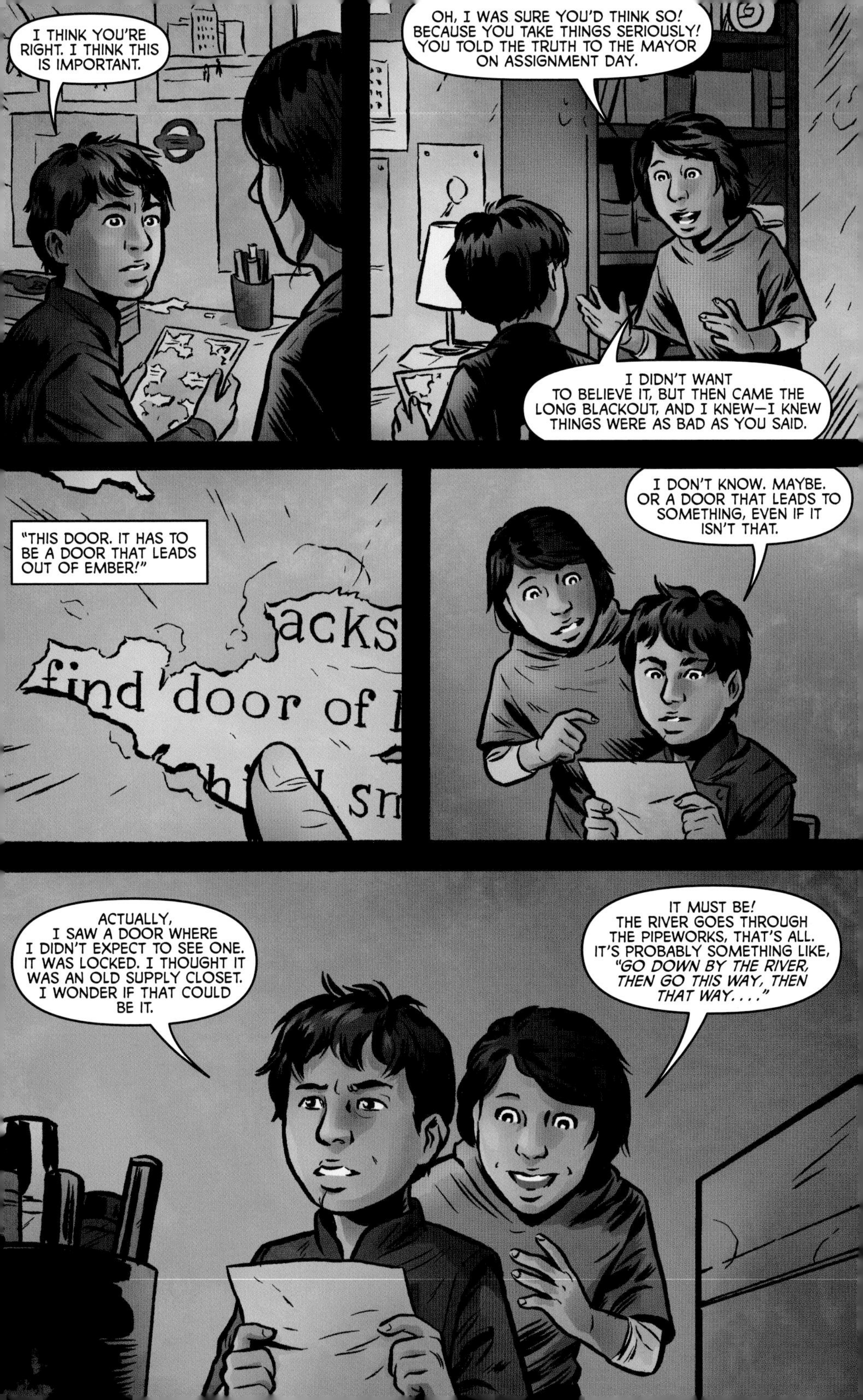

I THINK YOU'RE RIGHT. I THINK THIS IS IMPORTANT.
OH, I WAS SURE YOU'D THINK SO! BECAUSE YOU TAKE THINGS SERIOUSLY! YOU TOLD THE TRUTH TO THE MAYOR ON ASSIGNMENT DAY.
I DIDN'T WANT TO BELIEVE IT, BUT THEN CAME THE LONG BLACKOUT, AND I KNEW—I KNEW THINGS WERE AS BAD AS YOU SAID.
"THIS DOOR. IT HAS TO BE A DOOR THAT LEADS OUT OF EMBER!"
acks
find door of
I DON'T KNOW. MAYBE. OR A DOOR THAT LEADS TO SOMETHING, EVEN IF IT ISN'T THAT.
ACTUALLY, I SAW A DOOR WHERE I DIDN'T EXPECT TO SEE ONE. IT WAS LOCKED. I THOUGHT IT WAS AN OLD SUPPLY CLOSET. I WONDER IF THAT COULD BE IT.
IT MUST BE! THE RIVER GOES THROUGH THE PIPEWORKS, THAT'S ALL. IT'S PROBABLY SOMETHING LIKE, *"GO DOWN BY THE RIVER, THEN GO THIS WAY, THEN THAT WAY. . . ."*

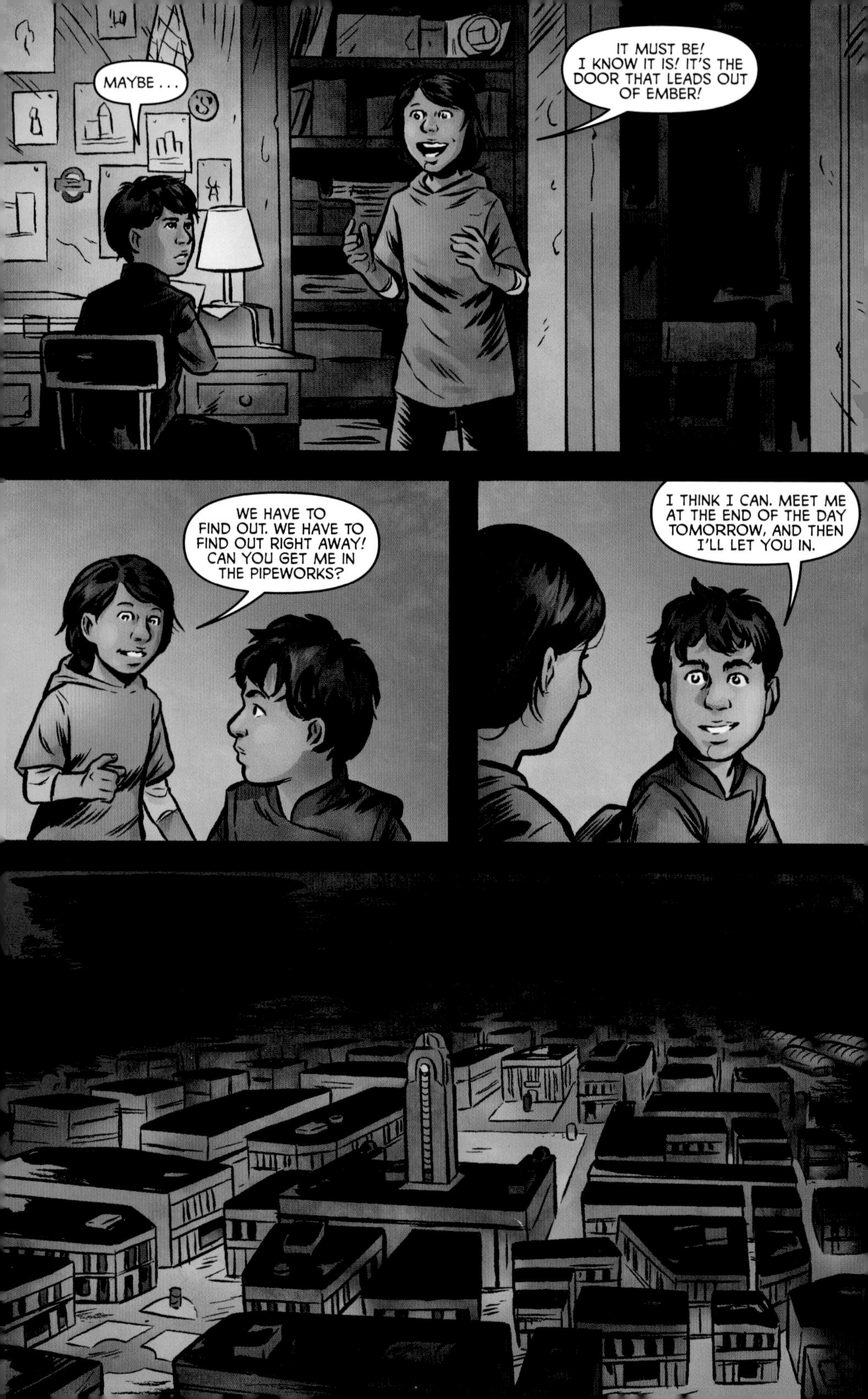
MAYBE . . .
IT MUST BE! I KNOW IT IS! IT'S THE DOOR THAT LEADS OUT OF EMBER!
WE HAVE TO FIND OUT. WE HAVE TO FIND OUT RIGHT AWAY! CAN YOU GET ME IN THE PIPEWORKS?
I THINK I CAN. MEET ME AT THE END OF THE DAY TOMORROW, AND THEN I'LL LET YOU IN.

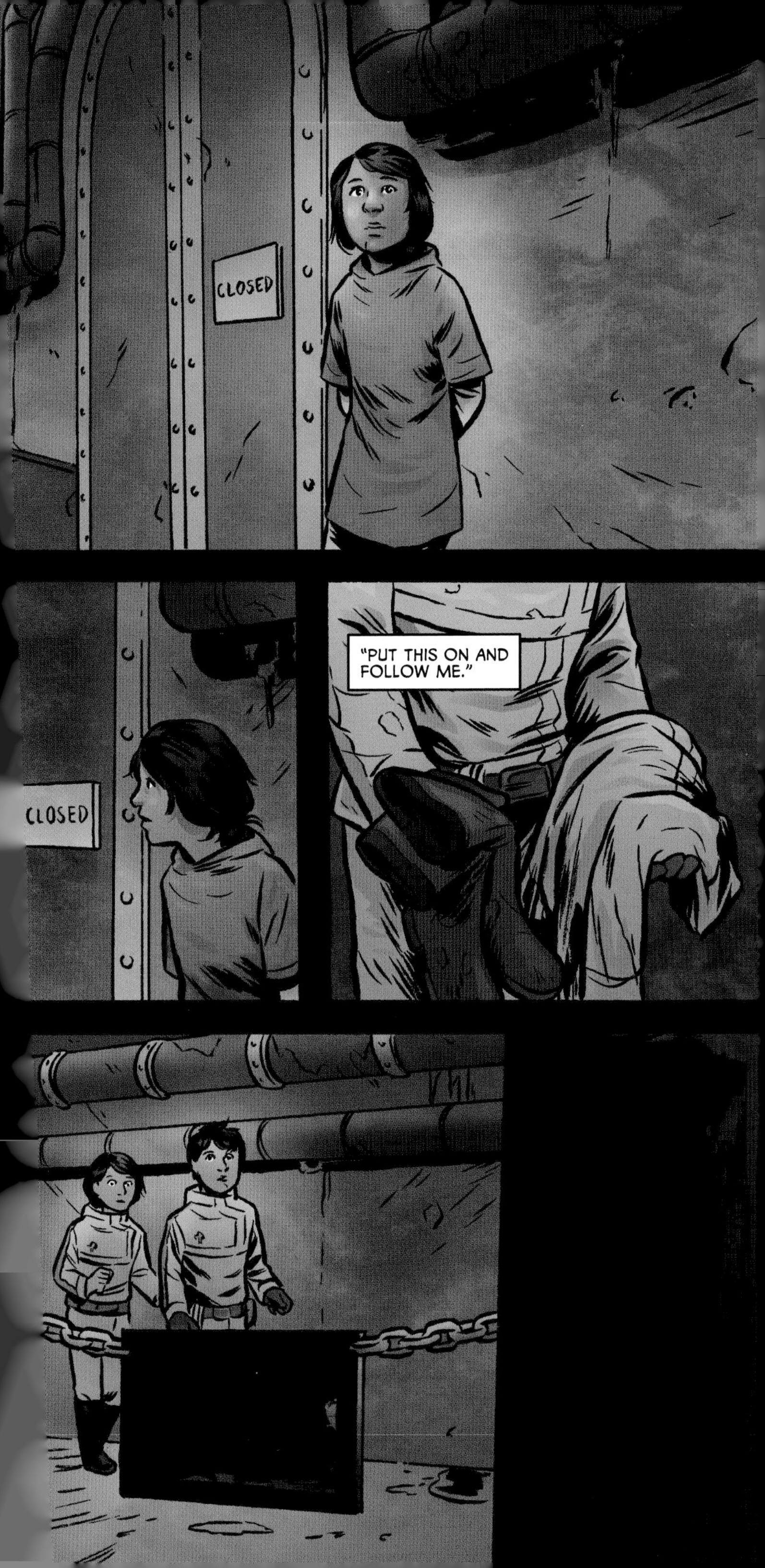
CLOSED
CLOSED
"PUT THIS ON AND FOLLOW ME."

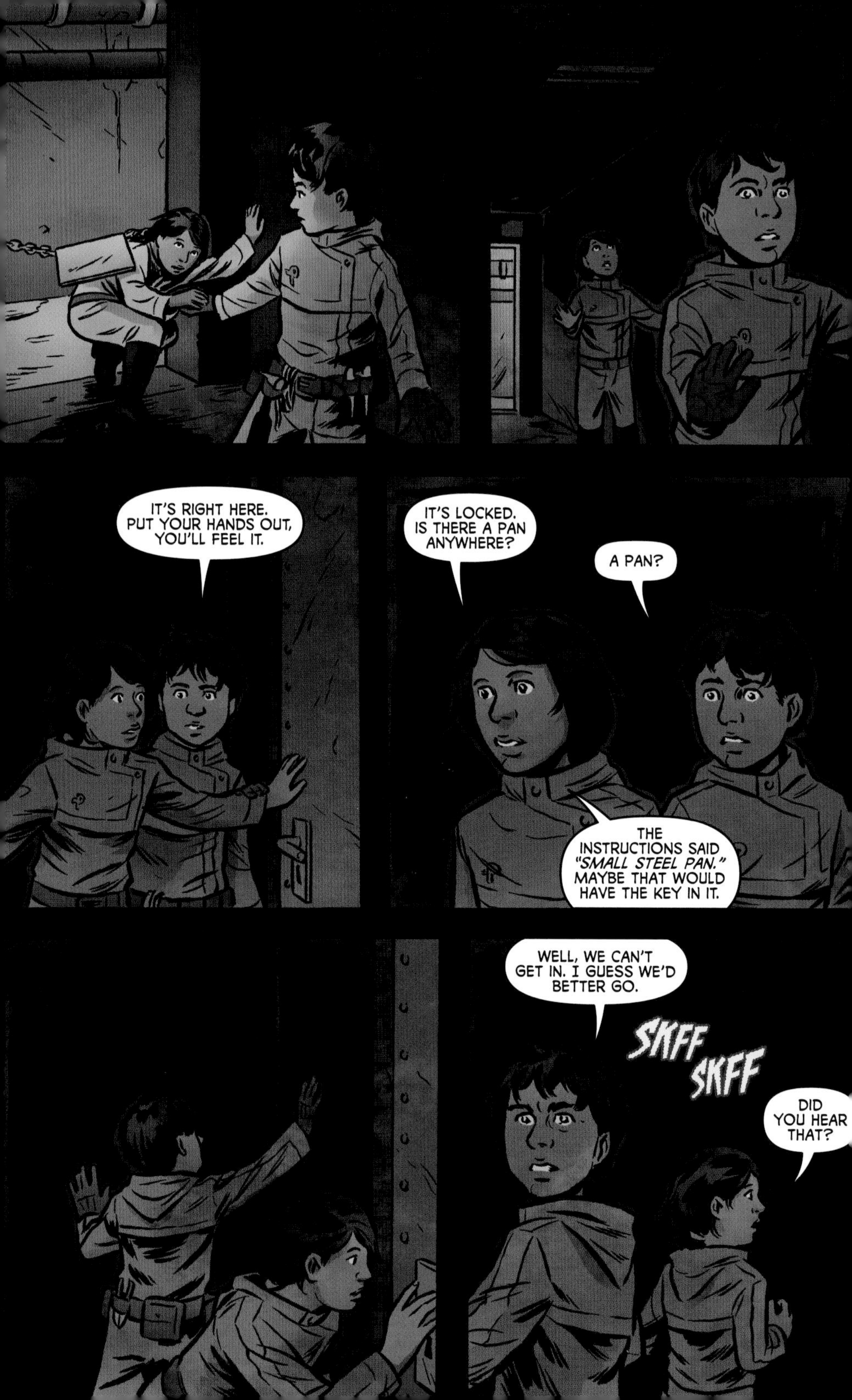
IT'S RIGHT HERE. PUT YOUR HANDS OUT, YOU'LL FEEL IT.
IT'S LOCKED. IS THERE A PAN ANYWHERE?
A PAN?
THE INSTRUCTIONS SAID *"SMALL STEEL PAN."* MAYBE THAT WOULD HAVE THE KEY IN IT.
WELL, WE CAN'T GET IN. I GUESS WE'D BETTER GO.
SKFF
SKFF
DID YOU HEAR THAT?

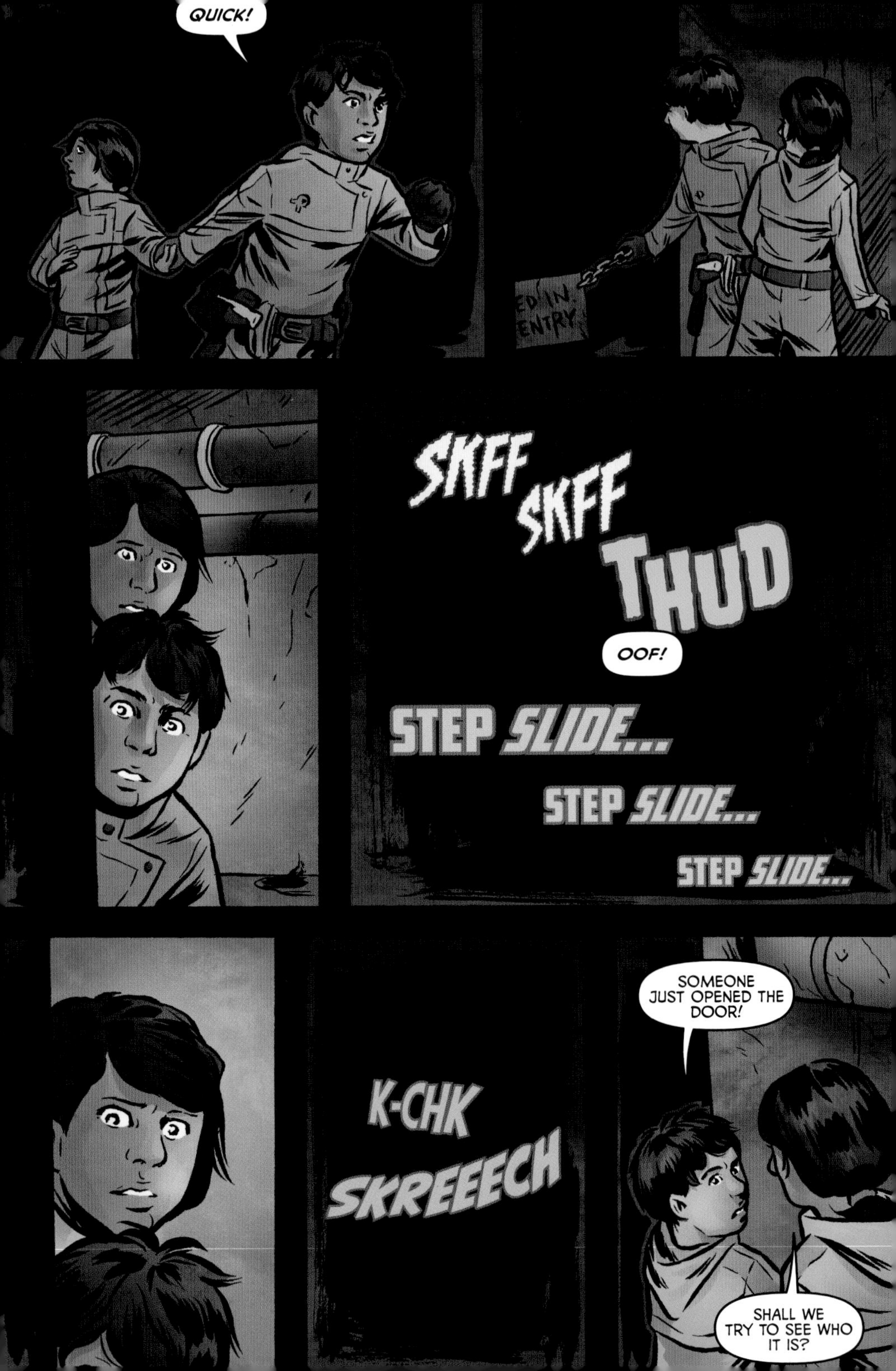
QUICK!
ED IN
ENTRY
SKFF
SKFF
THUD
OOF!
STEP SLIDE...
STEP SLIDE...
STEP SLIDE...
K-CHK
SKREEECH
SOMEONE JUST OPENED THE DOOR!
SHALL WE TRY TO SEE WHO IT IS?

I DON'T THINK WE SHOULD.
WE COULD JUST PEEK AROUND THE CORNER—
KLUNK!
STEP SLIDE...
STEP SLIDE...
STEP SLIDE...
LET'S HEAD BACK UP.

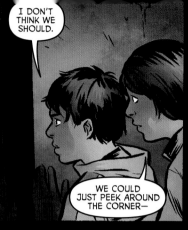

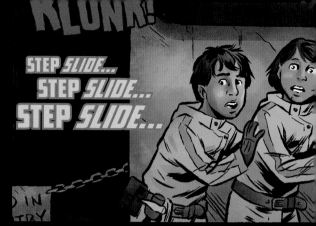

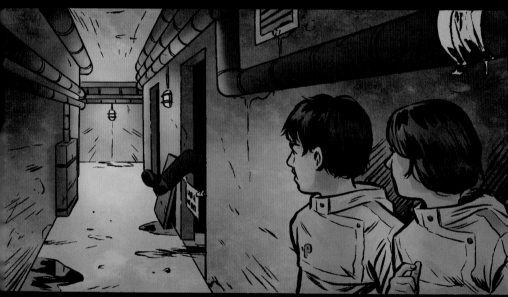

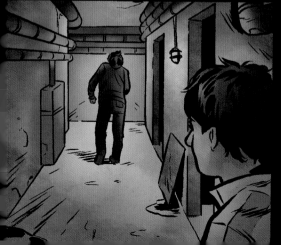

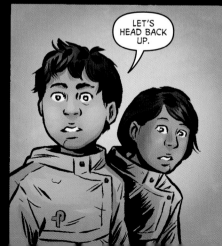

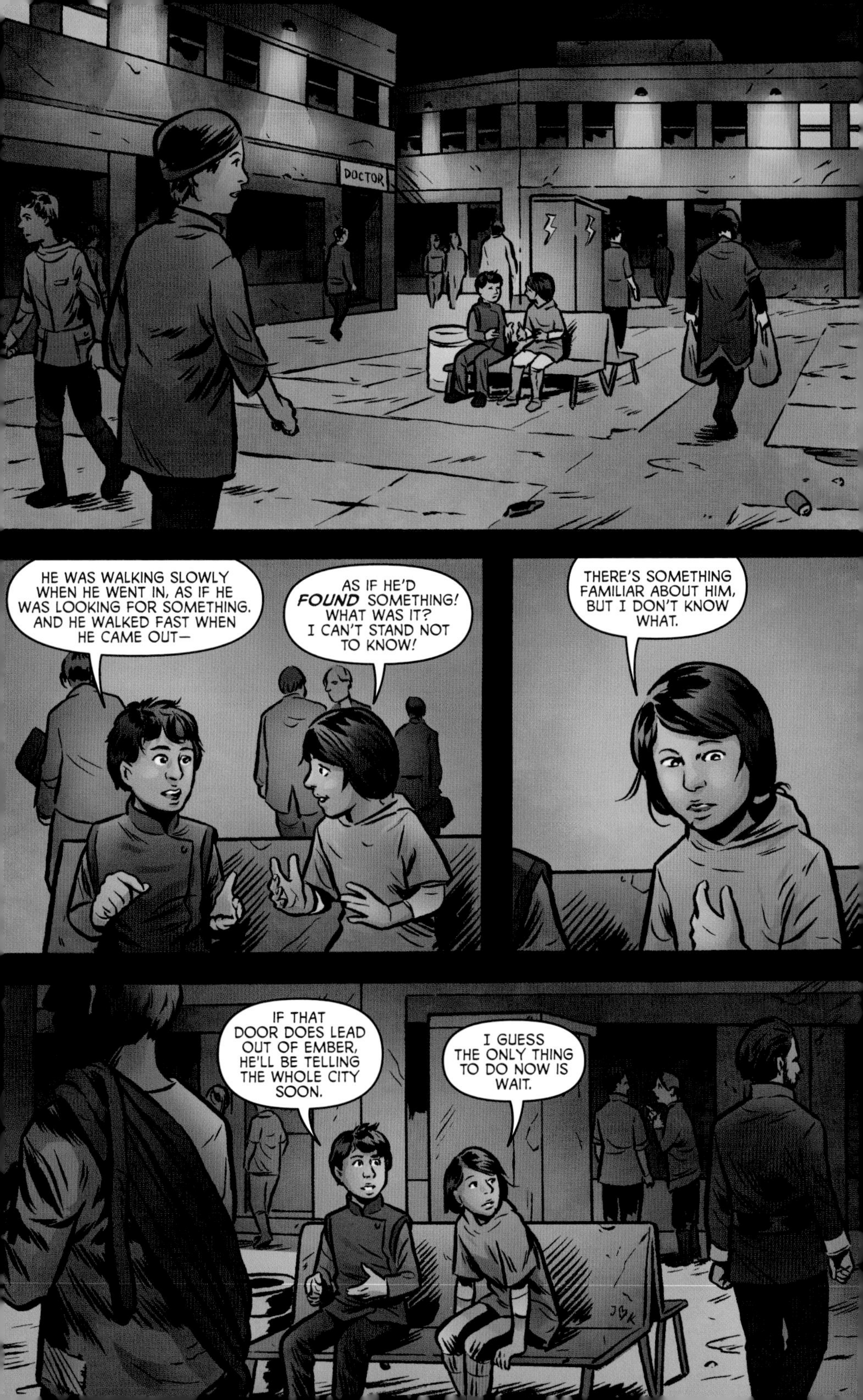
DOCTOR
HE WAS WALKING SLOWLY WHEN HE WENT IN, AS IF HE WAS LOOKING FOR SOMETHING. AND HE WALKED FAST WHEN HE CAME OUT—
AS IF HE'D *FOUND* SOMETHING! WHAT WAS IT? I CAN'T STAND NOT TO KNOW!
THERE'S SOMETHING FAMILIAR ABOUT HIM, BUT I DON'T KNOW WHAT.
IF THAT DOOR DOES LEAD OUT OF EMBER, HE'LL BE TELLING THE WHOLE CITY SOON.
I GUESS THE ONLY THING TO DO NOW IS WAIT.

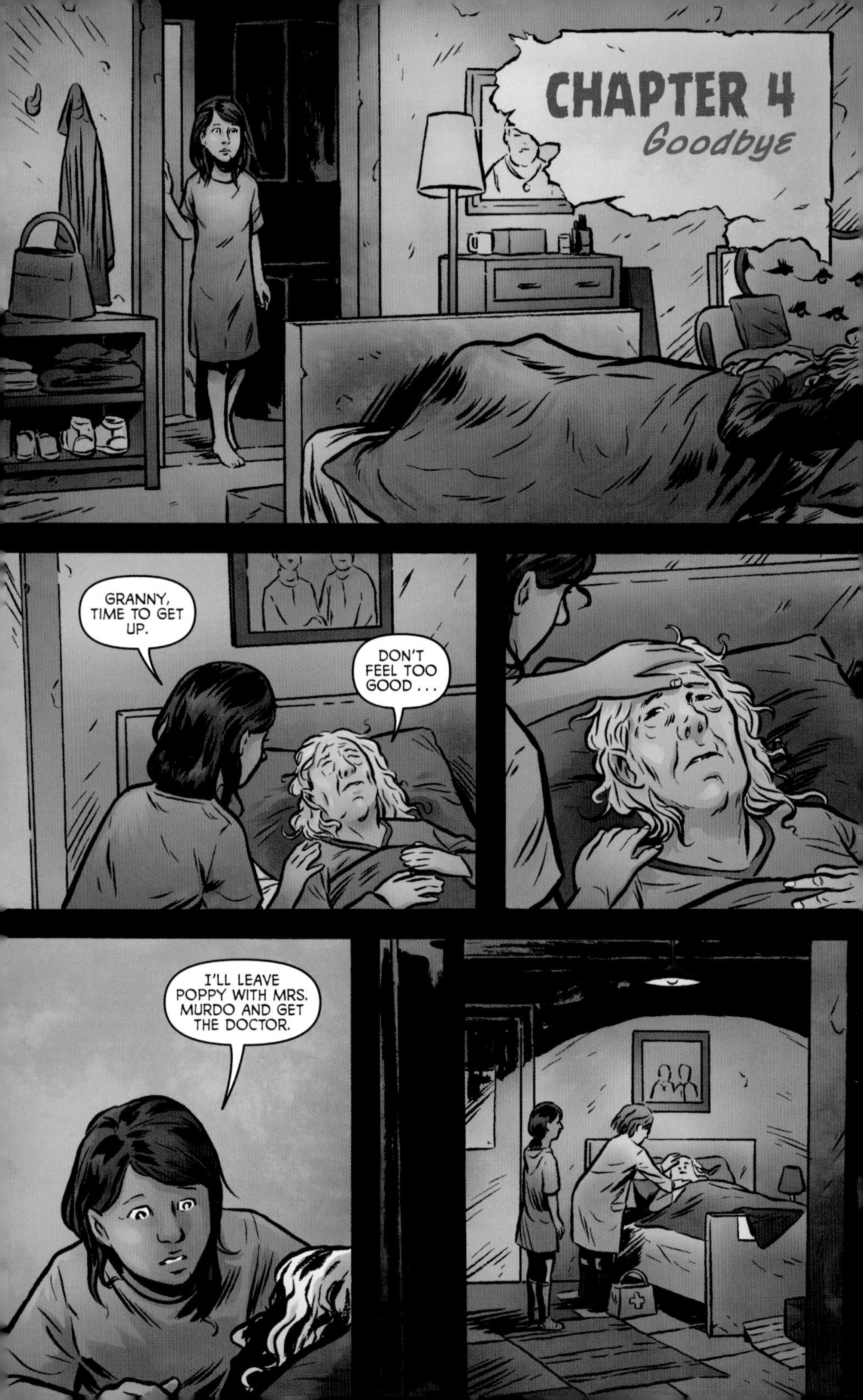
CHAPTER 4
Goodbye
GRANNY, TIME TO GET UP.
DON'T FEEL TOO GOOD . . .
I'LL LEAVE POPPY WITH MRS. MURDO AND GET THE DOCTOR.

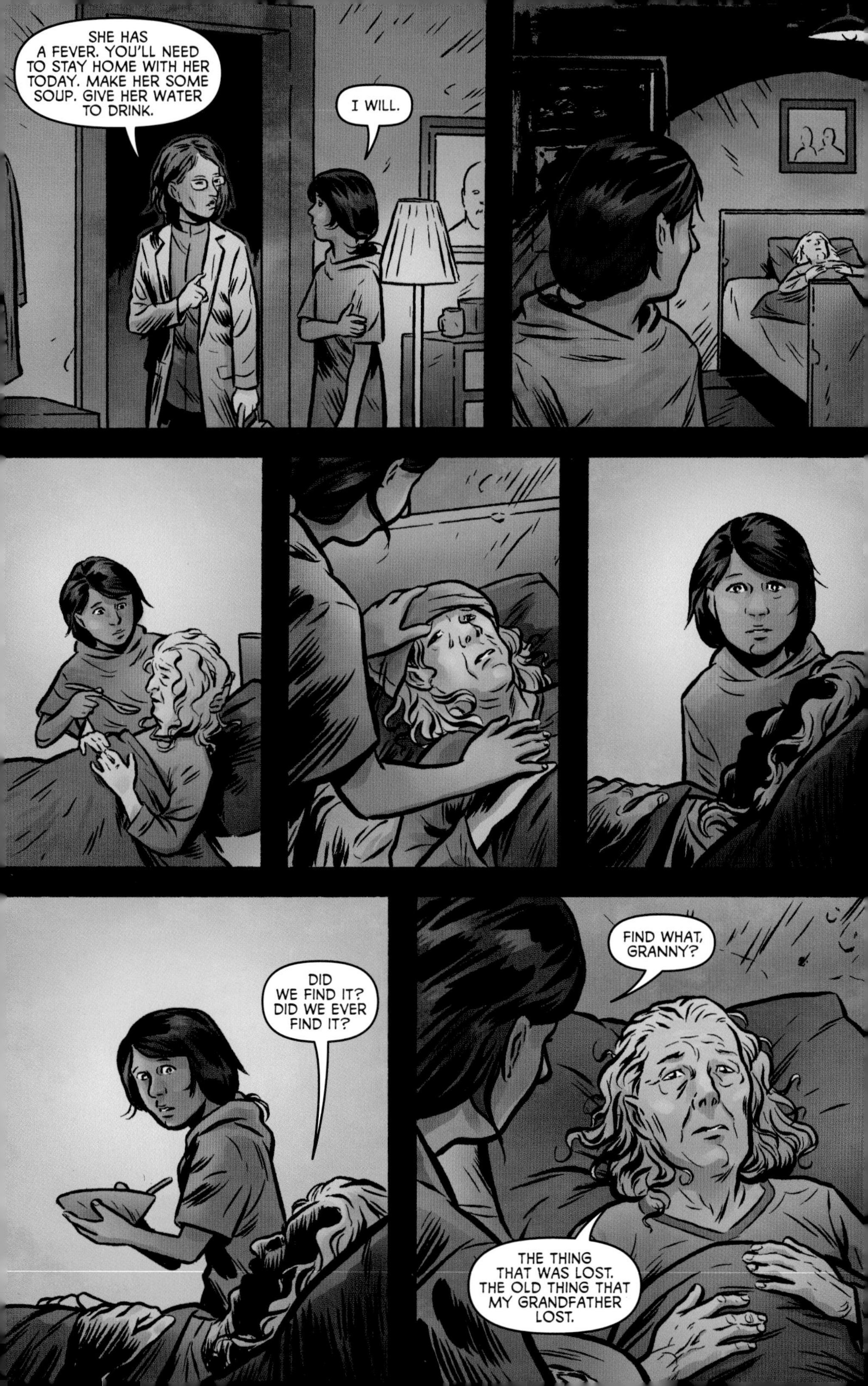
SHE HAS A FEVER. YOU'LL NEED TO STAY HOME WITH HER TODAY. MAKE HER SOME SOUP. GIVE HER WATER TO DRINK.
I WILL.
DID WE FIND IT? DID WE EVER FIND IT?
FIND WHAT, GRANNY?
THE THING THAT WAS LOST. THE OLD THING THAT MY GRANDFATHER LOST.

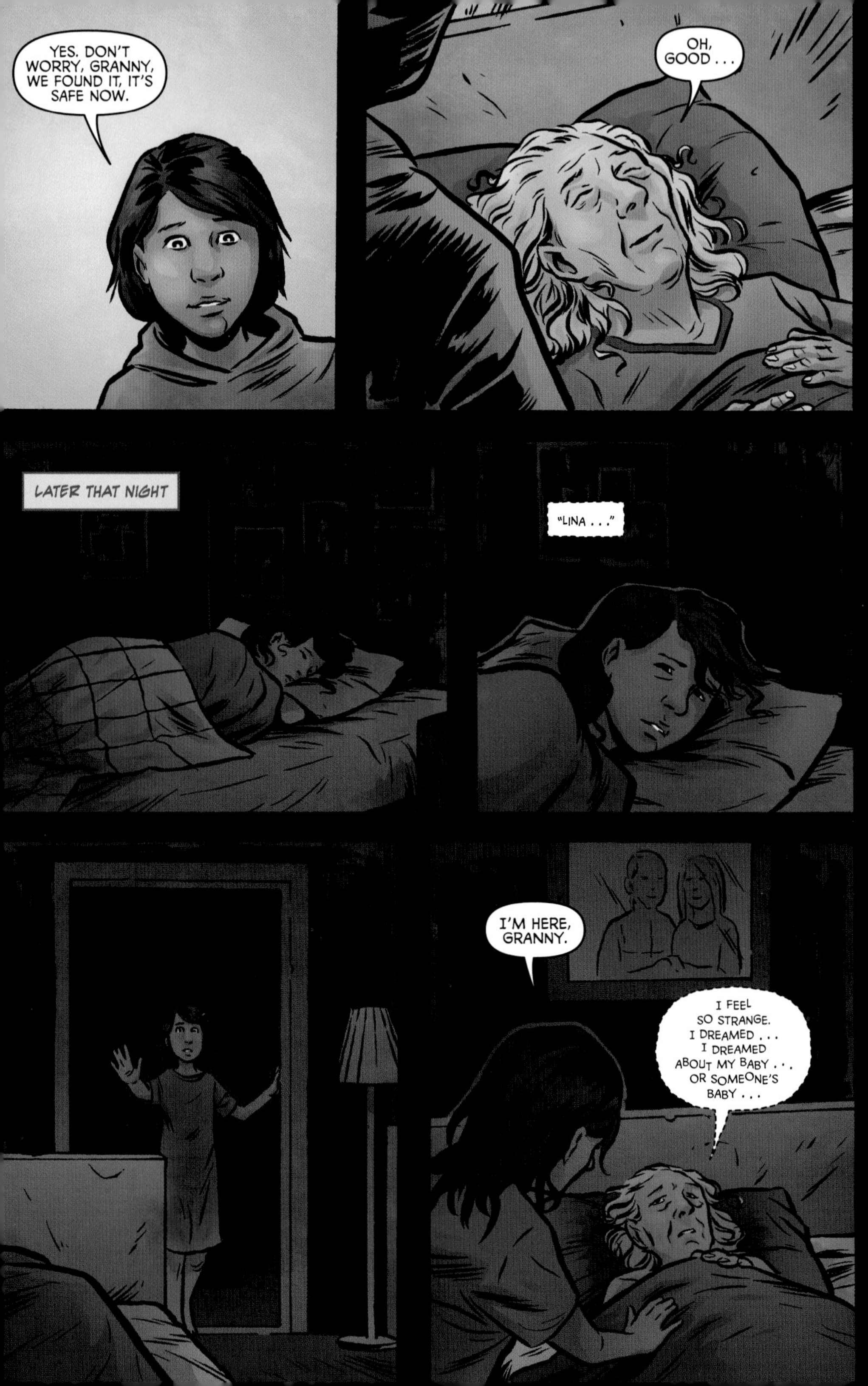
YES. DON'T WORRY, GRANNY, WE FOUND IT, IT'S SAFE NOW.
OH, GOOD . . .
LATER THAT NIGHT
"LINA . . ."
I'M HERE, GRANNY.
I FEEL SO STRANGE. I DREAMED . . . I DREAMED ABOUT MY BABY . . . OR SOMEONE'S BABY . . .

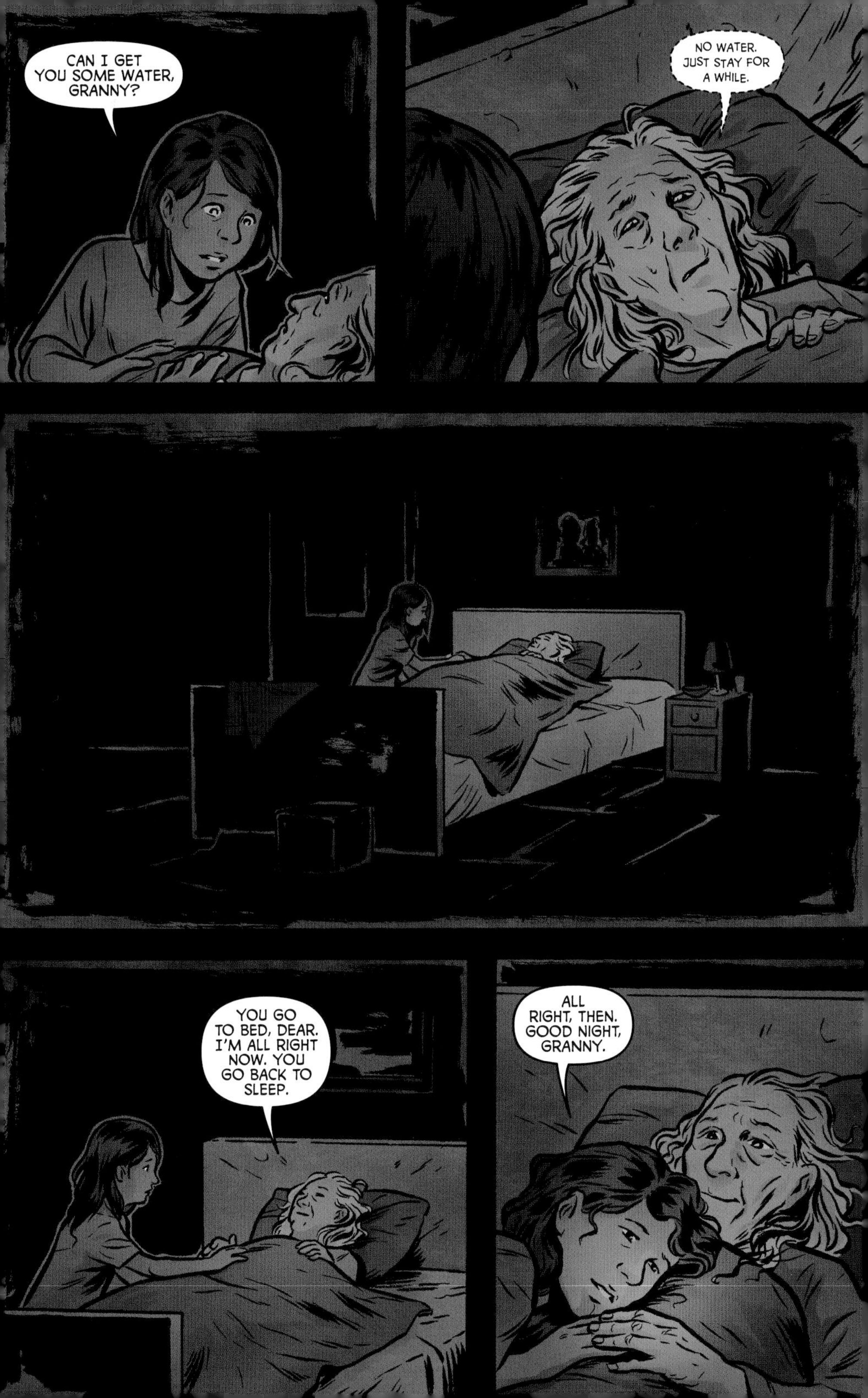
CAN I GET YOU SOME WATER, GRANNY?
NO WATER. JUST STAY FOR A WHILE.
YOU GO TO BED, DEAR. I'M ALL RIGHT NOW. YOU GO BACK TO SLEEP.
ALL RIGHT, THEN. GOOD NIGHT, GRANNY.

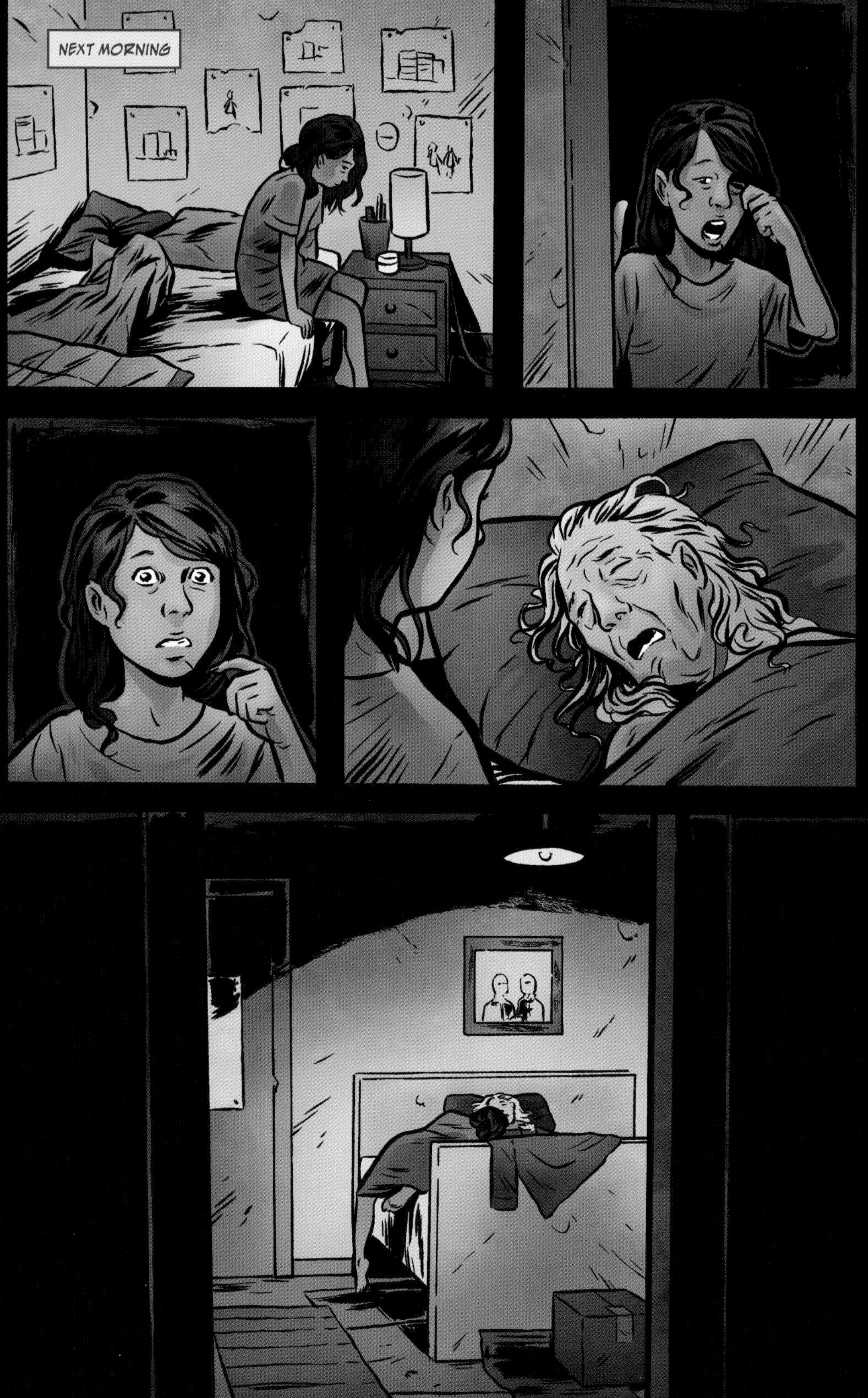
NEXT MORNING

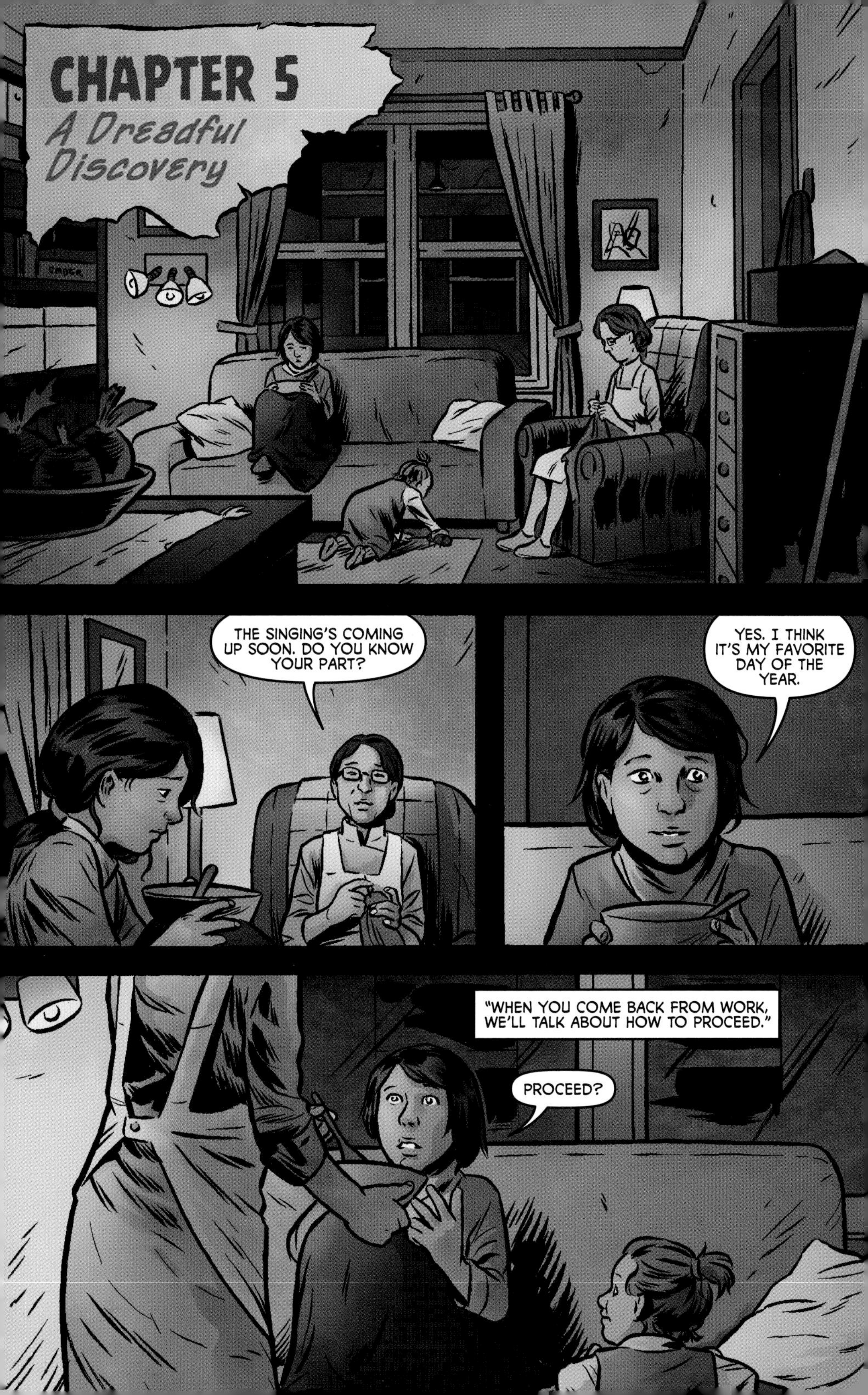
CHAPTER 5
A Dreadful Discovery
THE SINGING'S COMING UP SOON. DO YOU KNOW YOUR PART?
YES. I THINK IT'S MY FAVORITE DAY OF THE YEAR.
"WHEN YOU COME BACK FROM WORK, WE'LL TALK ABOUT HOW TO PROCEED."
PROCEED?

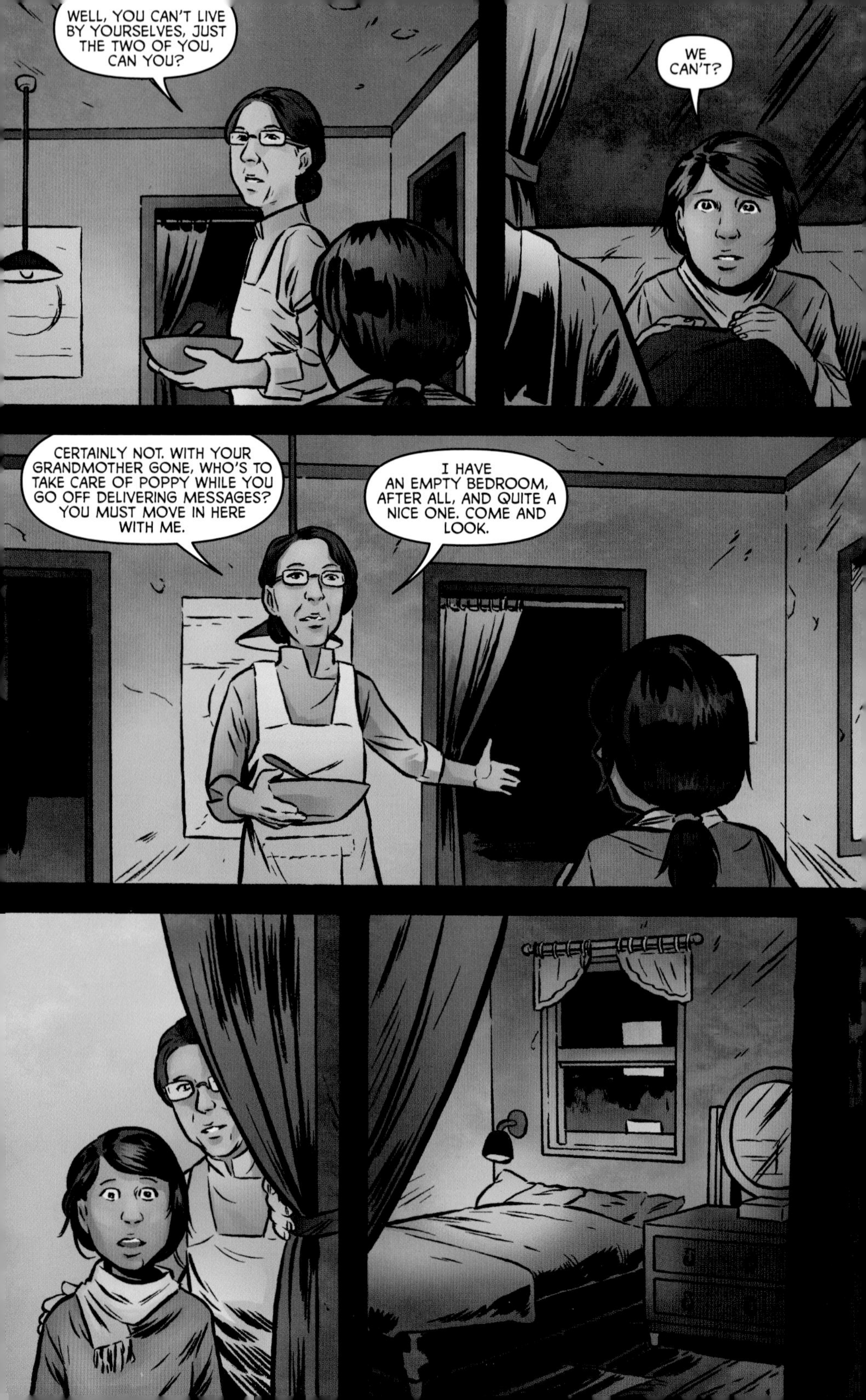
WELL, YOU CAN'T LIVE BY YOURSELVES, JUST THE TWO OF YOU, CAN YOU?
WE CAN'T?
CERTAINLY NOT. WITH YOUR GRANDMOTHER GONE, WHO'S TO TAKE CARE OF POPPY WHILE YOU GO OFF DELIVERING MESSAGES? YOU MUST MOVE IN HERE WITH ME.
I HAVE AN EMPTY BEDROOM, AFTER ALL, AND QUITE A NICE ONE. COME AND LOOK.

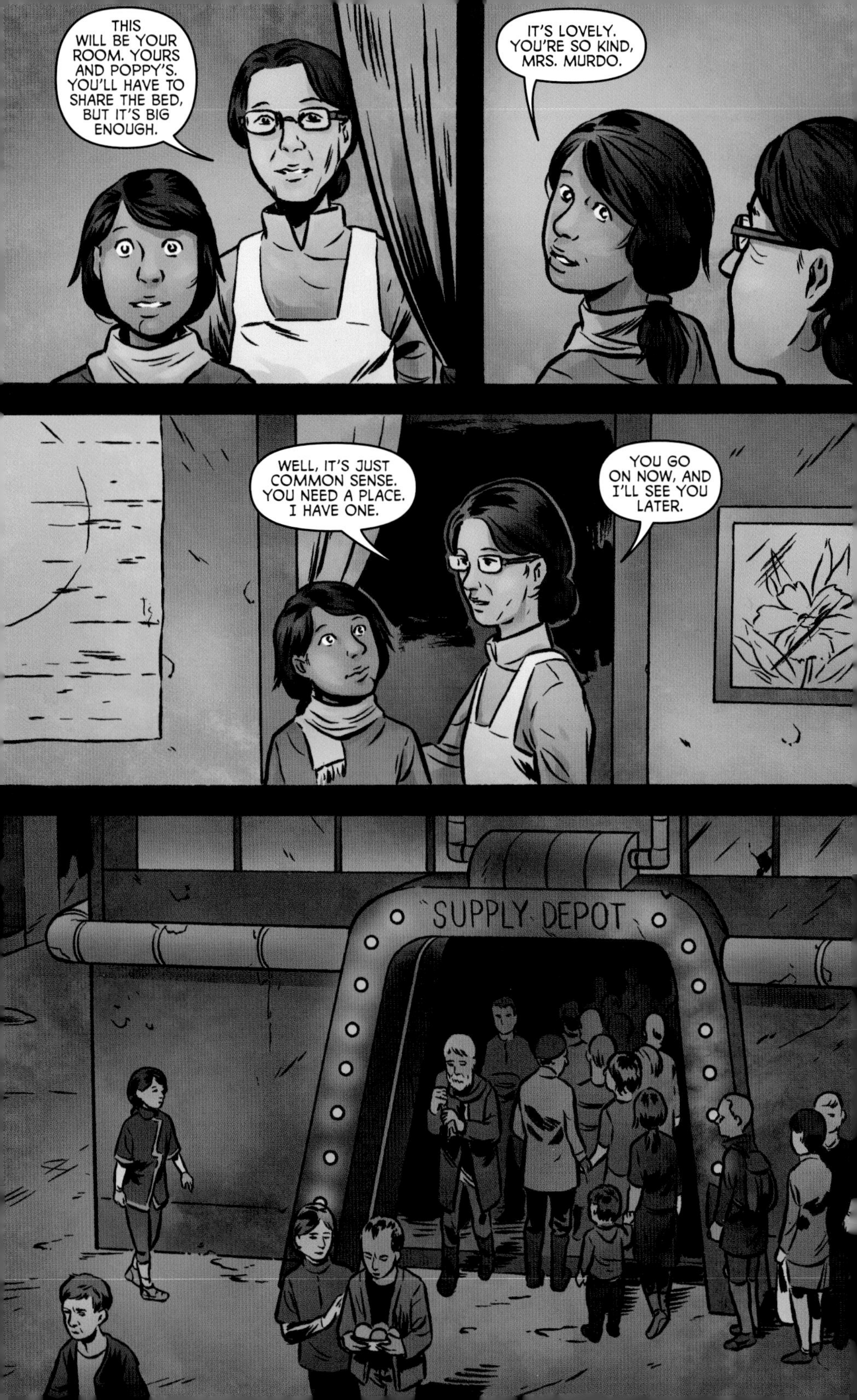
THIS WILL BE YOUR ROOM. YOURS AND POPPY'S. YOU'LL HAVE TO SHARE THE BED, BUT IT'S BIG ENOUGH.
IT'S LOVELY. YOU'RE SO KIND, MRS. MURDO.
WELL, IT'S JUST COMMON SENSE. YOU NEED A PLACE. I HAVE ONE.
YOU GO ON NOW, AND I'LL SEE YOU LATER.
SUPPLY DEPOT

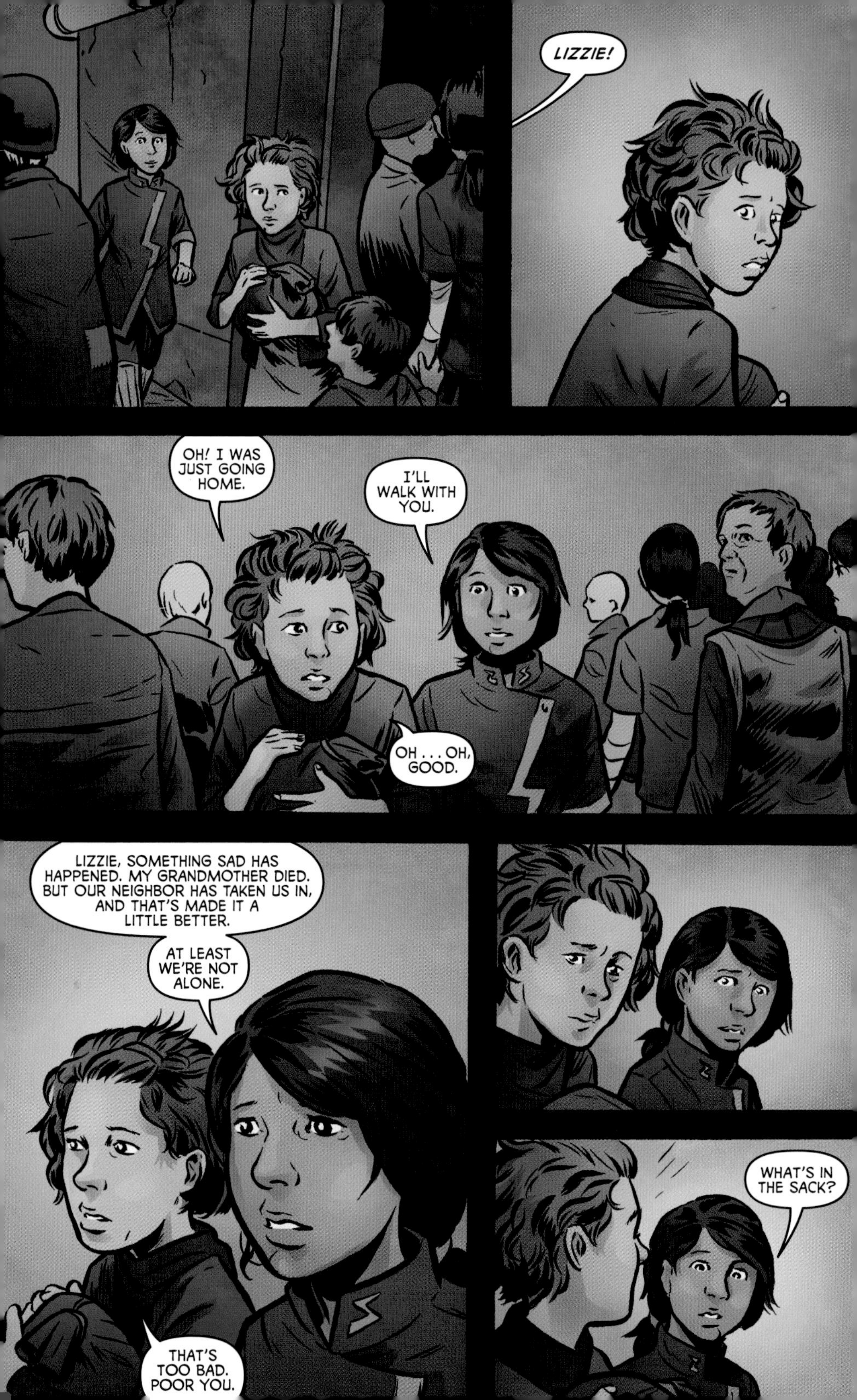
LIZZIE!
OH! I WAS JUST GOING HOME.
I'LL WALK WITH YOU.
OH . . . OH, GOOD.
LIZZIE, SOMETHING SAD HAS HAPPENED. MY GRANDMOTHER DIED. BUT OUR NEIGHBOR HAS TAKEN US IN, AND THAT'S MADE IT A LITTLE BETTER.
AT LEAST WE'RE NOT ALONE.
THAT'S TOO BAD. POOR YOU.
WHAT'S IN THE SACK?

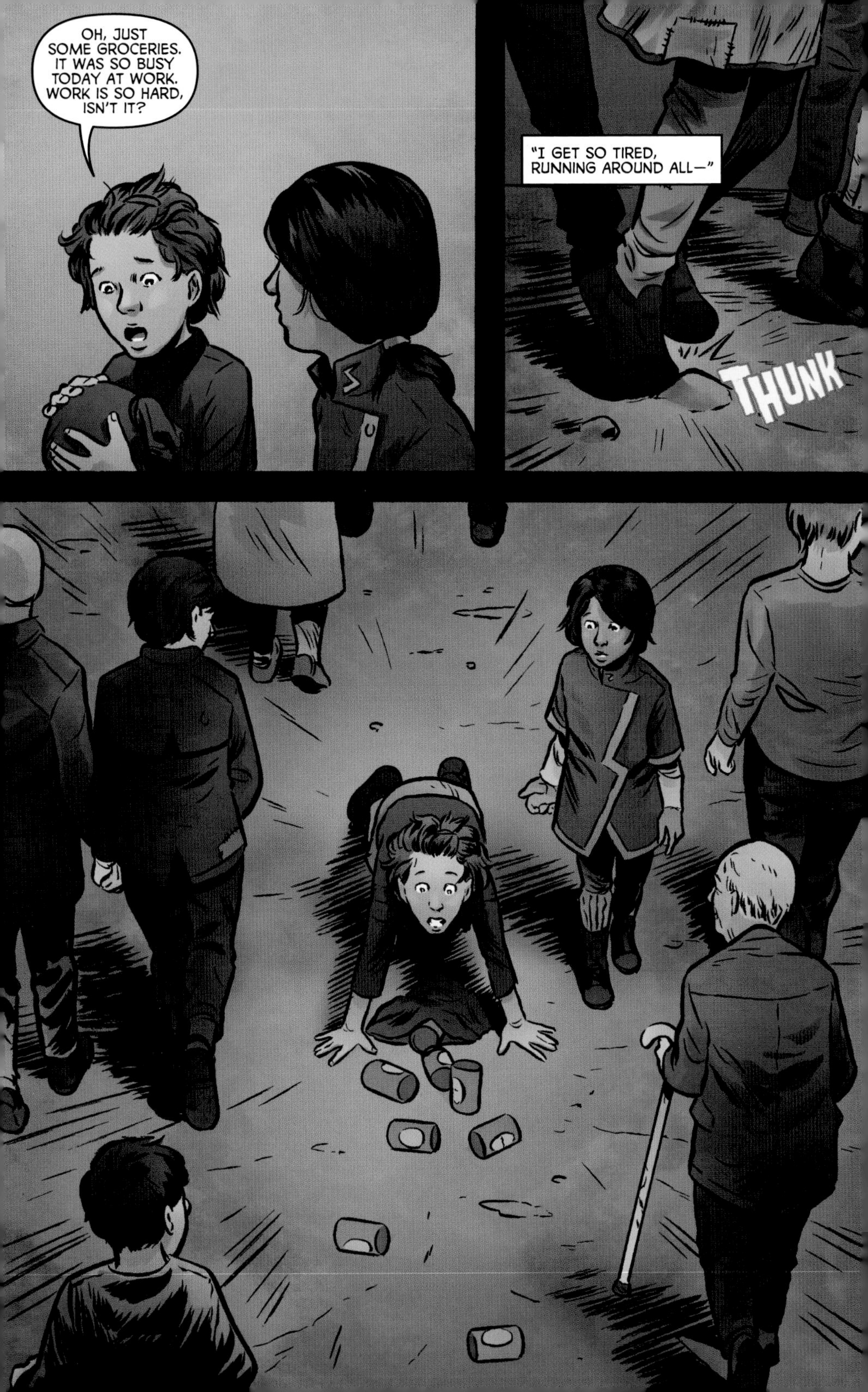
OH, JUST SOME GROCERIES. IT WAS SO BUSY TODAY AT WORK. WORK IS SO HARD, ISN'T IT?
"I GET SO TIRED, RUNNING AROUND ALL—"
THUNK

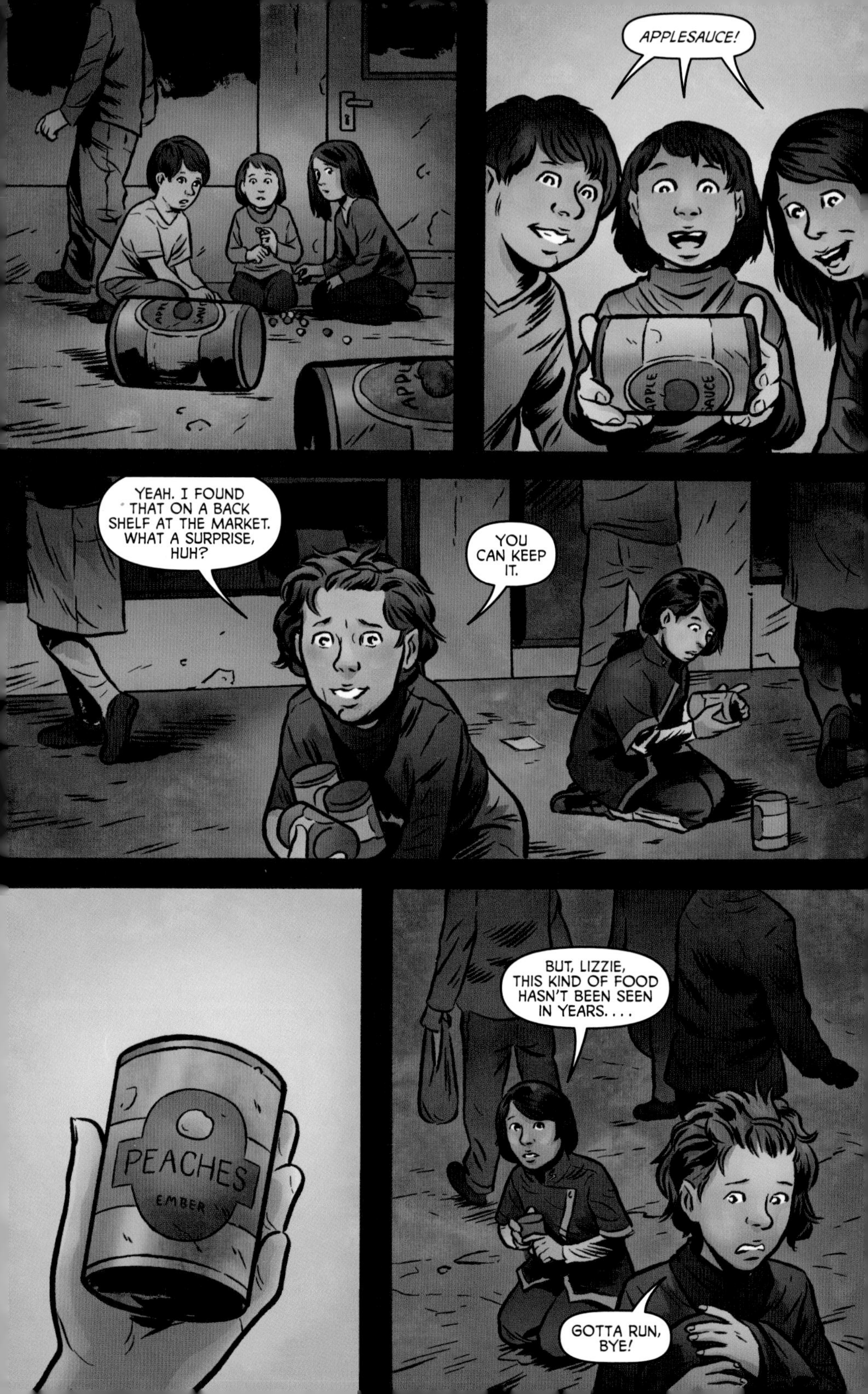
APPLESAUCE!
YEAH. I FOUND THAT ON A BACK SHELF AT THE MARKET. WHAT A SURPRISE, HUH?
YOU CAN KEEP IT.
PEACHES
EMBER
BUT, LIZZIE, THIS KIND OF FOOD HASN'T BEEN SEEN IN YEARS. . . .
GOTTA RUN, BYE!

LIZZIE, STOP! TELL ME THE TRUTH ABOUT WHERE YOU GOT THESE CANS!

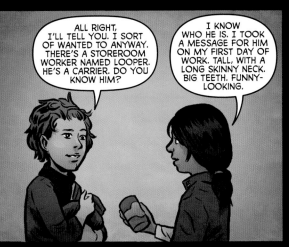

ALL RIGHT, I'LL TELL YOU. I SORT OF WANTED TO ANYWAY. THERE'S A STOREROOM WORKER NAMED LOOPER. HE'S A CARRIER. DO YOU KNOW HIM?

I KNOW WHO HE IS. I TOOK A MESSAGE FOR HIM ON MY FIRST DAY OF WORK. TALL, WITH A LONG SKINNY NECK. BIG TEETH. FUNNY-LOOKING.

WELL, I WOULDN'T DESCRIBE HIM THAT WAY. I THINK HE'S HANDSOME.

LOOPER EXPLORES THE STOREROOMS, LINA. HE WANTS TO KNOW THE TRUE SITUATION.

AND WHAT HAS HE FOUND OUT?

THAT THERE'S STILL A LITTLE BIT LEFT OF SOME RARE THINGS, JUST A FEW THINGS IN ROOMS HERE AND THERE THAT HAVE BEEN FORGOTTEN.

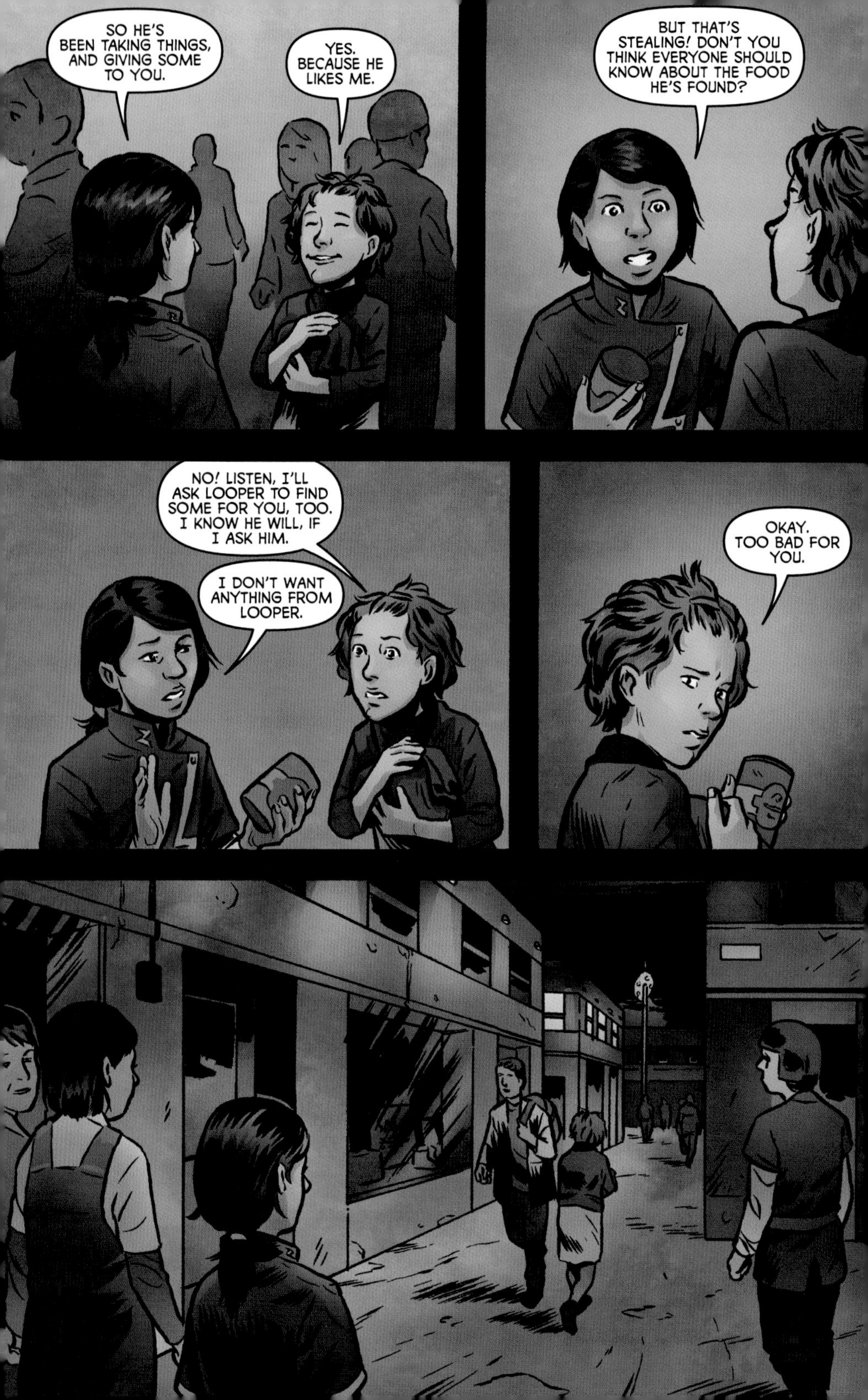
SO HE'S BEEN TAKING THINGS, AND GIVING SOME TO YOU.
YES. BECAUSE HE LIKES ME.
BUT THAT'S STEALING! DON'T YOU THINK EVERYONE SHOULD KNOW ABOUT THE FOOD HE'S FOUND?
NO! LISTEN, I'LL ASK LOOPER TO FIND SOME FOR YOU, TOO. I KNOW HE WILL, IF I ASK HIM.
I DON'T WANT ANYTHING FROM LOOPER.
OKAY. TOO BAD FOR YOU.

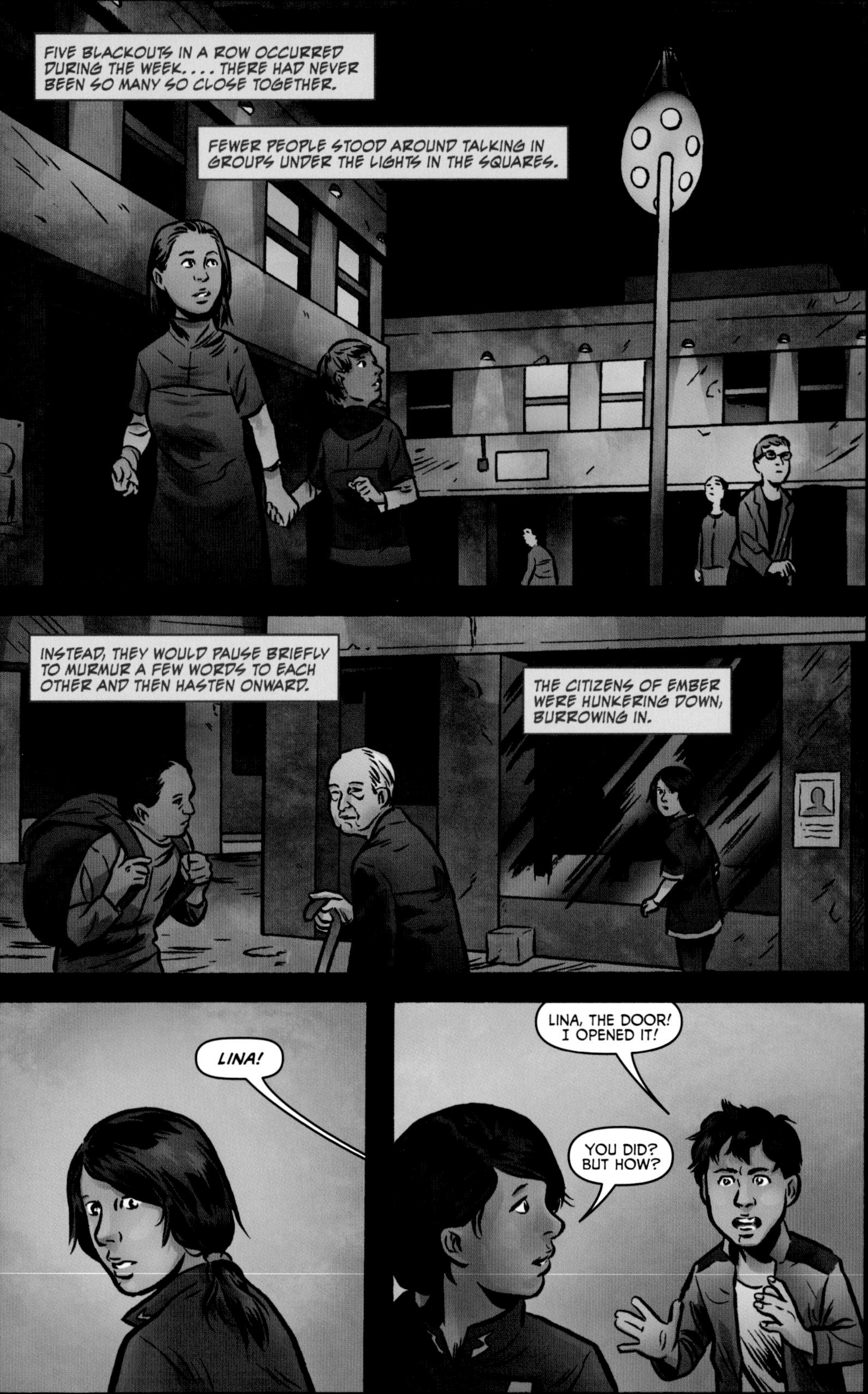
FIVE BLACKOUTS IN A ROW OCCURRED DURING THE WEEK. . . . THERE HAD NEVER BEEN SO MANY SO CLOSE TOGETHER.
FEWER PEOPLE STOOD AROUND TALKING IN GROUPS UNDER THE LIGHTS IN THE SQUARES.
INSTEAD, THEY WOULD PAUSE BRIEFLY TO MURMUR A FEW WORDS TO EACH OTHER AND THEN HASTEN ONWARD.
THE CITIZENS OF EMBER WERE HUNKERING DOWN, BURROWING IN.
LINA!
LINA, THE DOOR! I OPENED IT!
YOU DID? BUT HOW?

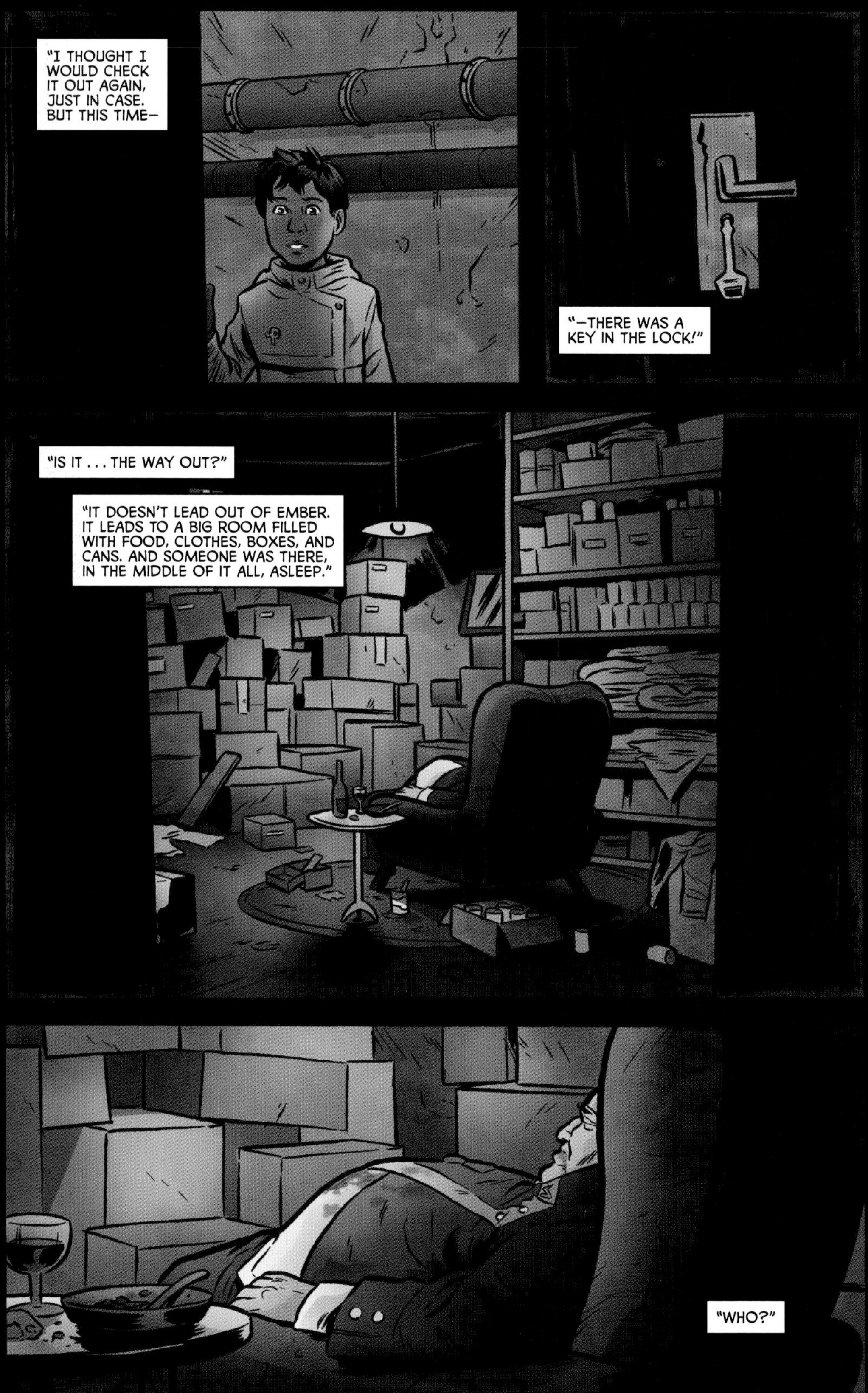
"I THOUGHT I WOULD CHECK IT OUT AGAIN, JUST IN CASE. BUT THIS TIME—
"—THERE WAS A KEY IN THE LOCK!"
"IS IT . . . THE WAY OUT?"
"IT DOESN'T LEAD OUT OF EMBER. IT LEADS TO A BIG ROOM FILLED WITH FOOD, CLOTHES, BOXES, AND CANS. AND SOMEONE WAS THERE, IN THE MIDDLE OF IT ALL, ASLEEP."
"WHO?"

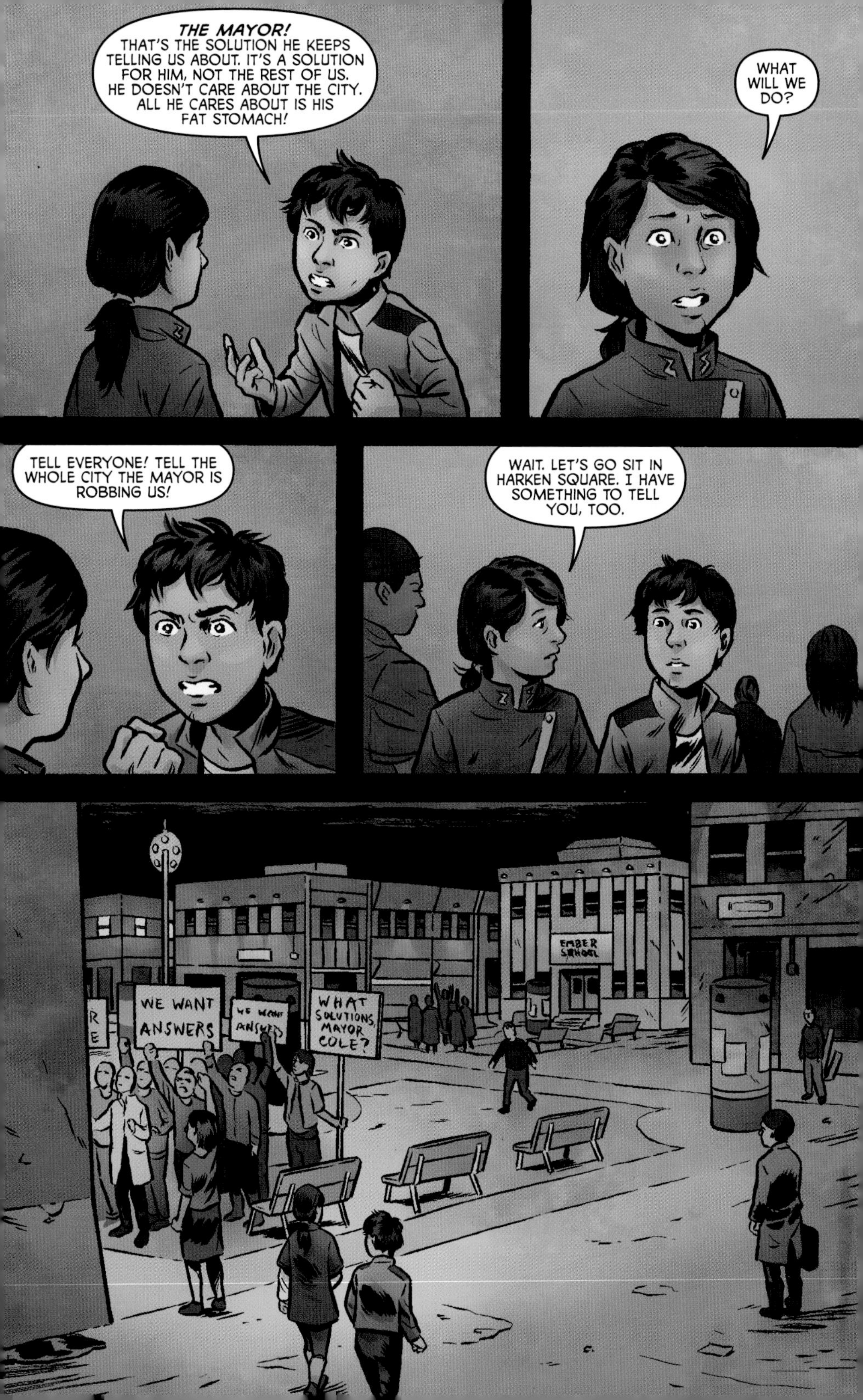
THE MAYOR! THAT'S THE SOLUTION HE KEEPS TELLING US ABOUT. IT'S A SOLUTION FOR HIM, NOT THE REST OF US. HE DOESN'T CARE ABOUT THE CITY. ALL HE CARES ABOUT IS HIS FAT STOMACH!
WHAT WILL WE DO?
TELL EVERYONE! TELL THE WHOLE CITY THE MAYOR IS ROBBING US!
WAIT. LET'S GO SIT IN HARKEN SQUARE. I HAVE SOMETHING TO TELL YOU, TOO.
WE WANT ANSWERS
WHAT SOLUTIONS, MAYOR COLE?
EMBER SCHOOL

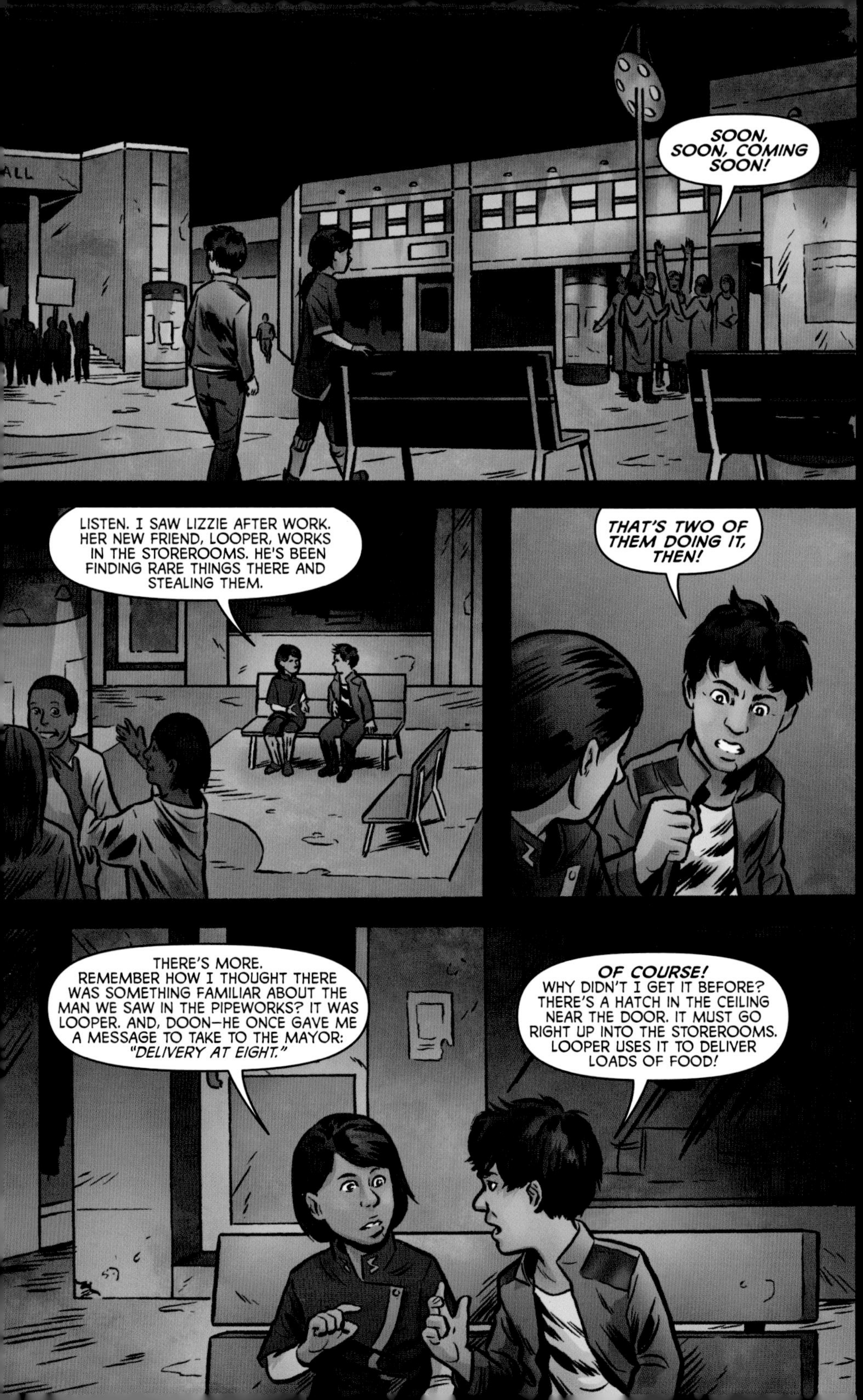

SOON, SOON, COMING SOON!
LISTEN. I SAW LIZZIE AFTER WORK. HER NEW FRIEND, LOOPER, WORKS IN THE STOREROOMS. HE'S BEEN FINDING RARE THINGS THERE AND STEALING THEM.
THAT'S TWO OF THEM DOING IT, THEN!
THERE'S MORE. REMEMBER HOW I THOUGHT THERE WAS SOMETHING FAMILIAR ABOUT THE MAN WE SAW IN THE PIPEWORKS? IT WAS LOOPER. AND, DOON—HE ONCE GAVE ME A MESSAGE TO TAKE TO THE MAYOR: *"DELIVERY AT EIGHT."*
OF COURSE! WHY DIDN'T I GET IT BEFORE? THERE'S A HATCH IN THE CEILING NEAR THE DOOR. IT MUST GO RIGHT UP INTO THE STOREROOMS. LOOPER USES IT TO DELIVER LOADS OF FOOD!

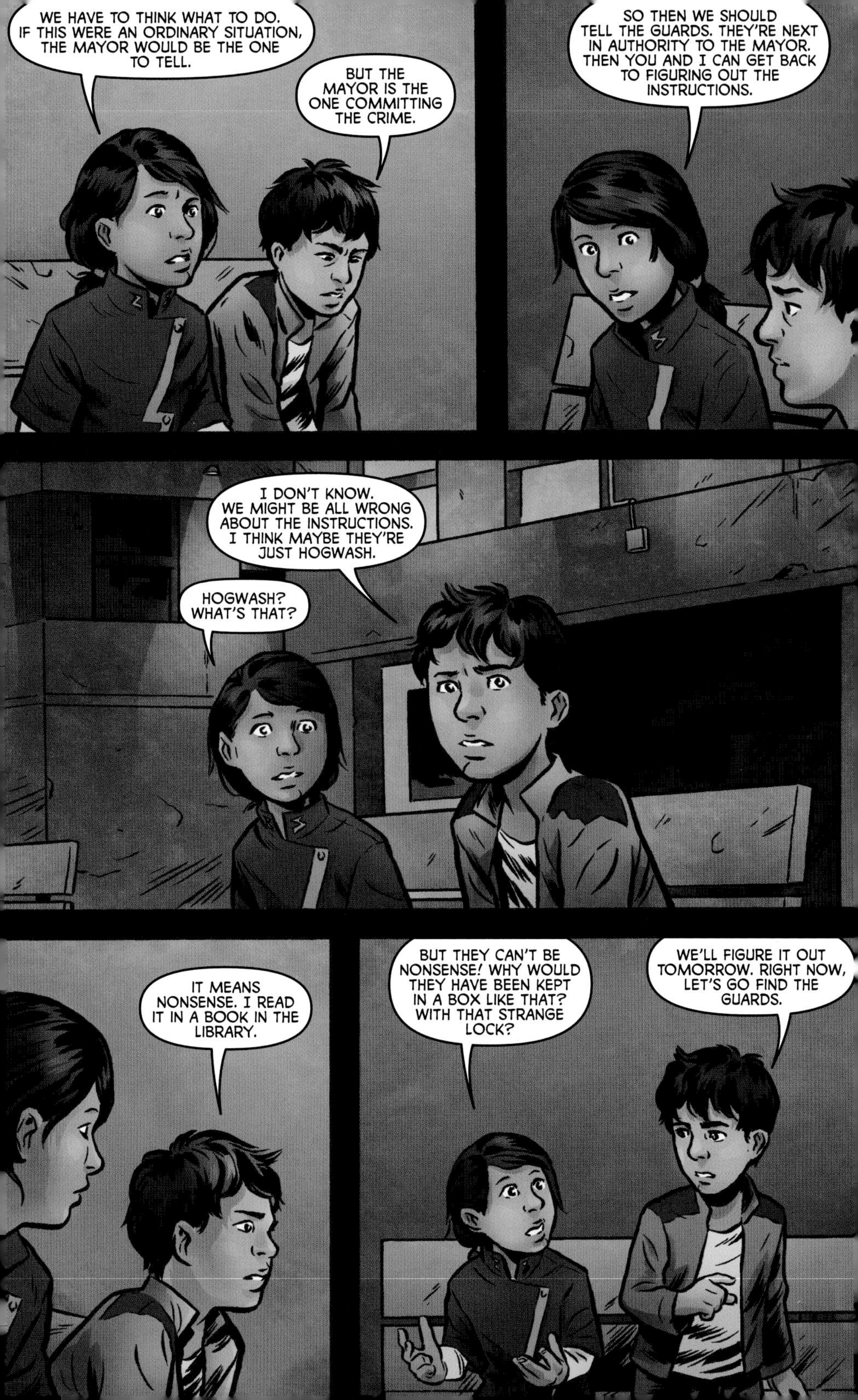
WE HAVE TO THINK WHAT TO DO. IF THIS WERE AN ORDINARY SITUATION, THE MAYOR WOULD BE THE ONE TO TELL.
BUT THE MAYOR IS THE ONE COMMITTING THE CRIME.
SO THEN WE SHOULD TELL THE GUARDS. THEY'RE NEXT IN AUTHORITY TO THE MAYOR. THEN YOU AND I CAN GET BACK TO FIGURING OUT THE INSTRUCTIONS.
I DON'T KNOW. WE MIGHT BE ALL WRONG ABOUT THE INSTRUCTIONS. I THINK MAYBE THEY'RE JUST HOGWASH.
HOGWASH? WHAT'S THAT?
IT MEANS NONSENSE. I READ IT IN A BOOK IN THE LIBRARY.
BUT THEY CAN'T BE NONSENSE! WHY WOULD THEY HAVE BEEN KEPT IN A BOX LIKE THAT? WITH THAT STRANGE LOCK?
WE'LL FIGURE IT OUT TOMORROW. RIGHT NOW, LET'S GO FIND THE GUARDS.

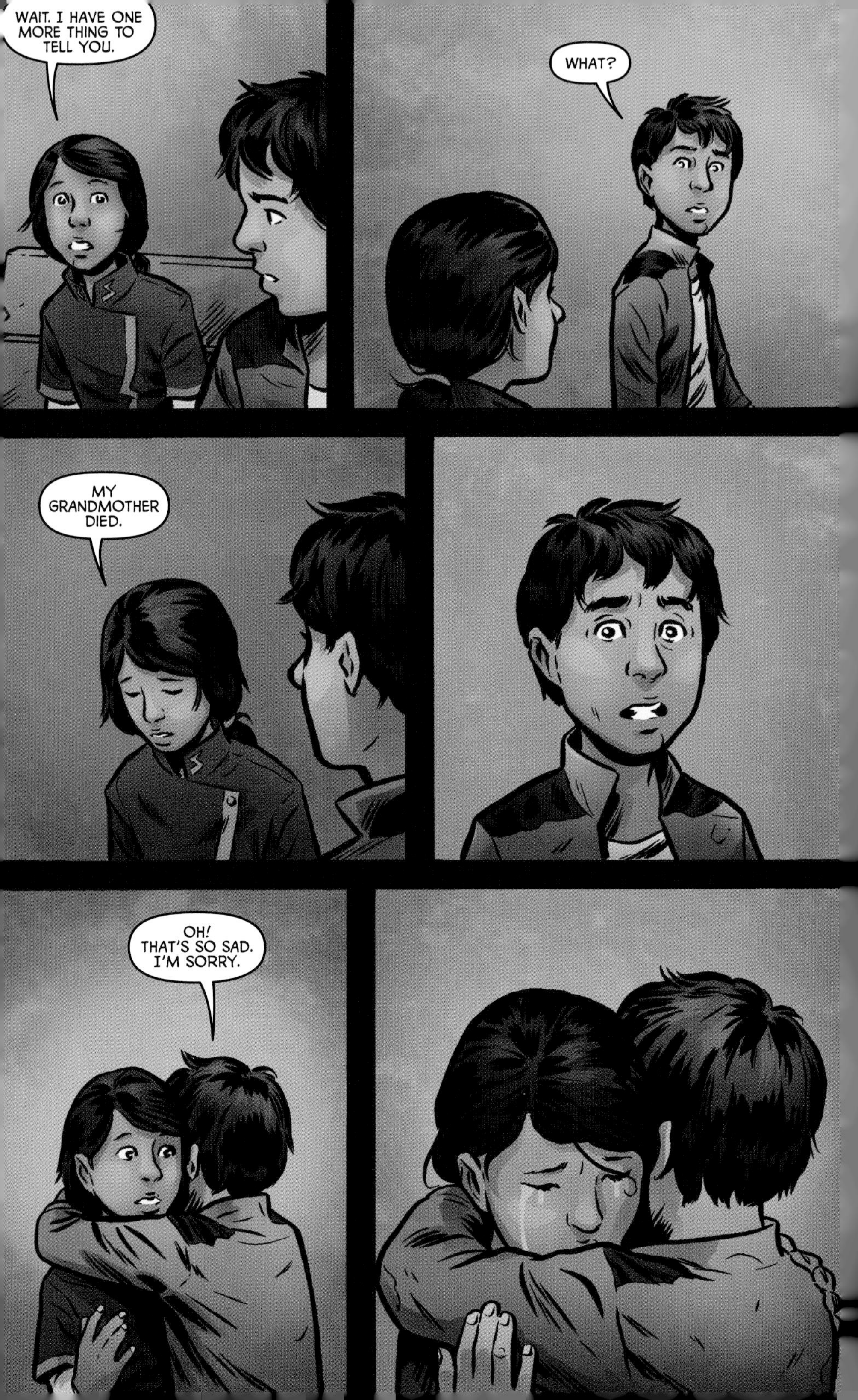
WAIT. I HAVE ONE MORE THING TO TELL YOU.
WHAT?
MY GRANDMOTHER DIED.
OH! THAT'S SO SAD. I'M SORRY.

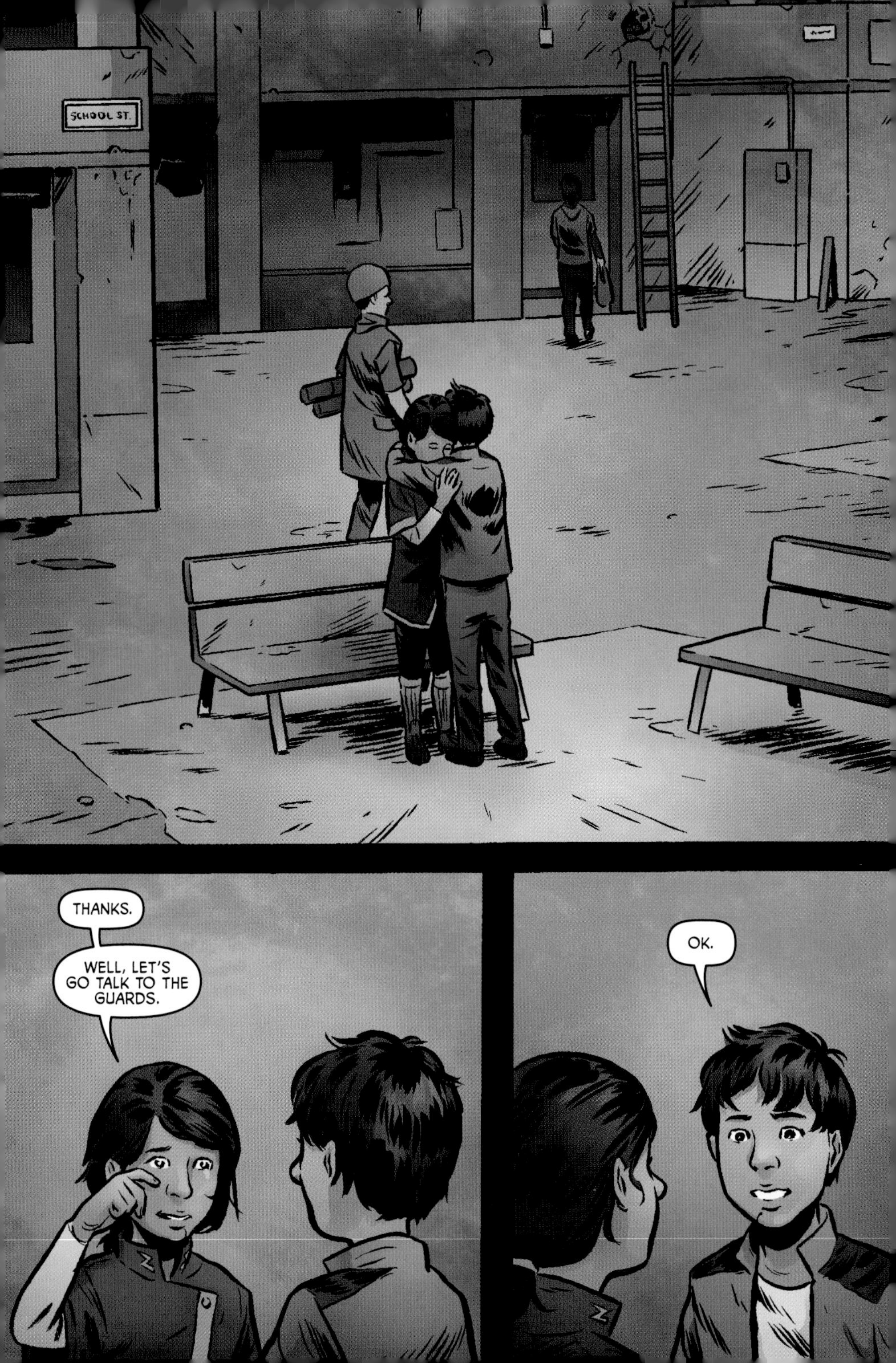
SCHOOL ST.
THANKS.
WELL, LET'S GO TALK TO THE GUARDS.
OK.

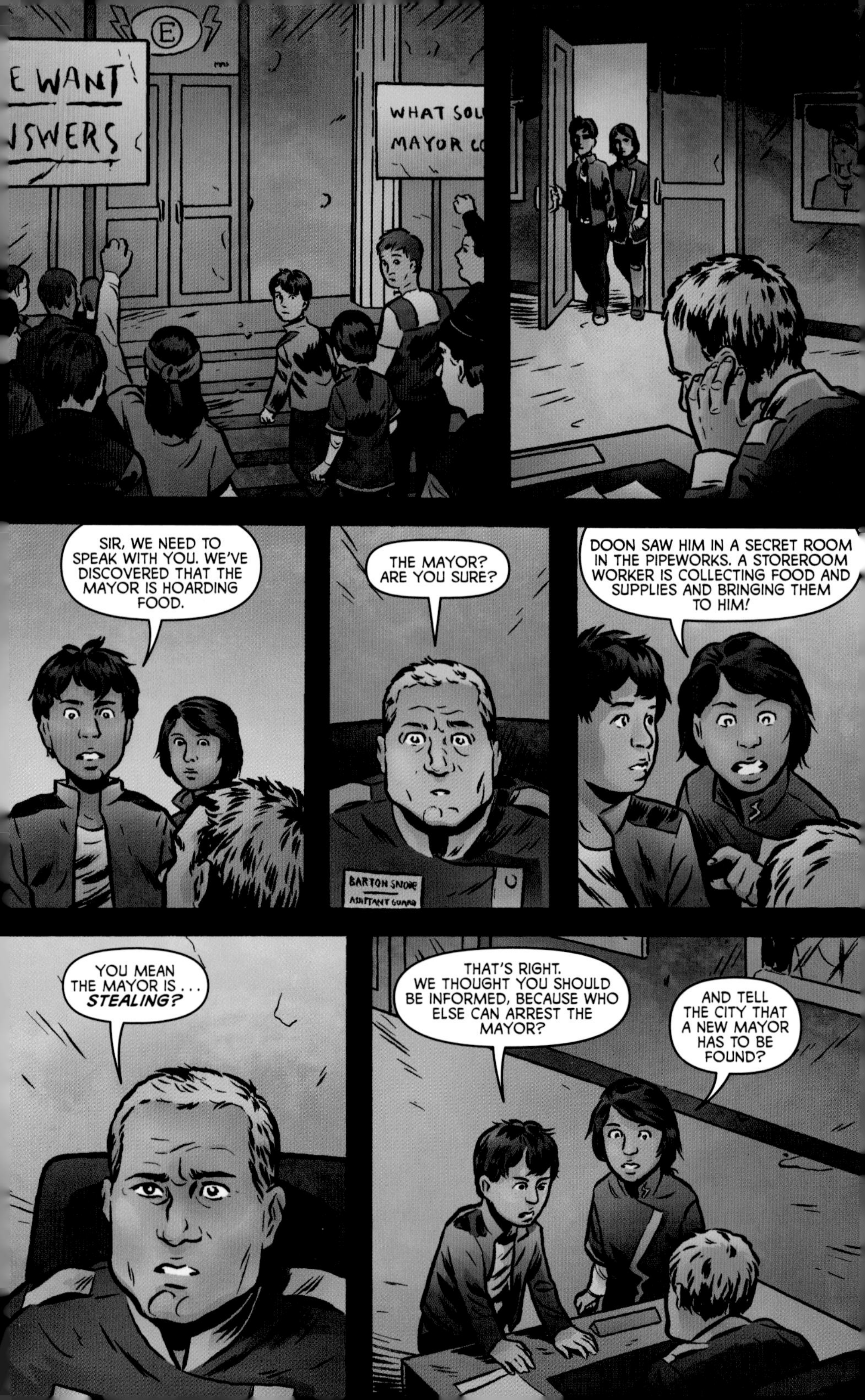
E WANT
NSWERS
WHAT SOL
MAYOR C
SIR, WE NEED TO SPEAK WITH YOU. WE'VE DISCOVERED THAT THE MAYOR IS HOARDING FOOD.
THE MAYOR? ARE YOU SURE?
BARTON SNODE
ASSISTANT GUARD
DOON SAW HIM IN A SECRET ROOM IN THE PIPEWORKS. A STOREROOM WORKER IS COLLECTING FOOD AND SUPPLIES AND BRINGING THEM TO HIM!
YOU MEAN THE MAYOR IS . . . ***STEALING?***
THAT'S RIGHT. WE THOUGHT YOU SHOULD BE INFORMED, BECAUSE WHO ELSE CAN ARREST THE MAYOR?
AND TELL THE CITY THAT A NEW MAYOR HAS TO BE FOUND?

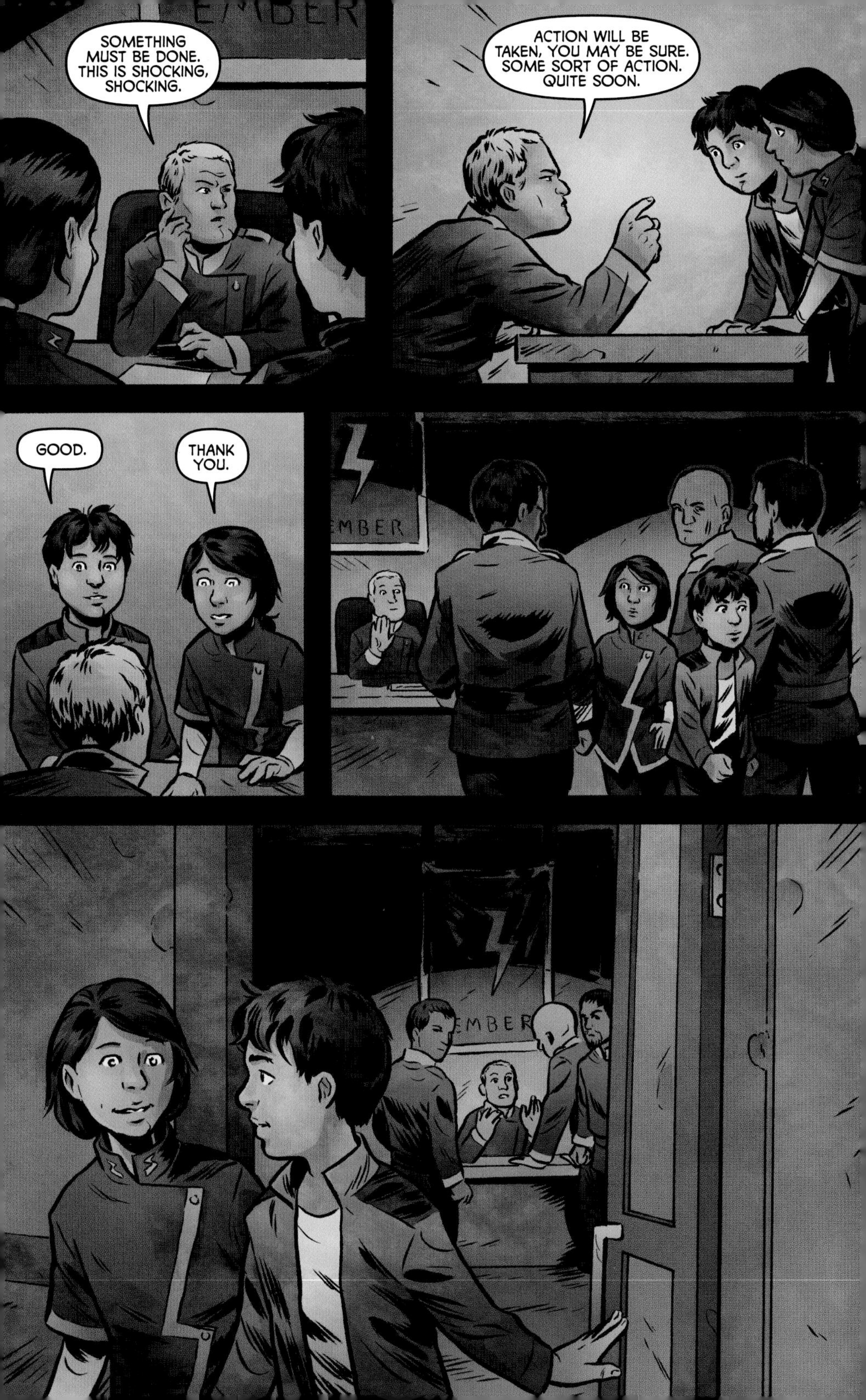
SOMETHING MUST BE DONE. THIS IS SHOCKING, SHOCKING.
ACTION WILL BE TAKEN, YOU MAY BE SURE. SOME SORT OF ACTION. QUITE SOON.
GOOD.
THANK YOU.

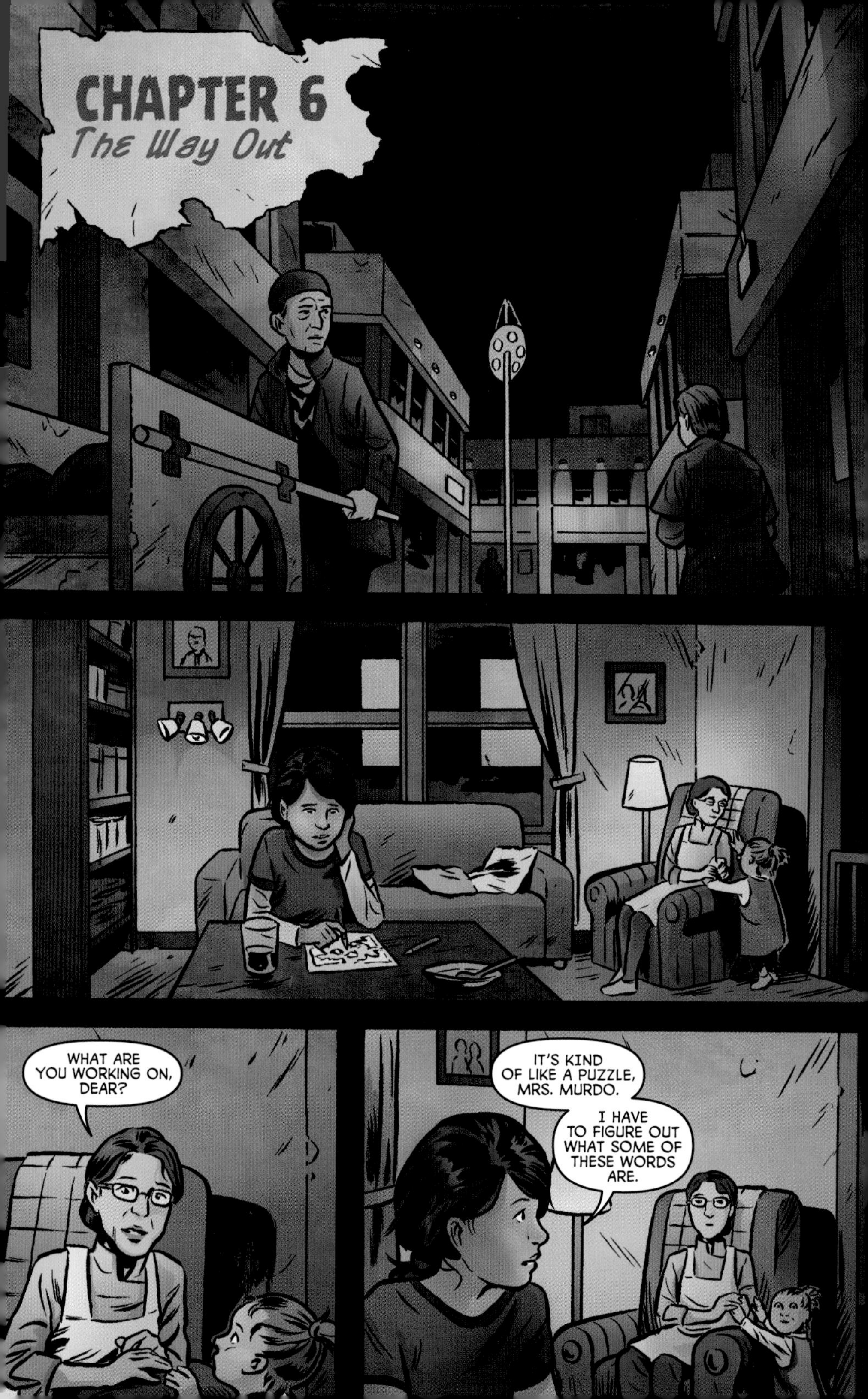
CHAPTER 6
The Way Out
WHAT ARE YOU WORKING ON, DEAR?
IT'S KIND OF LIKE A PUZZLE, MRS. MURDO.
I HAVE TO FIGURE OUT WHAT SOME OF THESE WORDS ARE.

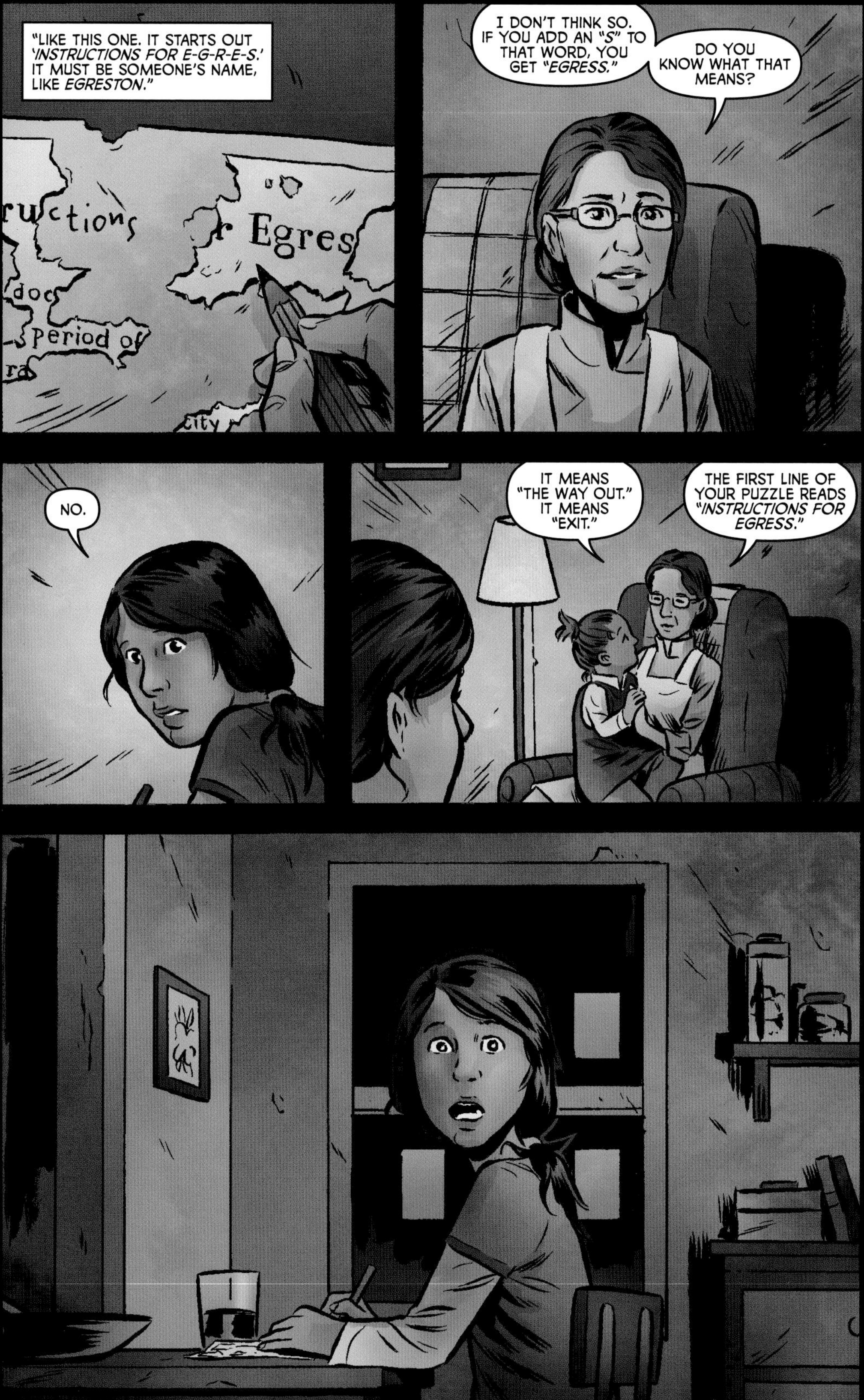
"LIKE THIS ONE. IT STARTS OUT 'INSTRUCTIONS FOR E-G-R-E-S.' IT MUST BE SOMEONE'S NAME, LIKE EGRESTON."
ructions r Egres
doc
period of
City
I DON'T THINK SO. IF YOU ADD AN "S" TO THAT WORD, YOU GET "EGRESS."
DO YOU KNOW WHAT THAT MEANS?
NO.
IT MEANS "THE WAY OUT." IT MEANS "EXIT."
THE FIRST LINE OF YOUR PUZZLE READS "INSTRUCTIONS FOR EGRESS."

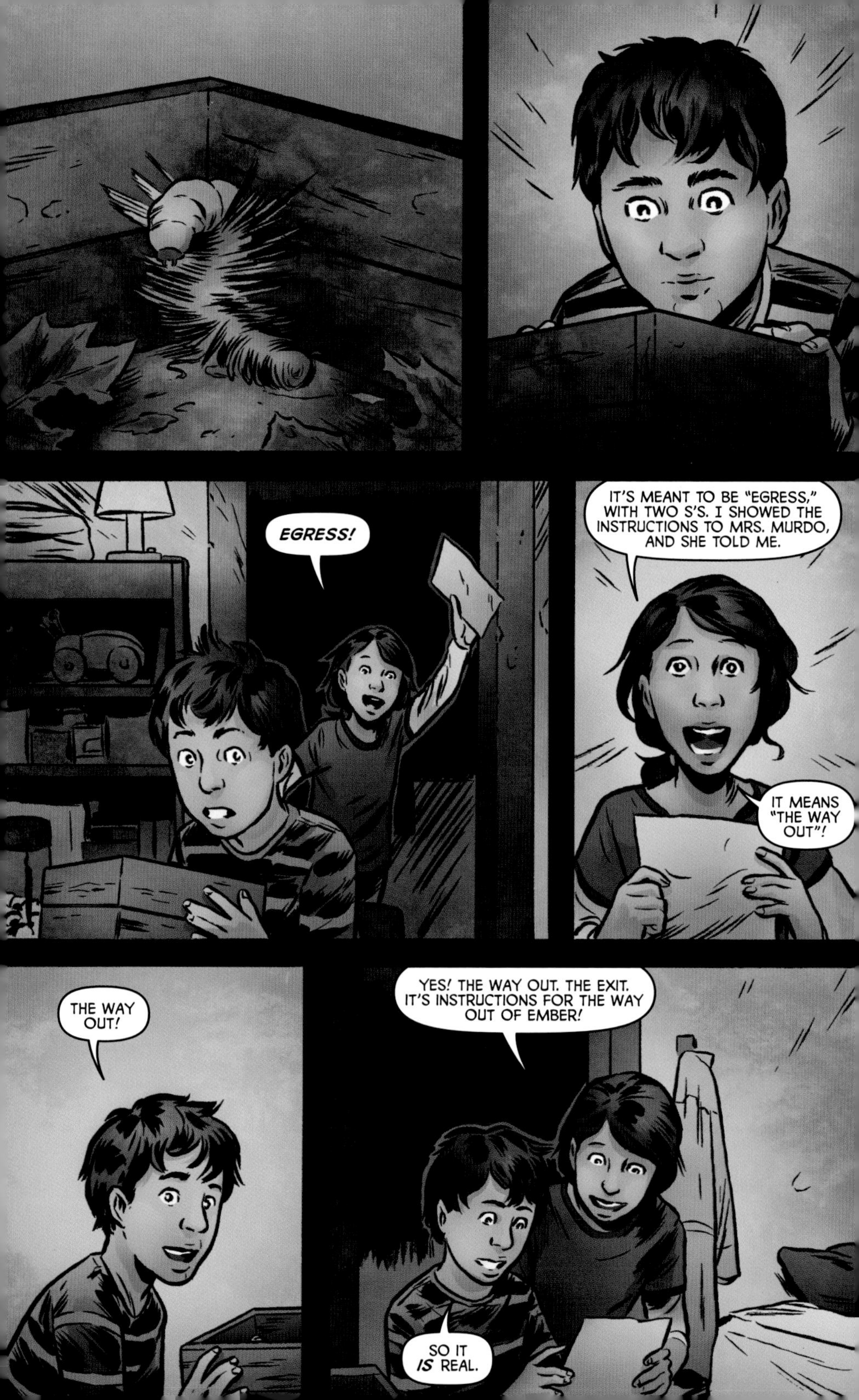
EGRESS!
IT'S MEANT TO BE "EGRESS," WITH TWO S'S. I SHOWED THE INSTRUCTIONS TO MRS. MURDO, AND SHE TOLD ME.
IT MEANS "THE WAY OUT"!
THE WAY OUT!
YES! THE WAY OUT. THE EXIT. IT'S INSTRUCTIONS FOR THE WAY OUT OF EMBER!
SO IT *IS* REAL.

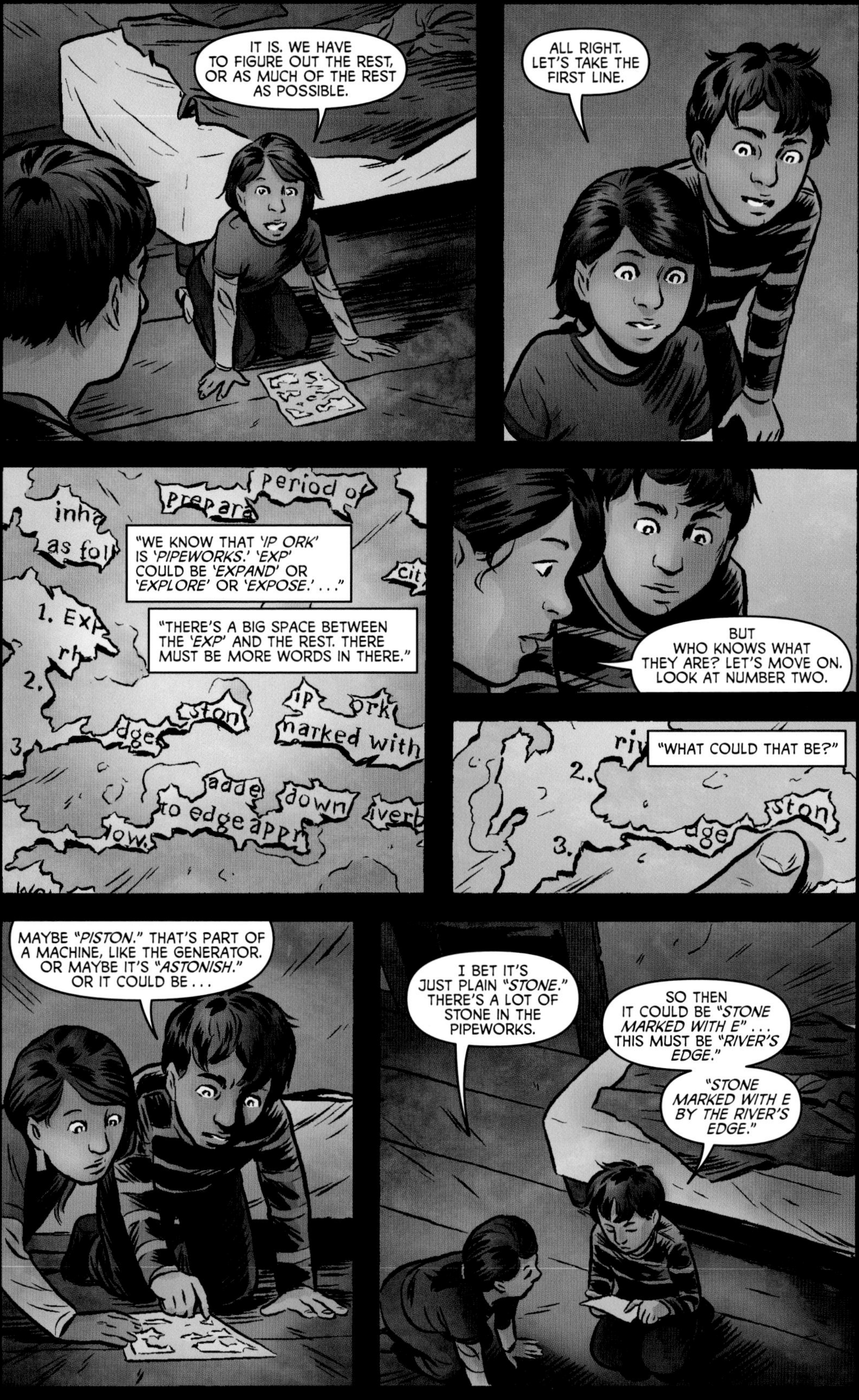
IT IS. WE HAVE TO FIGURE OUT THE REST, OR AS MUCH OF THE REST AS POSSIBLE.
ALL RIGHT. LET'S TAKE THE FIRST LINE.
Period of
prepara
inha
as fol
city
1. EXP
rh
2.
3.
"WE KNOW THAT 'IP ORK' IS 'PIPEWORKS.' 'EXP' COULD BE 'EXPAND' OR 'EXPLORE' OR 'EXPOSE.' . . ."
"THERE'S A BIG SPACE BETWEEN THE 'EXP' AND THE REST. THERE MUST BE MORE WORDS IN THERE."
ip ork
ston
dge
narked with
adde
down
to edge appr
iverb
low.
BUT WHO KNOWS WHAT THEY ARE? LET'S MOVE ON. LOOK AT NUMBER TWO.
riv
"WHAT COULD THAT BE?"
2.
ston
dge
3.
MAYBE "PISTON." THAT'S PART OF A MACHINE, LIKE THE GENERATOR. OR MAYBE IT'S "ASTONISH." OR IT COULD BE . . .
I BET IT'S JUST PLAIN "STONE." THERE'S A LOT OF STONE IN THE PIPEWORKS.
SO THEN IT COULD BE "STONE MARKED WITH E" . . . THIS MUST BE "RIVER'S EDGE."
"STONE MARKED WITH E BY THE RIVER'S EDGE."

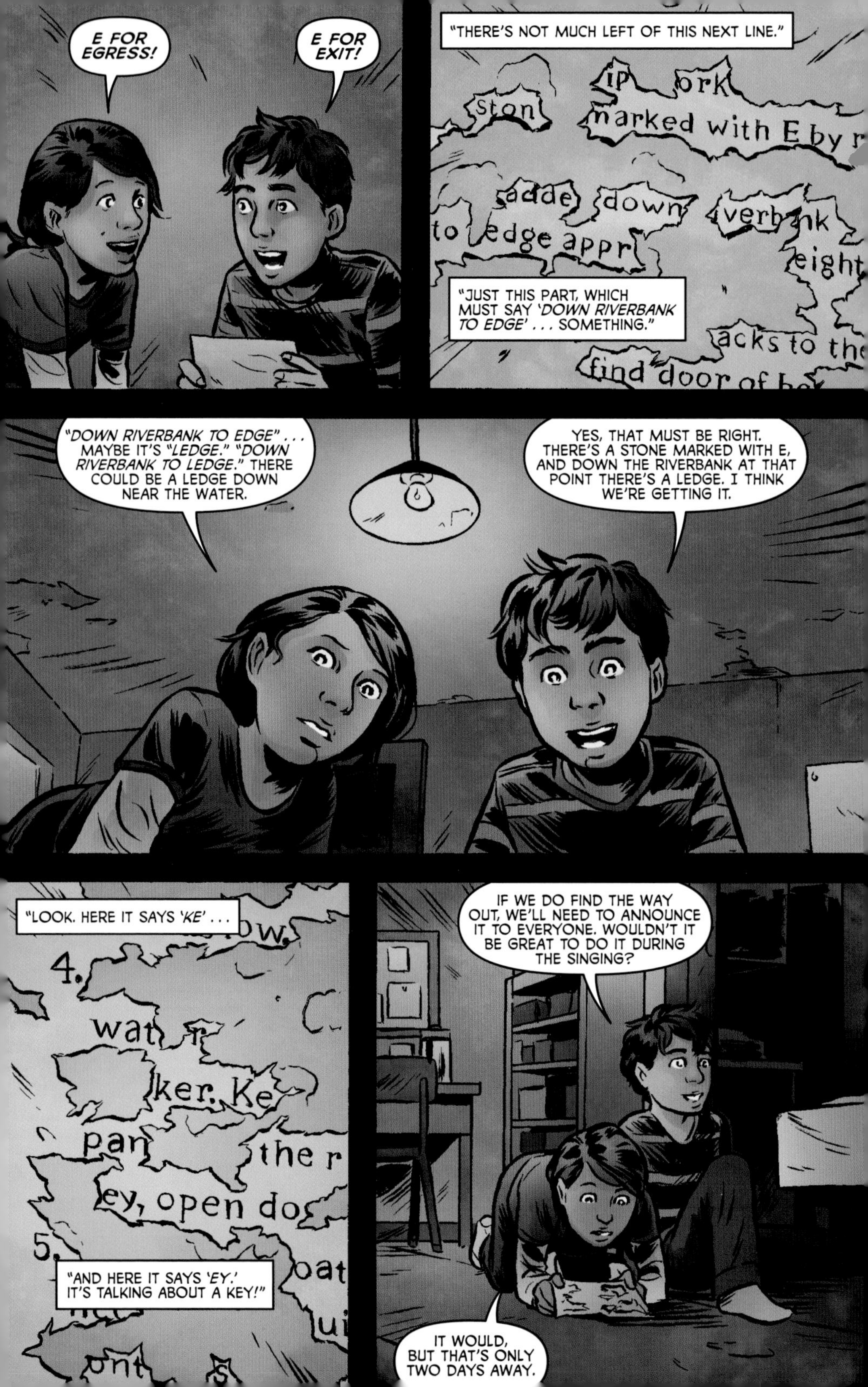
E FOR EGRESS!
E FOR EXIT!
"THERE'S NOT MUCH LEFT OF THIS NEXT LINE."
ston
ip ork
narked with E by r
adde down verbank
to edge appr
eight
"JUST THIS PART, WHICH MUST SAY '*DOWN RIVERBANK TO EDGE*' . . . SOMETHING."
acks to th
find door of h
"*DOWN RIVERBANK TO EDGE*" . . . MAYBE IT'S "*LEDGE*." "*DOWN RIVERBANK TO LEDGE*." THERE COULD BE A LEDGE DOWN NEAR THE WATER.
YES, THAT MUST BE RIGHT. THERE'S A STONE MARKED WITH E, AND DOWN THE RIVERBANK AT THAT POINT THERE'S A LEDGE. I THINK WE'RE GETTING IT.
"LOOK. HERE IT SAYS '*KE*' . . .
ow.
4.
wat r
ker. Ke
pan the r
ey, open do
5.
oat
"AND HERE IT SAYS '*EY.*' IT'S TALKING ABOUT A KEY!"
IF WE DO FIND THE WAY OUT, WE'LL NEED TO ANNOUNCE IT TO EVERYONE. WOULDN'T IT BE GREAT TO DO IT DURING THE SINGING?
IT WOULD, BUT THAT'S ONLY TWO DAYS AWAY.

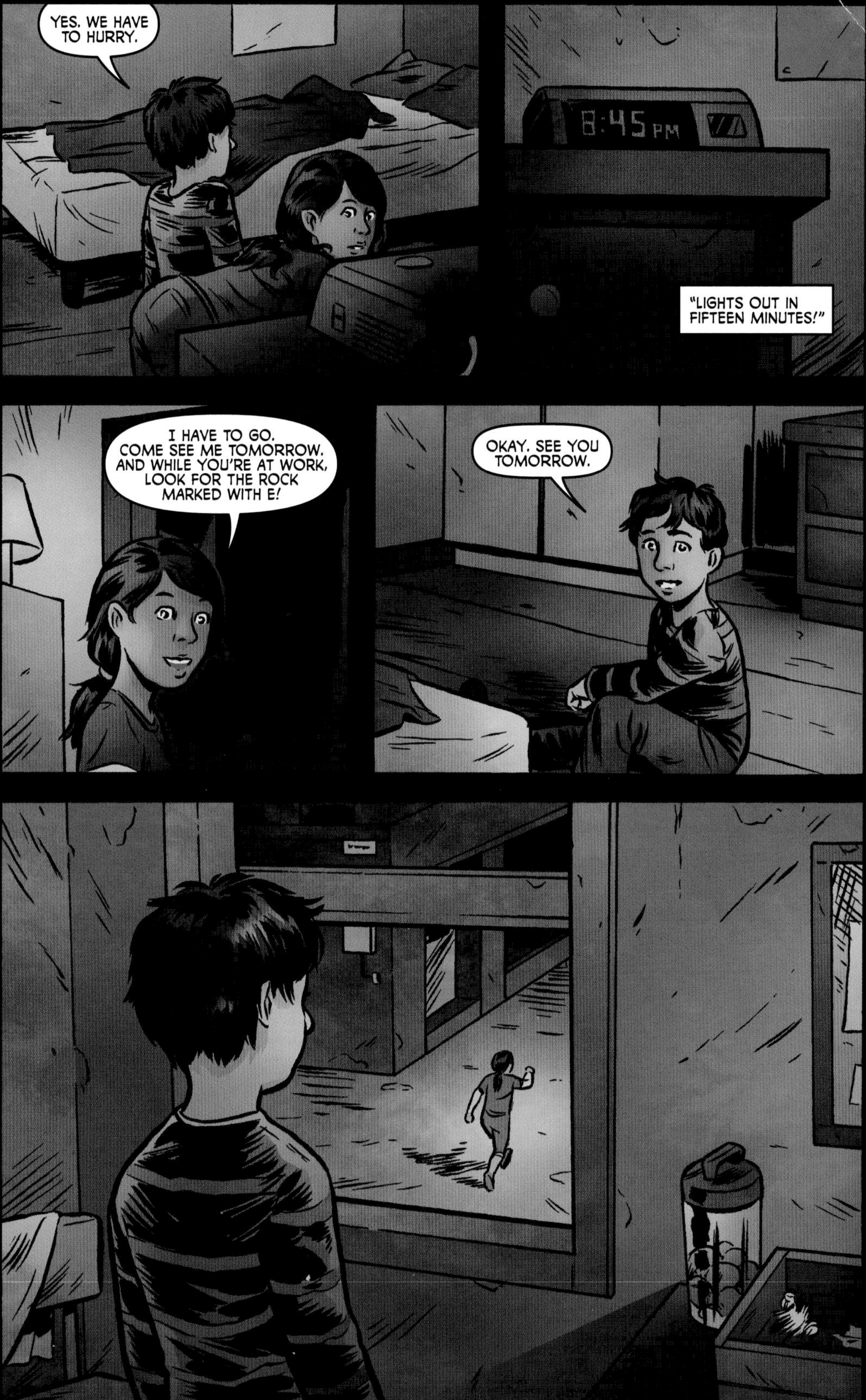
YES. WE HAVE TO HURRY.
8:45 PM
"LIGHTS OUT IN FIFTEEN MINUTES!"
I HAVE TO GO. COME SEE ME TOMORROW. AND WHILE YOU'RE AT WORK, LOOK FOR THE ROCK MARKED WITH E!
OKAY. SEE YOU TOMORROW.

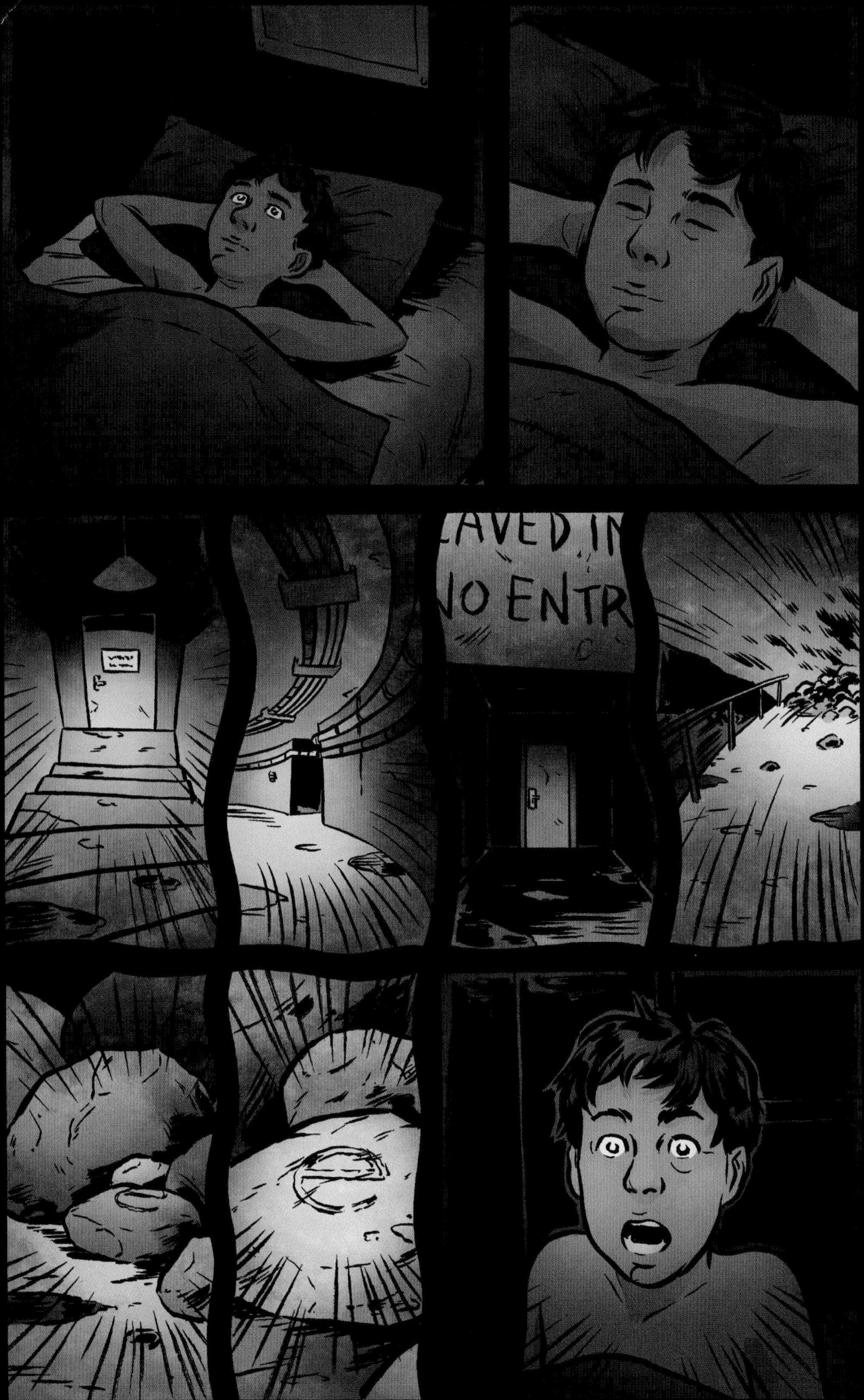
CAVED IN
NO ENTR

NEXT DAY

MESSENGER

"LINA!"

I'VE BEEN LOOKING ALL OVER FOR YOU! I'VE FOUND THE E! AT LEAST IT LOOKS LIKE AN E. IT MUST BE, THOUGH YOU WOULDN'T KNOW IT IF YOU WEREN'T LOOKING FOR IT.

WHERE IS IT?

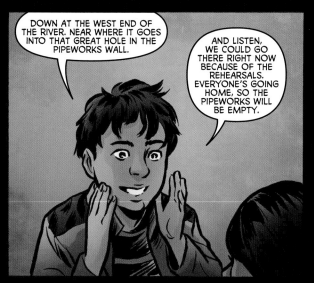

DOWN AT THE WEST END OF THE RIVER. NEAR WHERE IT GOES INTO THAT GREAT HOLE IN THE PIPEWORKS WALL.

AND LISTEN, WE COULD GO THERE RIGHT NOW BECAUSE OF THE REHEARSALS. EVERYONE'S GOING HOME, SO THE PIPEWORKS WILL BE EMPTY.

LET'S GO.

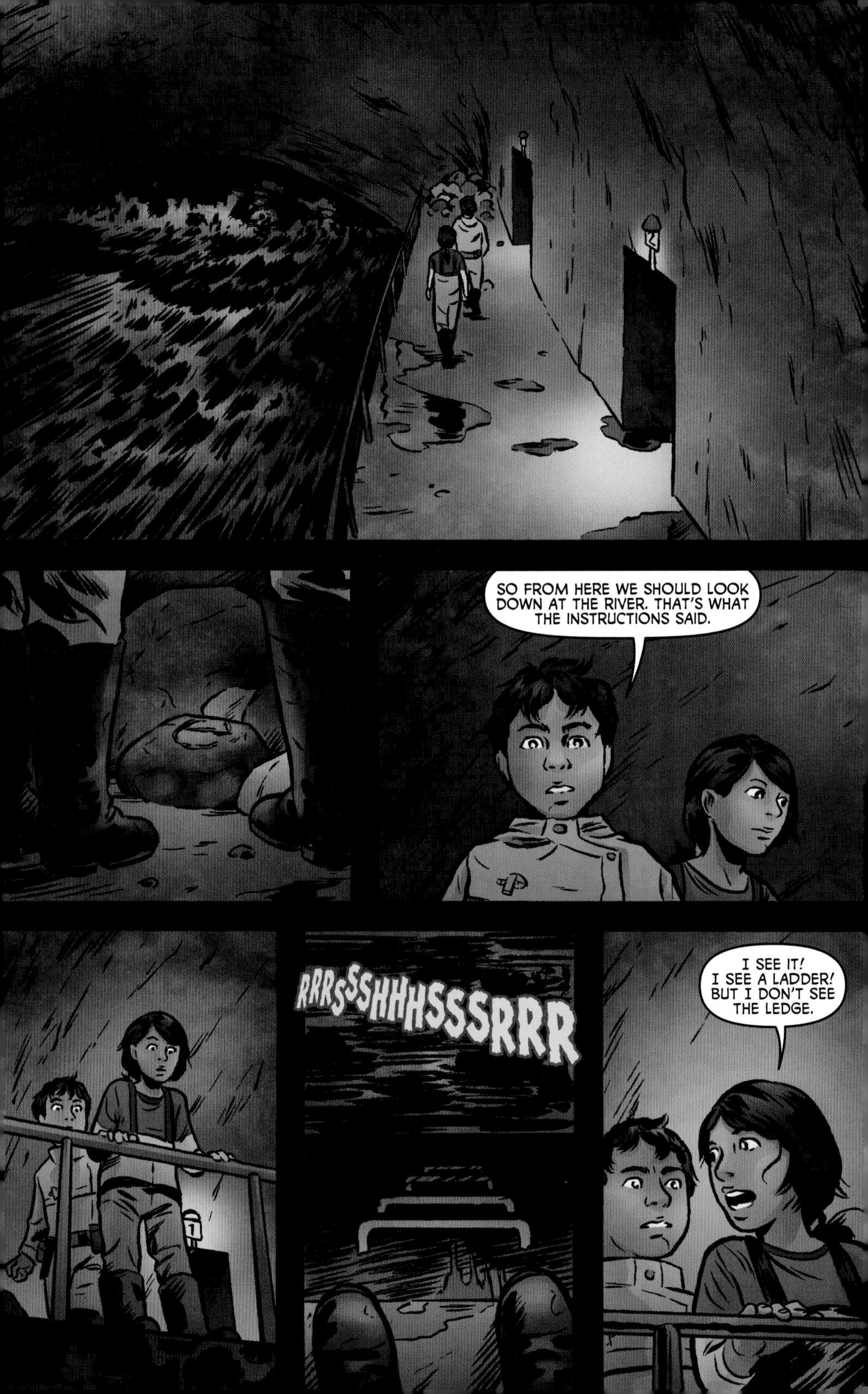
SO FROM HERE WE SHOULD LOOK DOWN AT THE RIVER. THAT'S WHAT THE INSTRUCTIONS SAID.
RRRSSSHHHSSSRRR
I SEE IT! I SEE A LADDER! BUT I DON'T SEE THE LEDGE.

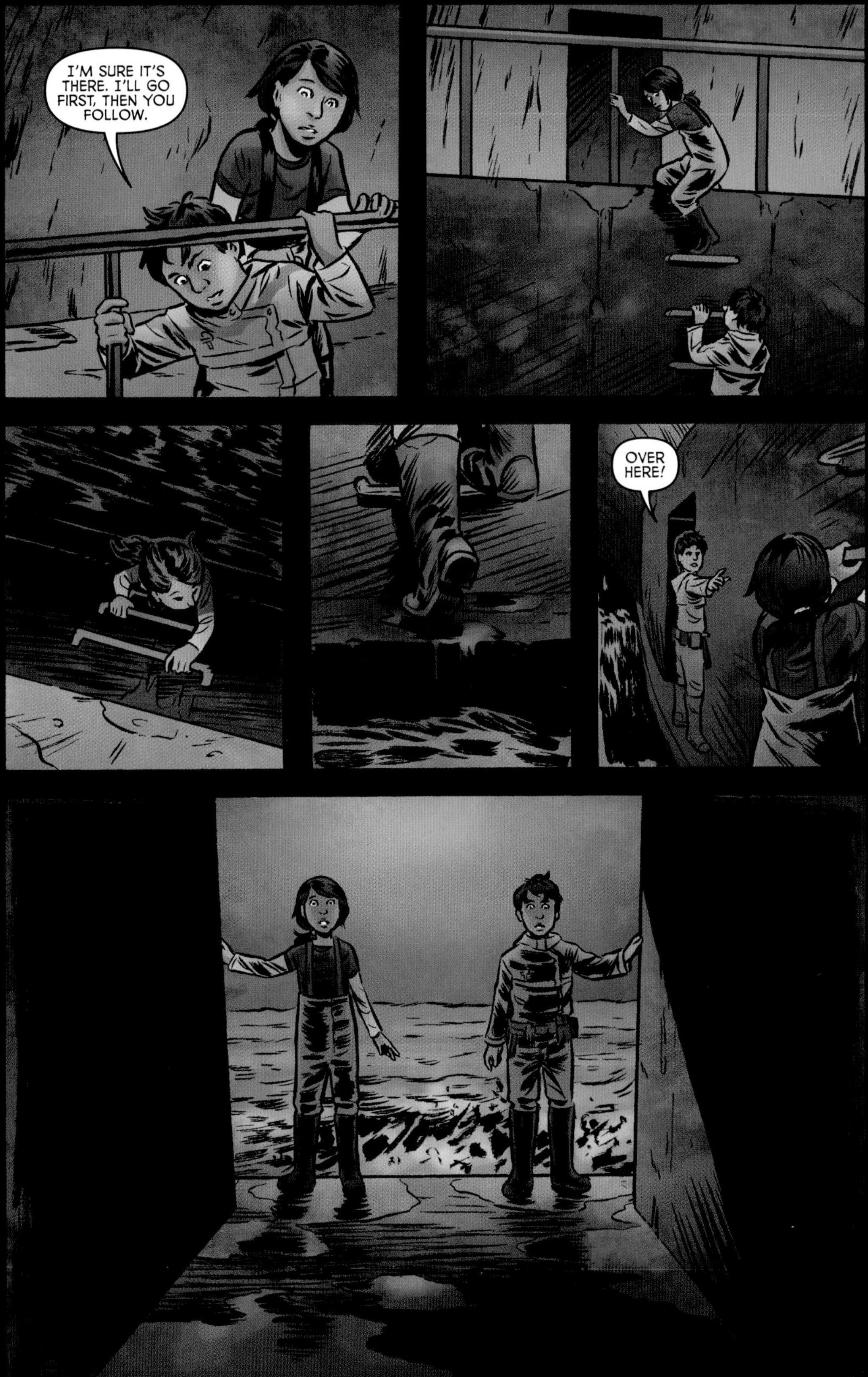
I'M SURE IT'S THERE. I'LL GO FIRST, THEN YOU FOLLOW.
OVER HERE!

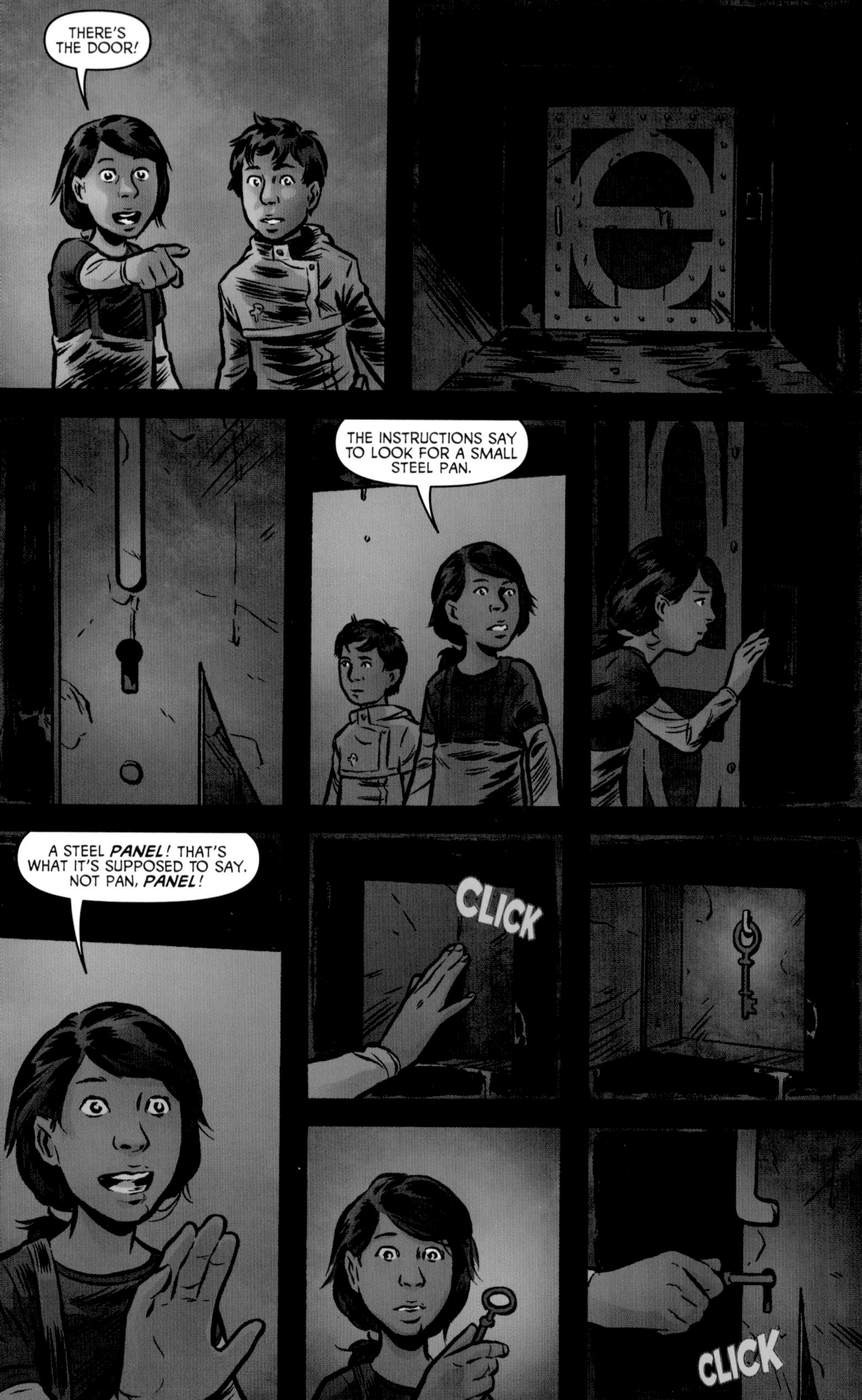
THERE'S THE DOOR!
THE INSTRUCTIONS SAY TO LOOK FOR A SMALL STEEL PAN.
A STEEL *PANEL!* THAT'S WHAT IT'S SUPPOSED TO SAY. NOT PAN, *PANEL!*
CLICK
CLICK

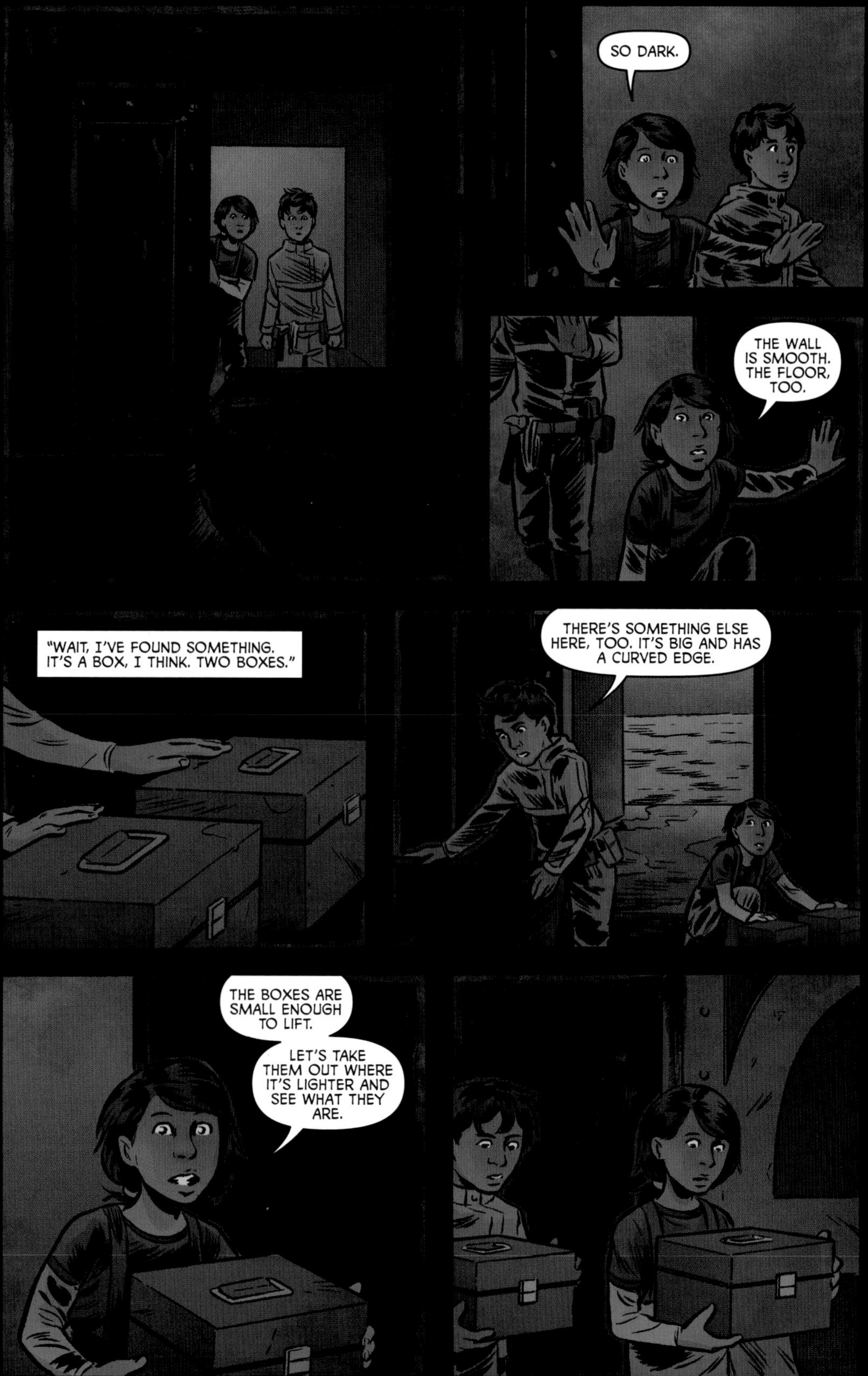
SO DARK.
THE WALL IS SMOOTH. THE FLOOR, TOO.
"WAIT, I'VE FOUND SOMETHING. IT'S A BOX, I THINK. TWO BOXES."
THERE'S SOMETHING ELSE HERE, TOO. IT'S BIG AND HAS A CURVED EDGE.
THE BOXES ARE SMALL ENOUGH TO LIFT.
LET'S TAKE THEM OUT WHERE IT'S LIGHTER AND SEE WHAT THEY ARE.

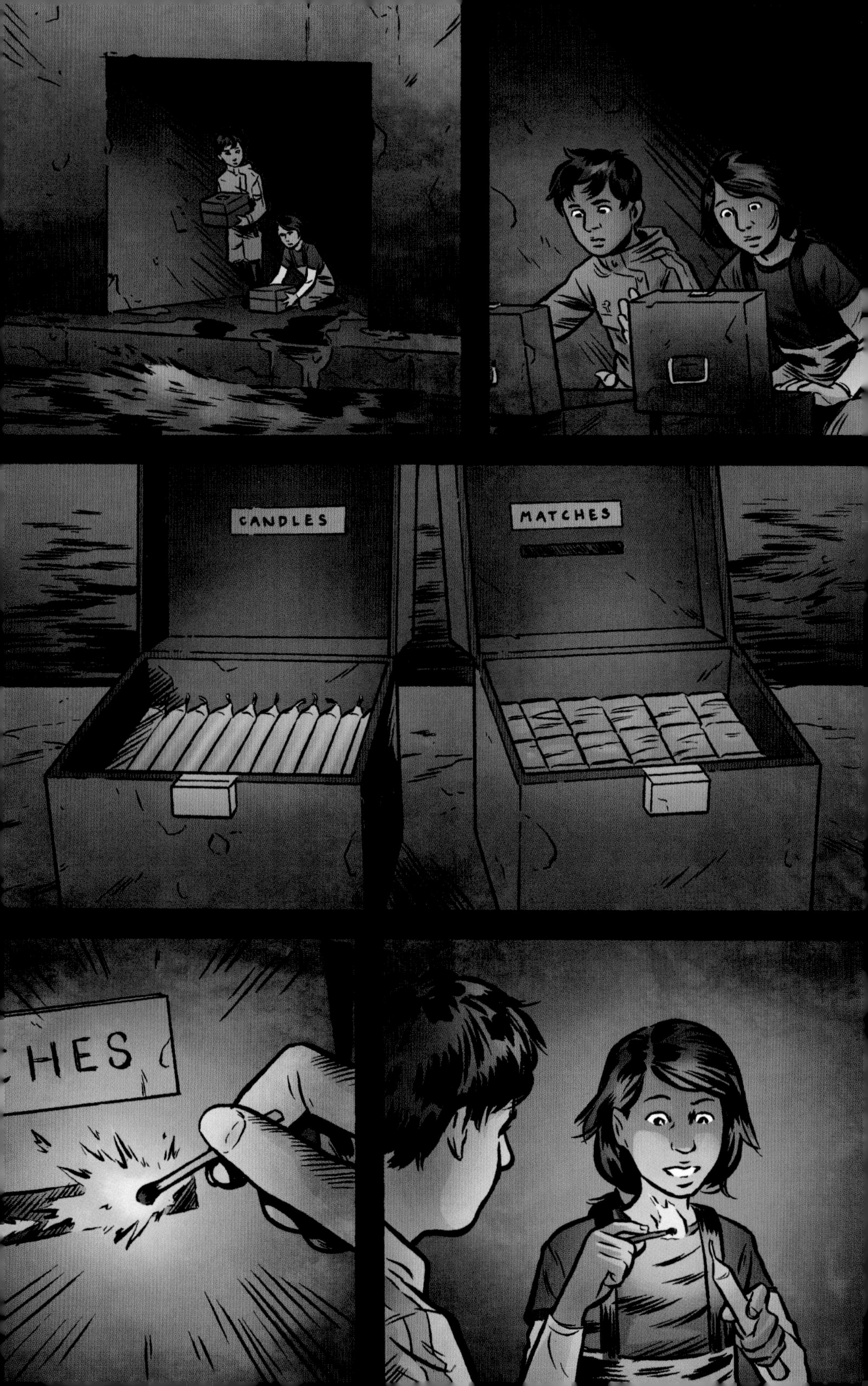
CANDLES
MATCHES
HES

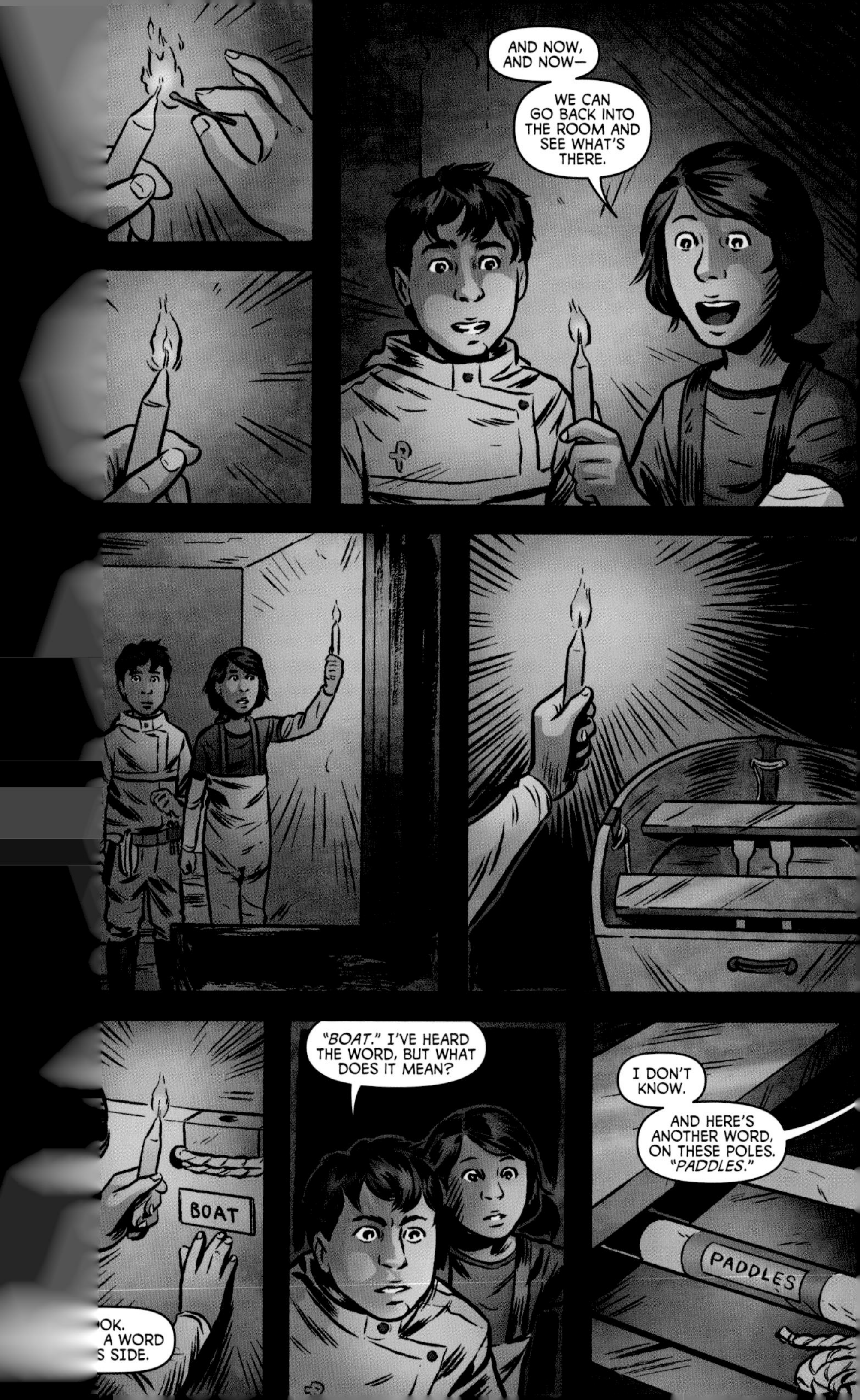
AND NOW, AND NOW—
WE CAN GO BACK INTO THE ROOM AND SEE WHAT'S THERE.
A WORD
BOAT
"BOAT." I'VE HEARD THE WORD, BUT WHAT DOES IT MEAN?
I DON'T KNOW.
AND HERE'S ANOTHER WORD, ON THESE POLES. "PADDLES."
PADDLES

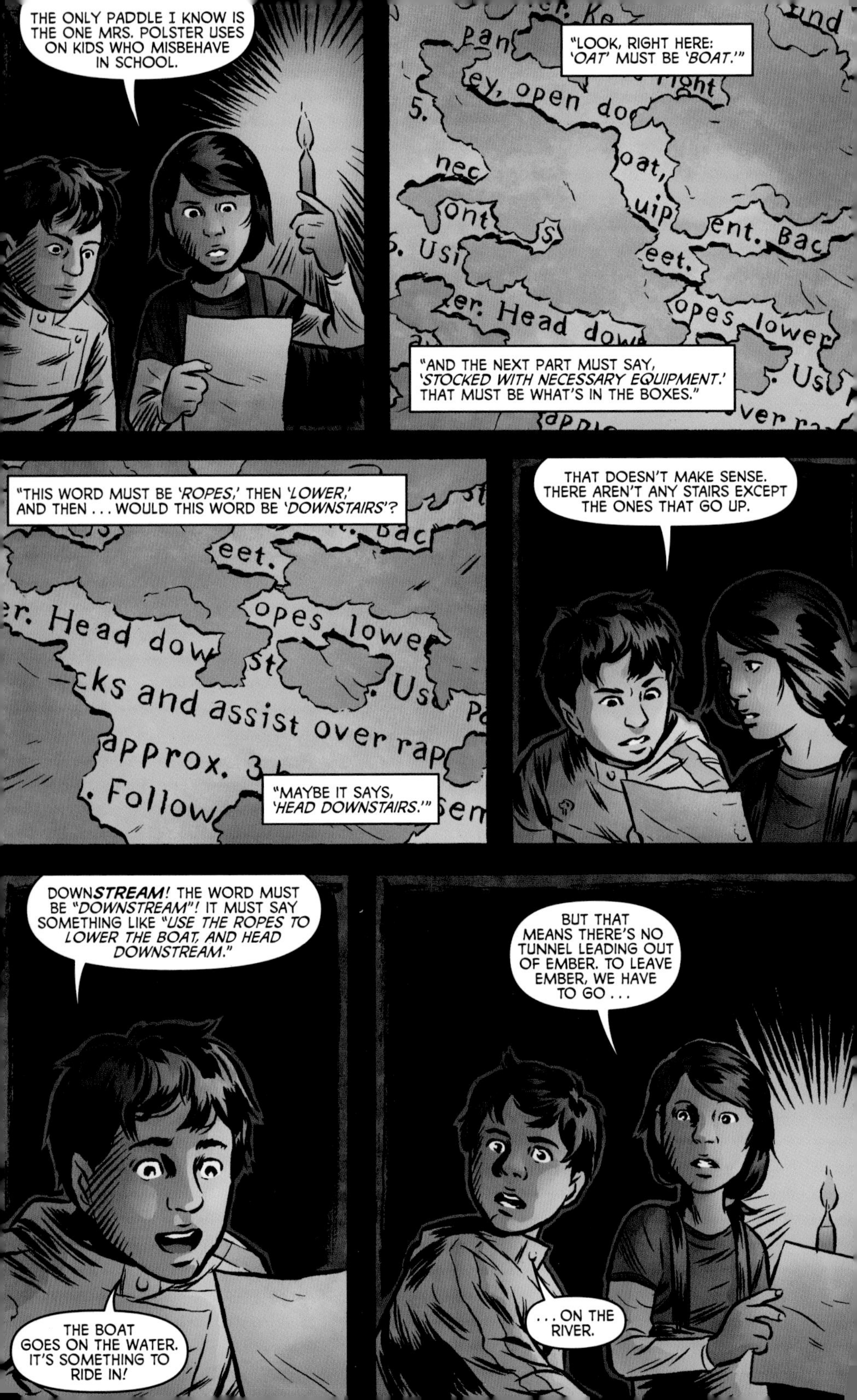
THE ONLY PADDLE I KNOW IS THE ONE MRS. POLSTER USES ON KIDS WHO MISBEHAVE IN SCHOOL.
"LOOK, RIGHT HERE: '*OAT*' MUST BE '*BOAT*.'"
"AND THE NEXT PART MUST SAY, '*STOCKED WITH NECESSARY EQUIPMENT*.' THAT MUST BE WHAT'S IN THE BOXES."
"THIS WORD MUST BE '*ROPES*,' THEN '*LOWER*,' AND THEN . . . WOULD THIS WORD BE '*DOWNSTAIRS*'?
"MAYBE IT SAYS, '*HEAD DOWNSTAIRS*.'"
THAT DOESN'T MAKE SENSE. THERE AREN'T ANY STAIRS EXCEPT THE ONES THAT GO UP.
DOWN***STREAM***! THE WORD MUST BE "*DOWNSTREAM*"! IT MUST SAY SOMETHING LIKE "*USE THE ROPES TO LOWER THE BOAT, AND HEAD DOWNSTREAM*."
THE BOAT GOES ON THE WATER. IT'S SOMETHING TO RIDE IN!
BUT THAT MEANS THERE'S NO TUNNEL LEADING OUT OF EMBER. TO LEAVE EMBER, WE HAVE TO GO . . .
. . . ON THE RIVER.

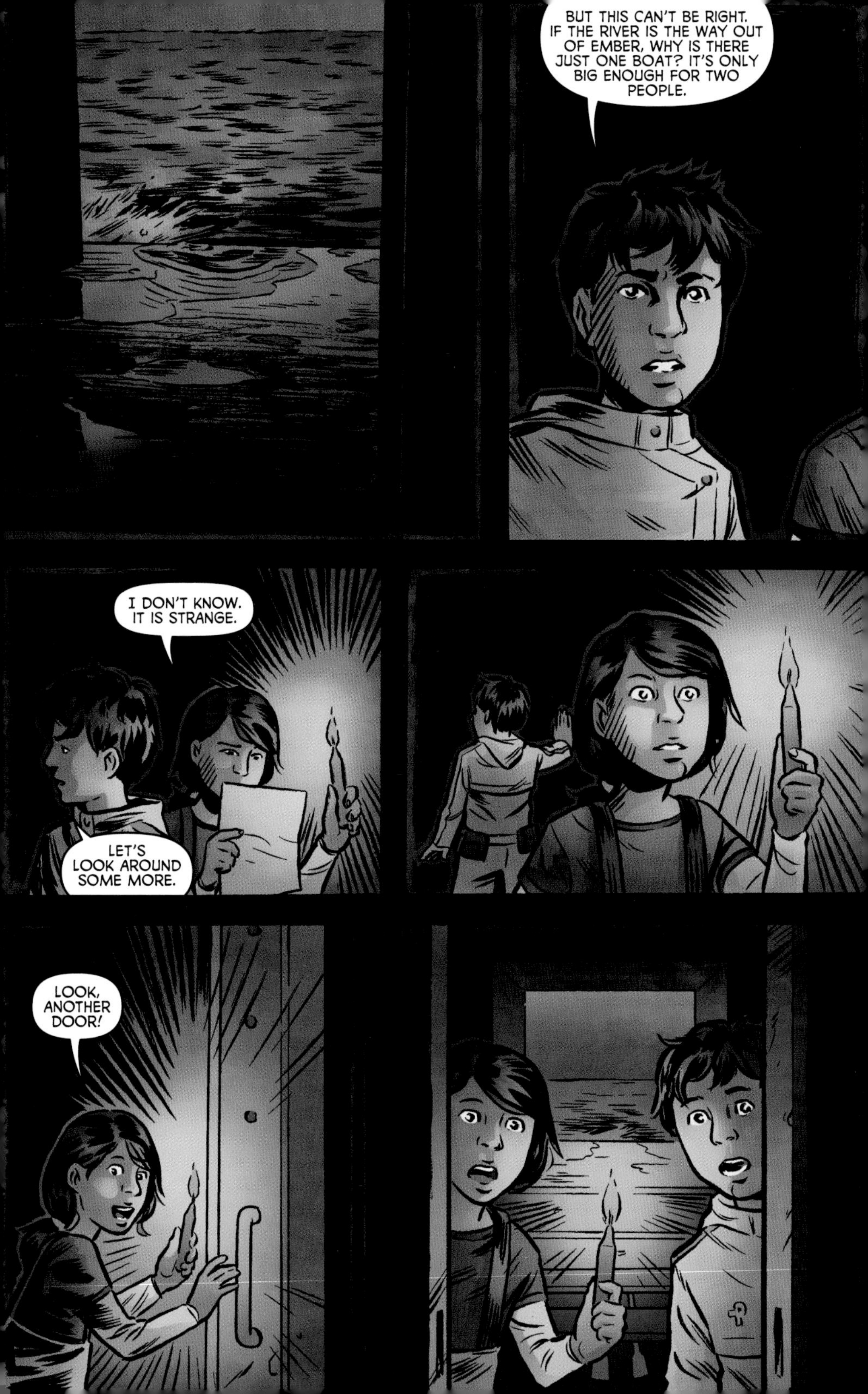
BUT THIS CAN'T BE RIGHT. IF THE RIVER IS THE WAY OUT OF EMBER, WHY IS THERE JUST ONE BOAT? IT'S ONLY BIG ENOUGH FOR TWO PEOPLE.
I DON'T KNOW. IT IS STRANGE.
LET'S LOOK AROUND SOME MORE.
LOOK, ANOTHER DOOR!

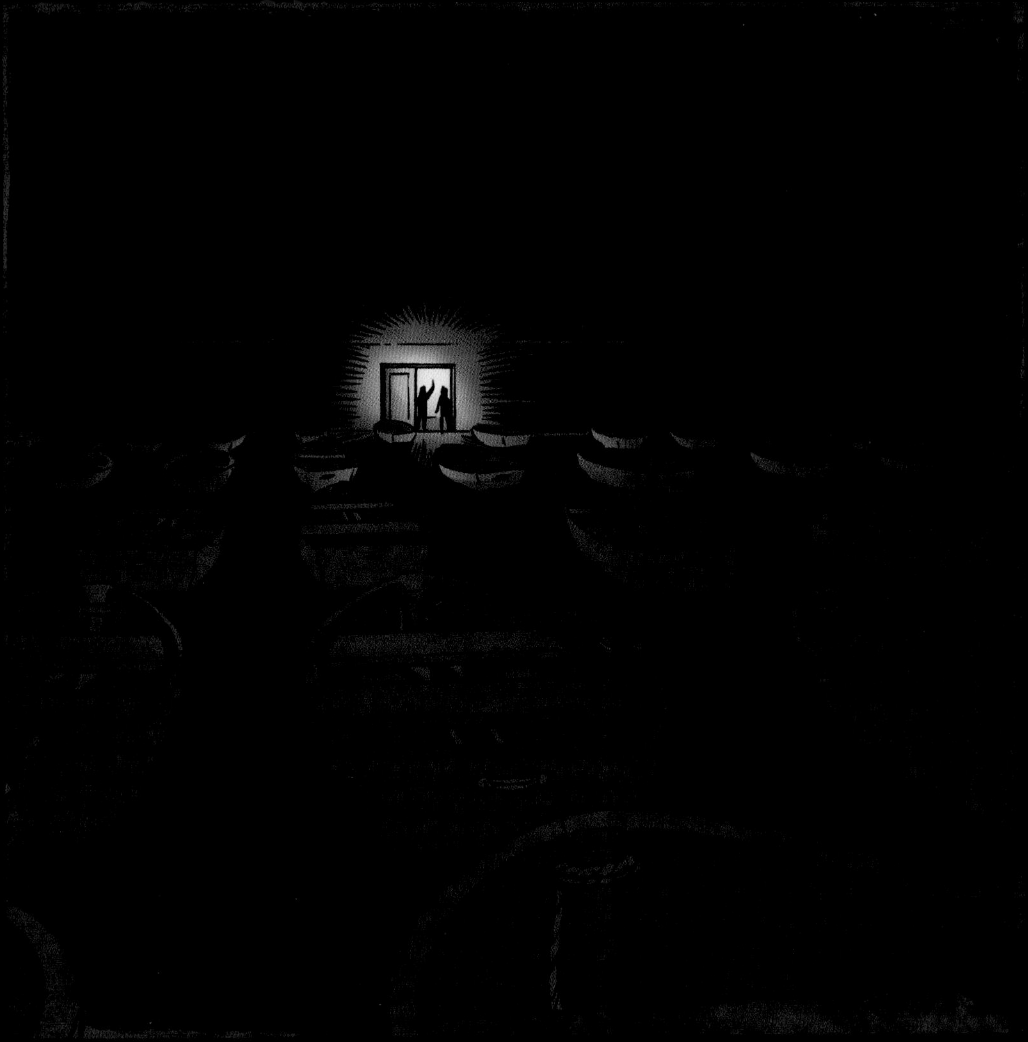

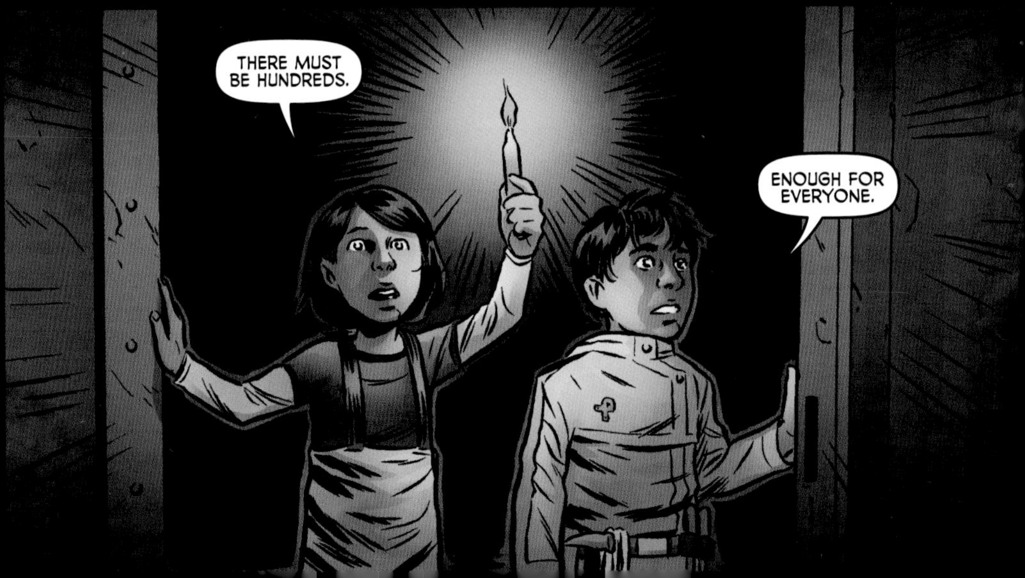
THERE MUST BE HUNDREDS.
ENOUGH FOR EVERYONE.

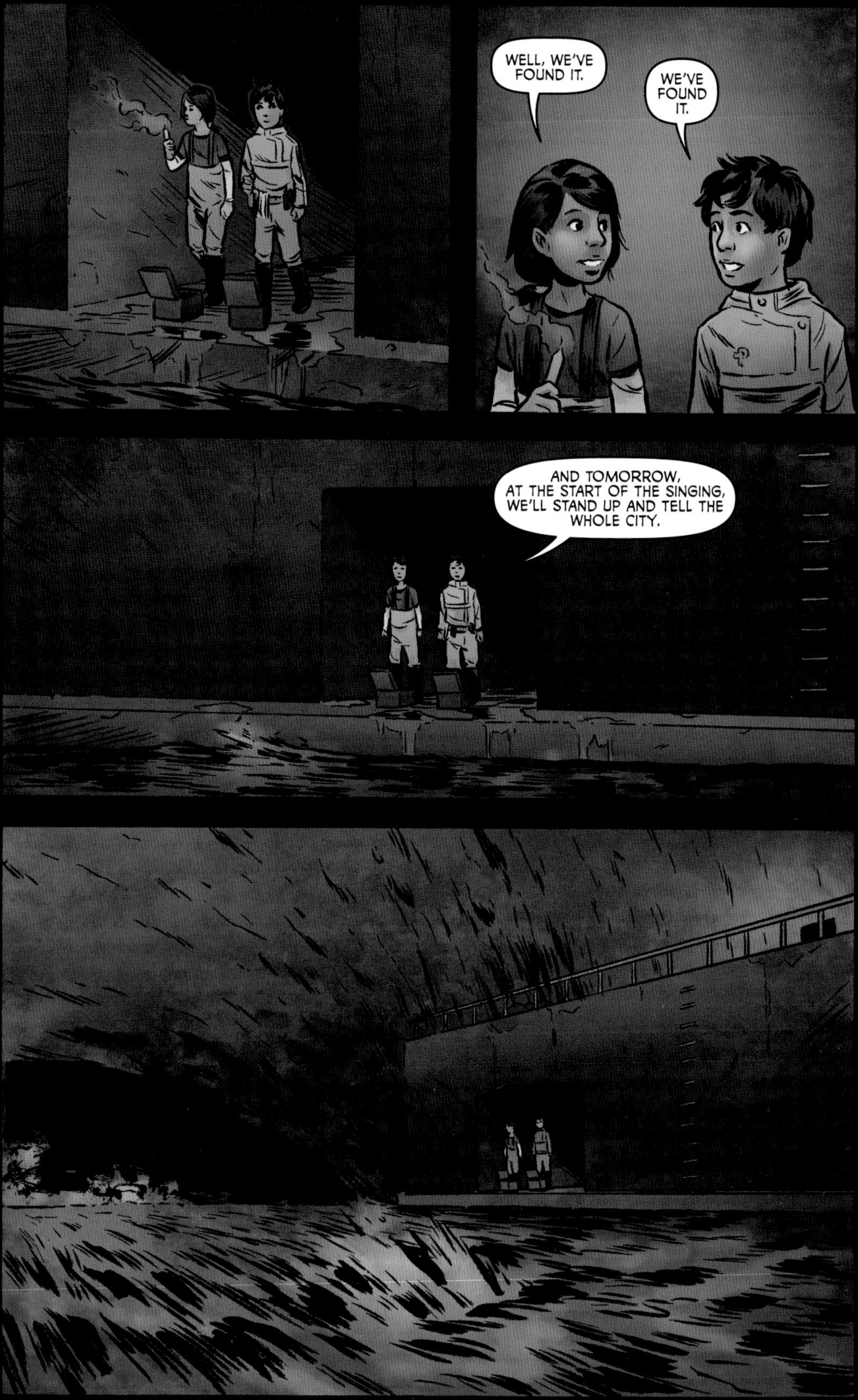
WELL, WE'VE FOUND IT.
WE'VE FOUND IT.
AND TOMORROW, AT THE START OF THE SINGING, WE'LL STAND UP AND TELL THE WHOLE CITY.

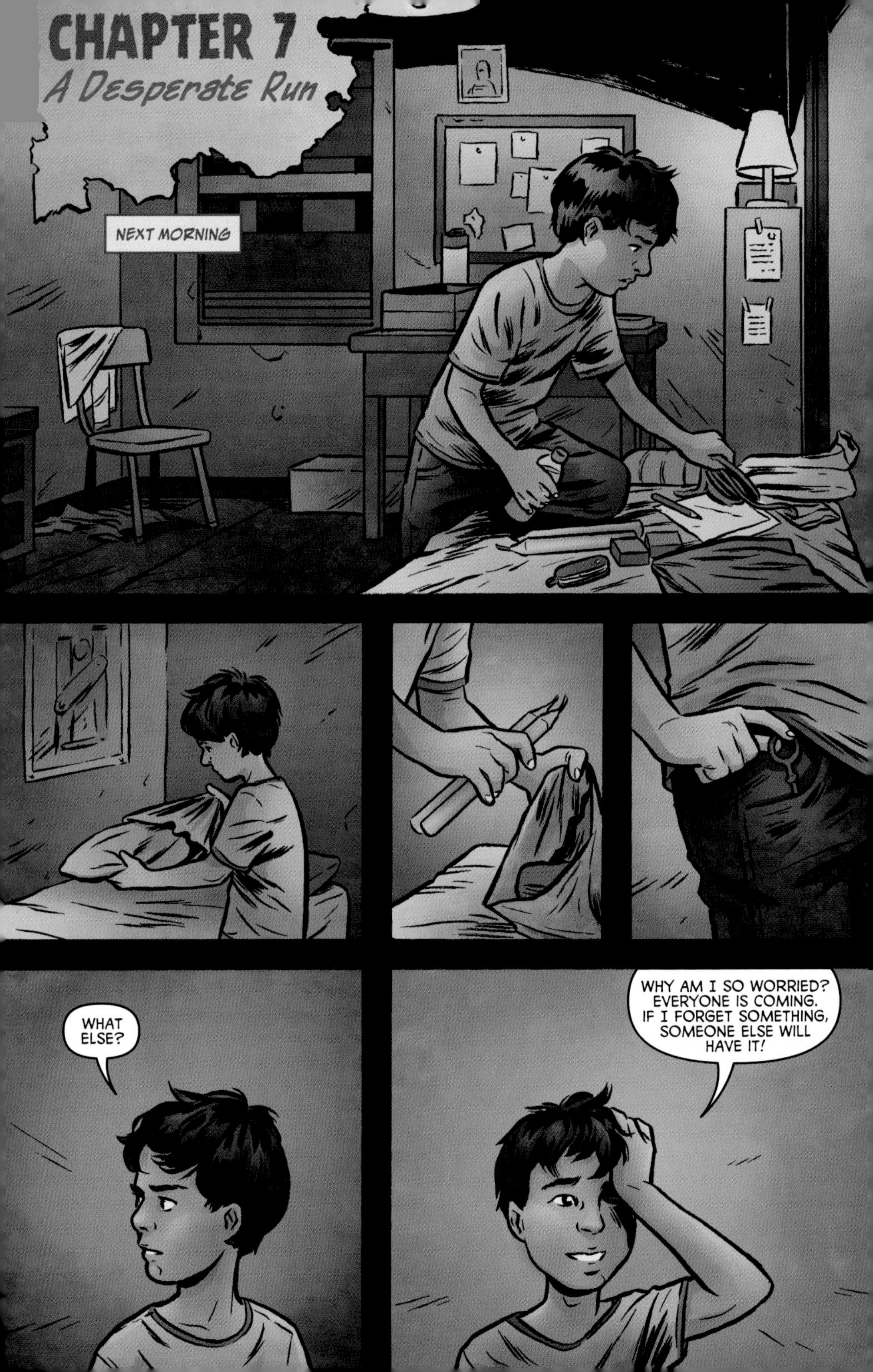
CHAPTER 7
A Desperate Run
NEXT MORNING
WHAT ELSE?
WHY AM I SO WORRIED? EVERYONE IS COMING. IF I FORGET SOMETHING, SOMEONE ELSE WILL HAVE IT!

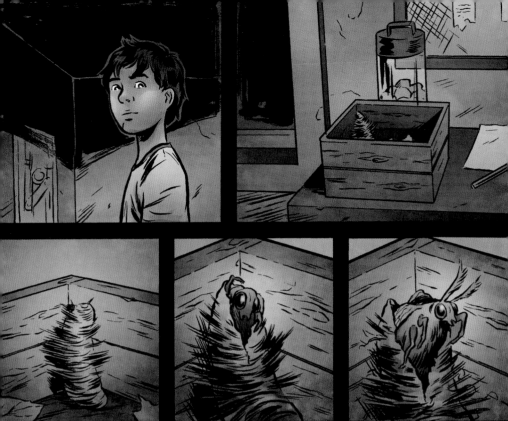

EGRESS.

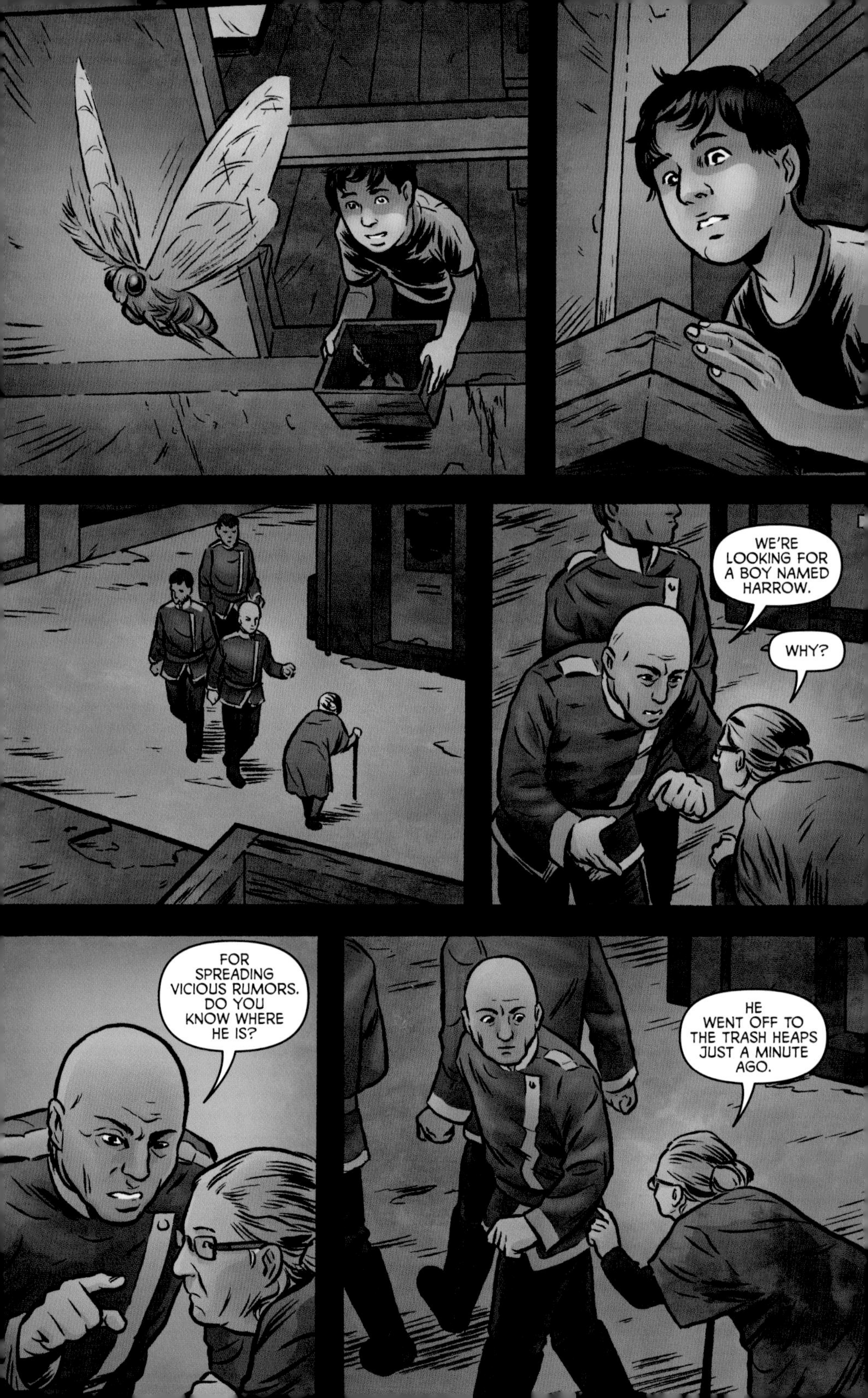
WE'RE LOOKING FOR A BOY NAMED HARROW.
WHY?
FOR SPREADING VICIOUS RUMORS. DO YOU KNOW WHERE HE IS?
HE WENT OFF TO THE TRASH HEAPS JUST A MINUTE AGO.

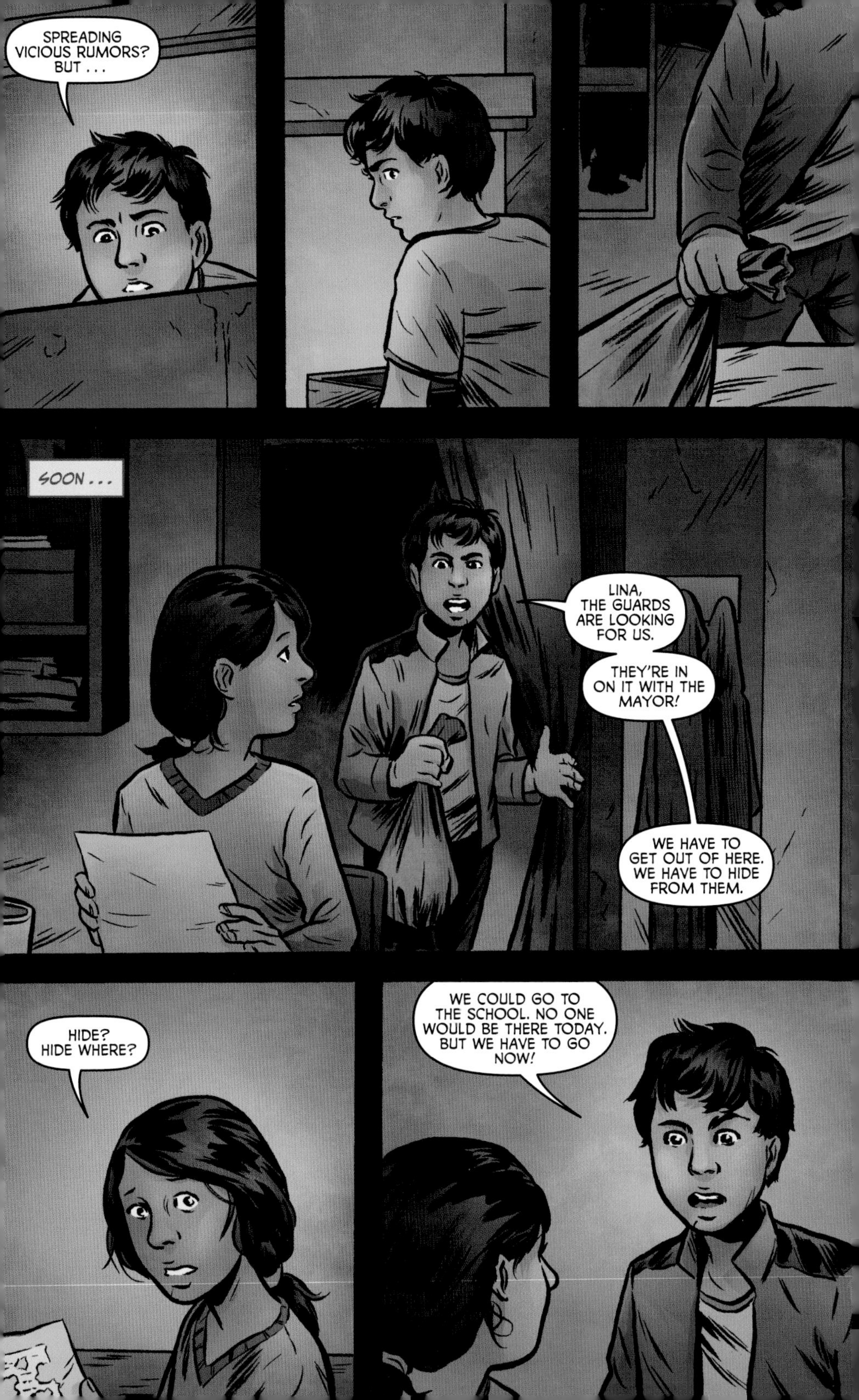
SPREADING VICIOUS RUMORS? BUT . . .
SOON . . .
LINA, THE GUARDS ARE LOOKING FOR US.
THEY'RE IN ON IT WITH THE MAYOR!
WE HAVE TO GET OUT OF HERE. WE HAVE TO HIDE FROM THEM.
HIDE? HIDE WHERE?
WE COULD GO TO THE SCHOOL. NO ONE WOULD BE THERE TODAY. BUT WE HAVE TO GO NOW!

DOON HARROW
AND
LINA MAYFLEET

WANTED FOR SPREADING
VICIOUS RUMORS

IF YOU SEE THEM, REPORT
TO MAYOR'S CHIEF GUARD

BELIEVE NOTHING THEY SAY

→ REWARD ←

RUMORS
THEM, REPORT
CHIEF GUARD
ING THEY SAY
WARD ←

DOON
LINA

WANTED
VICIOUS

IF YOU SE
TO MAYOR

BELIEVE
→ REW

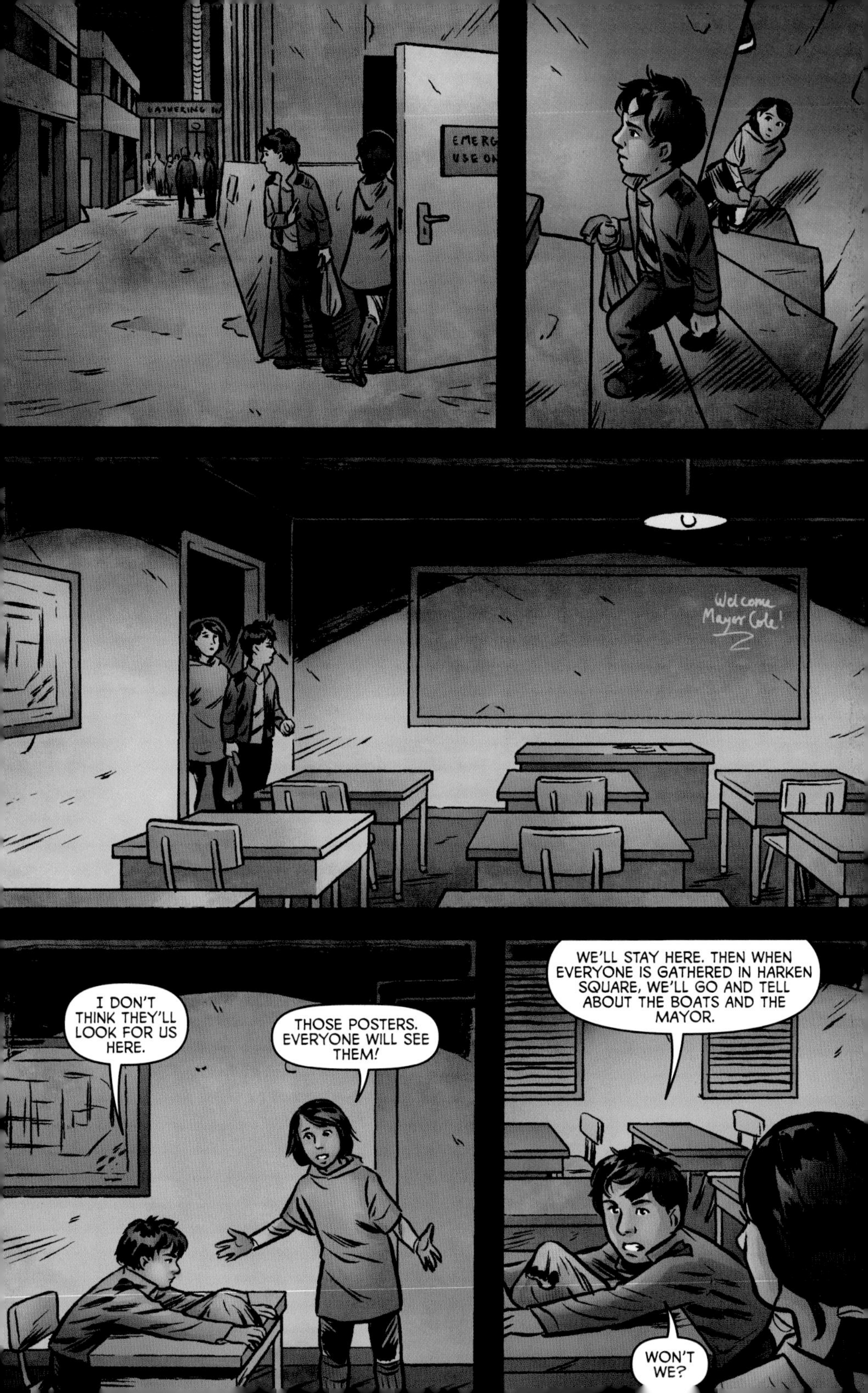
GATHERING
EMERG
USE ON
Welcome Mayor Cole!
I DON'T THINK THEY'LL LOOK FOR US HERE.
THOSE POSTERS. EVERYONE WILL SEE THEM!
WE'LL STAY HERE. THEN WHEN EVERYONE IS GATHERED IN HARKEN SQUARE, WE'LL GO AND TELL ABOUT THE BOATS AND THE MAYOR.
WON'T WE?

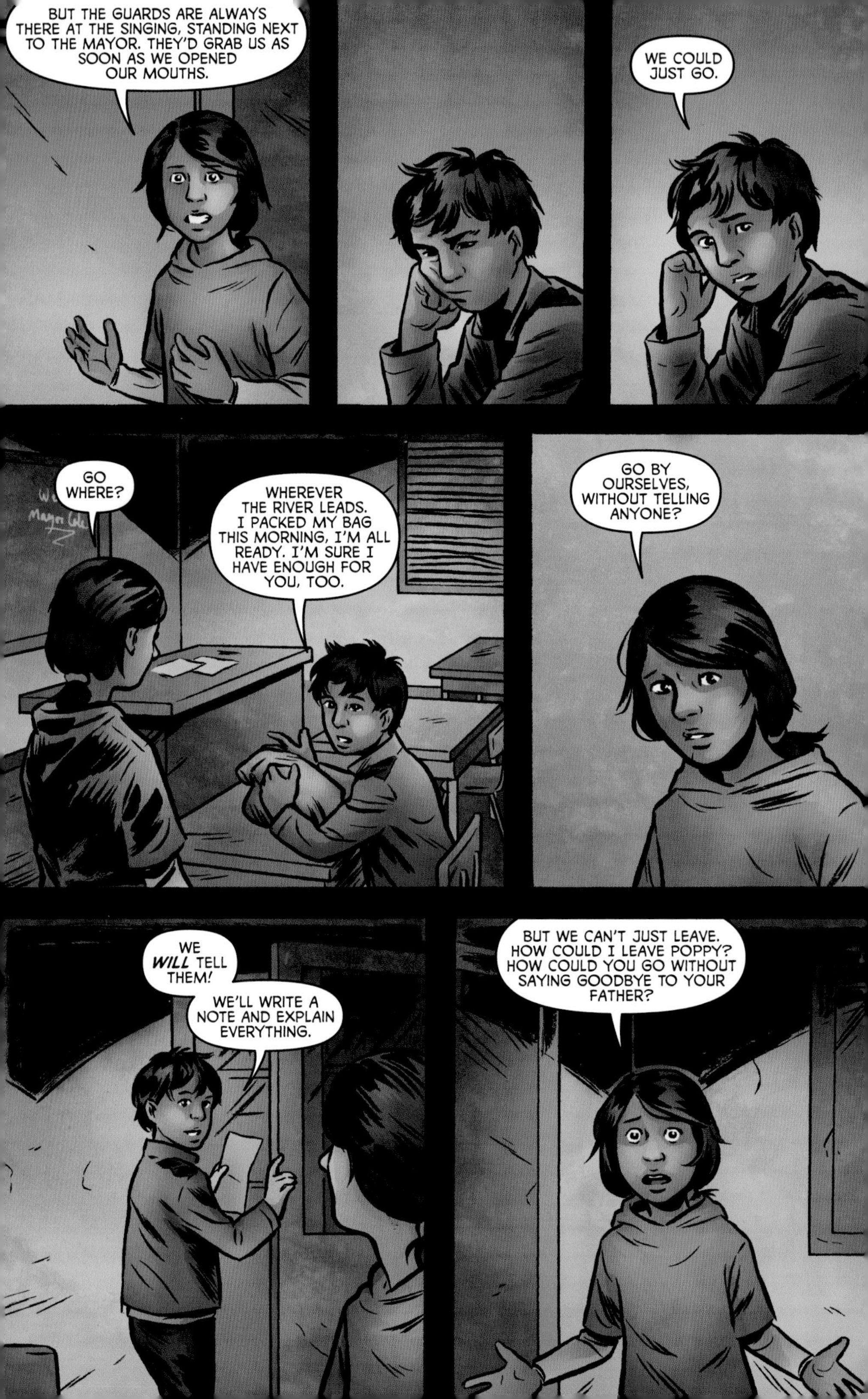
BUT THE GUARDS ARE ALWAYS THERE AT THE SINGING, STANDING NEXT TO THE MAYOR. THEY'D GRAB US AS SOON AS WE OPENED OUR MOUTHS.
WE COULD JUST GO.
GO WHERE?
WHEREVER THE RIVER LEADS. I PACKED MY BAG THIS MORNING, I'M ALL READY. I'M SURE I HAVE ENOUGH FOR YOU, TOO.
GO BY OURSELVES, WITHOUT TELLING ANYONE?
WE *WILL* TELL THEM!
WE'LL WRITE A NOTE AND EXPLAIN EVERYTHING.
BUT WE CAN'T JUST LEAVE. HOW COULD I LEAVE POPPY? HOW COULD YOU GO WITHOUT SAYING GOODBYE TO YOUR FATHER?

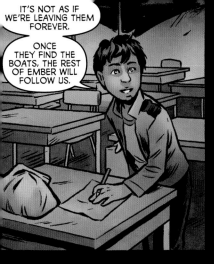

IT'S NOT AS IF WE'RE LEAVING THEM FOREVER.

ONCE THEY FIND THE BOATS, THE REST OF EMBER WILL FOLLOW US.

HOW LONG DO YOU THINK IT WILL TAKE? IT'S A LOT OF PEOPLE TO GET ORGANIZED. IT COULD BE A BIG MESS, DOON. POPPY WILL NEED ME.

POPPY HAS MRS. MURDO. SHE'LL BE FINE.

I'LL DELIVER IT. I KNOW BACK WAYS, WHERE NO ONE WILL SEE ME. I'LL TAKE IT TO MRS. MURDO.

BACK SOON.

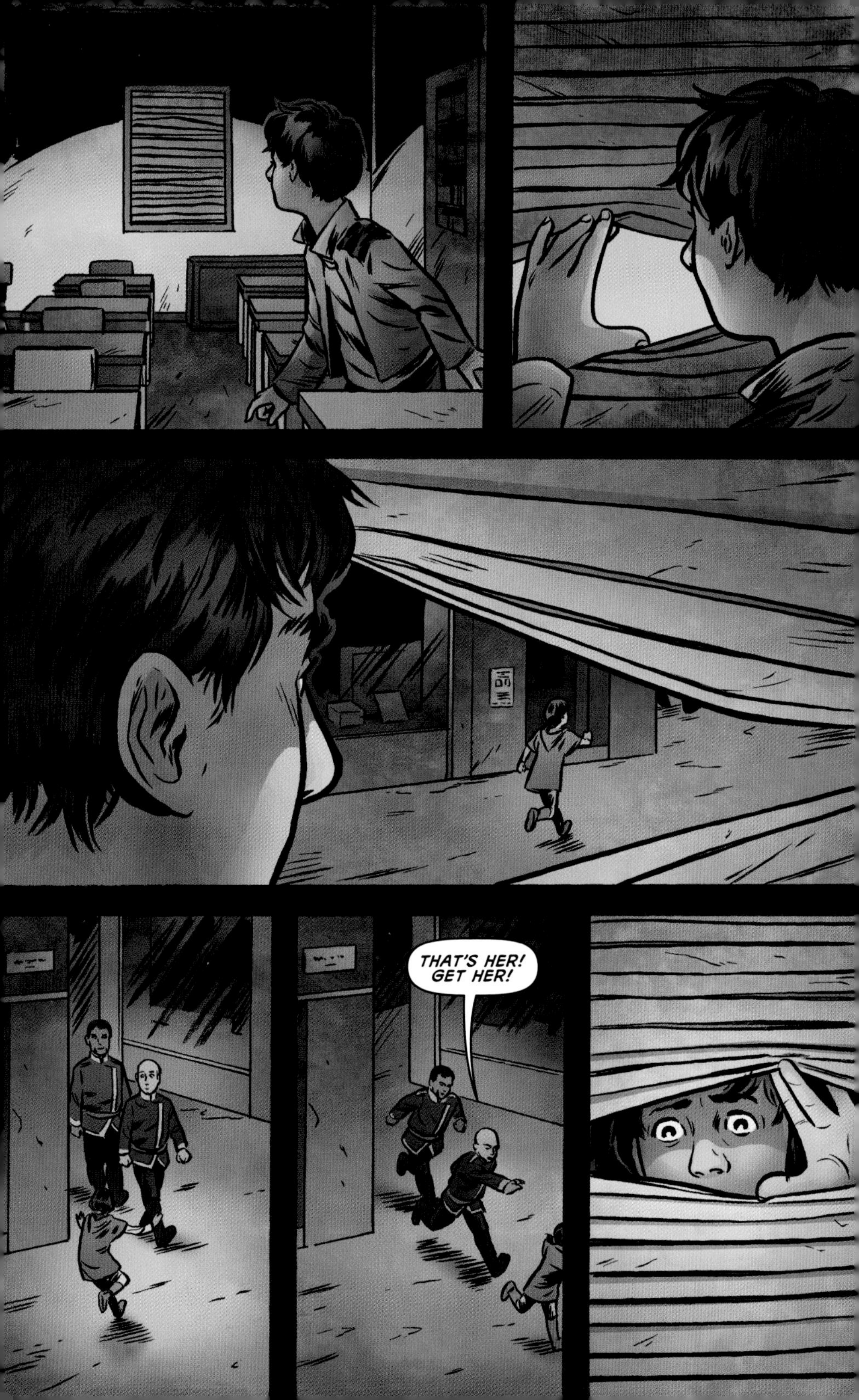
THAT'S HER! GET HER!

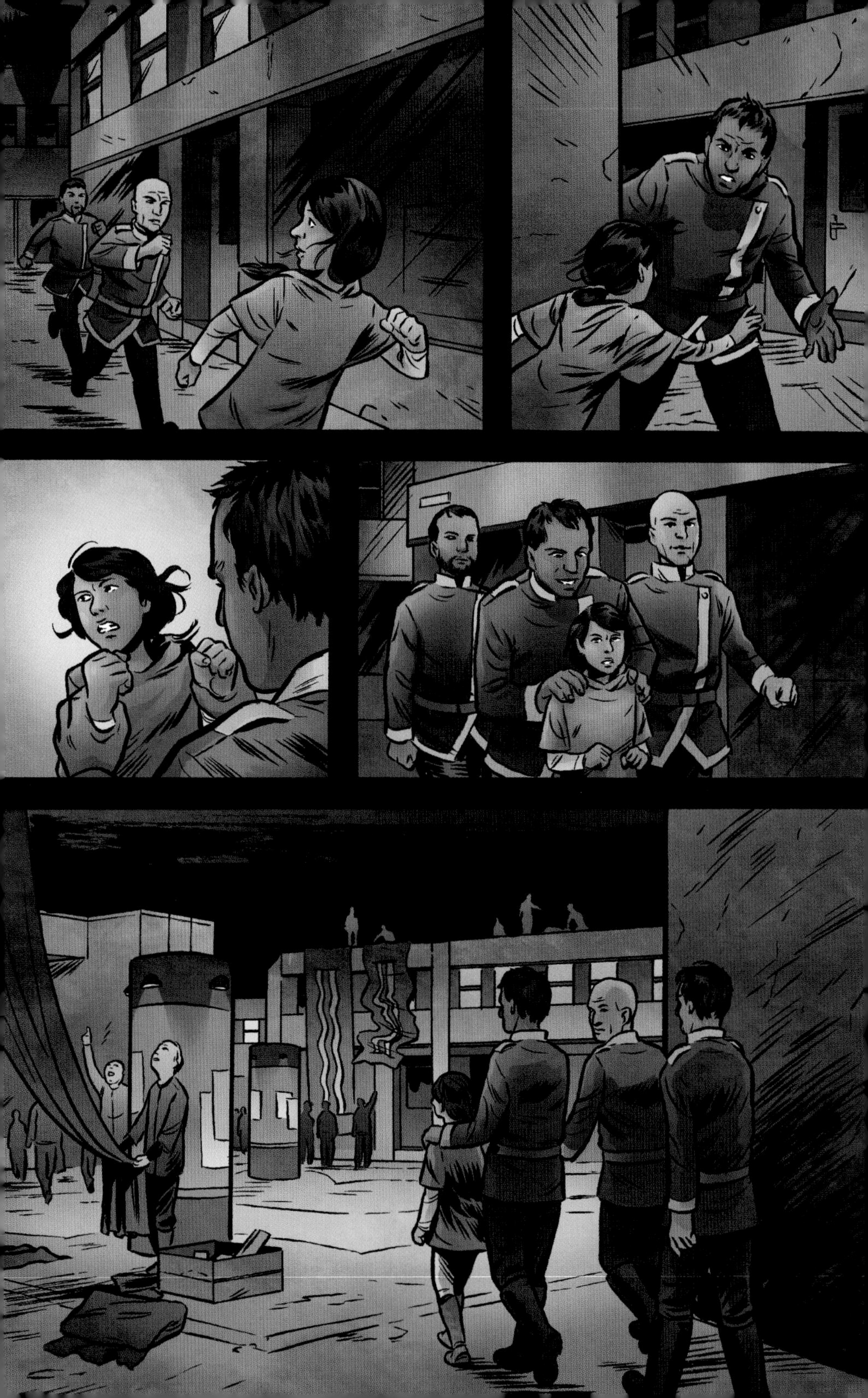

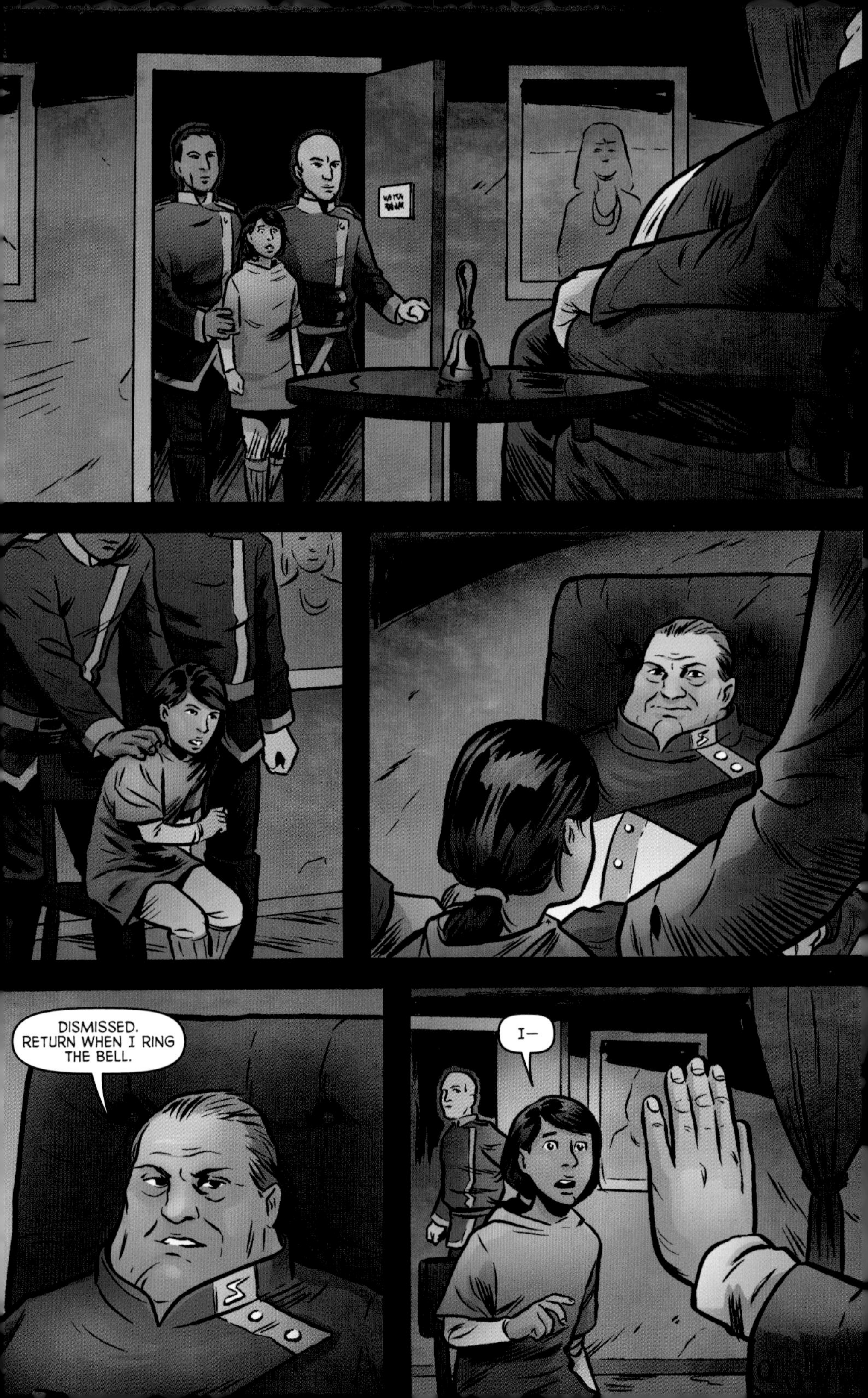
DISMISSED. RETURN WHEN I RING THE BELL.
I—

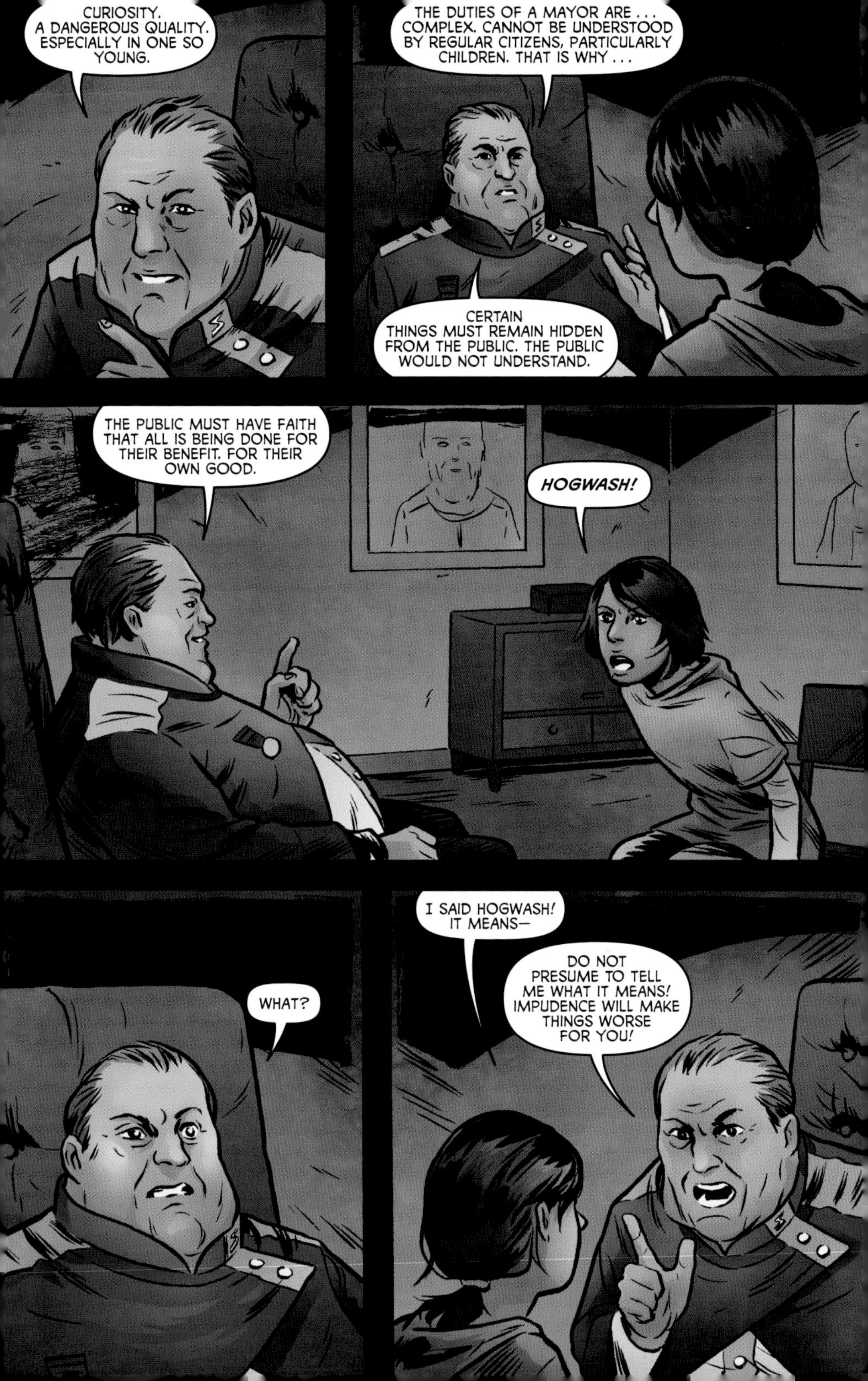

CURIOSITY. A DANGEROUS QUALITY. ESPECIALLY IN ONE SO YOUNG.
THE DUTIES OF A MAYOR ARE . . . COMPLEX. CANNOT BE UNDERSTOOD BY REGULAR CITIZENS, PARTICULARLY CHILDREN. THAT IS WHY . . .
CERTAIN THINGS MUST REMAIN HIDDEN FROM THE PUBLIC. THE PUBLIC WOULD NOT UNDERSTAND.
THE PUBLIC MUST HAVE FAITH THAT ALL IS BEING DONE FOR THEIR BENEFIT. FOR THEIR OWN GOOD.
HOGWASH!
WHAT?
I SAID HOGWASH! IT MEANS—
DO NOT PRESUME TO TELL ME WHAT IT MEANS! IMPUDENCE WILL MAKE THINGS WORSE FOR YOU!

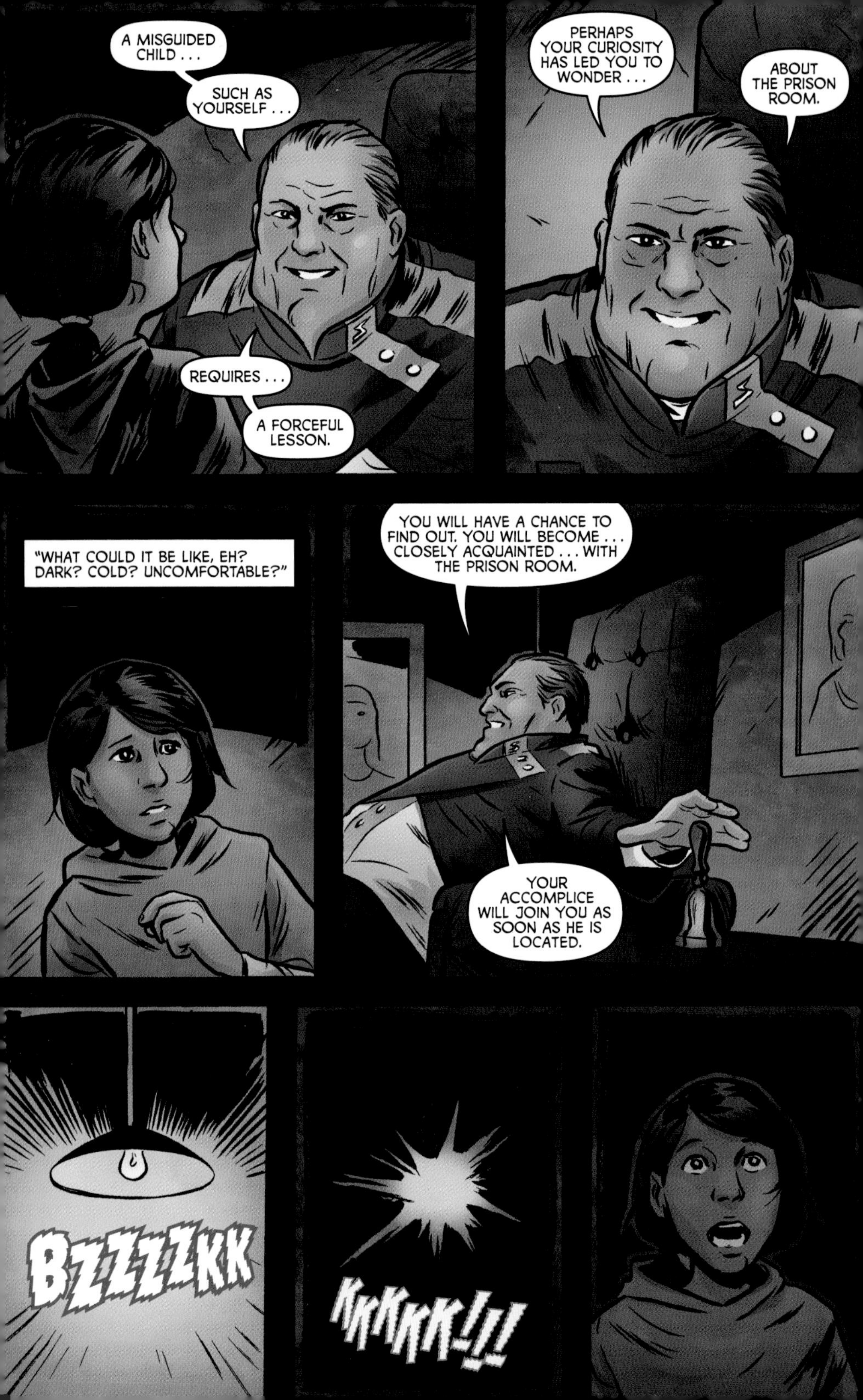
A MISGUIDED CHILD . . .
SUCH AS YOURSELF . . .
REQUIRES . . .
A FORCEFUL LESSON.
PERHAPS YOUR CURIOSITY HAS LED YOU TO WONDER . . .
ABOUT THE PRISON ROOM.
"WHAT COULD IT BE LIKE, EH? DARK? COLD? UNCOMFORTABLE?"
YOU WILL HAVE A CHANCE TO FIND OUT. YOU WILL BECOME . . . CLOSELY ACQUAINTED . . . WITH THE PRISON ROOM.
YOUR ACCOMPLICE WILL JOIN YOU AS SOON AS HE IS LOCATED.
BZZZZZKK
KKKKK-!!!

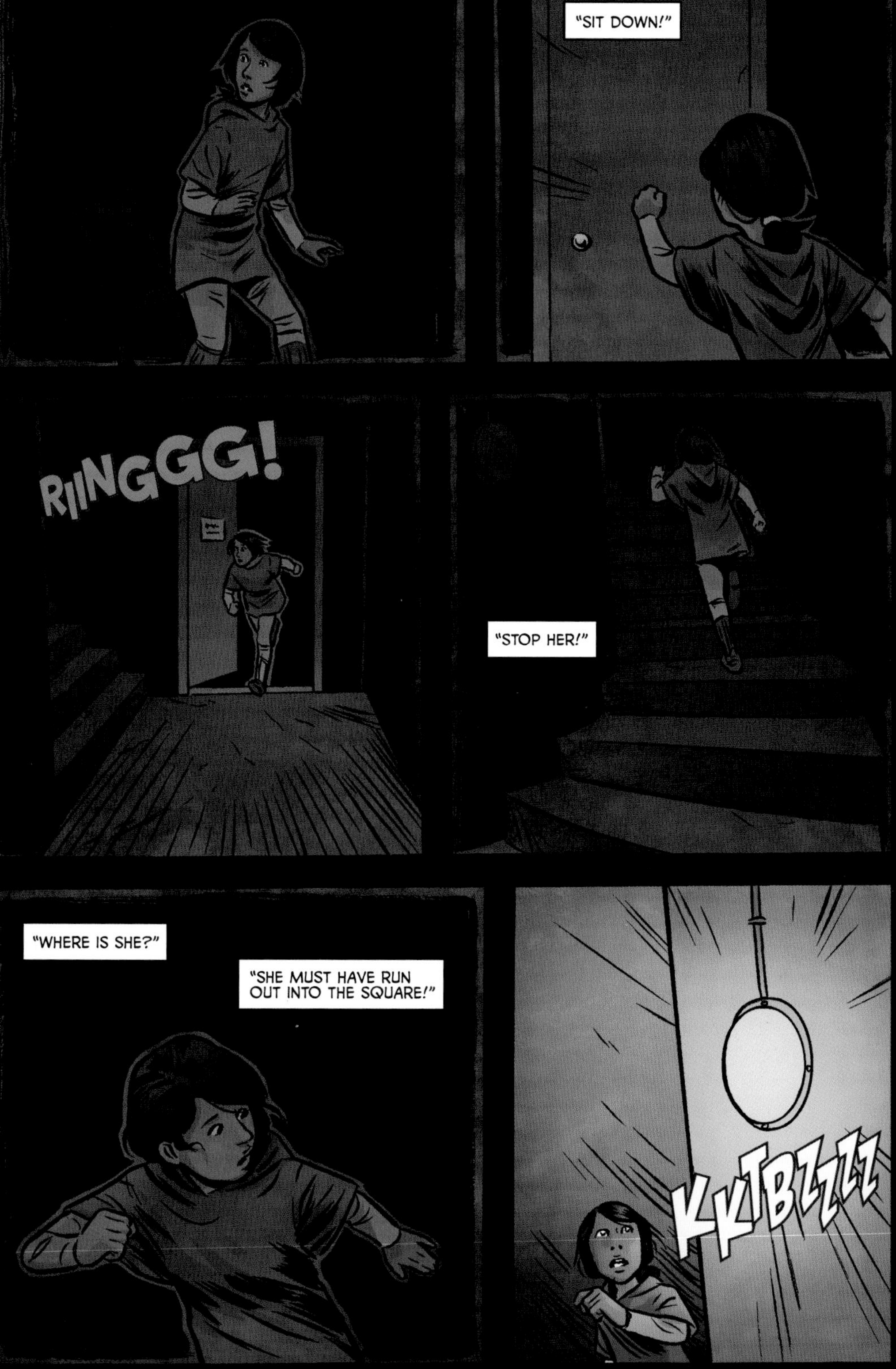
"SIT DOWN!"
RIINGGG!
"STOP HER!"
"WHERE IS SHE?"
"SHE MUST HAVE RUN OUT INTO THE SQUARE!"
KKTBZZZZ

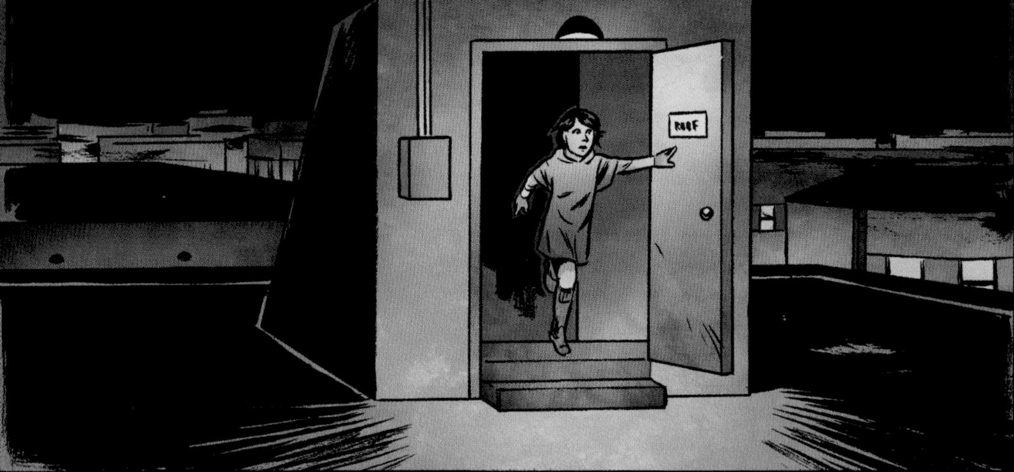
ROOF
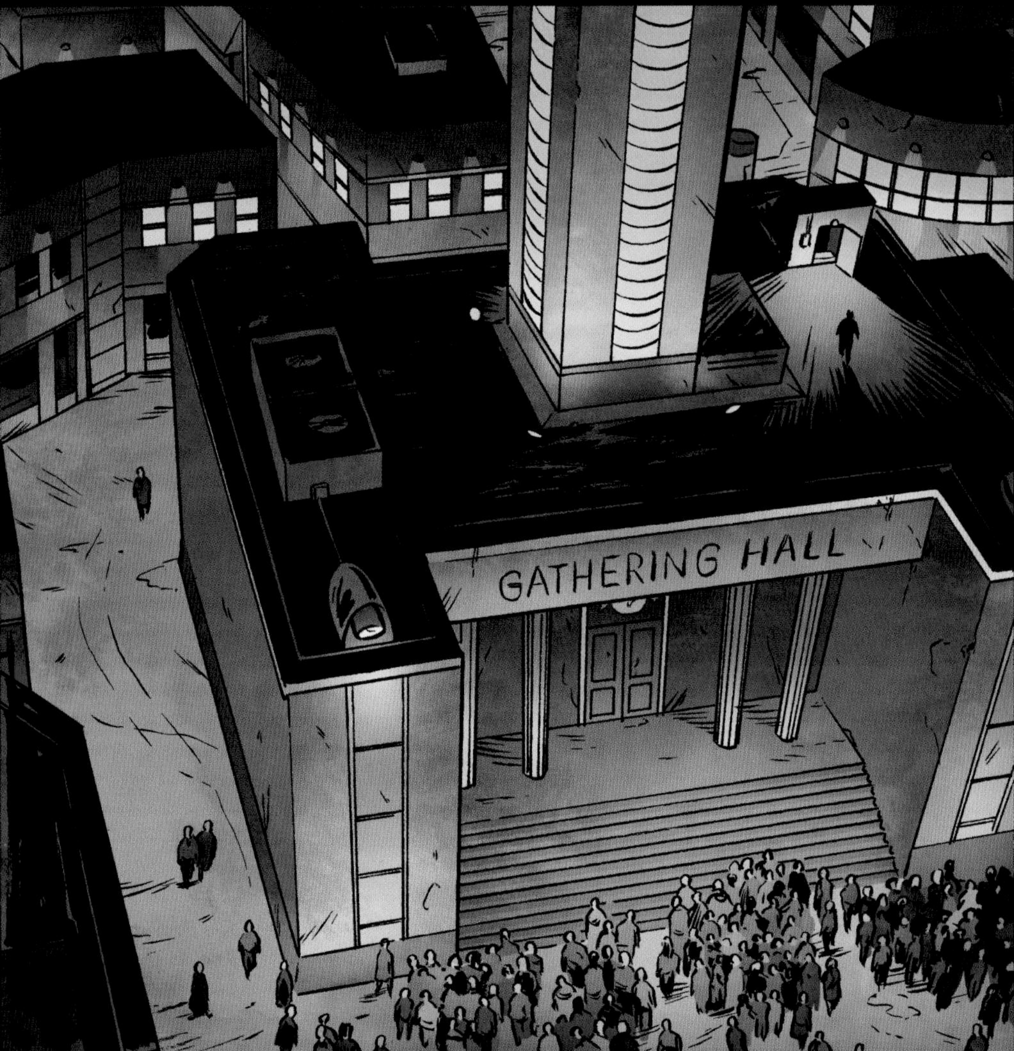
GATHERING HALL

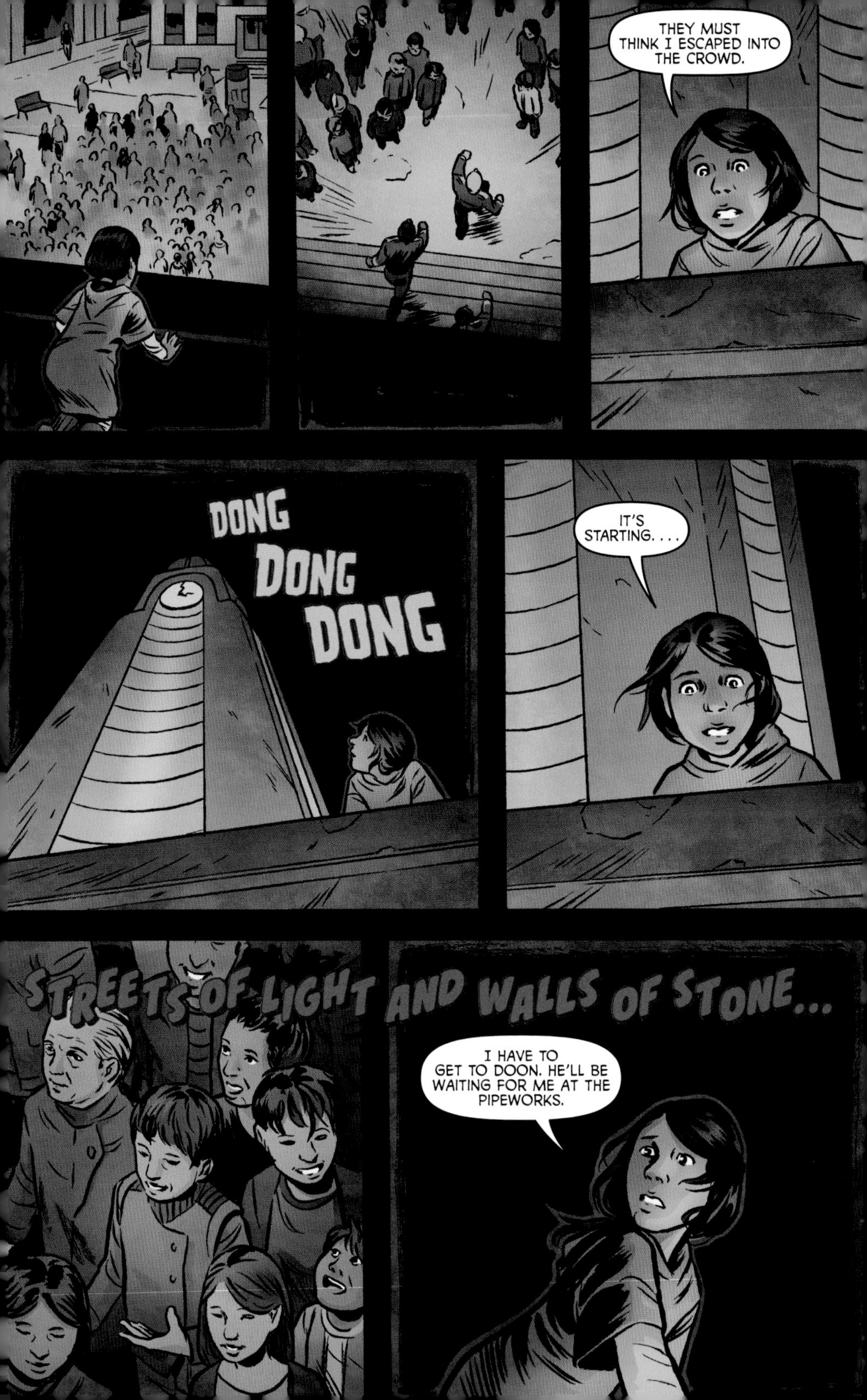
THEY MUST THINK I ESCAPED INTO THE CROWD.
DONG
DONG
DONG
IT'S STARTING. . . .
STREETS OF LIGHT AND WALLS OF STONE...
I HAVE TO GET TO DOON. HE'LL BE WAITING FOR ME AT THE PIPEWORKS.

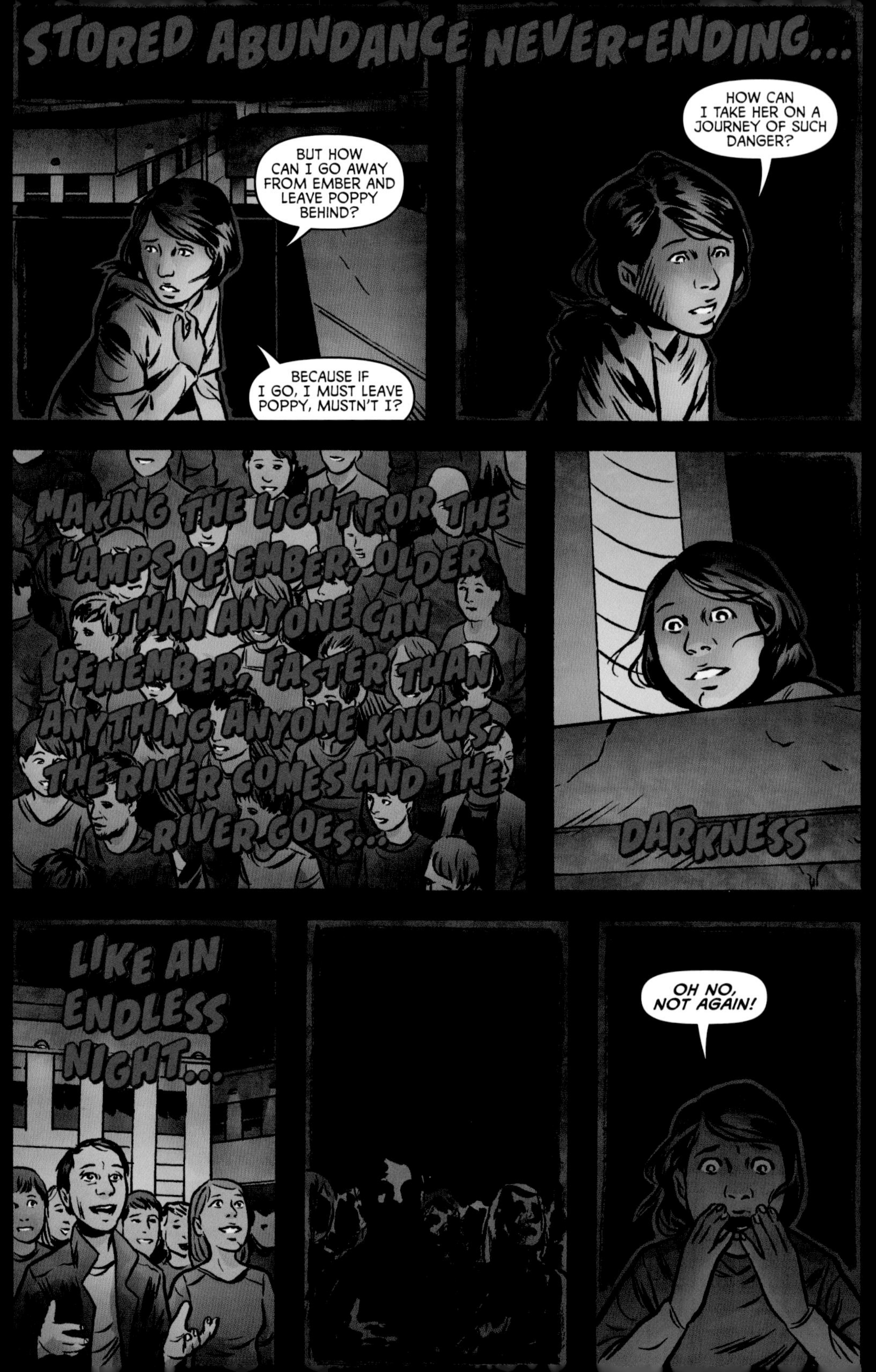
STORED ABUNDANCE NEVER-ENDING...
BUT HOW CAN I GO AWAY FROM EMBER AND LEAVE POPPY BEHIND?
BECAUSE IF I GO, I MUST LEAVE POPPY, MUSTN'T I?
HOW CAN I TAKE HER ON A JOURNEY OF SUCH DANGER?
MAKING THE LIGHT FOR THE LAMPS OF EMBER, OLDER THAN ANYONE CAN REMEMBER, FASTER THAN ANYTHING ANYONE KNOWS, THE RIVER COMES AND THE RIVER GOES...
DARKNESS
LIKE AN ENDLESS NIGHT...
OH NO, NOT AGAIN!

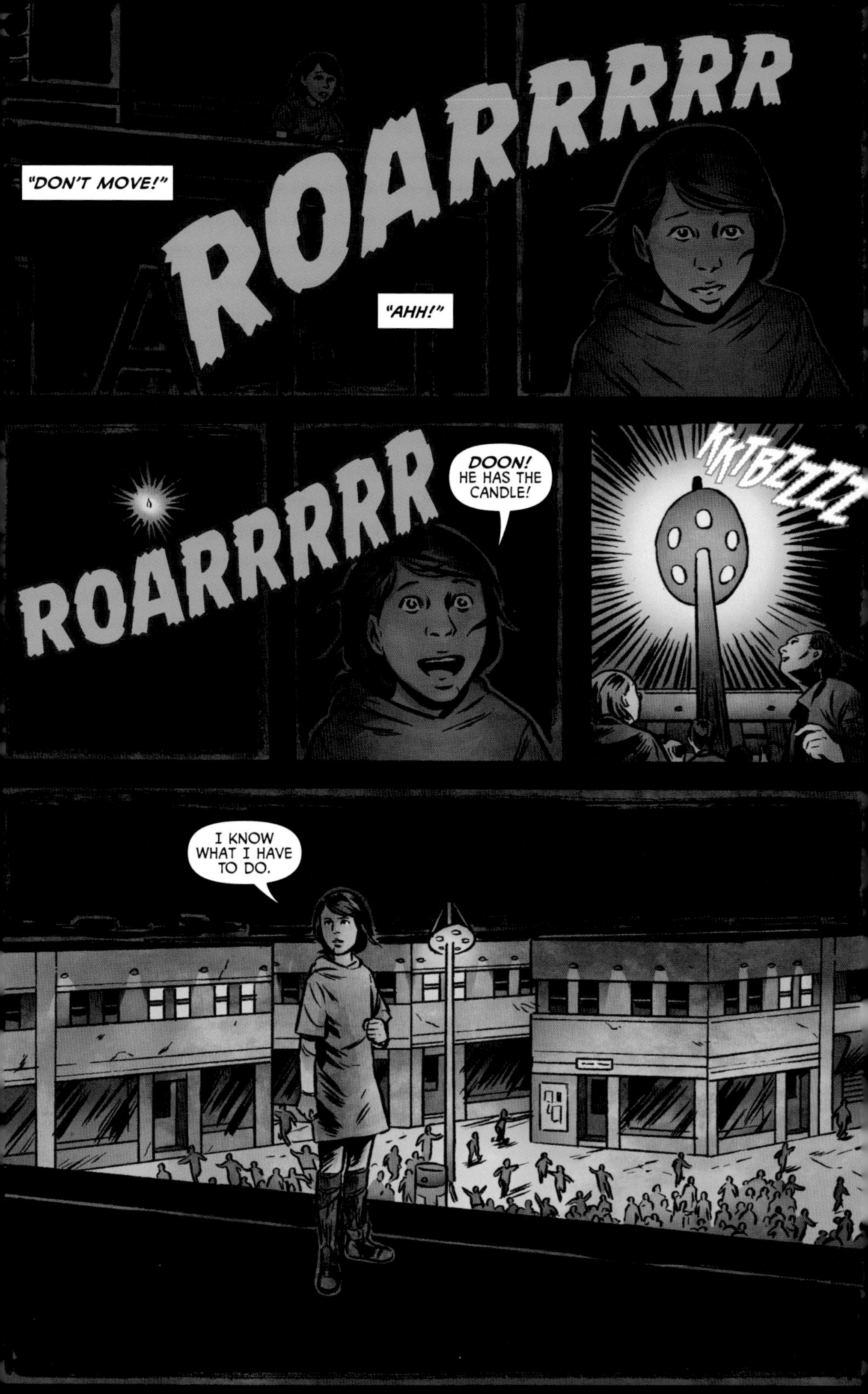
"DON'T MOVE!"
ROARRRRRR
"AHH!"
ROARRRRR
DOON! HE HAS THE CANDLE!
KKTBZZZZ
I KNOW WHAT I HAVE TO DO.

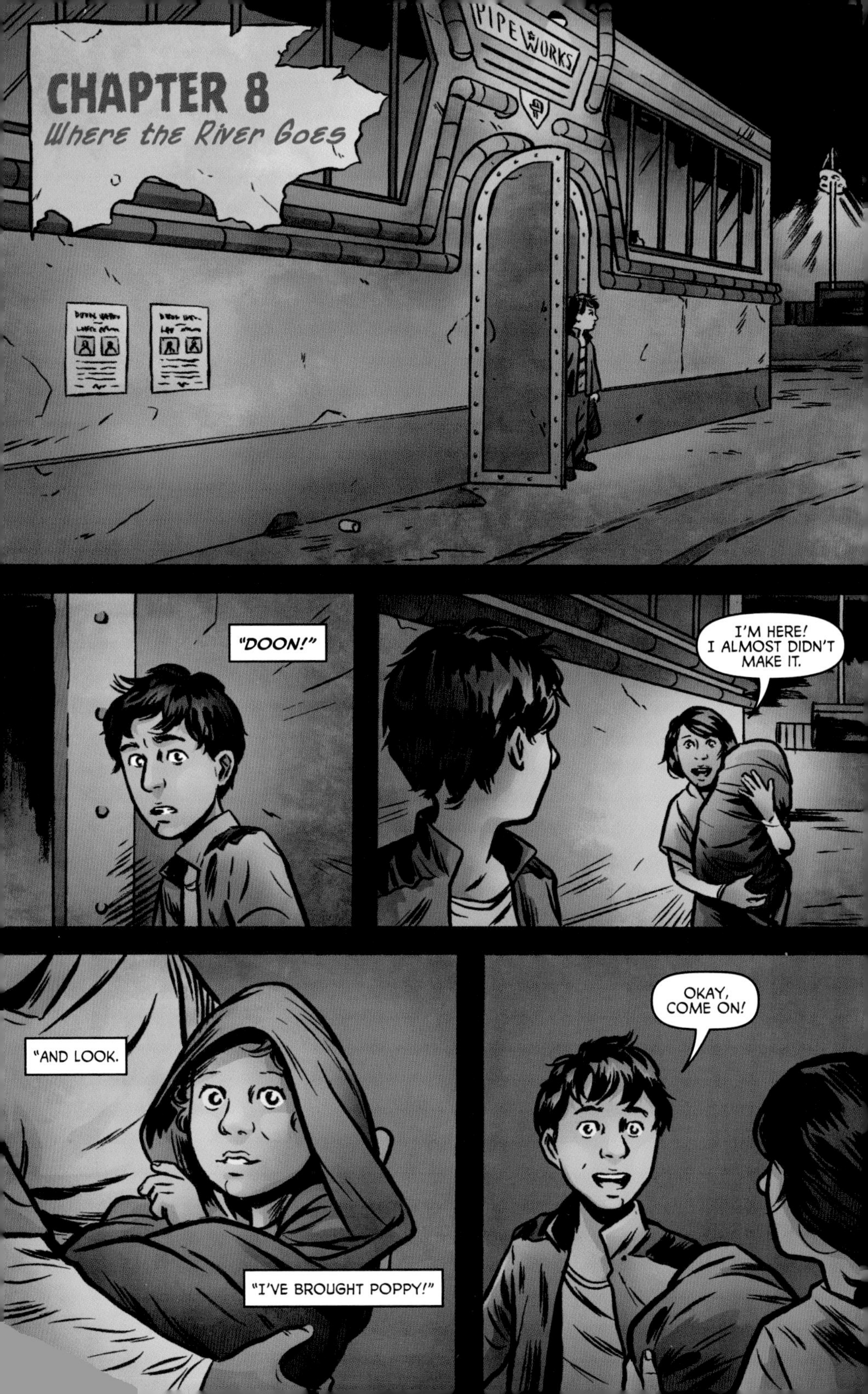
CHAPTER 8
Where the River Goes
PIPEWORKS
"DOON!"
I'M HERE! I ALMOST DIDN'T MAKE IT.
"AND LOOK.
"I'VE BROUGHT POPPY!"
OKAY, COME ON!

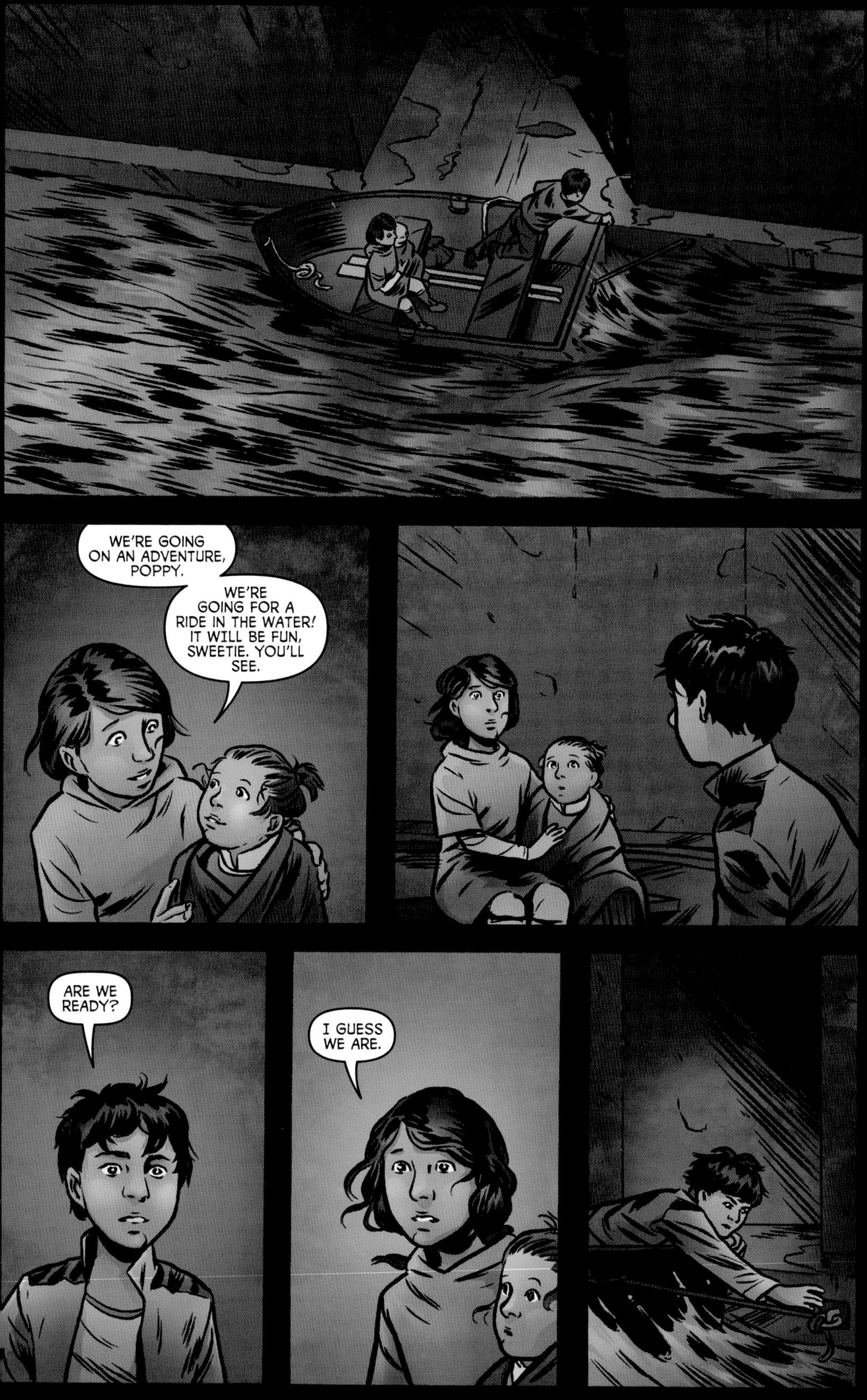
WE'RE GOING ON AN ADVENTURE, POPPY.
WE'RE GOING FOR A RIDE IN THE WATER! IT WILL BE FUN, SWEETIE. YOU'LL SEE.
ARE WE READY?
I GUESS WE ARE.

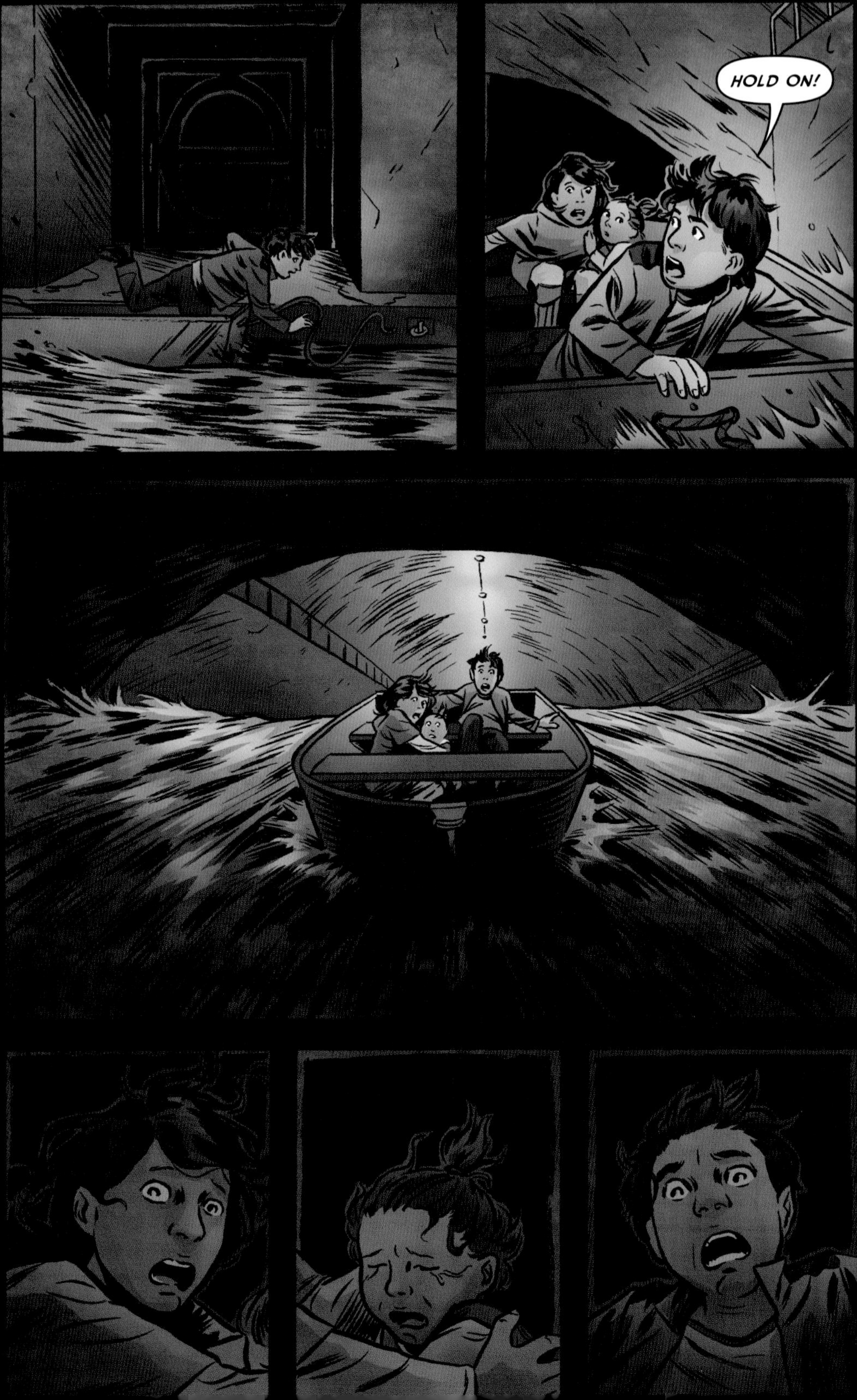
HOLD ON!

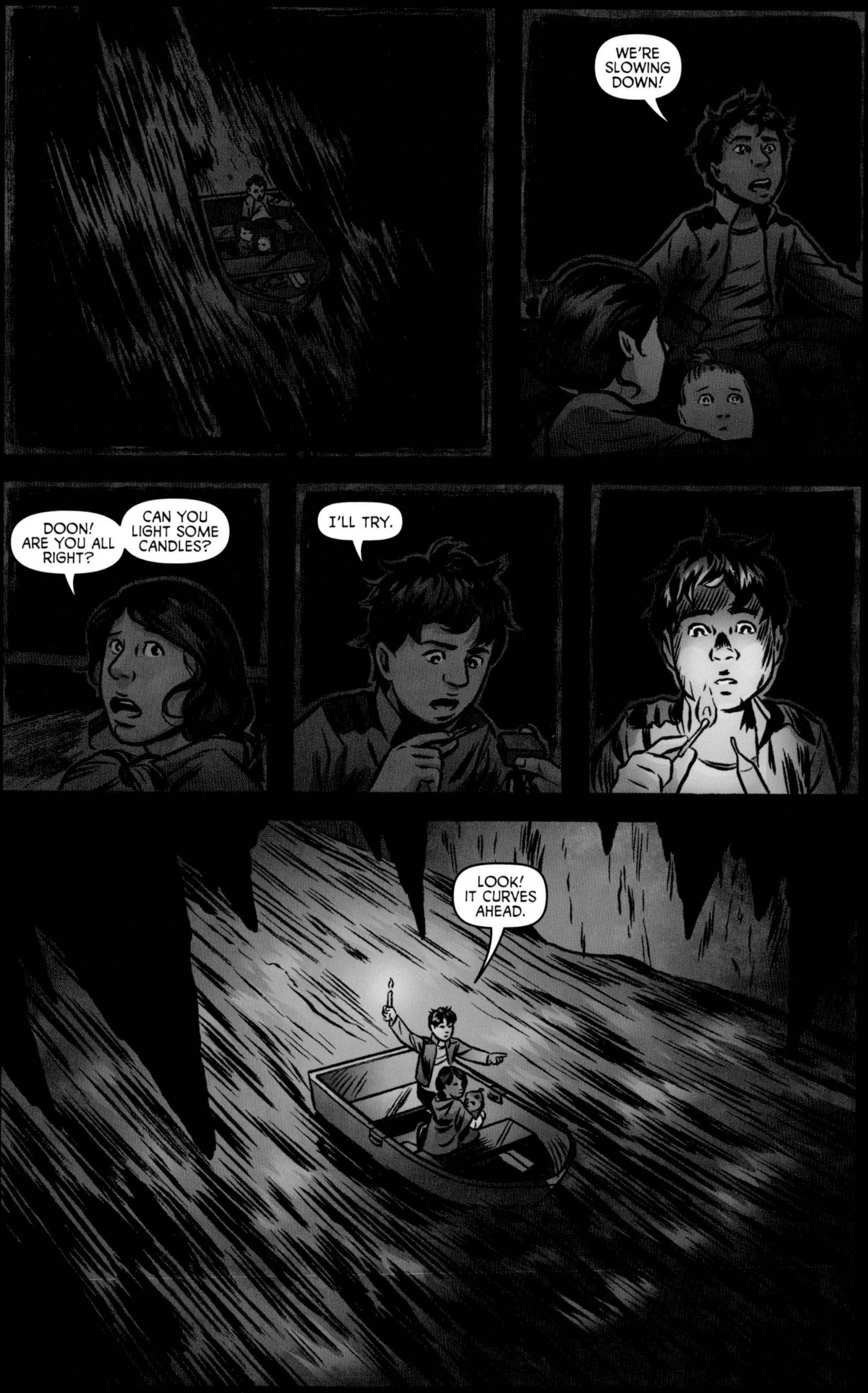
WE'RE SLOWING DOWN!
DOON! ARE YOU ALL RIGHT?
CAN YOU LIGHT SOME CANDLES?
I'LL TRY.
LOOK! IT CURVES AHEAD.

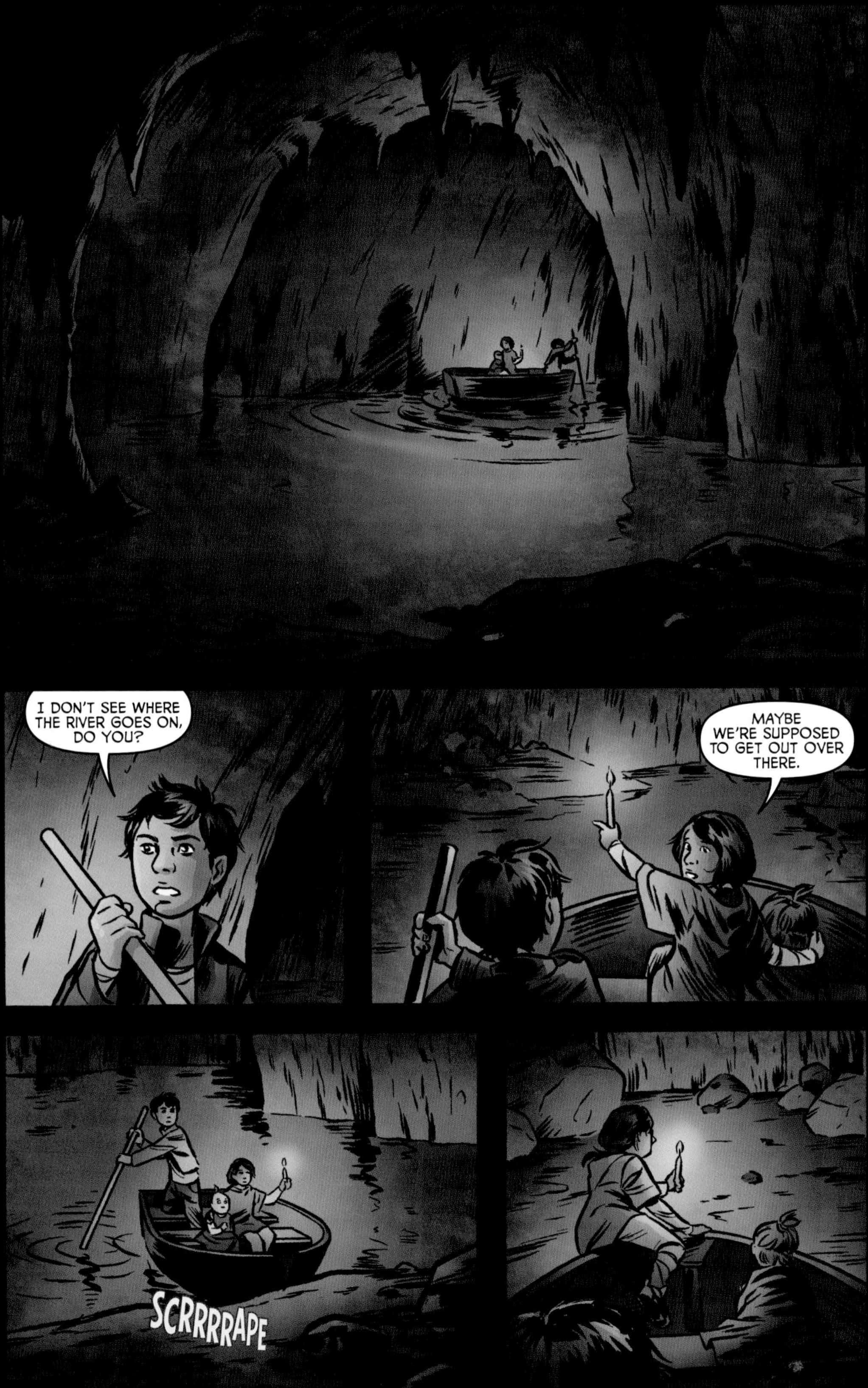
I DON'T SEE WHERE THE RIVER GOES ON, DO YOU?
MAYBE WE'RE SUPPOSED TO GET OUT OVER THERE.
SCRRRRAPE

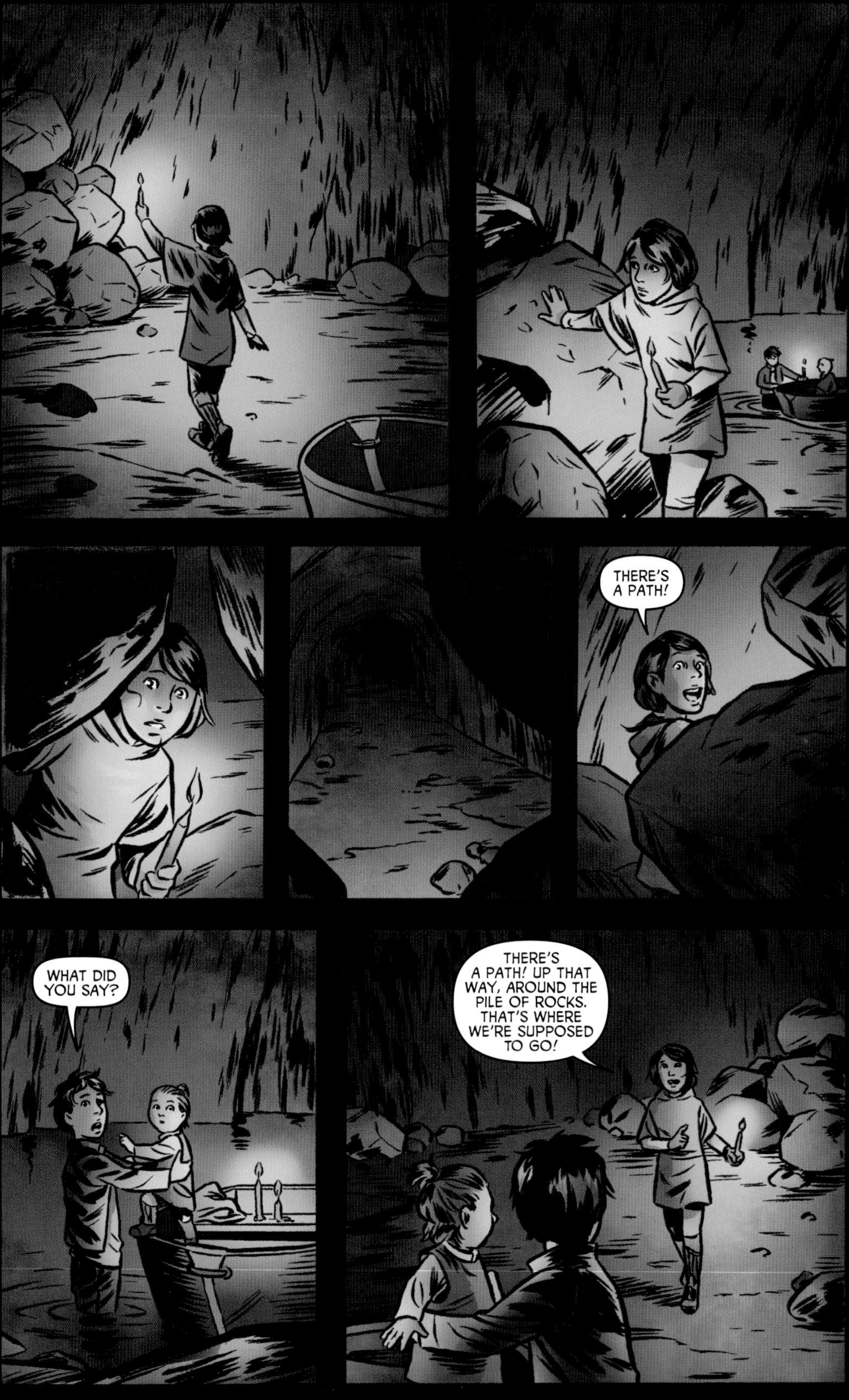
THERE'S A PATH!
WHAT DID YOU SAY?
THERE'S A PATH! UP THAT WAY, AROUND THE PILE OF ROCKS. THAT'S WHERE WE'RE SUPPOSED TO GO!

OKAY, BUT LET'S REST HERE AND EAT SOMETHING FIRST.

WHAT DID YOU TELL MRS. MURDO ABOUT POPPY?

I JUST SAID SHE MUST GIVE POPPY TO ME. THAT I WAS TAKING HER TO SAFETY.

BECAUSE THAT'S WHAT I REALIZED ON THE ROOF OF THE GATHERING HALL, DOON. I'D BEEN THINKING THAT I HAD TO LEAVE POPPY BECAUSE SHE'D BE SAFE WITH MRS. MURDO.

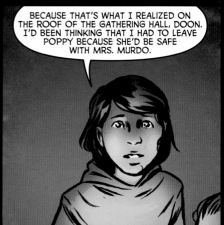

BUT WHEN THE LIGHTS WENT OUT, I SUDDENLY KNEW I COULDN'T LEAVE HER BEHIND.

WHATEVER HAPPENS TO US NOW, IT'S BETTER THAN WHAT'S GOING TO HAPPEN THERE.

SO YOU GAVE MRS. MURDO THE NOTE, THEN?

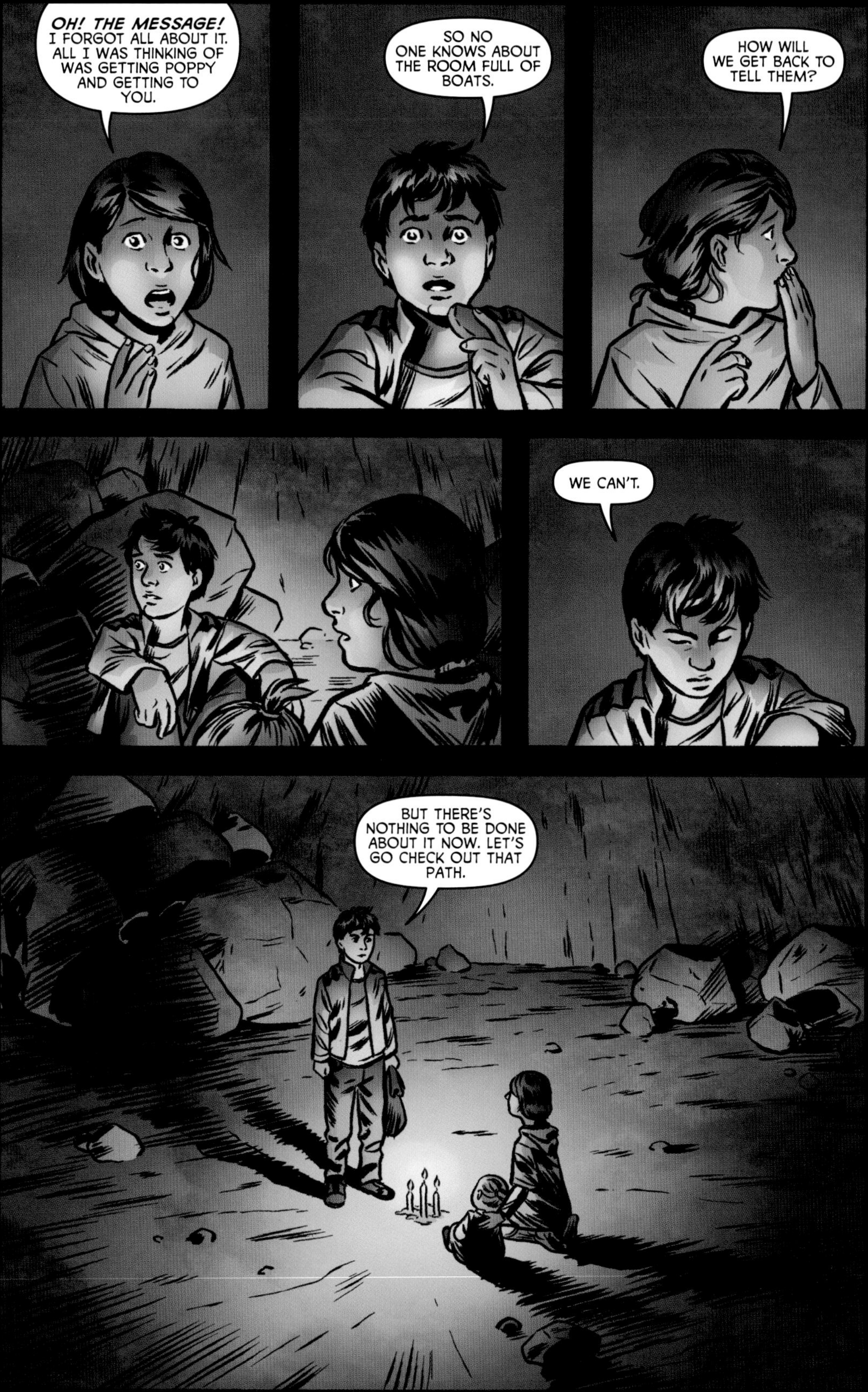

OH! THE MESSAGE! I FORGOT ALL ABOUT IT. ALL I WAS THINKING OF WAS GETTING POPPY AND GETTING TO YOU.
SO NO ONE KNOWS ABOUT THE ROOM FULL OF BOATS.
HOW WILL WE GET BACK TO TELL THEM?
WE CAN'T.
BUT THERE'S NOTHING TO BE DONE ABOUT IT NOW. LET'S GO CHECK OUT THAT PATH.

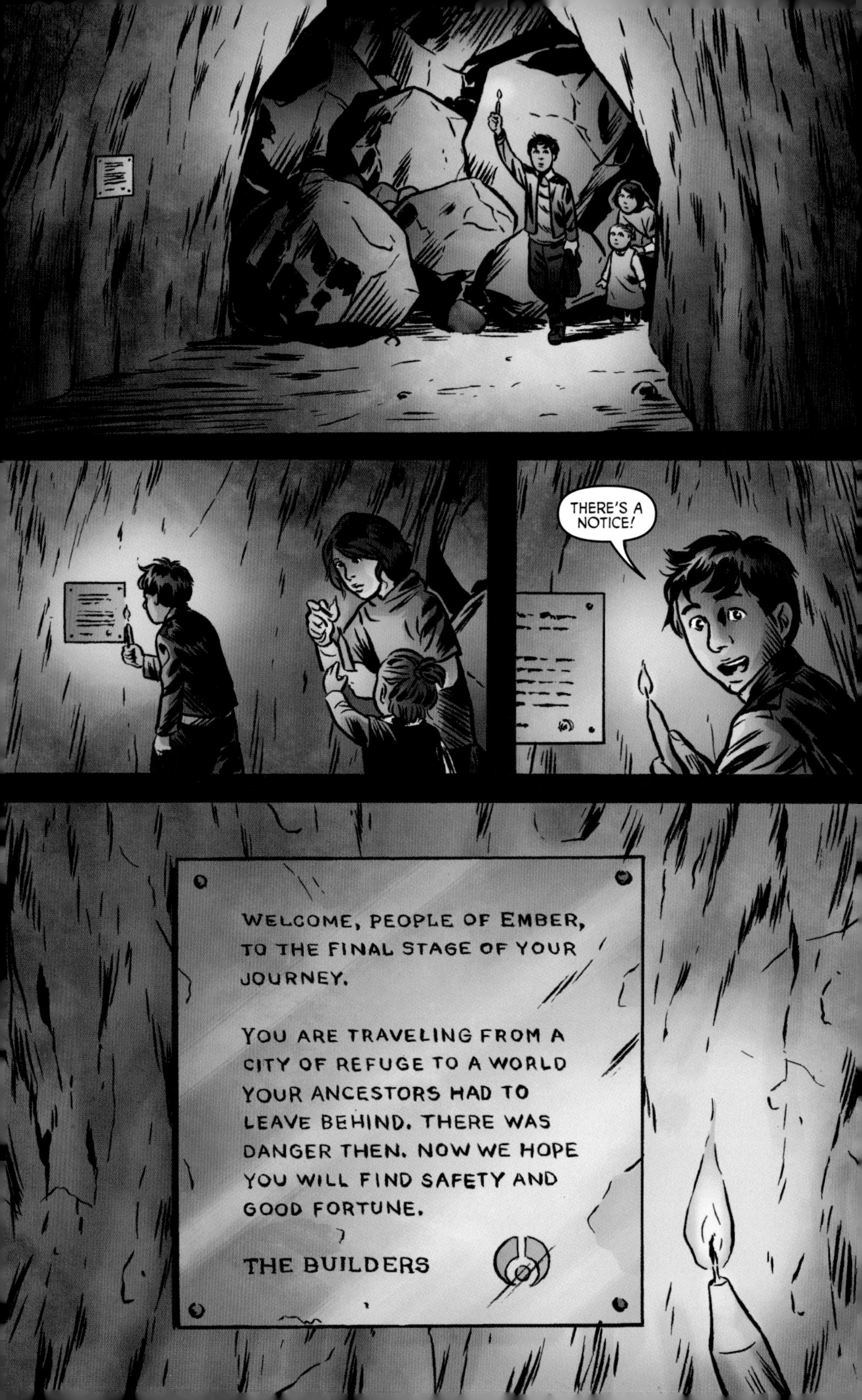
THERE'S A NOTICE!
WELCOME, PEOPLE OF EMBER, TO THE FINAL STAGE OF YOUR JOURNEY.
YOU ARE TRAVELING FROM A CITY OF REFUGE TO A WORLD YOUR ANCESTORS HAD TO LEAVE BEHIND. THERE WAS DANGER THEN. NOW WE HOPE YOU WILL FIND SAFETY AND GOOD FORTUNE.
THE BUILDERS

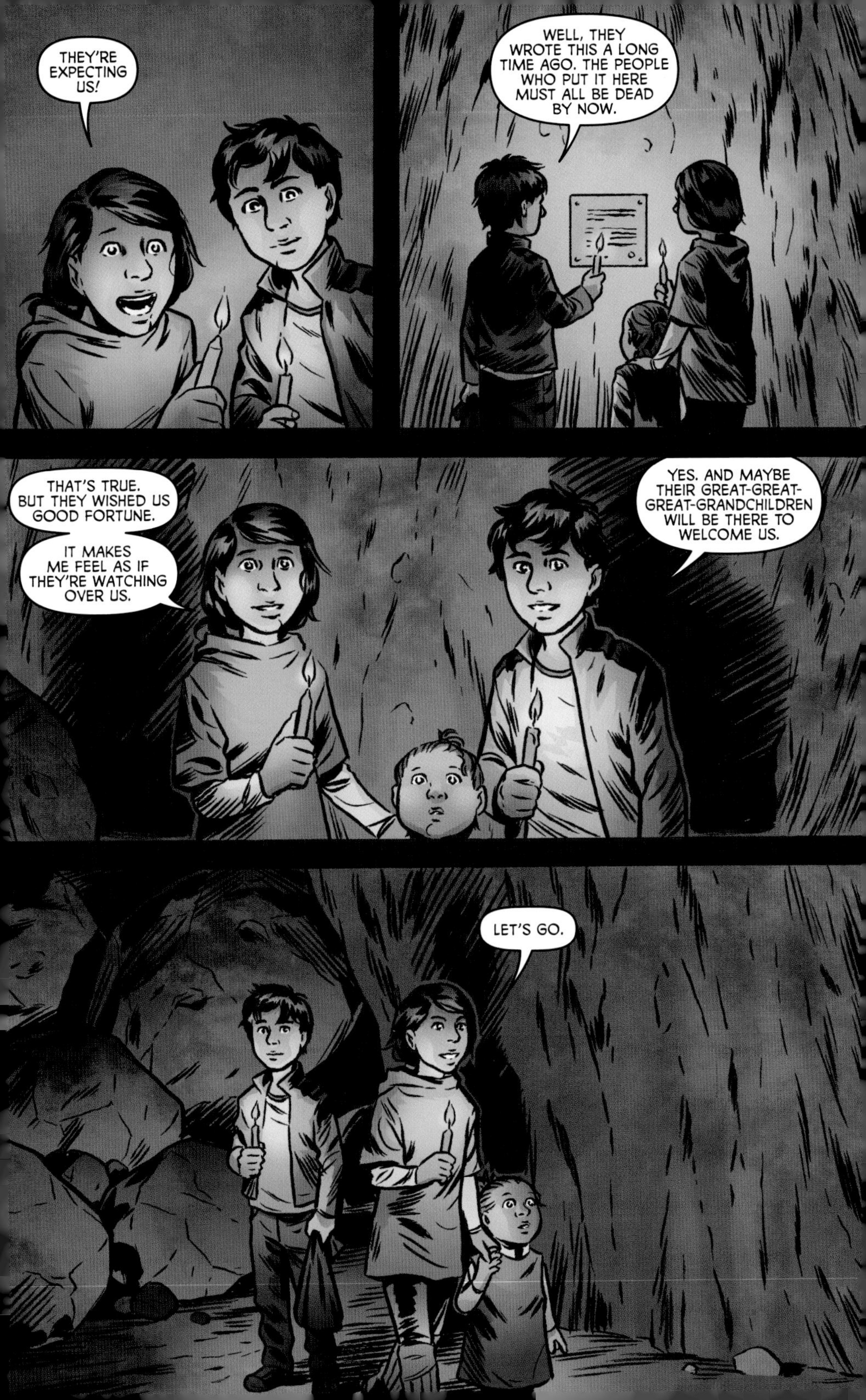
THEY'RE EXPECTING US!
WELL, THEY WROTE THIS A LONG TIME AGO. THE PEOPLE WHO PUT IT HERE MUST ALL BE DEAD BY NOW.
THAT'S TRUE. BUT THEY WISHED US GOOD FORTUNE.
IT MAKES ME FEEL AS IF THEY'RE WATCHING OVER US.
YES. AND MAYBE THEIR GREAT-GREAT-GREAT-GRANDCHILDREN WILL BE THERE TO WELCOME US.
LET'S GO.

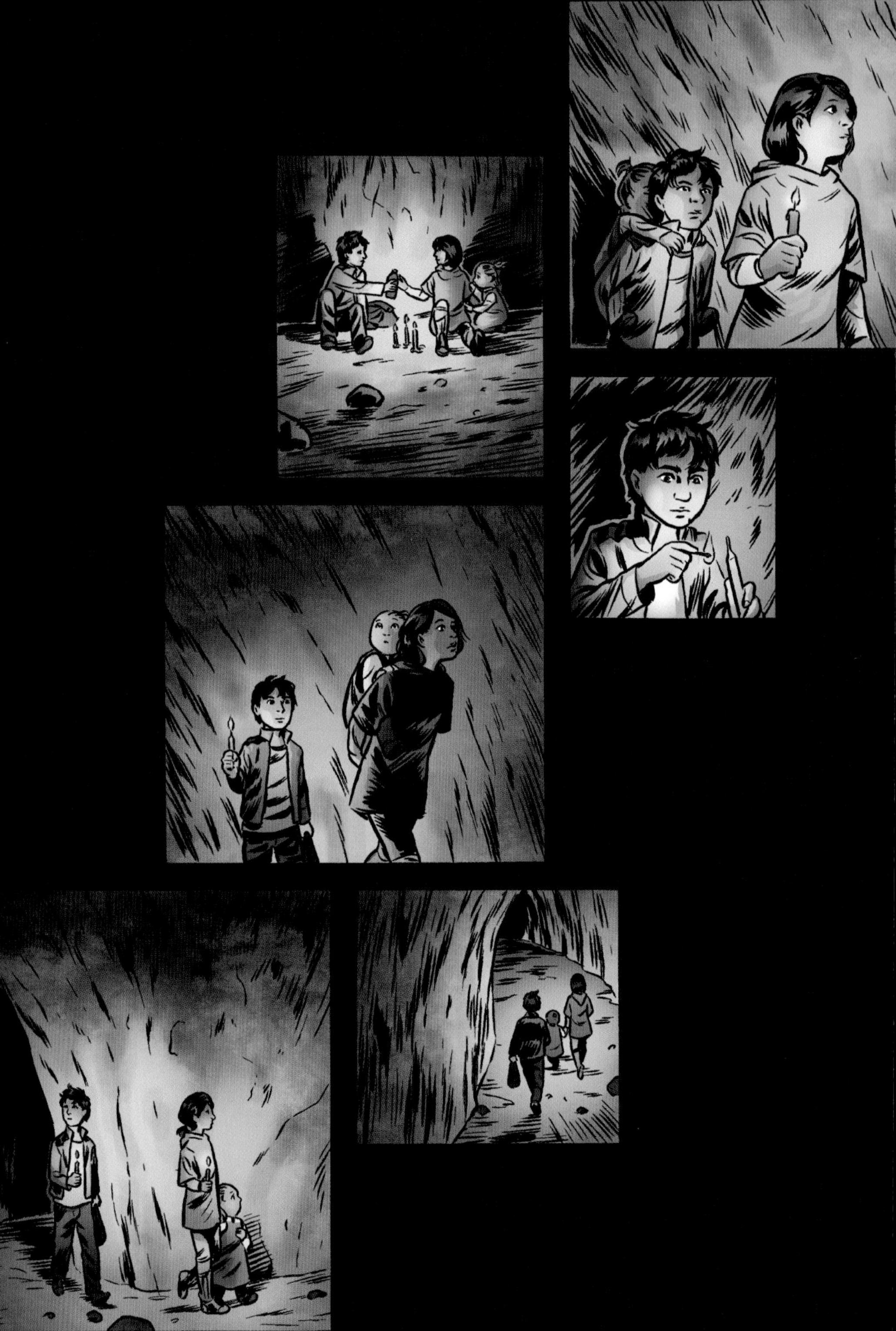

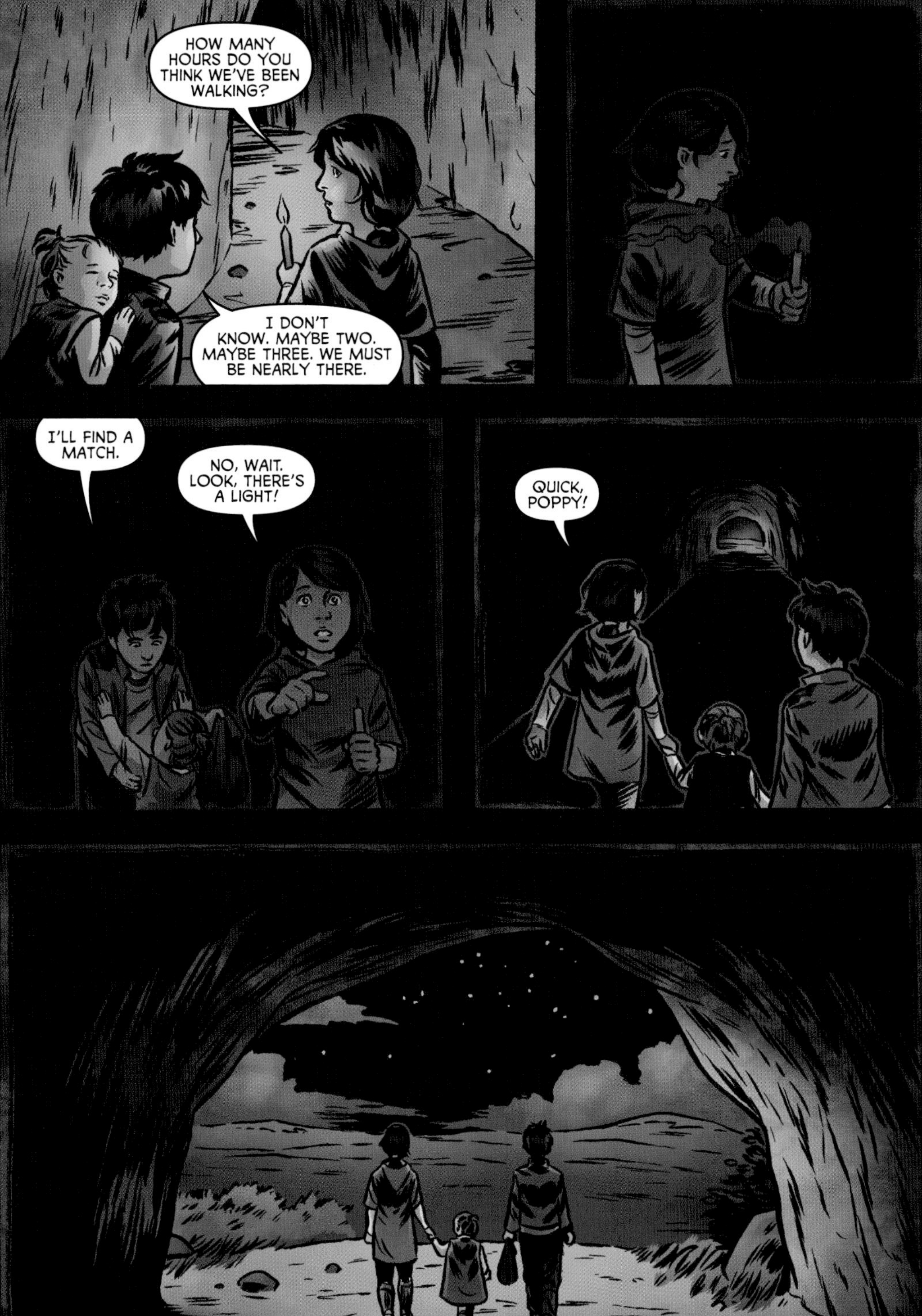
HOW MANY HOURS DO YOU THINK WE'VE BEEN WALKING?
I DON'T KNOW. MAYBE TWO. MAYBE THREE. WE MUST BE NEARLY THERE.
I'LL FIND A MATCH.
NO, WAIT. LOOK, THERE'S A LIGHT!
QUICK, POPPY!

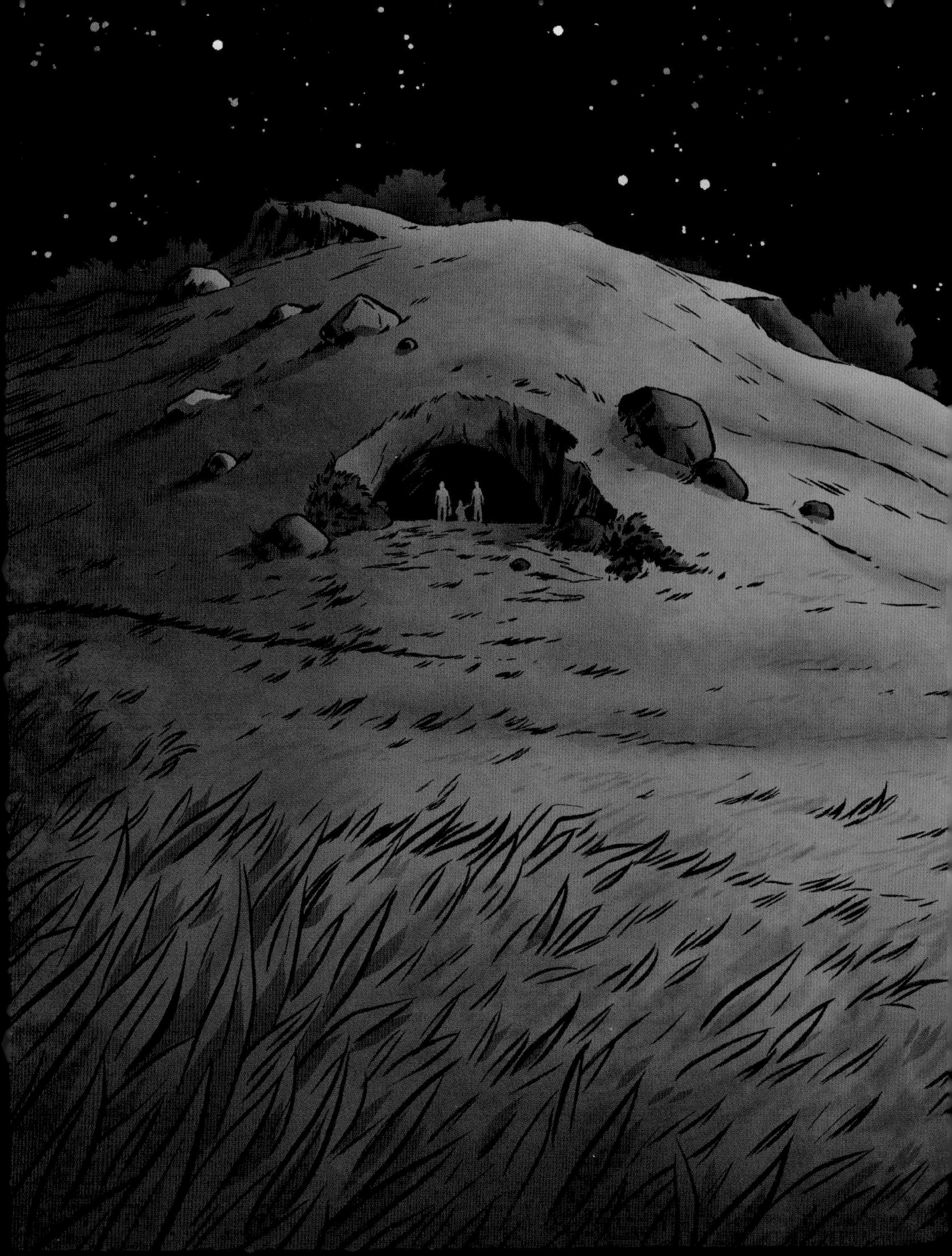

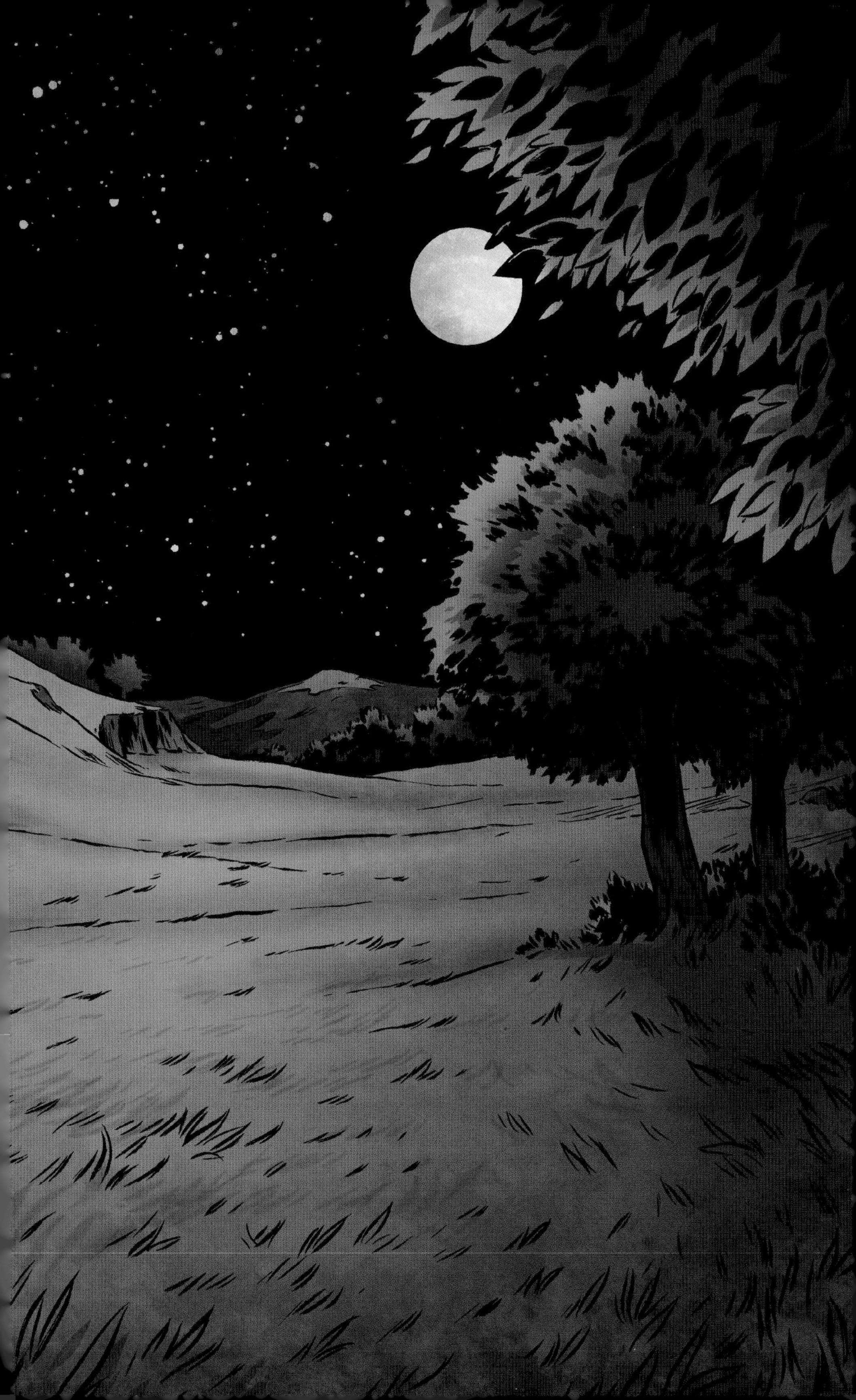

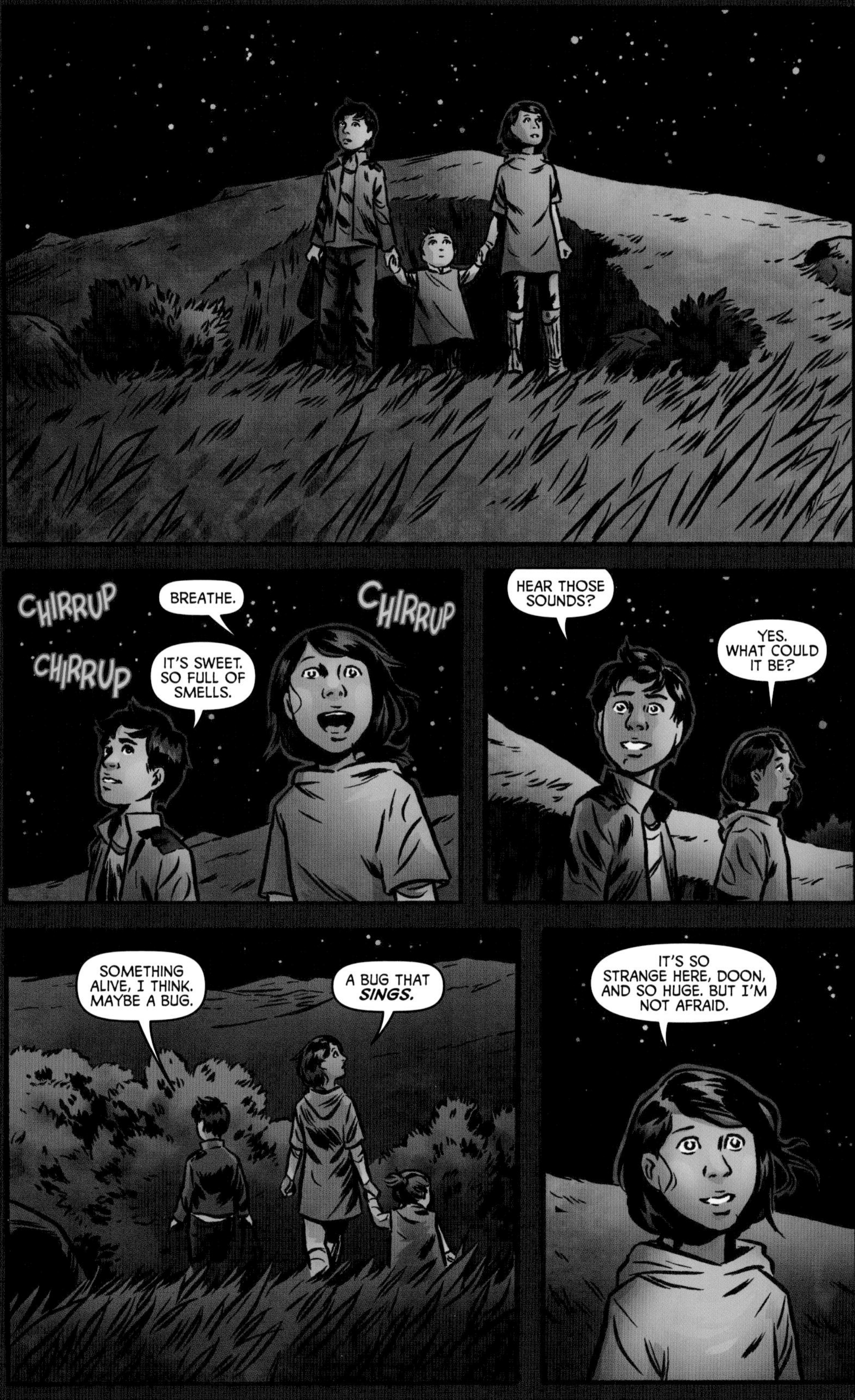
CHIRRUP
BREATHE.
CHIRRUP
CHIRRUP
IT'S SWEET. SO FULL OF SMELLS.
HEAR THOSE SOUNDS?
YES. WHAT COULD IT BE?
SOMETHING ALIVE, I THINK. MAYBE A BUG.
A BUG THAT *SINGS.*
IT'S SO STRANGE HERE, DOON, AND SO HUGE. BUT I'M NOT AFRAID.

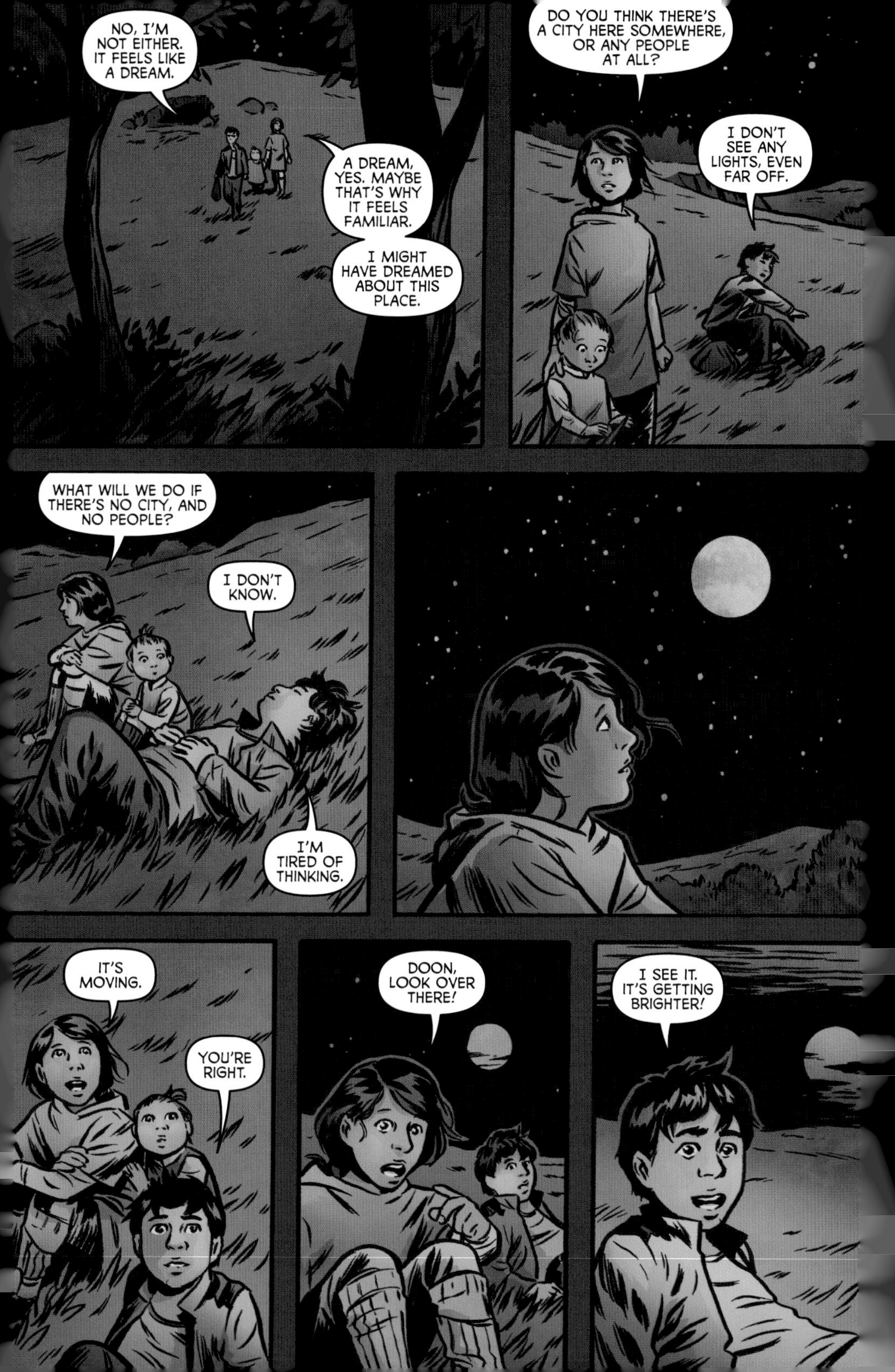
NO, I'M NOT EITHER. IT FEELS LIKE A DREAM.
A DREAM, YES. MAYBE THAT'S WHY IT FEELS FAMILIAR.
I MIGHT HAVE DREAMED ABOUT THIS PLACE.
DO YOU THINK THERE'S A CITY HERE SOMEWHERE, OR ANY PEOPLE AT ALL?
I DON'T SEE ANY LIGHTS, EVEN FAR OFF.
WHAT WILL WE DO IF THERE'S NO CITY, AND NO PEOPLE?
I DON'T KNOW.
I'M TIRED OF THINKING.
IT'S MOVING.
YOU'RE RIGHT.
DOON, LOOK OVER THERE!
I SEE IT. IT'S GETTING BRIGHTER!

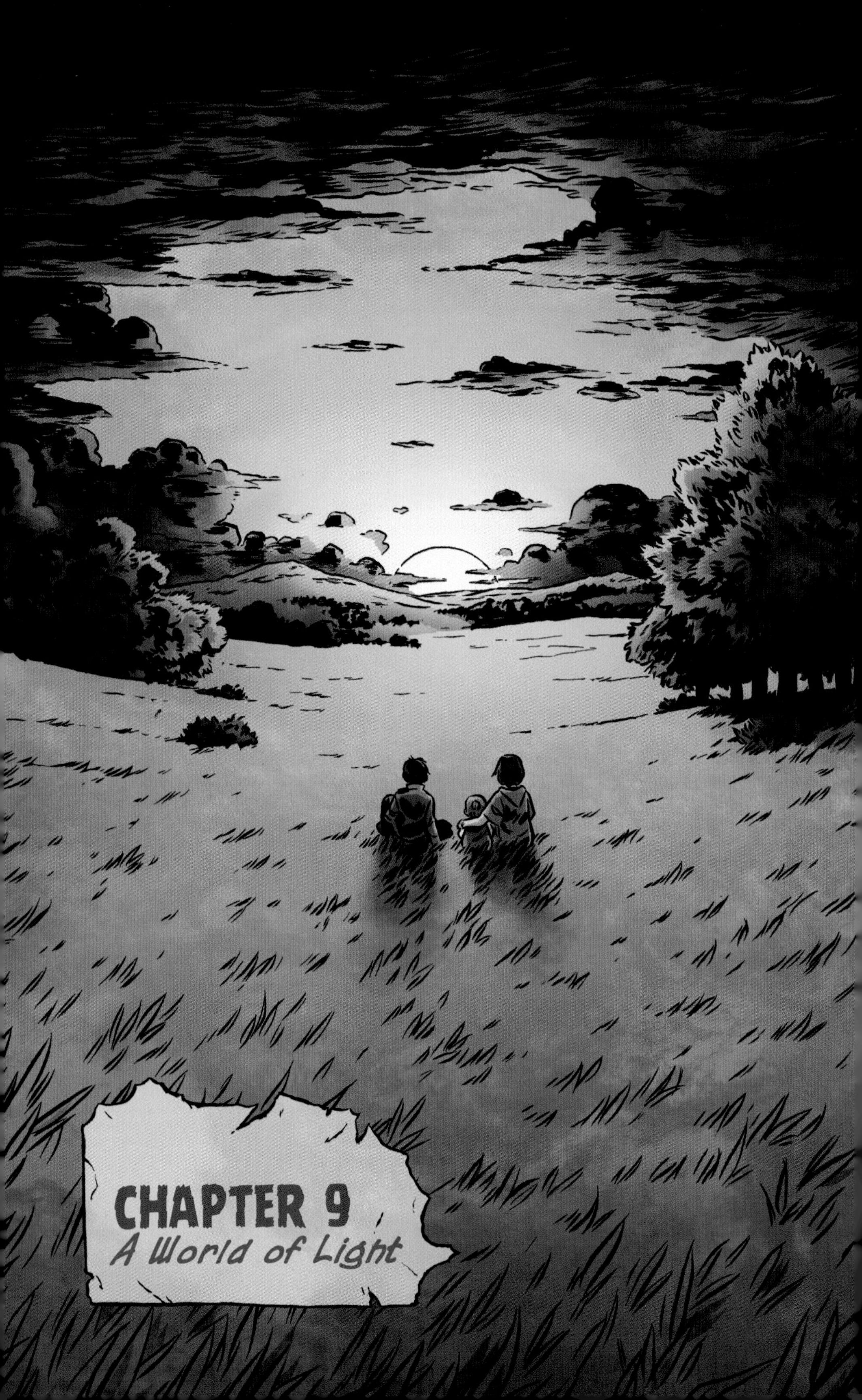
CHAPTER 9
A World of Light

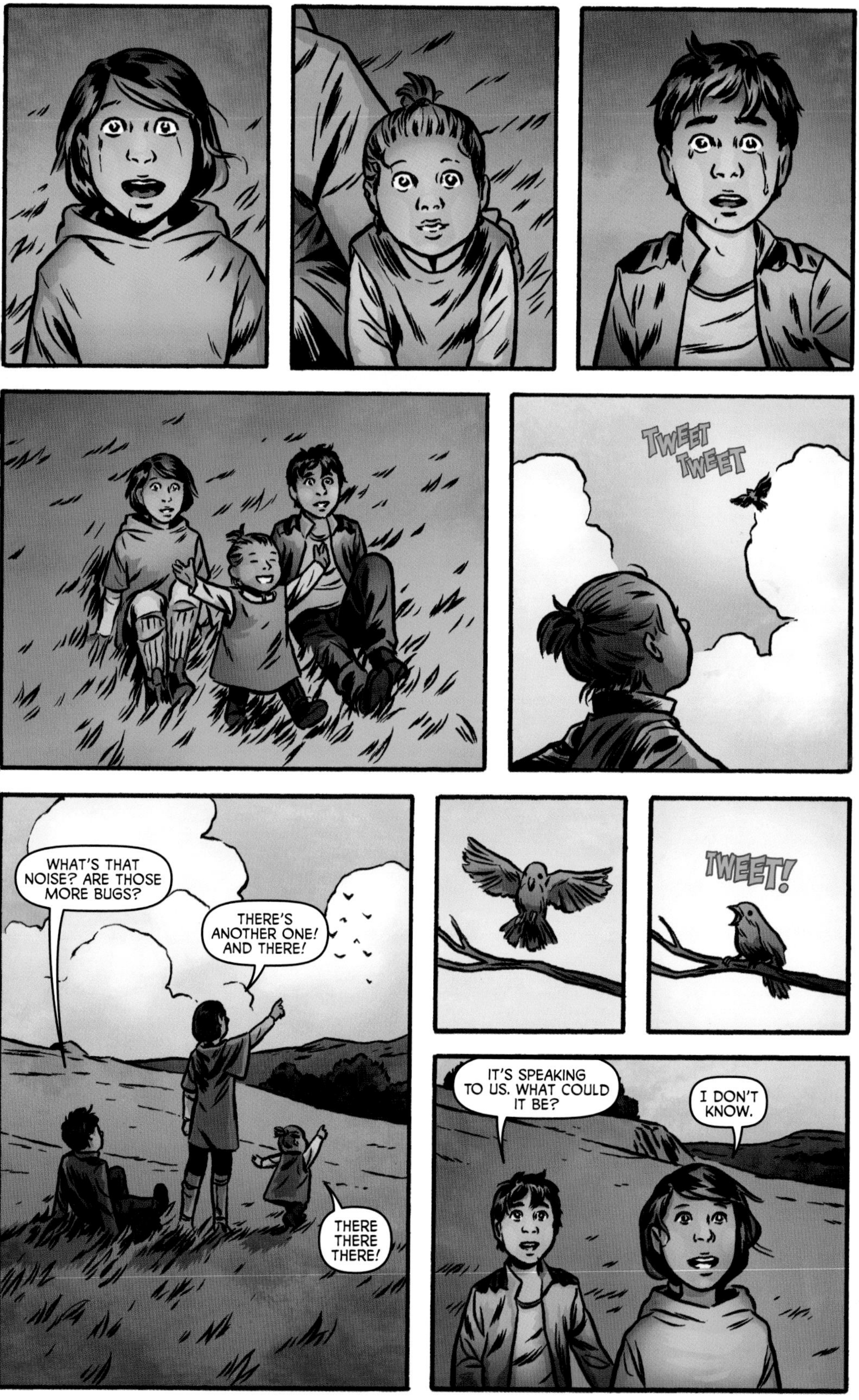
TWEET
TWEET
WHAT'S THAT NOISE? ARE THOSE MORE BUGS?
THERE'S ANOTHER ONE! AND THERE!
THERE THERE THERE!
TWEET!
IT'S SPEAKING TO US. WHAT COULD IT BE?
I DON'T KNOW.

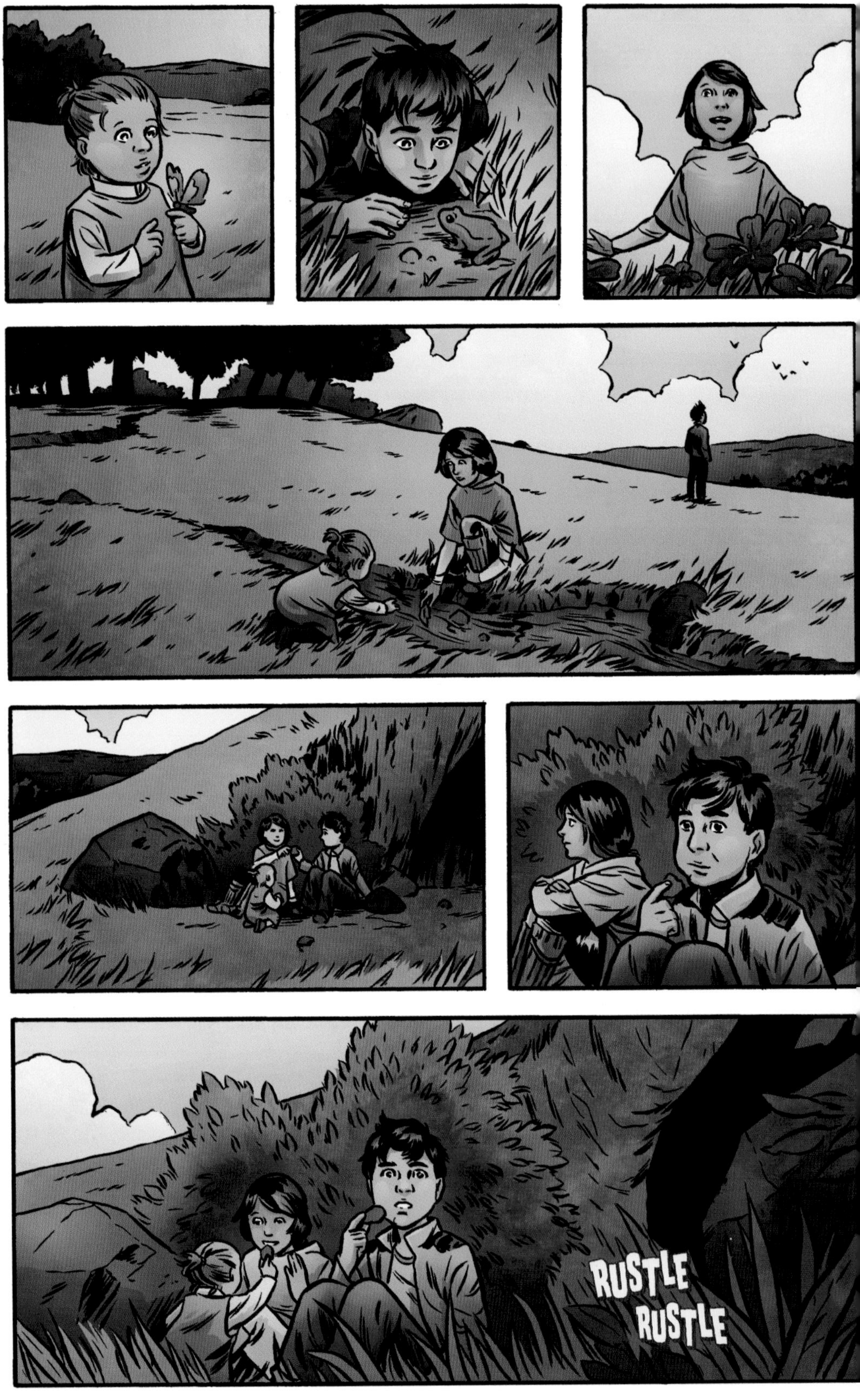
RUSTLE
RUSTLE

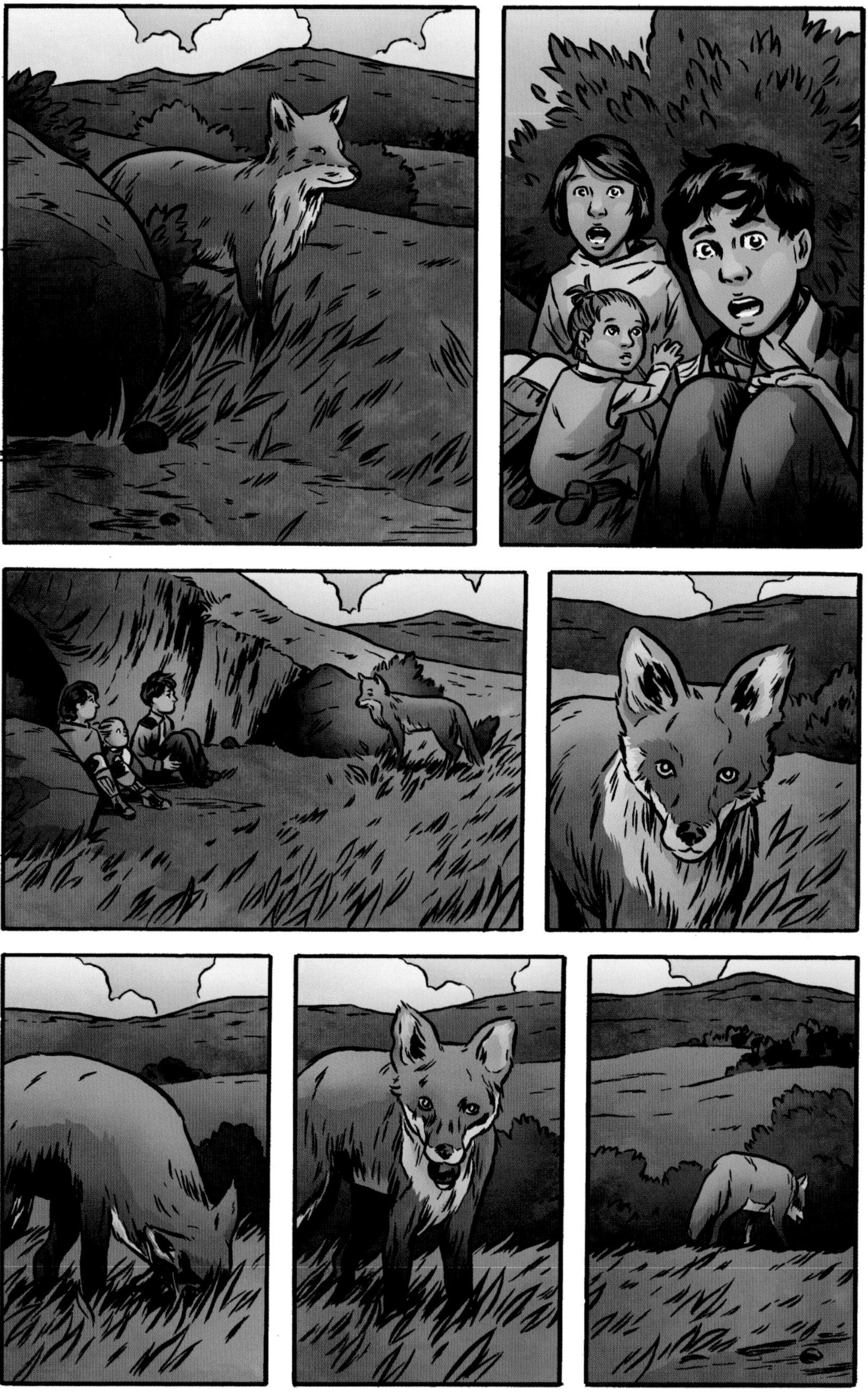

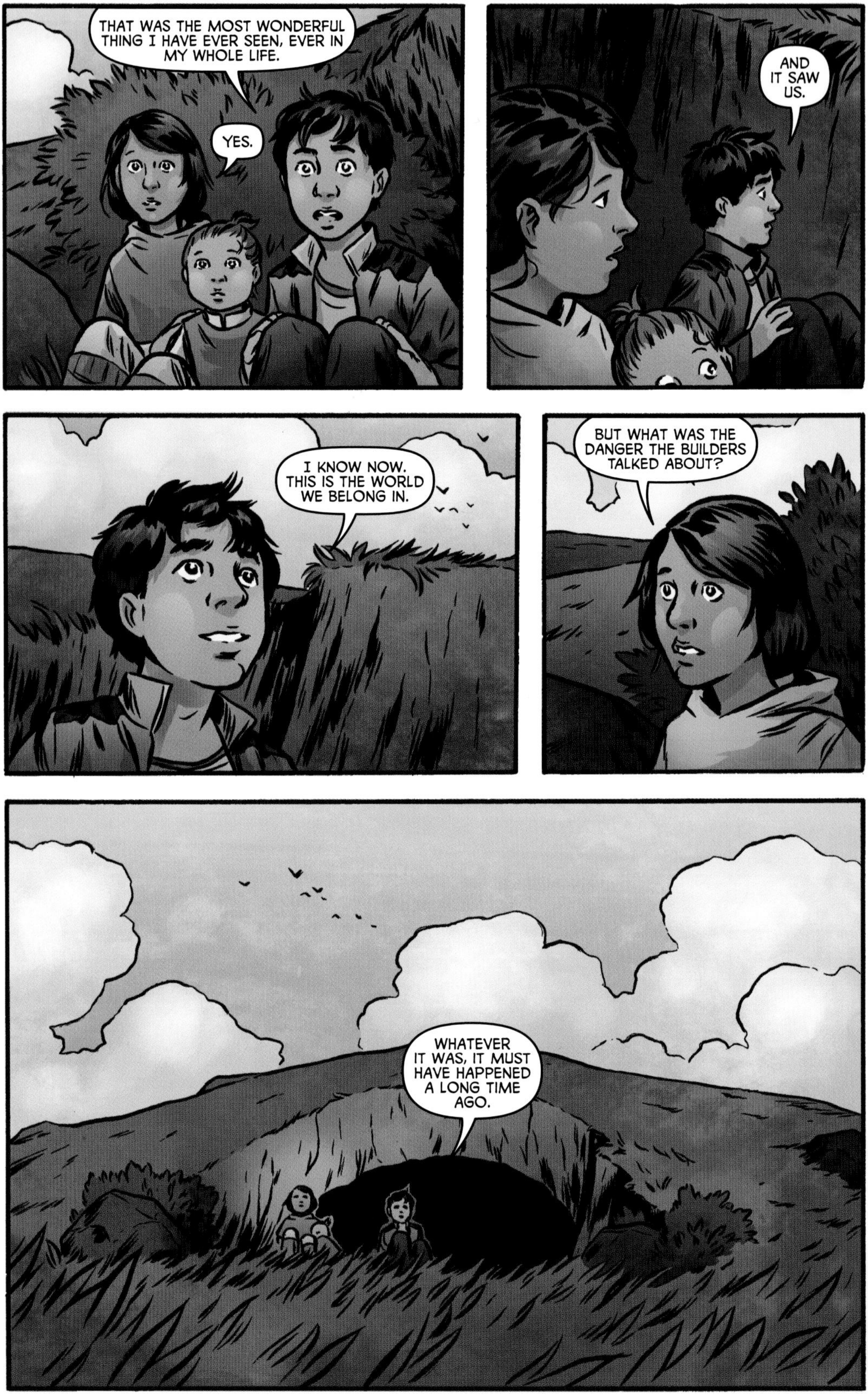
THAT WAS THE MOST WONDERFUL THING I HAVE EVER SEEN, EVER IN MY WHOLE LIFE.
YES.
AND IT SAW US.
I KNOW NOW. THIS IS THE WORLD WE BELONG IN.
BUT WHAT WAS THE DANGER THE BUILDERS TALKED ABOUT?
WHATEVER IT WAS, IT MUST HAVE HAPPENED A LONG TIME AGO.

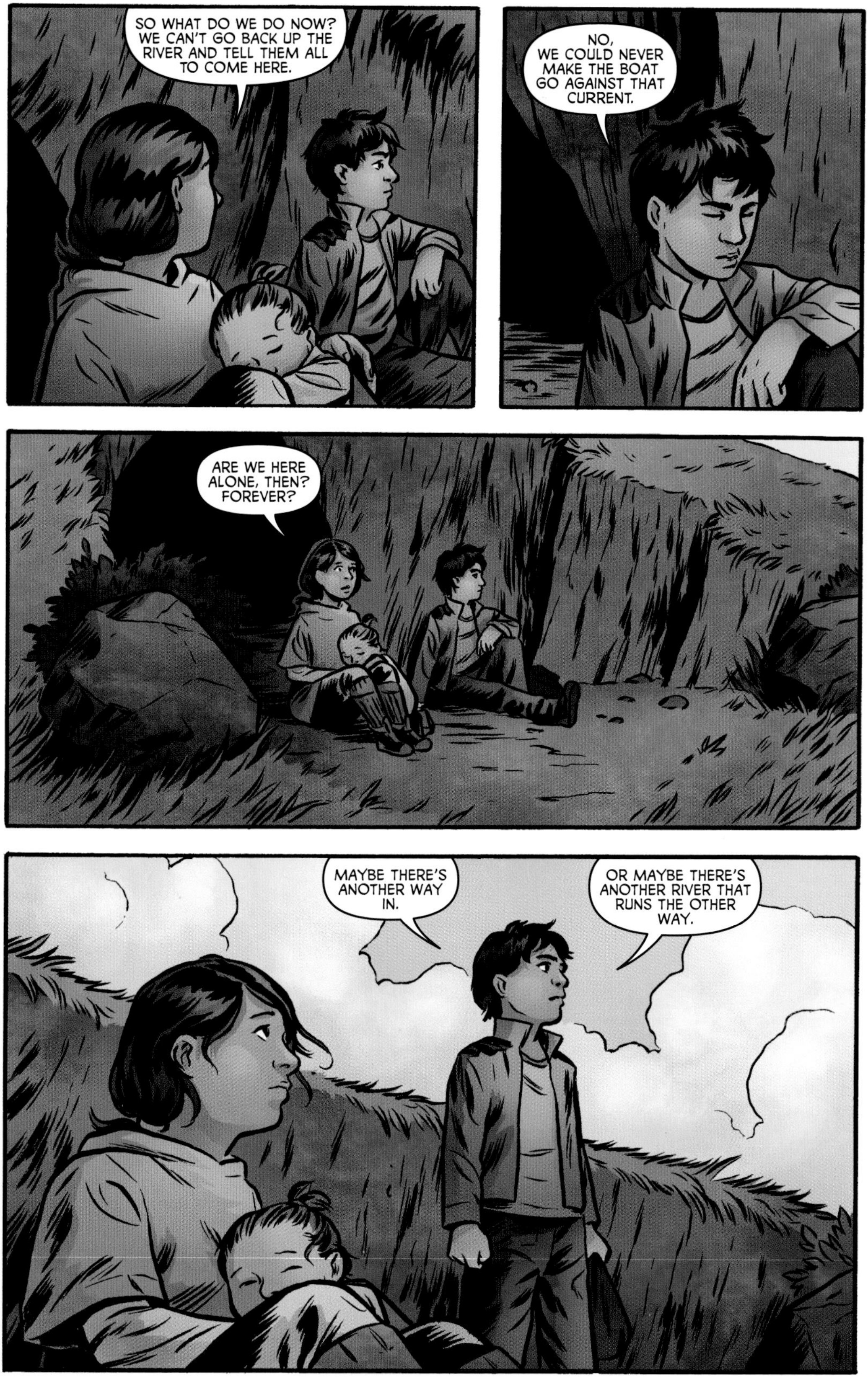
SO WHAT DO WE DO NOW? WE CAN'T GO BACK UP THE RIVER AND TELL THEM ALL TO COME HERE.
NO, WE COULD NEVER MAKE THE BOAT GO AGAINST THAT CURRENT.
ARE WE HERE ALONE, THEN? FOREVER?
MAYBE THERE'S ANOTHER WAY IN.
OR MAYBE THERE'S ANOTHER RIVER THAT RUNS THE OTHER WAY.

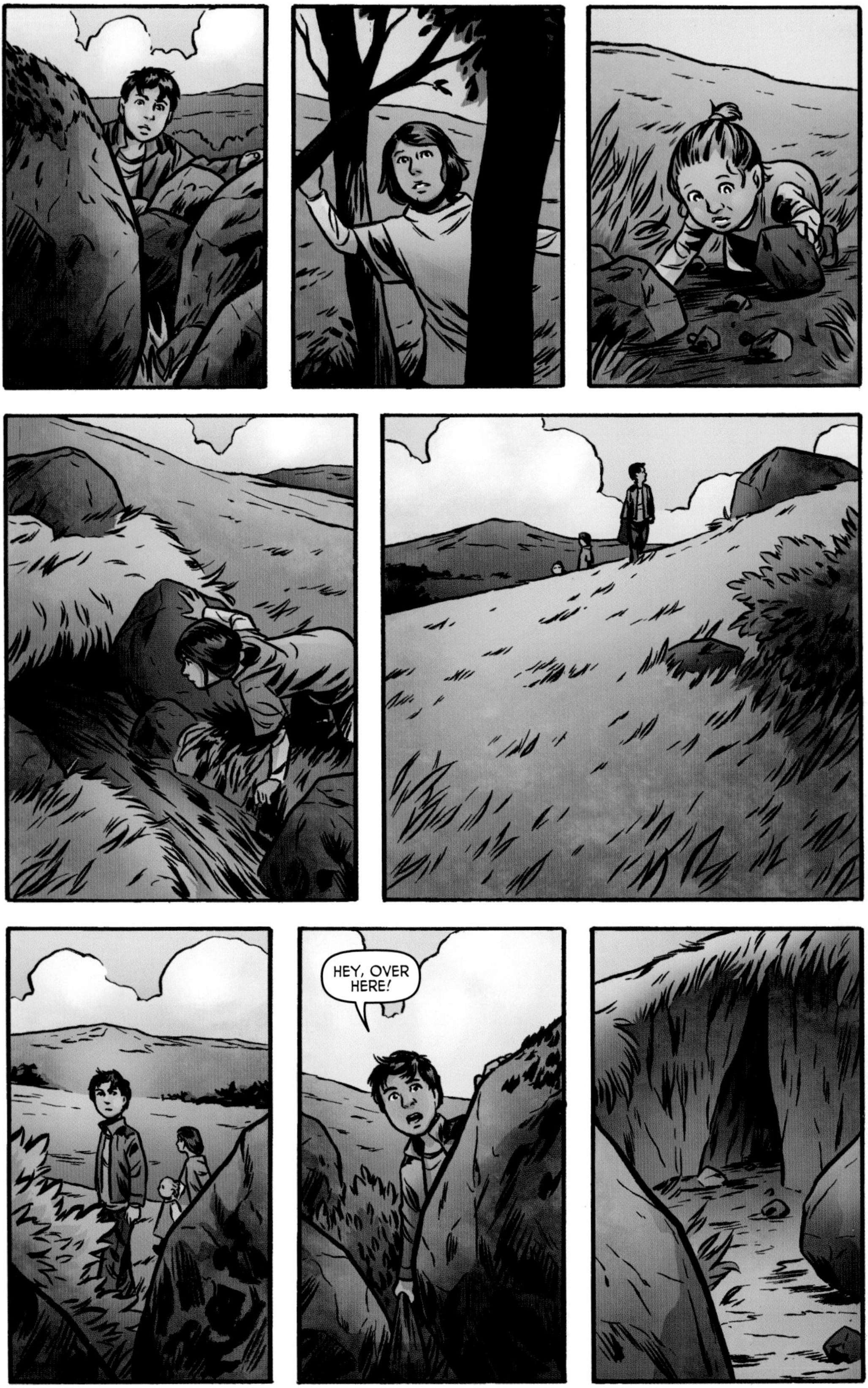
HEY, OVER HERE!

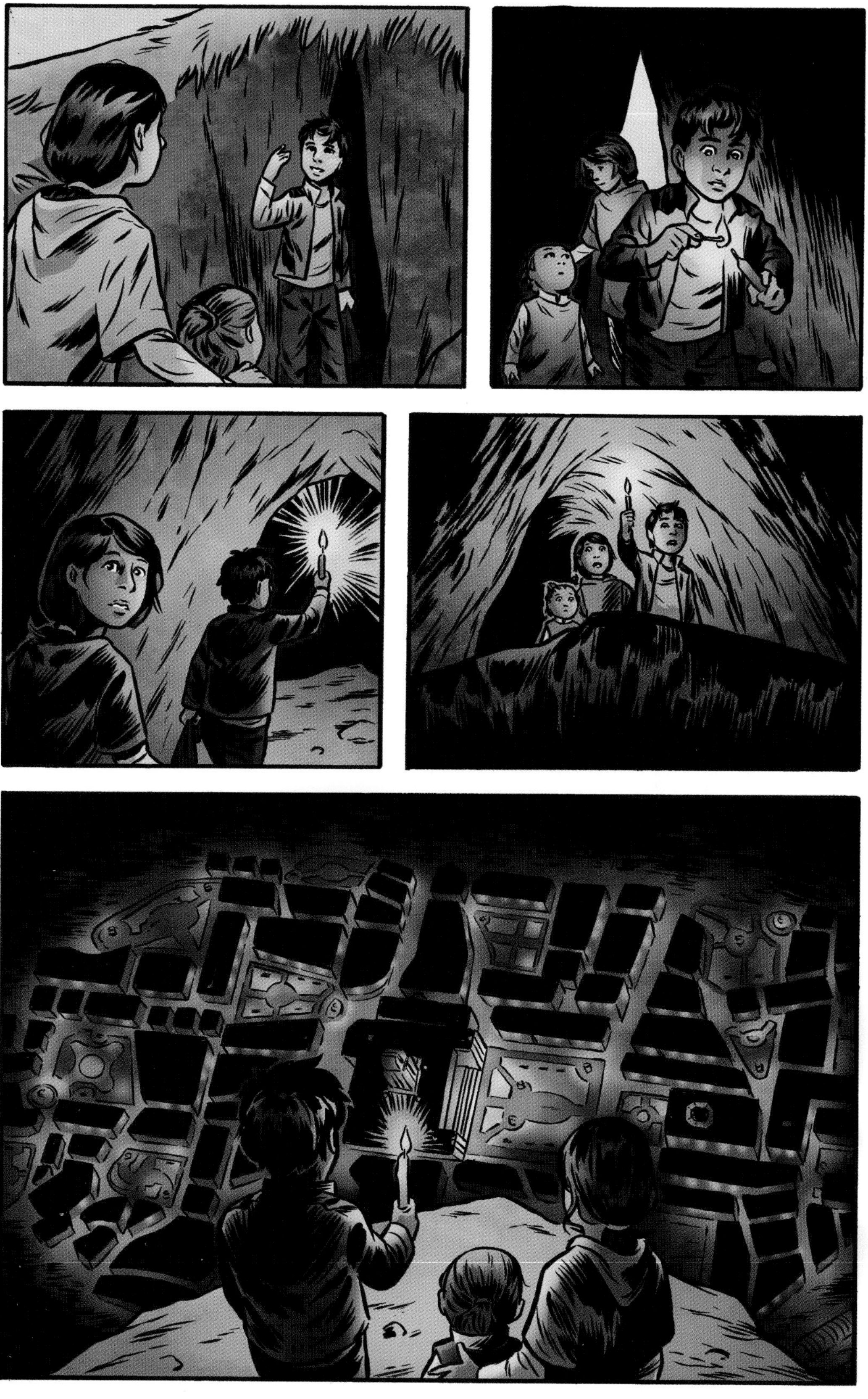

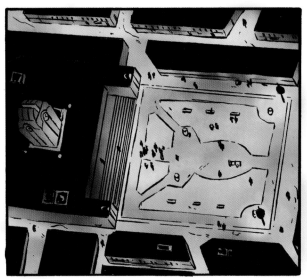

IT'S *EMBER!*

OH, OUR CITY, DOON. OUR CITY IS AT THE BOTTOM OF A HOLE! WE WERE UNDERGROUND. NOT JUST THE PIPEWORKS. EVERYTHING!

I WONDER WHAT'S HAPPENING THERE.

COULD THEY HEAR US IF WE SHOUTED?

I DON'T THINK SO. WE'RE MUCH TOO FAR UP.

BUT SOMEHOW, WE HAVE TO GET WORD TO THEM.

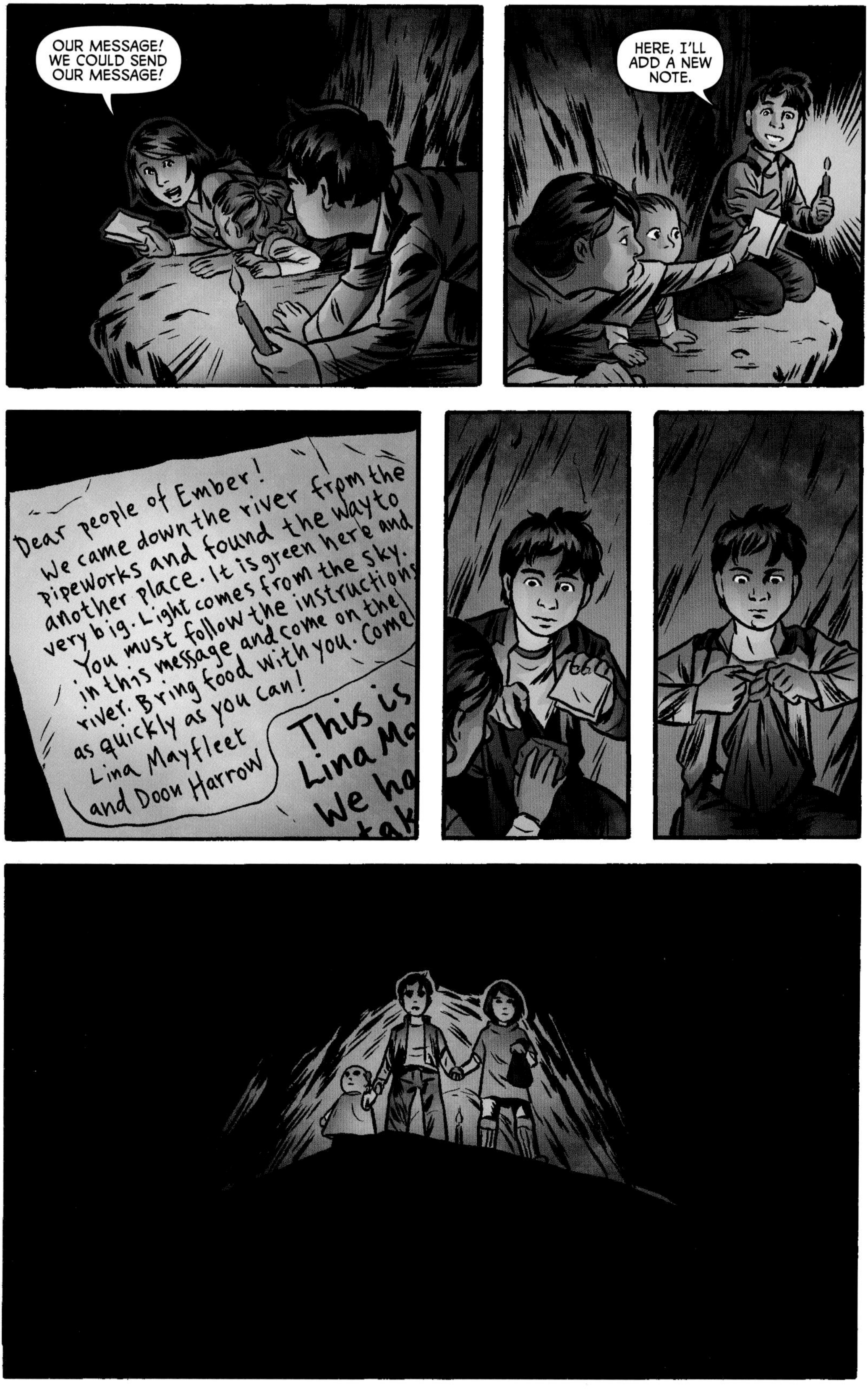
OUR MESSAGE! WE COULD SEND OUR MESSAGE!
HERE, I'LL ADD A NEW NOTE.
Dear people of Ember!
We came down the river from the
pipeWorks and found the way to
another place. It is green here and
very big. Light comes from the sky.
You must follow the instructions
in this message and come on the
river. Bring food with you. Come
as quickly as you can!
Lina Mayfleet
and Doon Harrow
This is

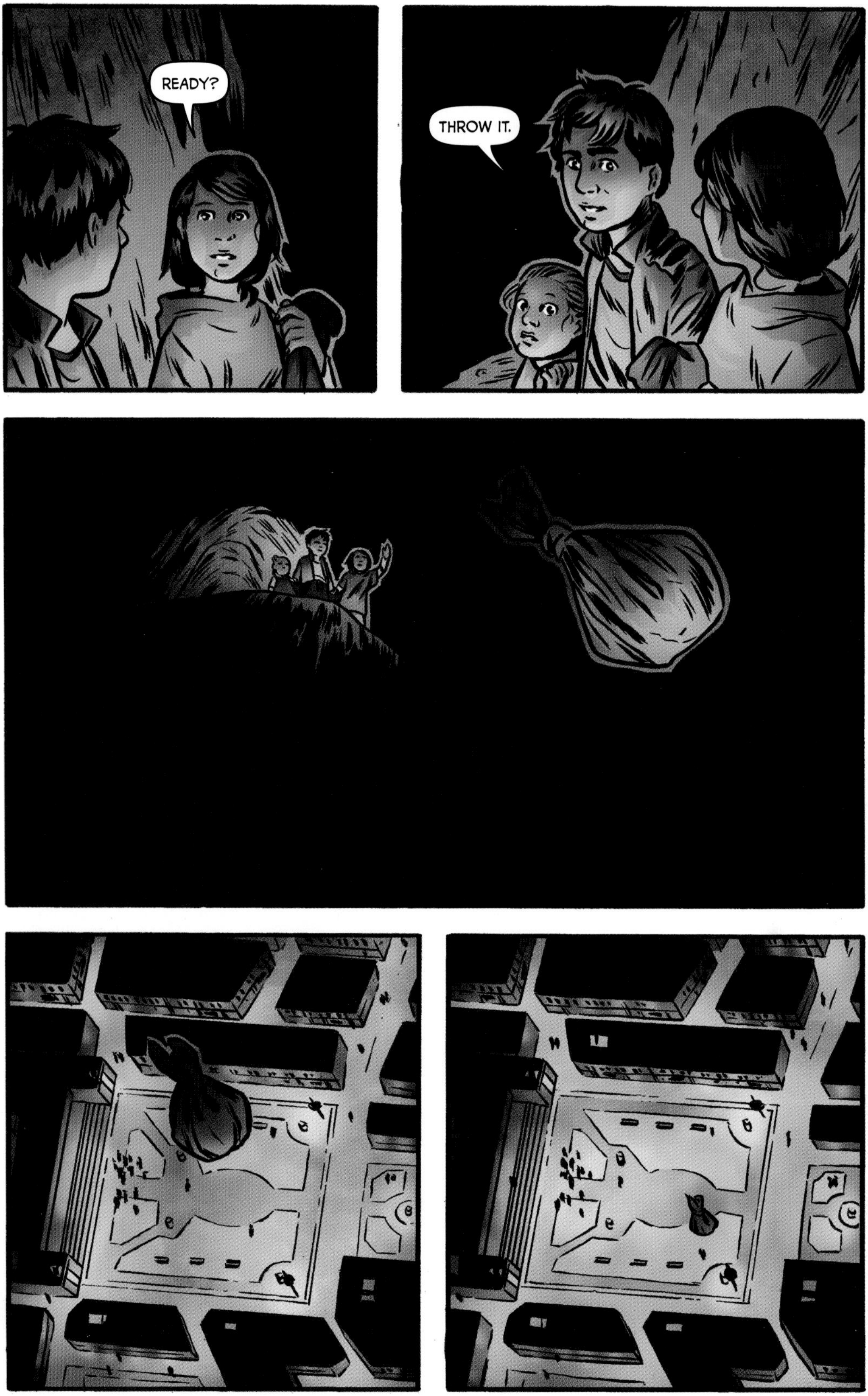
READY?
THROW IT.

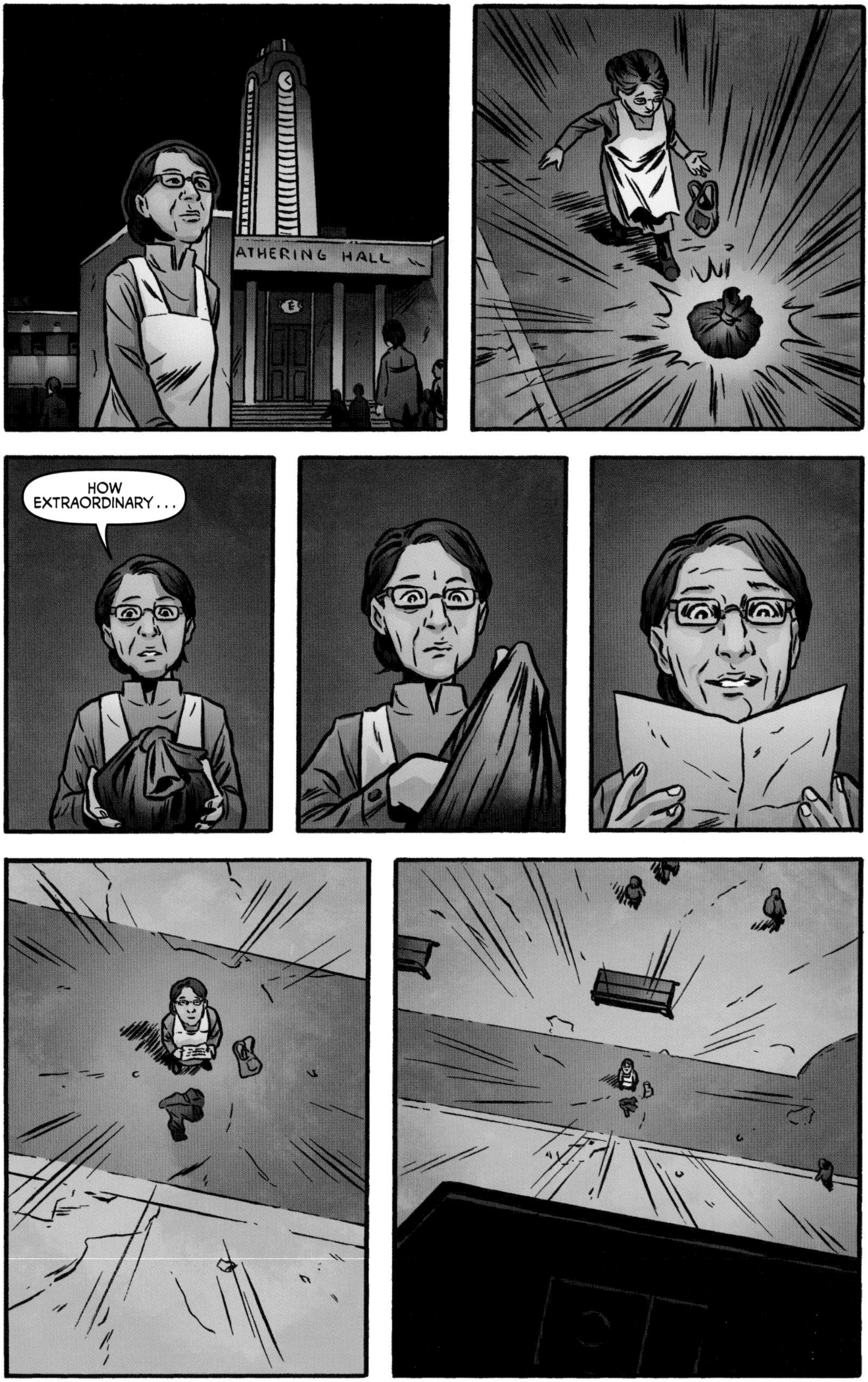
ATHERING HALL
HOW EXTRAORDINARY . . .

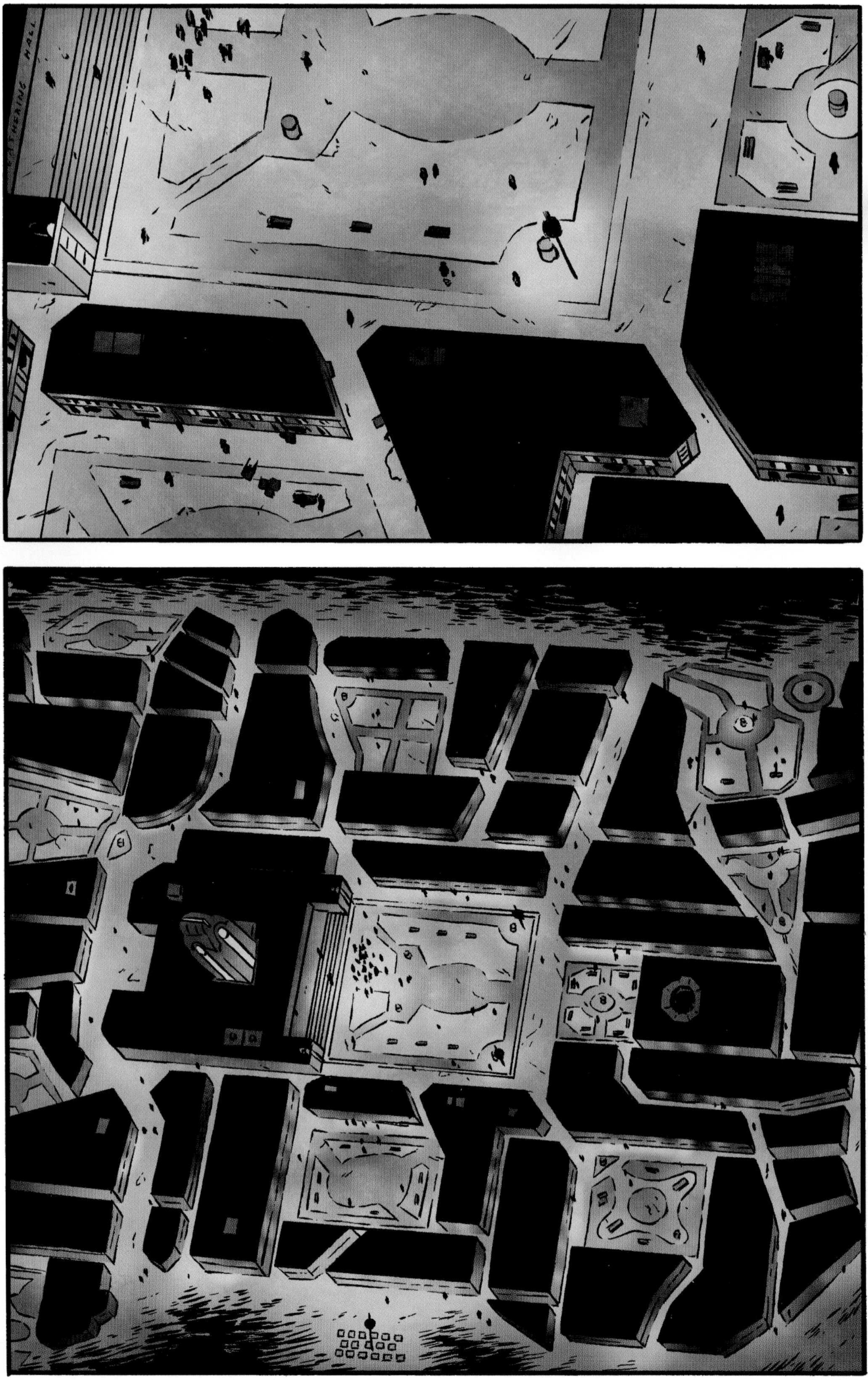
GATHERING HALL

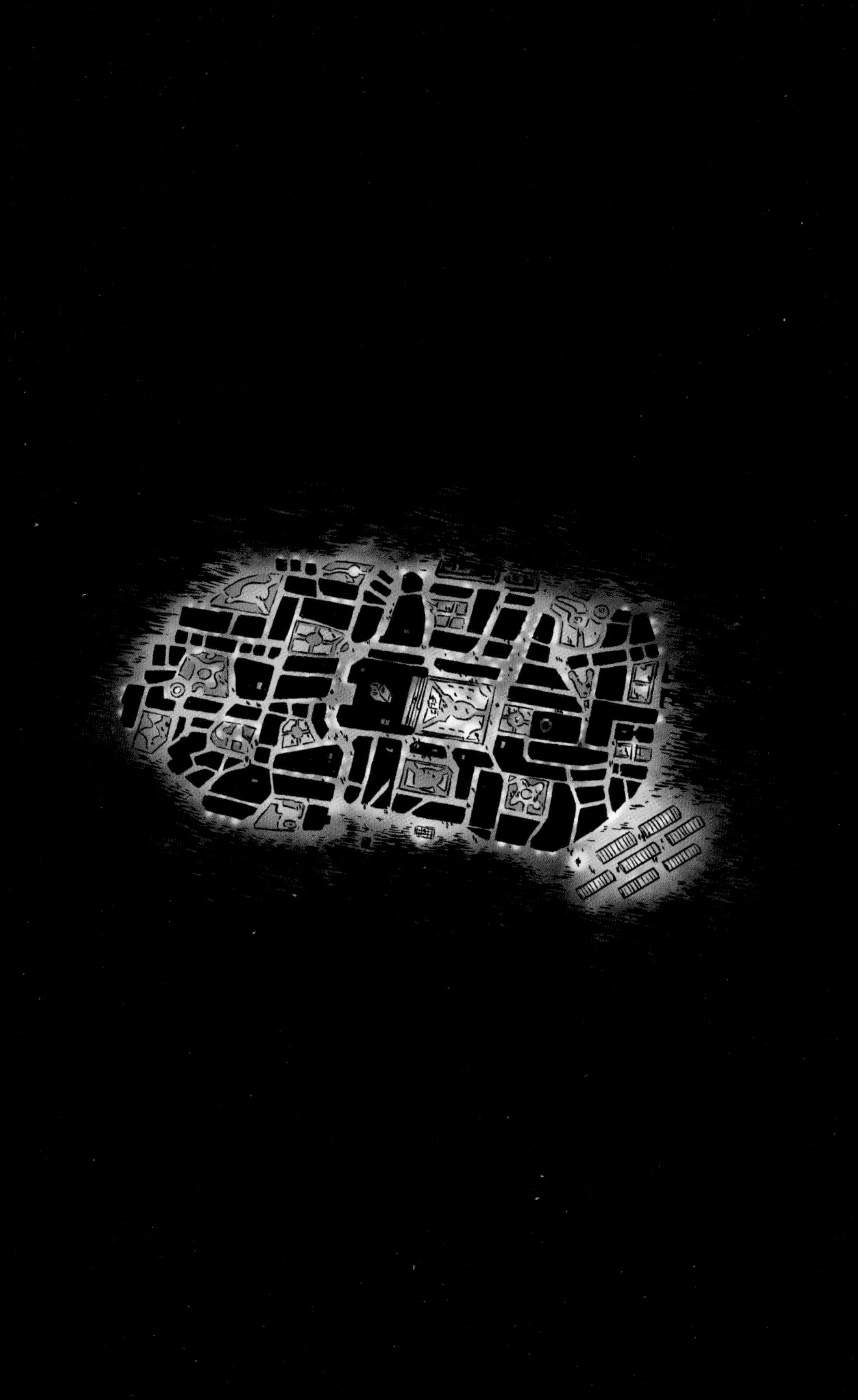

Text copyright © 2012 by Jeanne DuPrau
Cover art and interior illustrations copyright © 2012 by Niklas Asker

Visit us on the Web! randomhouse.com/kids

Educators and librarians, for a variety of teaching tools,
visit us at randomhouse.com/teachers

Library of Congress Cataloging-in-Publication Data
DuPrau, Jeanne.
The city of Ember : the graphic novel / [an abridgement of the novel by]
Jeanne DuPrau ; adapted by Dallas Middaugh ; art by Niklas Asker ; color
by Niklas Asker and Bo Ashi ; lettering by Chris Dickey. — 1st ed.
p. cm.
Summary: In the year 241, twelve-year-old Lina trades jobs on
Assignment Day to be a Messenger to run to new places in her decaying
but beloved city, perhaps even to glimpse Unknown Regions.
ISBN 978-0-375-86821-4 (trade) — ISBN 978-0-375-96821-1 (lib. bdg.) —
ISBN 978-0-307-97910-0 (ebook) — ISBN 978-0-375-86793-4 (pbk.)
1. Graphic novels. [1. Graphic novels. 2. Fantasy. 3. DuPrau, Jeanne. City of
Ember—Adaptations.] I. Middaugh, Dallas. II. Asker, Niklas, ill. III. Title.
PZ7.7.D93Ci 2012
741.5'973—dc23
2011051619

MANUFACTURED IN CHINA
17
First Edition